IRRESISTIBLE DESIRES

"Kurt," Nikki breathed, his name a bittersweet sigh on her lips. She watched him tense, and felt his coiled strength in the hand she rested hesitantly on his forearm. The muscles strained beneath her palm and her fingertips itched to feel more.

"Don't do this to me, Nicole," Kurt groaned, his voice husky. "I don't have the strength to fight you a second time. Not when I know it's a fight I can't win."

His palm cupped her cheek. Nikki closed her eyes, savoring the sensation of his warm, rough flesh. The smell of hay surrounded her, engulfed her, enveloped her in a blanket of desire.

Her resistance—if she'd ever really offered any—drained away in a hot rush when his hand slipped past her temple and his fingers buried themselves in her hair. She couldn't deny it anymore. She wanted Kurt now as much as she'd wanted him six years ago. No, she wanted him more . . . consequences be damned!

Contemporary Fiction From Robin St. Thomas

Fortune's Sisters (2616, $3.95)
It was Pia's destiny to be a Hollywood star. She had complete self-confidence, breathtaking beauty, and the help of her domineering mother. But her younger sister Jeanne began to steal the spotlight meant for Pia, diverting attention away from the ruthlessly ambitious star. When her mother Mathilde started to return the advances of dashing director Wes Guest, Pia's jealousy surfaced. Her passion for Guest and desire to be the brightest star in Hollywood pitted Pia against her own family—sister against sister, mother against daughter. Pia was determined to be the only survivor in the arenas of love and fame. But neither Mathilde nor Jeanne would surrender without a fight. . . .

Lover's Masquerade (2886, $4.50)
New Orleans. A city of secrets, shrouded in mystery and magic. A city where dreams become obsessions and memories once again become reality. A city where even one trip, like a stop on Claudia Gage's book promotion tour, can lead to a perilous fall. For New Orleans is also the home of Armand Dantine, who knows the secrets that Claudia would conceal and the past she cannot remember. And he will stop at nothing to make her love him, and will not let her go again . . .

Available wherever paperbacks are sold, or order direct from the Publisher. Send cover price plus 50¢ per copy for mailing and handling to Zebra Books, Dept. 2998, 475 Park Avenue South, New York, N.Y. 10016. Residents of New York, New Jersey and Pennsylvania must include sales tax. DO NOT SEND CASH.

PASSION'S WILD DELIGHT
REBECCA SINCLAIR

ZEBRA BOOKS
KENSINGTON PUBLISHING CORP.

ZEBRA BOOKS

are published by

Kensington Publishing Corp.
475 Park Avenue South
New York, NY 10016

Copyright © 1990 by Patricia F. Viall

All rights reserved. No part of this book may be reproduced in any form or by any means without the prior written consent of the Publisher, excepting brief quotes used in reviews.

First printing: May, 1990

Printed in the United States of America

*To Barbara Lewis,
for bonds that transcend* . . .

Chapter One

Spring, 1886
Coldbrook, Massachusetts

"Damn, damn, *damn!*"

Nikki Dennison sent an angry glare at the man slung over the pitch-black stallion beneath her. And if looks could kill, this man would be dead.

His arms dangled over the horse's sinewy back; they were so long they almost dragged the ground with each jostling step. His firm side pressed against her thighs. The warm stickiness of blood seeped through her coarse trousers, plastering the rough black fabric to her skin. His head hung down, the glow of moonlight casting his raven hair a rich silver. Sweat-dampened tendrils bounced around the cord of his neck and his eagle-sharp cheeks.

"I should have listened to Mike," she muttered under her breath. "He said not to go out tonight. He said it was too risky. Damn, but he didn't say a word about *shooting* the man!"

Tugging on the reins, she plunged the horse deeper into the hills, which were blanketed with towering pines, spruce, maple, and oak. Common sense was her guide. That, and an uncanny knack for directions. She coaxed her mount around a large, craggy rock.

Powerful hooves crunched over dried leaves and twigs. A chilly spring breeze, filled with the sweet scent of sap, rustled the ceiling of branches above. The sound was rivaled by Nikki's breathing, a noise that seemed abnormally harsh and ragged in her ears as it fogged the air in front of her face.

So far, no thunder of hoofbeats was heard from behind, no cry of alarm had been raised. She could be thankful for that, if for nothing else. Of course, pursuit would be difficult with no horses to follow on; setting them free was probably the only thing she'd done right all night. When the carriage driver awoke he would be nursing his wounded pride along with a lump on his head. It would be a long walk to town before he could share his humiliation with anyone; longer still before he could summon help. By the time her victim had managed to stumble his way that far, she would, with any luck, be long gone.

Victim. The brutality of the word hit her full force. Her large, cornflower-blue gaze flickered to the man she had forced the driver to toss over her saddle. Ah, now *there* was a victim if ever she'd seen one!

Her grip on the reins loosened when the man let out a pained groan. It was about time he woke up, she thought. Shifting her attention to the man, and letting the horse pick its own way through the shadows of sturdy tree trunks, she rested a palm on the hard length of his back.

A surge of unbidden memory washed up her arm, and lapped a tingling path down her spine. *Hay. Moonlight. Hands so tender she could feel a blush kiss her cheeks just thinking about them.* With a grunt of annoyance, she shoved the memory aside. Gone too was the warm, tingling feeling it evoked.

The muscles beneath her fingertips tensed. The dark head turned. A cold smile played on her lips as she wondered what the man's first reaction would be to his upside-down world.

Whatever it was, his response was immediate. She was in the process of pulling back on the reins when, in one lithe shove, he slipped from the stallion's back.

He stumbled backward, his legs making the awkward adjustment to solid ground. His stance was precarious, no doubt from loss of blood. His boots shuffled in the carpet of leaves as he reached out to steady himself against the bark of a nearby oak. One arm cradled his wounded side in a protective gesture.

Nikki wasted no time in gaining control of her mount and spinning the horse around. The stallion, trained for trail drives, immediately complied. An expert flick of her small wrist brought the powerful hooves to a stop. The other hand slipped the pistol from the cinched leather belt at her waist.

The dark head snapped up at the sound of clicking chambers. Steel-gray eyes sparkled in the moonlight filtering down through the trees. His assessive gaze raked the wide-brimmed hat, pulled low on a creamy brow, and the black silk scarf, knotted to conceal the lower portion of a delicately boned face. Wisps of spun silver framed high cheekbones, curled over a long, tapered neck—his kidnapper's sex was glaringly apparent. The stormy gaze shifted, narrowing on the deadly barrel of the pistol that was leveled at his chest.

"Welcome back," she greeted with only a trace of sarcasm. A very *large* trace. Her voice, slightly muffled by the scarf, was undeniably feminine—and as cold as ice. "I was beginning to think I'd killed you after all."

"Wasn't that your plan?" His voice was rich, deep, and filled with hostility. So he *did* remember what had happened back there, Nikki thought. She'd wondered if he would.

"To kill you?" She chuckled, her thumb unconsciously stroking the butt of the pistol. The carved mahogany was warm from her touch, nestling in her palm as though it belonged there. Tonight, it did. "Hell, no. I'd rather have you alive, but it would have been fine with me either way." One finely arched brow rose in her forehead as she cocked her head to the side and swept him with an assessing glare. The scarf hid the crooked smile playing over her full, moist lips.

His jaw tightened, but he made no reply. He lifted his hand. No emotion registered in his eyes when he looked at his thick, blood-soaked fingers. The other hand probed the steadily bleeding wound. Nikki made an effort to harden herself when she saw him flinch.

"The bullet will have to come out," she said, drawing his attention back to her. "It might get infected if it stays in, although I really don't—"

"Care either way," he ended flatly, leaning hard against the tree trunk. "So you've said. Should I ask if you're planning to take it out yourself? Or did you want me to do it? Loss of blood and trembling fingers go hand-in-hand, lady. The blade could slip and I might kill myself. Then where would you be?"

"Burying you, probably."

Nikki kept her gaze, as well as her pistol, trained on the man while she reached behind her and dug into the leather saddlebag. Her fingers closed around the strips of white linen she'd brought in abundance —just in case. Pulling a handful free, she tossed them to him. He made no move to take them.

"Bind yourself up," she ordered harshly. "And make the knots good and tight. We've still got a ways to ride yet, and I won't risk having you pass out on me again."

"Why not? Wouldn't it be easier for you if I did? If I'm unconscious you won't have to worry about being overpowered," his lips curled in a cold smile, "or worse."

"I won't have to worry about it if you're dead, either," she countered hotly, bristling under his threat. "And that's exactly what you're going to be if you don't shut up and do what you're told. Now, bind yourself up and be quick about it. We don't have all night."

His keen gaze flickered between the pistol and the clear blue eyes glaring at him from over the scarf. With deliberate slowness, he peeled the crushed velvet waistcoat from his shoulders. The frilly white shirt took longer to come off since the material refused to part with his blood-caked side.

"We could be here all night," Nikki sputtered under her breath. Reaching down, she grabbed the canteen she'd draped over the saddle horn. Soaking the wound should speed things up a bit, she reasoned as she tossed it to him. And this would be a great disinfectant.

He snatched it midair, scowling darkly at the pain the movement caused. Uncapping the canteen, he splashed a liberal amount of the crystal-clear liquid over his wounded side. His face drained to ash-white and he let out a bellow of pain laced with cold, hard fury.

"What the hell is that?!" He threw the canteen to the ground, where it bounced under a low, prickly bush and spilled its guts in the dirt. His hand clutched his stinging side.

"Gin," she replied blandly. Even at this distance she could smell the tang of alcohol, interwoven with the sap of trees. She chuckled dryly. "Why? What did you think it was, water?"

"Yes, I thought it was water. How the hell was I supposed to know? I see a canteen, I automatically think water!"

"The smell should have been a clue. Where I come from, gin and water don't smell alike."

He glowered at her, the pain abating. "Maybe not," he growled, and began passing a long strip of linen tightly around his waist. "Then again, I have no sense of smell. Next time warn me."

There won't be a next time, Nikki thought as, of its own accord, her gaze followed his fingers. The groove of the saddle horn had left an angry red outline on his taut stomach. She shifted uneasily in the saddle when her attention strayed to the muscles of his shoulders and chest. The silver sheen of moonlight made his skin glow a deep bronze. Each rippling tendon was iron-hard beneath the sun-kissed flesh and thick pelt of curling black hairs coating it. His gaze was shrewd, his height commanding, and with the raw sinew to back it all up, he made a more than worthy opponent.

Nikki swallowed hard as the memory of a body not quite so muscular flashed through her mind. He had changed, she thought, and changed a lot. The last six years had filled out a body that had, at one time, only held a great deal of promise. The promise had been fulfilled—twice over. Never lanky, Kurt Frazier now boasted a rugged form that bespoke a man close friends with hard work and sweat. A certain shrewdness had been added to his gaze, a keen awareness that hadn't been there before. His face had changed, too, although not as much. His jaw was harder, his cheeks sharper. Only the tiny lines shooting out from his darkly lashed eyes denied the somber set of his expression.

Swallowing the observation, Nikki waited patiently as he knotted the cloth beneath his left arm. He slipped the white linen shirt over his shoulders. He didn't button it or tuck it in as he shrugged on the stained waistcoat, then turned toward her.

"Ready?" he asked lazily. His feet crunched over the leaves when he slowly approached horse and rider. The thinning of his lips provided the only indication that he was in pain.

"If you think you're up to it." Her fingers tightened around the pistol when he stopped a scant few feet away.

"And if I say I'm not?"

She shrugged. "We ride anyway. If they haven't found your carriage yet, they will soon. I want to be as far away from here as I can get when they figure out you're gone." A stray moonbeam sparkled on something buried in the leaves near where he'd stood, snatching Nikki's attention. Scowling, she nodded to the spot behind him. "That wasn't very smart, Mr. Frazier. Go get your button, and while you're at it, be thankful I don't shoot you for pulling such a stupid stunt."

The gray eyes glinted with anger as he looked down the dark barrel of her pistol, still pointed at his chest. If he was surprised at her use of his name he didn't show it as, wordlessly, he did as he was told. Nikki wondered just how much longer he would comply. Probably for as long as it would take him to regain his strength. After that, who knew what he would do to free himself? Of course, by then it would be too late, she'd have already joined up with Mike and Willy. Between the three of them, they should have no trouble keeping one wounded man under control.

"I'll take that." She reached out a hand, palm up, when he started to slip the button into his trouser pocket. Reluctantly, he placed it on her palm. A quick glance assured her the rest of his buttons were still intact.

"If you think I'm getting back up on that damn horse, think again," he sneered, raking her masculine attire with a touch of disdain. "My stomach still aches from the last time."

Her fingers closed tightly around the ice-cold button. "I don't care if your entire body aches, you're getting on this saddle—peacefully. You'll do whatever I tell you," her eyes narrowed, "or did you forget, *I'm* the one holding the gun?"

"I didn't forget." A mirthless smile played over his sensuously thin lips. "You have a gun," he nodded, "and I know you can use it. But I think you want me alive, so you won't."

"Don't bet on it. Having you dead is better than not having you at all."

The smile was gone as quickly as it had come. "Lady, you want me on that horse, you're going to have to put me up there yourself. Personally, I don't think you're strong enough."

"Back up," Nikki barked, angrily waving the gun at the tree he had just leaned against. "I said, *back up!*"

Lifting his hands in supposed defeat, he slowly backed away.

She gave a disgusted sigh. Only a fool wouldn't see what he was doing. And Nicole Dennison was no fool. Reaching down in front of her left leg, she pulled a coil of braided hemp from where it was attached to the saddle, then slid lithely to the ground. With the rope in one hand and the gun in the other, she approached him. Her boots crunched over dry leaves and twigs as the moonlight played over the dark silk of her costume. The cool midnight breeze flicked at the scarf around her neck.

"Put your hands out, palms up where I can see them. And don't try anything cute. I'm already sick of you. If I have to put another bullet in your arrogant hide so you know I mean business, so be it."

A trace of a grin pulled at the man's lips as he held out his hands. He complied too easily. That should have warned her. She grabbed one end of the rope with her free hand and let the other end trail onto the hard-packed ground. With the gun precariously gripped in her right hand, she began wrapping the rough strip of hemp around his wrists.

"Loosen up," she barked when she felt his muscles bunching beneath her fingertips. Was it his insolence that disturbed her, or the feel of his warm, familiar flesh beneath her fingers?

She jerked the rope until it dug painfully into his wrists. He didn't flinch. "I said, loosen up! I know what you're doing. I tie this around your wrists the way you are now and the rope will be off before we clear the trees. Now, either you relax or you walk back to camp. And I don't think your fancy boots are made for walking that far, not in these conditions."

She glanced up to see him grinning lazily down at her. The moonlight played over his hair, making it glow like rich, dark satin in the twisting shadows. For a split second, Nikki was tempted to shoot the smile off his arrogantly handsome face. She settled for pulling the rope tighter instead.

The man wasted no time. When he made his move he made it fast, with cold precision. Before she knew what was happening, he raised his half-tied hands, fingers interlocked, and knocked her hard aside the head. The rope curled from his half-bound wrists, catching her around the ankles so she tripped when she stumbled backward from the bone-jarring blow. The hat flew from her head, freeing the quicksilver braid as the ground came up to meet her backside with a powerful thud. Her head snapped back and smashed into a solid maple trunk.

Air whooshed from her lungs, sparks of light flashed behind her eyes. She reached out a hand to steady herself, and felt the pistol wrenched from her grasp.

Never one to admit defeat, she stubbornly shook off the spinning in her head and lunged for his legs when he tried to disentangle himself from the rope. He must not have been prepared for further resistance, for he fell to the ground quite easily.

Nikki could feel the ground tremble beneath her hands and knees as hard body met harder earth. She took no time to savor his inhalation of surprise as she thrust herself on top of him.

He was rock-hard beneath her straddled thighs, but she noticed only the angry glint in his eyes and the pistol he stubbornly clutched in his hands—strong, solid hands that were aiming the gun in her direction.

With a strangled cry, she lunged for the pistol. Her knee purposely smashed into his wounded side as her fingers closed around his wrist. It took both her small hands to encompass the thick, trunklike appendage, but encompass it she did, and squeezed for all she was worth. The gun dropped onto the bed of trampled leaves.

She ground her knee into his side once more, then shoved herself off of him and scrambled after the gun. With a muffled groan, he was after her. His heavy body collapsed over her back, pinning her to the ground and forcing the breath from her lungs when she reached out for the pistol. Her fingers brushed the carved wooden handle, but it was still too far away to grab.

Sensing her intent, he shifted position, reaching his arm over hers and plucking up the gun with an ease that made her grit her teeth in frustration. The loose knot securing her scarf around her face twisted free. Leaves and twigs scraped her cheek and jaw when she twisted her head, fighting for every precious breath. She arched her back, trying to buck him off the way an angry bronco would a hated saddle. He wouldn't budge.

Again he shifted, and Nikki waited for her ribs to snap from the pressure of his weight. It was her only chance for thought. The waist-length braid was shoved aside, and nearly pulled from her scalp, then her arms were yanked painfully behind her back. She gasped when the rope was coiled tightly around her wrists.

She fought like a demon; twisting, kicking, and screaming every cuss she'd ever heard at his dark head—and making up others as she warmed to her subject. Occasionally, her foot made contact with his sinewy hip. The only reward for her sharp heel gouging into those rigid muscles was a stifled groan.

Not until he was satisfied she was securely tied did he roll off of her. Coiling the braid around his fist, he yanked her with him and flipped her onto her back.

Nikki lay rigid on the ground, stubbornly focusing all her attention on the sharp twigs biting at her skin through her ripped shirt. Her arms ached from the contorted position he'd tied her in. She refused to look at him, instead riveting her gaze to the leaves rustling overhead, and the pale moonlight that made each tree a dark, ominous silhouette.

It was the loud, metallic click of rotating chambers that finally snatched her attention. Her jaw was a tight, angry line, her eyes glistening a furious midnight blue when she glanced to the left and saw him tucking her pistol into his belt. A confident smirk twisted his lips. The sight of it made Nikki's stomach churn with fury.

"You haven't won, Frazier," she growled, squirming on the ground like a snake until she managed to pull herself up to a sitting position. Resting her back against a tree trunk, she glared at him with all the anger that coursed through her blood. "You have the upper hand now, but it won't last. I don't give up so easily."

When he turned toward her, Nikki was proud to see her struggles had reopened his wound. One side of his coat and trousers was smeared with fresh blood. The smell of it thickened the air.

"Thanks for the warning, lady," he sneered. "I'll keep it in mind." He plowed his tired fingers through his tousled raven hair. His piercing gaze never left her. "Now you can tell me what the hell this is all about. Why you're so all-fired set on killing me. Or should I guess?"

"You can guess until the cows come home, but if you haven't figured it out by now you'll just be wasting your time."

Scowling, he leaned back against a tree and slid slowly to the ground. He was losing blood fast. They both knew that if the bleeding in his side wasn't stopped soon, it would be only a matter of time before he lost consciousness again. Since it was her only hope of getting out of the mess she was in alive, Nikki decided to stall for time.

His gray eyes narrowed, traveling lazily from the top of her pale silver head, laced liberally with dried leaves and twigs, to the scuffed tips of her square-toed boots. Then back again. She wasn't sure, but she could have sworn a flicker of recognition glinted in his eyes. It was doused quickly as his attention focused on the full breasts, straining against her black silk shirt. His eyes darkened to a shade just shy of turqoise.

Nikki didn't blink, didn't flinch, didn't do anything but moodily return his stare when his gaze locked with her own.

"Do I know you?" he asked suddenly, his scowl deepening into angry crevasses. "You look familiar."

She smiled tightly, but refused to answer as she rested her head back against the rough bark. He *should* remember, Nikki thought. *Hay. Moonlight. The slow heat of passion.* But if he didn't, that was fine, too. Let him figure it out for himself. And while he was doing that, his wound was busy pumping blood onto the ground, making him weaker by the second.

A secretive smile pulled at her lips when she noticed the sickly pallor of his skin and the white line etching his mouth. She hadn't lied. She wasn't done with this man yet. Not by a long shot. The smile still in place, she inspected the knot at her wrists with cold, numb fingers.

Apparently, another thought occurred to him just then. His eyes flashed skeptically, his gaze settling on her perfectly curved, full pink lips. "You can start by telling me how you know my name. Then you can tell me what the hell you were trying to prove by single-handedly holding up my carriage."

"Figure it out yourself," she snapped, her grin broadening with sugary sweetness when her fingers played over the knot. It was firm, but not so tight it couldn't be pried free, given a little time.

"Well?" she pressed when he didn't reply. "Are you going to shoot me, have me arrested, or are we going to sit out here under the stars yapping all night? Since you've got me trussed up like a Christmas goose, and I seem to have lost my gun, I'd say it's your card to play." She shrugged, as though whatever his plans were, she couldn't care less. "I can't stop you no matter what you do," *yet*, she thought, "but, to be perfectly blunt, I do have other things to do right now. If you'd be so kind as to untie me . . . ?"

She started to turn her back toward him, as though offering him the ropes to untie, but his harsh laughter stopped her cold.

"Now who's being foolish?" he chided as she settled back against the tree. "I'd unleash a pack of half-starved wolves on a herd of fat, helpless sheep before I'd untie that rope." He fingered his wounded side for effect.

Nikki didn't so much as flush. "Suit yourself," she shrugged, holding back a smile when her thumb slipped free of the rope. The rough hemp scraped her wrists raw, but her mind was too set on freeing herself to notice. Just a little more time, that was all she needed, she thought. "Do you know who I am yet?"

Her index finger slipped free, and began picking at the knot that was loosening quickly.

His eyes glistened in the moonlight as his gaze played over her delicately molded features. "No. But give me time. I never forget a face."

This time Nikki did smile. Tightly. The last time she'd set eyes on Kurt Frazier she'd been seventeen years old. *Hay, laced with the tangy scent of male sweat*. If he didn't remember her yet, chances were he wouldn't; not without some help. *The no-good bastard!* Nikki thought. Was he so used to being seduced by young girls in barns that he couldn't remember one woman from the next?! That thought stung her raw, and the rawness was reflected in her voice. "Maybe. Then again, maybe I look like someone you know." The first layer of the knot peeled away under her insistent prodding. "Maybe you've never met me at all. You *are* wounded, after all. Loss of blood being what it is, there's always the chance your mind's playing tricks on you."

"That," his eyes narrowed shrewdly, his fingers straying to the gun handle jutting from his belt, "or *you* are."

"Hmmm. That too," she said. Her gaze followed his hands and she noted how long his fingers were; lean and powerful, with tiny black curls separating the knuckles on each sun-bronzed finger.

"I don't suppose you'll help jar my memory?"

It wasn't meant as a question. She answered him anyway. "Not a chance."

He nodded, as though that was exactly what he'd expected her to say.

She glanced down, feigning acute interest in the dusty toe of her boot, and felt the second layer of the knot fall away, followed immediately by the third—and last. She saw him move but didn't dare look up for fear he'd see the victory shimmering in her eyes. Circulation rushed through her fingers, the blood beneath her skin tingled as warmth flowed through her hands. As inconspicuously as possible, she shook the rope free. It dropped onto the leaves that scattered the base of the tree at her back. Her glance snapped up. Had he heard the barely distinguishable sound? If he did, he gave no sign.

Nikki chaffed her stinging flesh and wondered how she was going to get her pistol back, then get this no-good murderer back to camp without having to kill him first. Since she would have killed him an hour ago if that had been her intent, and since no clear-cut plan leapt to mind, she reacted on gut instinct. Pulling her legs up in what appeared to be a casual motion, she tightened her cramped muscles and prepared to pounce.

The chance came faster than she'd hoped. The scowl marring Frazier's brow told Nikki he was still trying to place where he'd seen her before. She doubted he was aware of her balancing her weight on the balls of her feet a split second before she lunged at him.

Simultaneous grunts shattered the air as she slammed into his firm chest. They toppled to the ground as one, and again Nikki found herself straddling a firm, iron-hard waist.

Her hands were everywhere at once—arms, shoulders, blood-soaked side—as she fought desperately to regain control of her gun. His defense was weakened from loss of blood, but even at half-strength she was no match for him. Everywhere she searched, his hands were there first, thrusting her smaller hands aside, trying to wrap steely fingers around her wrists.

Nikki beat him in dexterity, though, and before he could grab her arms, she'd managed to squirm away. It was only by sheer luck that she felt her fingers brush the handle of the pistol as she rolled off of him.

Not one to spit in fate's face, she snatched up the

weapon and leveled it at the wide target of his chest. A surge of power pumped through her veins as her thumb twitched over the hammer. She smiled victoriously into his glare of outrage.

"I wouldn't try it," she warned coldly when he readied himself to rush her. A cocky half-smile tugged at her lips. "You already have one of my bullets in your side. I'd be more than happy to give it company, but I'll warn you, the next one goes for your heart . . . if you have one."

"I thought you wanted me alive," he growled, rolling back on his haunches. His gaze shifted restlessly between the woman and the gun, neither of which seemed to please him.

Shrugging, she pushed a curled wisp of silver from her brow. "I changed my mind. Dead will do me just fine at this point." To punctuate the words, she jerked the hammer back. The metallic click was loud against their ragged breaths.

"Come on, big man," she sneered, her soft voice thick with long-suppressed hatred. "Lunge for me. I'd take any reason I could get to put a bullet through that cold heart of yours."

"If you could find it," he snapped.

"If I could find it," she echoed. Her gaze sparkled with loathing, her thumb grazed the wooden butt nestled so perfectly in her palm. "Maybe you could draw me a map."

"Why you little—!"

Everything happened at once. Not only did the man rush her, he pounced on her like a tiger attacking its smaller, weaker, half-starved prey.

Seeing his broad chest closing in, Nikki did what came naturally—she jerked the trigger back with her index finger and waited for the stinging blast of the gun to cut the night. Three times in rapid succession she pulled the trigger, and each time her only reward was an empty clink of metal chambers.

He emptied my gun!

She had barely enough time to roll to the side before his body crashed to the ground. Pain exploded in her shoulder when his sharp jaw smashed into her tender flesh. She was flung back, her head barely missing the wide trunk of a tree.

"No-good bastard!" she hissed on a swift exhalation. One arm was trapped beneath his considerable weight. She didn't try to free it. Instead, she deftly twirled the pistol on her index finger and let the barrel snap into her palm. Her fingers closed around the weapon in a white-knuckled fist that cut a deadly arch toward his temple.

The gun never made it that far. The rumble of horse hooves made Nikki hesitate for the length of one throbbing heartbeat. Not long, but enough time for her opponent to roll to the side. The gun whipped through the dead air where his head had been.

Kurt Frazier was in the process of stumbling to his feet, clutching his side with one hand while the other scrambled for the gun, when two riders broke through the thick line of trees. He never had time to retrieve the bullets he'd hidden beneath the blanket of brittle twigs.

"Nikki!" the first rider cried. Sliding from the horse, he cleared the distance between them in five quick strides. Like his sister, Michael Dennison wore a hat low on his brow and a dark scarf tied securely around the lower half of his face. He made ready to enfold Nikki in a relieved embrace, but she quickly sidestepped him. Her gaze was trained on Kurt Frazier, and nothing on heaven or earth was going to make her shift it.

"Watch him close, Willy," she called to the rider who was still seated, the same black hat and scarf obscuring his features. "And don't trust him for a minute, even if he looks like he's ready to keel over." Satisfied that their captive was being suitably guarded, Nikki glared at the tall man hovering by her side. "And where the hell have you been? This idiot could have killed and buried me in the time it took you two to figure out I was in trouble!"

"But I thought you said—?"

"Thought!" Her furious glare swept to the boy on the horse, stopping Willy cold. He swallowed hard and averted his gaze to Frazier. "Well, isn't this a fine time for you two to start thinking!" With a disgusted sigh, she stalked over to Frazier and plucked the empty pistol from his slackened grasp. "You got lucky this time," she spat. Shoving the pistol under her belt, her angry gaze raked him head to toe. "Don't get used to it, it won't happen again."

Kurt's gaze snapped up. Again, the nagging suspicion that he'd met this woman before tugged at his gut. His ears perked to the sound of her voice when she berated the young riders' tardiness. His gaze roved over her hair, which shimmered like a sparkling white rope in the moonlight . . . where had he seen it before?

This time it was Kurt's turn to inspect. Starting with the top of her head, he let his attention wander with slow precision down the length of her petite frame. Silky, sun-bleached hair. Valleys and curves that even the bulky, masculine shirt and trousers she wore couldn't disguise. A delicately pointed chin and high, carved cheekbones. A nose that was just a touch too long, breaking the gentleness of her features as it hovered above lips a man could lose his soul in.

Nikki, he thought, his mind whirling. *The tall one had called her Nikki.*

In the end, it wasn't anything physical that kindled the first spark of recognition in his gut. Instead, it was her furious pacing and the brittle sound of leaves, crunching like dried hay under her boots.

"Nicole Dennison." The name rolled over his

tongue, rushed past his lips, and came out as something just shy of a cuss. As though to prove him right, she glared over her shoulder, sending him a look that said it was about time he figured it out.

Nicole Dennison, his mind raged. How had he missed recognizing her, even disguised as she was? His *body* should have known, should have reacted. Six painful years was no excuse. And then, once the fog of surprise cleared, replaced by harsh reality, he thought more slowly, *Well, I'll be a son of a bitch!*

Chapter Two

"Why didn't you kill him, Sis? You had every chance."

Michael Dennison's words, as he plopped onto the ground next to his sister, managed to grab Kurt's attention. His dark head snapped up, his narrow gaze piercing the shadows to his right. Without the scarves obscuring their faces, or the hats to shadow eye and brow, it was obvious the two were related.

Scowling, he turned his attention to the third boy, who was stretched on the ground, snoring loudly. The youngest of the three sported the same mane of golden hair as his brother, wild and short, but his height resembled Nicole's. The shoulders were round, the stomach paunchy. As a man he would be wide, not tall and lanky like his brother, nor as recklessly handsome.

"I tried. He stole the bullets from my gun." Nikki shrugged, biting into the tough sliver of salted jerky Mike had shoved into her hand. "I don't know, maybe it's better this way. Looks like I'll get my trial after all."

"Trial?" Mike sputtered around a mouthful of dried meat. "What good would that do? Frazier had Sheriff Hardy wrapped around his little finger back when he worked for Pop. Hardy wouldn't convict him of kicking a dog."

The cornflower gaze narrowed, traveling to the man who'd murdered her father. A hint of surprise flashed in Kurt's eyes, but was quickly hidden. When he returned her stare, it was to shoot her a glance of raw challenge.

"They *will* hang him," she snapped. "We've got a witness who saw him do it. And he left the ranch with no explanation the morning the murder took place. That alone should earn him a visit to the hangman's noose. Hardy may have liked Frazier just fine *six years ago*, but even *he* can't overlook evidence like that."

"You won't be needing evidence if somebody doesn't feed me pretty soon." Kurt's mocking voice cut the air like a knife. His mouth curved into a lazy grin as he continued to hold Nikki's stare. "Or are you afraid I'll jump you if you get too close?"

"Afraid? *Nikki?*" Mike chuckled as though that was one of the funniest things he'd ever heard—and got a ribful of his sister's elbow as reward.

"Shush up," she hissed in his ear. Leaning to the side, she reached for the saddlebag. Another slab of tasteless meat was produced. "Go check the horses, Mike, they'll need to be fed and watered. And fill up the canteens while you're at it." She nodded past the murky line of trees, and the river that gurgled beyond. "We're running low."

Ignoring Mike's grumbling complaints, Nikki pushed herself to her feet. Her aching legs protested; a hazard of spending too many hours in the saddle. Her back felt permanently crimped, but it couldn't be helped. Frazier had wasted too much time while they rode. To compensate, Nikki made them ride on when they should have been sleeping. She'd been desperate to put distance between them and anyone who might be following.

The first fingers of morning tinted the sky a pale

gray. Pretty soon she'd have to wake Willy up and press on. Neither she nor Mike had gotten a wink of sleep, but it was better to be dog-tired and achy in the saddle than to wake up and find Frazier gone or, worse, rescued. Their lives wouldn't be worth a chunk of rotten timber if that happened. No matter what part of the country one was in, only the sentence for kidnapping changed, not the crime.

"Here," Nikki muttered. She dropped the slab of jerky onto his bloodstained lap. "Enjoy it. You won't be getting more until sundown."

"Could be tough."

"No worse than any other piece of dry meat you've ever had, I'll wager." She started to turn away.

"I meant eating it." He nodded to his hands, bound together at the wrist and tied securely around his hips. The rope ran down his legs and joined the one coiled around his ankles. It was obvious that Nikki wasn't taking any chances.

Ah, well, she'd supplied the meal. Eating it was *his* problem, wasn't it? She made ready to plop back down on the leaves to snatch a quick nap, but instead found herself sending him another assessing glance. She may like seeing him this way just fine, but he couldn't eat tied up like that. Lord, he could barely *move* the way he was trussed up like a fat hen ready for roasting! Of course, Nikki had no intention of either loosening his ties, or freeing him of them. She wasn't stupid.

Sighing, she moved to his side and squatted beside him. He smelled of dried blood, leather, and sweat, with the faintest aroma of spicy cologne scenting the air near his head. It was an expensive, earthy smell that seemed right at home mingling with the aroma of pine sap and brush.

Her sparkling blue gaze shifted between his bound hands and the chunk of meat in his lap. Without thinking, she reached to snatch up the piece of jerky.

Her hand stopped, poised in midair. A tremor shot up her arm. She didn't want to touch that lap.

"Go ahead," he prompted huskily. "I don't bite. At least, not women who shoot the way you do."

Her jaw tightened. Sending him a quelling glare, she picked up the salty meat. Her fingers brushed his rock-hard thigh, and she pulled back as though she'd just snatched up a handful of flames. She scowled into his confident smile.

"Open your mouth," she snapped, and was surprised when he readily complied. Her fingers were trembling—from anger, or something else? She shoved half of the strip between even white teeth, and tugged when he bit into it. The piece was severed so abruptly she almost fell on her backside.

"Not bad," he muttered, grinning cockily and eyeing her. She looked tired. Her skin was drawn tight over high, regal cheekbones that more than one proper Bostonian miss of his acquaintance would give her eyeteeth to possess. Dark circles smudged her eyes, while dirt smudged her cheeks.

His strong, square jaw worked the tough piece of meat. Like a magnet, Nikki's attention was drawn there. The muscles beneath the sun-bronzed skin flexed with each leisurely chew. His firm chin was peppered with a new growth of whiskers, and had just the barest trace of a dimple dead center. It was a jaw that made a woman want to reach out and run her palm over it, just to see if the flesh was really as smooth and as warm and as hard as it looked. The dimpled chin was the one thing about Kurt Frazier that hadn't changed a bit.

Sucking in a ragged breath, she lifted her gaze, letting it rove over his sculpted cheeks, wide brow, and straight, narrow nose before meeting his gaze. His eyes, darkly intent, searched her face.

"You've grown up, Nicole Dennison," he said, his

voice soft and throaty, slightly muffled by the piece of jerky. "Last time I saw you, you had a pair of braids that bobbed to your waist and a smattering of freckles on your nose." His gaze dipped to her breasts, which strained against the black silk shirt. Although no mention was made of *those* changes, the insinuation was there.

"And I used to follow you around like a lost pup," she reminded him coldly. Shifting, she settled cross-legged on a bed of leaves, far enough away so she wouldn't have to touch him.

"Hmmm," he sighed, rolling the salty meat over his tongue and gazing thoughtfully into space. "You did at that. I'd almost forgotten."

The words stung. "I didn't," she snapped. "In fact, there isn't much I have forgotten about you, Kurt Frazier."

One dark brow slanted high. "Should I take that as a compliment?"

"Take it any way you like," she shrugged. "You ready for more yet?" She held the jerky to his mouth, but he turned away and shook his head. Her hand, greasy from the meat's fat as it melted in her palm, dropped back to her lap.

"Mickey's changed a lot, too. Last time I saw him, his head barely grazed my collarbone."

"He doesn't like to be called Mickey anymore," she corrected stiffly. "He's nineteen years old now and says the nickname makes him sound like a kid. You'd be smart to remember that."

Kurt nodded, swallowing the lump of tasteless meat. It had all the flavor of a piece of dry bark as it carved a path down his throat, but he knew better than to complain. Again, he refused the rest when Nikki offered it. If he ate all the meat now, his excuse for keeping her near would be gone. Of course, she'd leave even if he *didn't* eat, Kurt reasoned, but he was willing to take that chance. "How long have you been looking for me, Nicole? I left the ranch years ago."

"Six years, off and on," she answered flatly. "We got word a few months back you'd been seen near Cambridge, so we decided to risk a trip. Turned out to be a good risk."

"And the ranch?" he pressed, watching as a range of emotions played over her deceptively young features. "How's everything at the Triple D? Shouldn't you be bringing the longhorns back to summer ground right about now?"

Nikki's grip tightened on the piece of meat that was growing steadily warmer in her palm. Her eyes sparkled with an emotion Kurt didn't dare give a name to. Pain? Betrayal? Loathing? All three?

"They won't miss me on one round-up. As for the rest . . . ?" she shrugged. "Pete's holding things together the best he can, but it's been tough since Pop died. Not that *you* care." Her gaze dropped to the stain marring his coat and trousers.

Kurt nodded slowly. "Pete's a good man. He'll do your father proud. And Brian? You haven't mentioned him at all. All grown up with a wife of his own, I'll bet." His gaze searched the lightening shadows. "Where are they, Pete and Brian? Why didn't they come with you?"

"Someone had to stay home." She didn't mention that she, Mike, and Willy had been forced to sneak off the ranch to make the trip. Pete's bellow of rage had probably been heard all the way to Yellowstone when he'd found them gone. She picked up a small twig and began to snap pieces off the end as if she were shucking a green bean. "Like you said, it's time to move the herd. The ranch won't run itself, and Mike and Willy sure wouldn't know what to do if something went wrong."

"What could go wrong? Sounds to me like you've

got it all under control . . . as always."

The snideness in his tone made her gaze sharpen. She threw the piece of twig into the trees and ignored his sarcasm. "Did you hear me talking to Mike before?" she asked tightly. "Do you know where I'm bringing you and why?"

"I heard," he answered evasively. His gaze drifted to the piece of jerky she'd set aside on her lap. "I'll take that last bite now. And a drink too, if you can spare one."

She pushed the rest of the meat into his mouth, snatching her hand back when his warm, moist lips closed around the tip of her fingers. "M-Mike's filling the canteens. You can have a drink when he gets back." She wiped the feel of his lips off on her dusty trousers. "Well?" she asked moodily, plucking up another stick and snapping it. "Aren't you going to defend yourself? Aren't you going to convince me you didn't kill my father? That I've made a mistake and I should let you go free? Maybe even untie you and return you to your carriage?"

Kurt smiled around the piece of meat he worked between his strong, white teeth. "Why bother?" he shrugged, his gaze locking with hers. His eyes hardened to cold slivers of ice, the color accentuated by the newborn light of day. "I haven't forgotten how determined you are, Nicole. Not for a minute. I know nothing I do or say is going to change your mind once it's set. And I know you must have some sort of proof or you wouldn't have hunted me down this far. Am I right?"

Nikki snapped what was left of the twig in two, then threw the jagged pieces away. Sweeping the silver hair from her brow, she glared at him defiantly. "That depends. Is an eyewitness proof enough for you, or do you need more?"

Kurt's dark brows furrowed. "So who is this witness, anyway?"

"Ben Rollison. You didn't see him, but he was there. He watched you put a bullet through my father's heart, then came to get me when he saw you riding hell bent away from the ranch. He'll testify to it if he has to, and when he does . . ." Her voice trailed away suggestively. All the anger she harbored for the man shimmered in her eyes as she waited for him to deny the accusation.

"I'll hang," Kurt supplied. "Is that what you're trying to tell me? You're bringing me back to Snow Creek for a farce trial, then you'll get the satisfaction of watching me dance." His gaze softened, but his voice remained hard, unyielding. "You've changed more than I thought, Nicole. You used to be a sweet little kid who'd creep around a spider when other people would've smashed it under their boot heel. You used to cry every time you saw me break a horse, and when I asked you why you'd say you were afraid I was breaking its soul. Do you still remember those days, kid, or did your need for revenge wipe all that out?"

Kid, Nikki thought. That was all she was in Kurt Frazier's eyes. All she ever would be. She was a woman now, thanks to him, but he refused to see it. "I remember. I just don't dwell on it. And I don't like to think about how naive and gullible I used to be . . . although I should have guessed you'd remind me."

Kurt studied her long and hard, but made no reply. Her gaze was no longer innocent, he thought, but bitter and calculating. Her words no longer soft, but delivered with timed precision to achieve her desired end. The coy, level-headed girl who would, as often as not, look away when spoken to had been replaced by a breathtakingly attractive woman who faced her speaker head on and returned a gaze unflinchingly. There was a hardness about her now, a cold inflexibility in her stance and carriage that hadn't been there before.

Then, of course, there was her inexplicable lack of fear. Kurt knew few men who would rush him while he was the one holding the gun. But this girl had. There was no logical reason for *that* beyond sheer stupidity . . . yet he knew of her intelligence first hand.

Nikki pushed to her feet and stood towering over him, boots spread wide in the crinkling leaves. Small, capable fists straddled her shapely hips. It was a masculine stance, yet it looked right at home on her. "Mike will be back with the water soon," she said. Turning away, she stifled a yawn. "I'll send him over. Try and get some sleep. We all need it."

Kurt's eyes narrowed. He watched her go, noticing how her feet dragged tiredly through the leaves and twigs. The ache in his side from where Mickey had dug out the bullet was starting to fade, but the annoying twinges didn't stop him from smiling when his gaze dropped to the gentle sway of her hips. There were some things that Nicole Dennison was powerless to deny or disguise. The fact that there was a woman's softness lurking beneath her crusty exterior and masculine clothes was one of them.

With a ragged sigh, he leaned his head against the rough bark and closed his eyes. He'd lost blood, and he was tired; dead tired. But his mind kept churning. Memories of the sweet, innocent Nicole he'd once known pushed at him from all sides. He was powerless to stop them.

Too tired to fight, he let the recollections wash over him in slow, languid waves. The years had erased a lot from his mind about the small, light-haired beauty. Too much, he thought. And then there were things Kurt couldn't have forgotten if someone had put a gun to his head and demanded it. Like the feel of her soft body nuzzling his naked side. The feel of her quicksilver hair slipping through his fingers like a rich bolt of satin. The look of slaked passion hooding the lids of eyes so rich and vibrant a man could drown in them. The taste of her mouth, of lips so sweet and moist they were like the gentle kiss of rain under a broiling desert sun.

No, there were some things about Nicole Dennison that even time couldn't erase from Kurt Frazier's mind.

The memories, spun like the fragile silk of a spider's web, wove their way into his dreams. By the time Mike returned to offer him a sip from the freshly filled canteen, Kurt was already asleep, a contented grin turning his lips as the cool breeze tossed raven-black hair around his sleep-softened face.

Nikki's head throbbed. The dull ache was timed to coincide with each clomping hoofbeat of the horse swaying steadily beneath her. Her eyes stung as though someone had rubbed the insides of her eyelids with a coarse piece of sandpaper. Her throat was dry and parched from thirst, her teeth gritty from the unavoidable dirt she'd swallowed. Every muscle in her body screamed at the long hours she had spent straddling a saddle.

Willy and Mike fared no better. Both boys sported dark circles beneath their bloodshot eyes. Their normally erect backs were slumped in twin humps. Twice they had complained of the hectic pace Nikki set, and twice she'd told them exhaustion was a hell of a lot better than being shot at, which is exactly what would happen if last night's adventure was discovered. They were quick to snap their mouths shut, and kept any further protests to themselves for the rest of the afternoon.

Kurt Frazier did not feel so inclined. He'd started the day by complaining that his fingers were turning blue. Nikki had loosened the ropes. Then he'd griped about the lack of food. Nikki had given him her last piece of jerky, which meant she went hungry. He couldn't ride the horse without his legs free, but Nikki refused to take the chance of him slipping away from them. She'd had Willy tie him into the saddle. Two hours out, he'd developed a headache from the sun. Nikki had given him her hat, which was laughably small for his head. The last time he had opened his mouth to complain, Nikki had gagged him.

Nikki glanced over her shoulder, and stifled a chuckle. Her black leather hat sat atop Kurt's head, the ties securing it bouncing against the thick cord of his sun-kissed neck. The scarf that had been tied around her face the previous night was jammed into his mouth, with Mike's scarf securing it in place—just in case he tried to push it free with his tongue. His waistcoat had been stored in her saddlebag, and the whiteness of his shirt glowed like a ghost beneath the blinding sun until she had to squint from the brightness.

"Nikki, we gotta do something about Frazier. His wound's starting to bleed again, and I don't like the looks of it."

Lips tight, she shifted her attention to Willy. He had abandoned his post as Kurt's guard in order to impart to her what he considered a vital bit of information. Mike didn't look happy about having to fall back and take his brother's place.

Nikki shrugged, guiding the horse around a rock. "I don't hear him complaining."

"He *can't*. You've got your scarf shoved down his throat. Maybe you should take the gag off and ask him how he's doing."

"What, and listen to his endless list of complaints? No thank you! Next he'll be griping because his saddle is too hard, or the horse goes too slow. I don't care if he bleeds to death, just so long as he does it *quietly*."

A scowl creased Willy's pudgy brow. His eyes, never terribly alert, fixed on his sister in alarm. "Come on, Nikki, you don't mean that."

"Wanna bet?" The look she shot her youngest brother said she meant every word. "Look, if you're so concerned, *you* ungag him. While you're at it, you can wash and rebandage his wound, toss some water down his throat, and let him eat *your* lunch. I'm not doing it."

Nikki kicked her horse into a trot and Willy watched his sister speed out in front of him. A cloud of dirt puffed up behind her. Swiping off his hat, he mopped his sweaty brow on his sleeve. "All right," he called, "maybe I'll do just that."

"Be my guest!" she yelled over her shoulder. Her answer was faint, rivaled by the thunder of hoofbeats.

Nikki could feel Willy's eyes boring indignant holes in her back almost as keenly as she could sense his confusion. But she didn't turn around. Instead she let the stallion have its head, enjoying the feel of the wind stinging her cheeks. A few wisps of sun-bleached silver pulled from the quick bun she'd twisted at her nape. The silky curls tickled her cheek and neck as she leaned low over Stetson's back. Her breathing was ragged as she mentally urged the stallion on.

When she was sure she was out of view, she slowed the horse to a restless trot. Given the choice, she would have kept going. Unfortunately, cold logic chose that moment to rear its ugly head. Logic that said her spirited mount would not stay fresh by being pushed to its limits merely to vent her own growing frustration.

Following her ears, she guided the stallion through a layer of trees, and over to the bank of a crisp, gurgling river. She slipped from the sinewy back as the dark nose dipped thirstily into the cool mountain water.

Kneeling on the grassy bank, Nikki splashed the revitalizing liquid on her face and neck. Drops of moisture splattered her hair, trickled down the front of her shirt. The icy water pooled between her breasts, the feeling at once annoying and exhilarating.

After taking a hearty drink, she backed away from the bank and sat cross-legged in the tall, swaying grass. Her gaze lit on the pitch-black stallion, the color of which reminded her much too clearly of Kurt Frazier's silky hair.

Kurt Frazier. Everything in her life these past six years came back to *him*. She'd thought every feeling she'd had for her father's killer—short of hatred—died the day Ben Rollison took her out onto the range to show her Hugh Dennison's lifeless body. But she was wrong. Her ties to Kurt, so carefully concealed, ran deep. Deeper than she cared to admit. And emotions so solidly rooted were nearly impossible, she knew, to kill.

She lowered herself onto the bed of prickly grass, drinking deeply of the soft breeze, laced liberally with pine sap. The call of a sparrow shrieked in her ears.

In less than a month they'd be back at the ranch, and while she craved the crisp fresh air of the Dakota Territory, and the company of the brothers who'd been left behind, she found herself reluctant to hurry. Bringing Kurt back to Snow Creek would cause nothing but trouble. Ever since her father's death, the town had been split to the point of violence over who had done the man in. It had all blown over eventually, of course, but dragging him back for a trial would reopen those partially healed wounds.

That thought brought with it another more pressing problem. What was she going to do with him? In her wildest dreams, she'd never thought to catch him. Now that she had, she was at a loss. Of course she would see he paid for what he'd done to her father—town support or no town support. That went without question. But how, exactly, was she going to do that without . . . well, without hurting Beth?

"So this is where you got yourself off to."

Nikki cupped a hand over her eyes, blocking out the blinding midday sun, and looked up to see Mike leading his horse to the riverbank. Her stallion sidestepped the intruder as the dapple gray dipped its nose in the refreshing water.

"I needed time alone," she muttered pointedly.

Mike ignored her as he plopped down in the tall grass by his sister's side. His fingers plucked out a thick green stalk, which he immediately shoved between his teeth. If there was one thing he knew, intimately, it was women. He could read them like a book and, sister or not, the look on this one's face spoke volumes. "Frazier's really getting to you, isn't he? Maybe you should've killed him when you had the chance."

"I tried," she reminded him coldly, "but he doesn't have the decency to die. Why'd you follow me, Mike? What do you want?"

He shrugged, rolling the sweet-tasting stalk over his tongue. "Nothing. Willy got soft and untied Frazier's gag. I needed a break from his wagging tongue as much as you did, and I figured that wherever you went, it was bound to be quieter than where I was. You don't mind, do you?"

"Do I have a choice?"

His Dennison-blue gaze swept the clearing as he shook his head. It was quiet here. Peaceful. Only the soft murmur of conversation, the insistent squawk of birds, and the gurgle of the river for company; and not a one of them griped or complained. It would take a stick of dynamite to budge him now.

"Nope, guess you don't at that," he replied with his most charming smile. It was a grin that had managed to coax more than one innocent Snow

Creek female out behind the barn at night.

Nikki groaned. Even family wasn't immune to *that* grin! "Make yourself at home," she sighed reluctantly. "And don't even think of complaining— about anything. I don't want to hear it."

Mike chuckled. Uncurling his long frame, he stretched out on his side. A cushion of knuckles supported his head as he sent his sister a thoughtful look. What has gotten into her? he wondered absently. He'd have thought she'd be on top of the world once they finally caught up with Frazier, yet she seemed angrier than ever. Why? Wasn't it what she wanted most in the world, to see their father's murderer hanged for what he'd done?

"Your friend back there sure flaps his gums a lot," he said. His gaze narrowed on her, watching as her cheeks flooded a furious shade of crimson.

"He isn't my friend," Nikki snapped through gritted teeth. Her fingers closed around a handful of grass and she yanked the thick stalks from the ground and let them flutter onto the dirty lap of her trousers.

"Not now, maybe, but he used to be. I always thought you liked Kurt. And didn't I hear Pop say once that he hoped you two would settle down together? Said you'd make a right fine couple. Handsome as all get out." He scowled. "Pop was right."

Nikki cursed her brother's infernally good memory and shot him a look that would have made a lesser man flinch. But Mike was too accustomed to womanly mood swings to be bothered by his sister's anger.

"Pop was smart, but he wasn't right about everything," she replied tightly. "What you just said proves it. When it came to me, he never thought straight. You know that. Either he was trying to marry me off to every young man of age in Snow Creek or he was busy introducing me to his old cronies hoping one of *them* would catch my eye. I've never met a man so anxious to see his daughter married and gone."

"He didn't want you gone, he just thought a husband and kids would help you settle down to life. He was doing what he thought was best for you."

"*I* can decide what's best for me, thank you very much. And what *isn't* best for me is being around Kurt Frazier for one more minute than I have to be."

"His jabbering bother you that much?"

Nikki scowled. "No," she said truthfully. "I won't let it bother me. I know what he's doing. The Kurt Frazier I used to know never said one more word than was absolutely necessary. And he *never* talked like that; never whined, never complained. Right now he's just trying to annoy me, and I refuse to give him the satisfaction of seeing he's succeeded."

Mike turned his head and spit the soggy stalk of grass off his tongue. Wiping his mouth on his sleeve, he turned back to Nikki. "And Beth?" he asked, his tone deceptively smooth and even. "How's all of this going to affect her? Or haven't you thought of that yet?"

Nikki stiffened, her widened gaze raking her brother as her mind raced. Mike didn't know who Beth's father was. No one did. Had he guessed? "Leave my daughter out of this, Mike. This has nothing to do with her."

His expression hardened. "Knock it off, Nikki, I'm not Willy. I'm not stupid. You put Beth and Frazier in the same room and the whole town's going to know who the kid's father is. They might not've guessed while he was gone and they had no one to compare her to, but the resemblance is there. She has his hair, his smile." His tone softened as he stroked the long, thin line of her arm. "Face facts, Sis. Your secret's going to be out the second you and Frazier set foot in Snow Creek, whether you planned it that way or not."

"I know," Nikki sighed tiredly. She quickly abandoned any pretense of denying her daughter's parentage. What good would it do? Mike was right, the resemblance was there. She felt suddenly overwhelmed by the repercussions that would be caused by dragging Kurt back home. "But there's damn little I can do about it now."

"You could let him go."

"Let him go?! Why the hell would I do that?" Nikki stormed to her feet and began angrily pacing the grass. She clutched her hands so tightly behind her back that she half-expected her fingers to snap from the pressure. "Hugh Dennison was your father too. You should be as eager as I am to see his killer swing!"

"I am." Mike nodded solemnly, turning his face away. He'd never been sure, the way Nikki was, that Kurt had killed their father. But he couldn't tell *her* that! Brother or not, she'd probably shoot him between the eyes for what she considered traitorous sentiments. He added guardedly, "If Kurt Frazier killed Pop, he *should* be made to pay."

"If? *If?!* We have an eyewitness who *saw* him do it. Or isn't Ben Rollison's word good enough for you anymore?"

"I'm not just thinking of the off-chance that we might be hanging an innocent man here, Sis, I'm thinking of you. Of what bringing Kurt back to Snow Creek is going to do to your life."

"I can take care of my own life, Michael James."

"Like you have already?" he challenged, pushing to his feet. He didn't try to conceal his anger. With Nikki, he didn't have to. "Oh yeah, from what I can see you've done a bang-up job of taking care of your life. Getting pregnant without a husband, delivering a baby who has no father, and alienating an entire town in the process. Yup, just grand. Bang-up job."

"That's enough," Nikki hissed.

"No," he growled, "it isn't. Because now you want to bring the kid's father back so you can get him strung up. Hell of a lot of good that's going to do your daughter! Or hadn't you thought of how Beth would feel after Kurt swings?"

Nikki's cheeks whitened, but she stood her ground. "She's only five years old, Mike. She won't remember any of this."

"She won't have to!" he bellowed. "The town will remember for her. When she's ten, she'll start hearing stories of how her mother hunted her father down like a dog, dragged him back to town, forced him through a mock trial, then sat back and laughed while she watched him do a jig at the end of a rope. By the time she's twelve, the story'll have gotten better, juicier. By the time she's sixteen it won't even sound like the truth anymore!" His steely gaze pierced her. "She's going to hate you, Nikki."

"I'll explain it to her," she defended weakly. Was he right? *Would* Beth hate her for what she was about to do? Nikki couldn't bear the thought of that. "She'll understand once she's old enough to know the truth."

Mike dragged his fingers through his tousled blond hair and shook his head sadly. The pain in his sister's eyes doused his anger. "The only thing she'll understand is that her mother hated her father enough to put a rope around his neck. *No* kid is going to understand why."

"He killed Pop. He cold-bloodedly murdered *her* grandfather," she cried with renewed vigor. "He's got to pay for that. I can't let him go free now that I've finally got him. Even for Beth."

"I didn't say that. Have your trial if you must, just don't have it in Snow Creek. He won't get a fair hearing there anyway. We both know it. The town's split down the middle on this one." Stalking over to his sister, he yanked her stiff form into a rough embrace. "Pull into the next town we come to and turn him over to the sheriff there. That way your sense of justice will be served, and you won't have to go through the humiliation of revealing to the world who Beth's father is. Snow Creek's barely learned to live with this thing, Nikki. By the time Beth grows up, people will have forgotten about her father—unless you keep giving them reminders."

She shook her head. "I can't. There are still a lot of people back home who think Kurt's innocent. I want them to see how wrong they are." Sucking in a ragged breath, she buried her face in his shoulder and hugged him close. "I'm bringing him back, Mike. I *have* to. I made this decision years ago."

Mike stroked his sister's back, while battling the urge to strangle her stubborn little neck, and nodded reluctantly. He knew Nikki, knew when a subject was dropped. But as far as he was concerned, the discussion wasn't over—not by a long shot. He'd work on her every step of the way back to the ranch if that's what it took. Not that his argument would do any good, he thought grimly. Talking logic to Nikki was next to useless once she had her mind set. The most he could do was try to convince her she was wrong and, barring that, hang back and catch her when she fell. And she would fall, he thought. She may not have planned it, but she was going to fall hard this time.

"Suit yourself," he sighed. Squeezing her shoulders, he led her back to the horses, now sloshing knee deep in the river. "I just hope you know what you're doing."

So do I, Nikki thought. She gave her brother a reassuring hug, then stepped from the circle of his arms. She felt suddenly cold as she grabbed the reins, now dripping wet from where they'd dragged in the water, and swung lithely into the saddle.

Turning her mount in the direction she'd come, Nikki told herself she *was* doing the right thing. At the same time, she prepared herself for another of what would undoubtedly be many encounters with the detestable Kurt Frazier.

Chapter Three

"I didn't think you were ever coming back," Willy sighed, his expression softening to one of utter relief when he saw the two horses weaving past trees and brush. They'd been gone so long, he'd started to think they were going to leave him alone in the woods with a man he was quickly beginning to hate—again.

Hunkered down beside his bound and regagged prisoner, Willy wiped his bloodstained hands on his trousers and stood. He approached the skittish stallion just as Nikki slid from the horse's back.

Swiping a stray silver curl from her brow, she sent Willy a condescending glare. A teasing smile played over her lips. "What's the matter, Willy? He talk too much for you?"

"Talk?" the boy whined. "He never shut up. He wanted to know where you two went, when you'd be back, what we were cooking for supper, how long it would take to reach the ranch . . . the list goes on."

Mike stepped to Nikki's side as her grin broadened. His lanky body dwarfed his sister's smaller, slender form. "You didn't answer him, did you?"

Willy stiffened, planting his balled fists on fatty, shapeless hips as his gaze clashed with Mike's. "Course not. What kind of fool do you take me for? If

Nikki wanted him to know, she'd have told him. Or she'd have had one of us tell him."

"Good," Mike said with a nod. As always, he was reluctant with his praise where this particular brother was concerned. He turned to Nikki. "Well? What do we do now? Our supplies are almost gone, the canteens need to be refilled, the horses are dead on their hooves, and your friend's wound has opened up again. Do we camp here for the night, or move on?"

Her gaze shifted to Kurt, who was watching them closely. His wound *had* reopened. The fresh strip of cloth wrapped around his waist was already stained with blood. The thick black hair, so silkily inviting last night, now hung around his face with only a limp trace of its former curl. Dark circles smudged his eyes and his skin was ashen.

"We stay," she said finally, not missing the shimmer of relief that flashed in steel gray eyes. "This is as good a place as any, I suppose. Mike, bring the horses to the river we just left and leave them for the night. Tie them up good. I don't want to wake up in the morning and find them gone. Bring Kurt's dirty bandages, you can rinse them while you're there. We're running low." She turned to Willy. "Take one of the bags of greenbacks in my saddlebag, the small one, and ride into town. After you clear the trees, it should be right over the hill," she nodded in the direction from which she and Mike had come. "Buy as many supplies as you think we'll need. I don't want to have to stop again for at least a week, so be sure you get enough."

"What are you going to do?" Mike asked as he grabbed the reins of three of the horses and started leading them toward the trees. His heels crunched over dry leaves and twigs as he looped the reins to a tree and started unstrapping the saddles.

"Leave me one of the rifles. I'll take care of our *friend* here, and see about rustling up some dinner.

Go on," she prodded, when both brothers sent her a skeptical look. "I can take care of myself. And you two better hurry. We'll be running out of daylight in about two hours, and I want you both back by then."

"Uh, Nikki . . . ?"

She looked up to see Willy standing a few feet away, his big feet shuffling in the underbrush. He'd taken the cracked leather pouch from her saddlebag; it now dragged from his fingers. Looking at him expectantly, she relieved him of the rifle, and took the box of bullets tucked beneath his meaty arm. "Well?"

"I—uh—what, exactly, do you want me to buy?" he asked, spitting out the question as though he was confessing his innermost sins to a preacher. "I never bought supplies before. That's your job."

"Regular stuff, Willy," she said tightly. Couldn't the boy do *anything* without having it spelled out for him? "I don't know. Buy things you think we'll need." He looked at her blankly. "Cornmeal," she said, waiting for the light of comprehension to flicker in his dull eyes. "Dried meat, coffee, beans." No light. "Forget it, I'll go myself."

She started to shove the gun and bullets into his hands, only to have Willy jump back as though she'd just pushed a coiled rattler on him. His gaze shifted between Frazier and his sister. "I can do it," he cried, "just tell me what you need."

Nikki glanced up at the sky, clear and cloudless, and gauged the distance between the sun and rustling treetops. She counted to ten and when her temper was firmly in check offered with strained patience. "How about a list? Would that help?"

Willy nodded and followed her to the saddlebags, peering over her shoulder as she dug inside the shadowy leather. Finding the second pouch, she emptied the contents into the saddlebag, then tucked a pinch of cornmeal, a grain of coffee, a corner of their last piece of meat, and a small amount of the rest of what she wanted inside. It was half full when she yanked the leather thongs closed, and handed the pouch to Willy.

"Pay attention to what you're doing now, and make sure you pay for the stuff with the bag of *greenbacks*, Willy," she warned with a lightness she did not feel. "Decent merchants frown on being paid with old coffee beans. And when decent merchants frown, they do it with their rifles loaded."

Willy nodded, grinned ear to ear, then strutted with youthful confidence to his horse.

Shaking her head, Nikki watched him go. She etched a mental note to do something about Willy as soon as they reached the ranch. Drastic measures would be called for. Lord, if he couldn't even ride into a strange town and buy supplies for a week of riding, he was in worse shape than she'd thought! Maybe she'd force him to go on the fall cow-hunt. The company of hardened ranch hands, the difficulty of the trail, the exertion the drive necessitated; all might combine to show Willy that self-reliance wasn't the monster he had made it out to be.

That decided, she crouched down and retrieved the rifle and bullets she'd left on the bed of leaves. She was halfway to the trees when Kurt's muffled voice stopped her.

"*Un-i-mmm-i-cn-brf!*" His heel stamped the ground for emphasis. Nikki slowly turned around.

A steely gaze glared at her from over the scarf, tied around the lower half of his face. The black silk made his eyes glisten like sparkling chips of ice. His wrists, chafed from the rough hemp, strained against the bindings. He looked as if he was about to attempt to push himself to his feet. He could try, but he wouldn't get far, she thought. His feet were still tied together in a knot that even she would have had trouble undoing. He must have given Willy more problems than she'd thought if the boy had figured out how to tie *that* knot!

"Problems, Frazier?" she asked with feigned sweetness. She tossed the rifle under her arm and eyed him innocently. "You'll have to speak up. I can't understand a word you're saying."

Kurt's reply came in the form of an angry reddening of his chiseled cheeks, and a hardening of the angry slits of his eyes.

She might have left him sitting there until nightfall if he hadn't started wiggling around on the ground like a snake, trying to gain his footing. The white bandage around his naked waist darkened with each movement. Muffled words issued forth from around the scarf, and Nikki didn't need to understand them to know he was cursing her with gusto.

"You're going to kill yourself if you keep that up," she warned him coolly. Shoving the box of bullets into her trouser pocket, she deposited the rifle on the ground and carefully approached him. "Not that it matters to me, mind you."

"*N-mm-gnng-t-kl-oo-ff-i-vr-gt-mm-hns-n-oo, oo-ttl-btt!*"

He was on his knees now, sort of, doubled at the waist, with his hands securely bound in front of him. His legs were bent, back arched, his forehead firmly planted on the ground. He was not wearing a shirt. Scrapes marred the firmly worked muscles of his shoulders and back from where sharp twigs had bitten into his flesh.

Nikki thought she could grow to like him that way; tied up and at her mercy. The steely, upside-down eyes said he didn't like her at all.

She plopped down next to him, and returned his gaze measure for furious measure. "If you want fresh meat for supper, you'd better knock off the nonsense and let me get to my hunting. Otherwise, we're back to dried jerky again . . . *if* Willy remembers to buy it."

Kurt didn't reply. The scarf holding the gag in place had worked its way down on his face when he'd tried to stand, and he was busy scraping his cheek against the leaves, pushing it lower. When it cleared his chin, he gave a sigh of relief and worked the moist cloth shoved between his teeth—halfway down his throat!—with his tongue. It plopped out at the same time he resignedly lowered himself to the ground. His breathing was ragged.

"Be thankful my hands are tied, Nicole," he panted, his cheeks and hair gritty with dirt, "because I have an overpowering urge to strangle you right now."

She regarded him coldly. "No stronger than the one I've battled for the last six years, I'll wager."

Squelching the urge to check his wound, she pushed to her feet and headed for her rifle. She told herself she didn't care if he ripped his entire side open. His voice stopped her cold.

"Do you hate me that much?"

Her spine stiffened, her chin tilted, but she didn't turn around. "More," she replied flatly, and wondered where the familiar surge of hatred had gone; the one she always felt when she thought of Kurt Frazier and what he'd done to her father.

She heard him sigh, the sound almost buried in the dry leaves crunching beneath him. Instinctively, she knew he'd flipped to his back and pushed to a sitting position. "I remember a time when you didn't," he said, his tone mildly suggestive. "A time when you liked me just fine."

This time Nikki did turn; slowly, precisely. A spark of self-loathing shimmered in her narrow, cornflower-blue eyes as she hugged the rifle to her waist. "Some things are better left forgotten, buster. And this is one of them."

A dark brow cocked high. "Do you think I could forget—?"

"Why not?!" she demanded angrily, swiping the hair from her forehead in one jerky motion. She didn't want to discuss it with him, but she had a feeling he wasn't going to let the subject drop. At least she could be thankful he'd waited until they were alone. "It isn't as though it *meant* anything to you. Nothing *means* anything to you. I was just another stupid girl who gave you something you probably thought you deserved. Well, I'm not stupid anymore. I've smartened up in the last six years. I can see things the way they really are now."

Kurt's tone softened as a spark of confusion flickered behind his eyes. "It wasn't like that and you know it. You meant something to me. You—"

"I *meant* something to you?" she snapped. *Meant*. Past tense. Good, Nikki thought. That was exactly where their relationship belonged. In the past. "The only thing I *meant* to you was one more notch in your saddle horn. Something to brag about to the other hired hands. A good time with the boss's daughter, no strings. How many other women have you bedded since me, Kurt? One? Two? A dozen? Do you remember their names? Or didn't they *mean* anything to you?" Her tone turned venomous. "And did you kill their fathers too, or was I *special?*"

"Go hunt your rabbits," Kurt growled, his eyes spitting fire. "Talking to you is like talking to a milk cow. You both make about as much sense."

Nikki swallowed the insult and spun on her heel, her back painfully straight. Again, Kurt's voice stopped her. Only this time it wasn't anger that surged through her blood, but something else. Something she didn't dare give a name to.

"Do you remember the tornado that set down in seventy-six, Nicole? Just a little one, only wiped out half of Main Street, but people talked about it for years. Probably still do. How old were you then, kid? Thirteen? Fourteen?"

"Thirteen," she answered suspiciously. *Kid.* There it was again, that veiled insinuation. "And yes, I remember it. Why?"

"And do you remember where you hid? Do you remember me finding you curled up under your bed crying and shivering because you were so scared? No one looked for sweet, stubborn, clever little Nicole. They thought she could take care of herself, that she'd know what to do. They didn't look for you, baby . . . but I did. I found you under your bed and had to pick you up and carry you like a sack of potatoes over my shoulder down to the cellar where it was safe. As I recall, you fought me every step of the way. Do you remember any of that?"

"Yes, of course," she repeated weakly, cautiously. God, she remembered it like it was yesterday. "It happened a long time ago, Kurt. What does it have to do with anything now?"

Kurt pursed his lips and shook his head. A glint of pain flashed in his eyes. "Not a thing," he answered on a husky sigh. His voice was as deceptively smooth as a glass of aged brandy. "Go chase your rabbits, Nicole. I'll be here when you get back."

Nikki concentrated on putting one foot in front of the other, until the line of trees became a strong barrier between her back and the feel of Kurt Frazier's eyes boring into her rigid shoulders. Her neck was straight, as though it were encircled by an invisible iron band. But as soon as she was out of sight, her chin sagged wearily to her collarbone and her shoulders slumped.

Why had he brought up the tornado? she wondered as she picked her way slowly around tree and shrub. Why that particular memory, and why now? He had a reason, she knew. Kurt never did or said anything without a reason. But what, exactly, was it? And why was her own reaction so strong?

A jackrabbit darted out from the underbrush, then,

on seeing her, scampered back in the direction from which it had come. She didn't shoot it, but kept on walking. The rifle propped over her right shoulder stayed pointed harmlessly at the sky.

She was still deep in thought when she came to the river. Mike was nowhere to be seen, and she assumed he'd tethered the horses upstream. Good. She would finally have some time alone.

Sighing, she propped the rifle against the trunk of a towering oak and plopped herself down beneath its rustling shade. The hard-packed ground was cool against her backside, the dirt hard. She plucked up a thick stalk of grass, stuck it between her teeth, enjoying the sweet taste of it on her tongue. Resting her head against the coarse bark, she focused on the ever-changing river current.

The didn't look for you, baby . . . but I did.

He was right, no one had looked for her. Her family had assumed that intelligent, level-headed little Nicole had done the wise thing, as always, and scurried down to the safety of the cellar when she'd heard the twister was coming.

But she hadn't. She'd panicked. For the first time in her life, Nicole Dennison had done the unwise thing. She'd hidden under her bed, even knowing that, should the tornado succeed in felling the house, she'd be trapped if not killed in the rubble.

Kurt had found her, crying and shivering and acting like anyone but herself. He'd dragged her out from under the bed and held her so close to his chest she could hear his heart pounding. He'd stroked her back, kissed her hair, and whispered words of comfort that Nikki couldn't even hear over her breathless sobs. But the tone was comforting, even if she didn't hear the words. And she'd clung to him for dear life.

Looking back, Nikki couldn't recall ever feeling so safe, so protected, as when she'd been held in the strong circle of his arms. It was that feeling, and the frightening newness of it, that made her fight him so hard when he'd suggested she hide in the cellar. She hadn't wanted him to leave, afraid that the twister would wreak its destruction by carrying him out of her life forever. In her naïveté, she'd fought to stay in the security of his embrace. It hadn't worked. He'd tossed her over his shoulder as though she weighed no more than a scrappy kitten, and forcefully carried her down the stairs.

Nikki shivered when she remembered the cold mustiness of the cellar and the long hours spent huddled in a corner there. A lifetime passed before it was safe enough for Pete to ferret her out. Long, torturous hours spent contemplating broad shoulders, raven hair, and the sweet rush of breath that still singed her cheek. How could she ever forget arms so comforting and strong that they made her forget she wasn't a woman yet? That made her *want* to be a woman. *His* woman.

As a child, she'd respected Kurt. As a young girl, she'd admired his ability as the best broncobuster in Dakota. As an adolescent, she'd been infatuated with him. And as a girl bordering on womanhood, her feelings for him had blossomed that day into love. In the next year and a half, the emotion flourished to an obsession. It took four more years for her to bolster up the courage to bring their relationship to its culmination one moonswept night on a bed of hay in her father's barn.

A fish peeked its head over the river's currents. Nikki was too caught up in her memories to spare it more than a passing glance. Her thumb reached up and brushed her full lower lip. She grew uncomfortably warm, stirring restlessly against the hard tree when she remembered the feel of Kurt's mouth on hers, and the gentle guidance of his hands over her naked flesh.

She should hate him for what he had taken from her that night, Nikki thought, spitting the stalk of limp grass to the ground. And perhaps if he had forced his attentions on her, she would. But the only force used had been hers. The only seduction that of her own making. Even a man of stone couldn't have refused what she'd so eagerly offered—not for long, anyway. And that was exactly what Nikki had counted on. After his initial adamant refusal, Kurt had surrendered and taken from Nikki only that which had been freely given.

Once, she thought, shoving herself to her feet and snatching up the rifle. That single night of passion had created the one person Nikki loved above all else. The only person she knew of who could cause actual fear to pump through her blood. And now she had to do everything in her power to protect Beth from the hideous crimes of the child's father.

An hour and a half later, as the first threads of dusk stole across a sailor's sky, Nikki strolled back into camp. A string of four wild rabbits, cleaned and ready for roasting, dangled from her fingers.

She dropped the bounty onto the bed of leaves beside the campfire and instructed Willy to start them cooking. He looked at her with an expression just short of horror. The determined glint in his sister's eyes made him swallow his argument and start about the chore.

Mike sat propped against a tree, sharpening the point of a branch that would eventually be used as a spit for the rabbits he never doubted his sister would bring back. He chuckled heartily, watching his brother fumble clumsily with their supper.

Nikki stood in the center of the camp, hands on hips, and let her gaze flicker accusingly between her two brothers. "Did either of you think to change his bandages lately?" she asked.

"I just got back," Willy chirped, holding up a dead rabbit and wondering what to do with it. "Got everything you wanted except the beans. They didn't have none."

"He was sleeping when I got back," Mike added, not looking up as he drew the sharp blade of his knife down the length of the branch. A curling peel of bark fluttered to the ground. "I didn't want to wake him."

She nodded, heaving a sigh and snatching up the canteen propped next to Mike's feet. She should have expected as much. Without constant prodding, her brothers were about as useful as a pack of schoolboys on summer vacation.

Deciding she would have to do the chore herself if she wanted it done, Nikki crossed to where Kurt sat and dropped the canteen next to his muscular thigh. His broad back slumped against an oak tree, shoulders forward, feet crossed at the ankle. The large hands were clasped limply in his lap and his head dipped in sleep, his chin pillowed atop his rock-hard chest.

The bandages wrapped across his stomach were bright in the rustling shadows, the material stained with dirt from his afternoon struggles and splotched with blood. His pants were torn from the twigs and stones scattering the ground. Some of the scratches visible through the tears were dark and crusted, as were the ones on his arms and shoulders. His shirt was tossed in a wrinkled heap at his side. Obviously, no one had seen fit to put it back on him. The sun-kissed flesh had a distinctly pink tinge to it from where it had baked under a midday sun.

A handful of mosquito bites welted on his neck and torso. She noticed the ugly bumps as she dropped to her knees at his side. His hands were tied. He couldn't scratch the annoying bites. For a split second she felt a stab of guilt. The emotion was just as quickly shoved away. She couldn't afford to feel sympathy for this man, she reminded herself harshly. She couldn't afford to feel *anything* for this man but hatred.

Kurt must have sensed her presence, for suddenly his head snapped up and Nikki found herself captured by his haunting gray eyes. The hands she had extended with the intent of loosening his bandages hesitated. She could feel the heat of his body seep into her fingertips. The sweaty, leathery scent of him was strong as it stung her nostrils.

"Sit forward," she ordered, the harshness of her words countered by the breathless huskiness lacing her tone. "Your wound needs to be washed and the bandages need changing. I can't do it with your back sticking like glue to that tree."

He sat forward, and Nikki lifted her trouser leg, pulling out the long, curved-blade knife tucked in the leather cuff of her boot—a knife she had started carrying for extra protection since the night she'd kidnapped him. His skin felt warm against her knuckles as she carefully sliced away the moist knot holding the linen in place. It was no use trying to untie it since his blood had tightened the knot beyond loosening.

The steely gaze narrowed, focusing on a shapely knee, boldly exposed beneath the midnight-black hem. "Nicole, do you remember the time—?"

"Shush up," she growled. Replacing the knife, she yanked her trouser leg in place. Her skin burned from where his gaze had seared it. "I don't want to talk about old times with you, Kurt. I don't even want to *think* about those days."

"Why not?" he asked as she shoved him back against the tree trunk and reached for the canteen. "Are you embarrassed?"

"Of course not," she lied as she uncapped it and raised the narrow rim to his lips. "I just think talking about it's a waste of time." She waited until he had quenched his thirst before pulling the canteen away. "Grit your teeth, because it's going to hurt when I peel these bandages away. Some of the blood's dried. The cloth will probably stick to your skin worse than Buckeye Burt's biscuits stick to a skillet."

He chuckled at the memory of the one-eyed cook and his hard, tasteless biscuits. It was a wonder anyone on the drive survived to tell the tale with Buckeye going along to cook the meals. Kurt's mirth evaporated as the cold mountain water splashed over his side. He gasped as slender fingers began gently probing his wound.

Nikki scowled. The bullet hole itself was harmless, the bleeding not as excessive as it looked. The wound, as close to the taut waist as it could get, had missed all vital organs. Mike had removed the bullet cleanly. Nikki would have been proud of his handiwork if the wound would just heal and stop bleeding!

"Damn!" she muttered under her breath, taking the wet, dirty linen strips and tossing them into the leaves. What could she expect, really? It wasn't as though they'd taken very good care of Kurt since they'd kidnapped him. The wound needed to be cleaned and dressed twice as many times as they'd done it. And he hadn't been fed enough to keep a pigeon alive, let alone allow him to build up the strength to clot the blood. The wound had to form a clot. That went without question. And if it wouldn't do it itself, then . . .

The tantalizing aroma of roasting meat invaded the camp, making Nikki's stomach grumble hungrily. Squashing a wave of guilt, she fixed her attention on a dozing Willy. "Whiskey!" she hollered. "I want a bottle and I want it now."

Her brother's head snapped up, and there was a telltale darkening of his rounded cheeks when he looked at Nikki as though he didn't know what she was talking about. "Whiskey?" he gulped. "Gosh, Nikki, we don't got no—"

Her eyes narrowed threateningly. "Don't tell me you rode into a town filled with saloons and didn't stop to buy yourself a bottle, William Andrew. I know you too well. Just like I know whose canteen I took last night by mistake. You know, the one filled with gin? Now, either you hand over the whiskey, rum, or whatever else you bought, or I'll make you wish you had. Which will it be?"

With uncanny speed, Willy dug into his saddlebag. He produced a tall bottle, three quarters full of sloshing amber liquid, which he tossed to his sister. Nikki snatched it out of midair.

"We'll talk about this later," she spat. Clamping the cork between her teeth, she yanked it from the bottle. The pungent smell of liquor made her catch her breath as she raised the lip of the bottle to Kurt's smiling mouth. "Stop your grinning and drink," she ordered, giving him no choice in the matter as she poured a goodly portion of the firewater down his throat.

A drop of dark amber trickled down his stubbled chin. Nikki unconsciously wiped it away. Her hand brushed his liquor-moist lips. His flesh quivered beneath her fingertips. She snatched her hand back when she felt her knuckles graze the dark whiskers coating his jaw, but not before she saw a glint of raw challenge sparkle in his eyes.

"What are you going to do?" he queried, eyeing her carefully. "Get me drunk and have your way with me? I won't stop you, if that's what you think. Not this time."

His voice, throaty and raw from the liquor, shot up Nikki's spine. She met his gaze unflinchingly. "As I recall, you don't need a bottle to be taken advantage of," she countered with a boldness that startled even herself.

His lips curved into a devilish grin that made her heart skip a beat. "So you *do* remember," he said lazily, his gaze warming her head to toe. "I was starting to wonder."

She gave him no time to say more as she dumped another gulp of whiskey down his throat. He hadn't eaten since noon, and even then, not much. It shouldn't take long to get him drunk.

"Hey, Nikki, don't let him drink it all," Willy whined from where he crouched next to the roasting rabbits. The glow of fire played off his rounded features, making him look even fatter.

"Shut up, fool," Mike growled, saving his sister the trouble. He'd gone from sharpening branches to whittling a squared-off chunk of dried pine.

Nikki turned her attention back to Kurt, whose gaze never wavered. "As soon as the whiskey starts working, I'm going to cauterize that wound. Unless you're lucky enough to pass out drunk, it's going to hurt. I can't stop that."

"Would you?" Kurt asked softly, his whiskey-laden breath grazing her cheek and neck. "I mean, if you could stop it from hurting . . . would you do it?"

Nikki rocked back on her heels as though he'd just clipped her jaw. *He* hadn't. The answer that immediately tumbled from her lips, had. "Yes," she said, "I suppose I would."

His lips turned up in a cocky grin as one hand inched toward her cheek. The rope connecting the thick, powerful wrists to his ankles brought him up short. Kurt's hands dropped to his lap. His gaze flashed with the disappointment he felt at not being able to touch her.

"You still don't step on spiders, do you, Nicole?" he asked, his voice slurring from the whiskey. His eyelids thickened, then drooped shut. A long minute passed before they swooped up again. "Maybe you haven't changed so much, after all." This time when his eyes closed, they stayed closed.

Maybe not, Nikki agreed silently. Pushing to her feet, she began to search for something that could be used to cauterize his wound. *Maybe I haven't changed at all. Maybe I'm just better at covering my weaknesses now.*

Chapter Four

"Nicole? Ouch! Nicole, wake up!"

Nikki stirred under the blanket, muttered a curse under her breath, then drifted back to sleep.

Kurt scowled and tried again. "Come on, honey, wake up. *Nikki!*"

Wrinkling her nose, she swatted at a pesky fly buzzing near her cheek, then slowly opened her eyes. She rubbed at eyelids that were reluctant to pry themselves apart as the gentle sounds of the night washed over her. She stifled a yawn with the back of her fist and squinted into the darkness. With the moon hiding behind a layer of inky clouds, it was hard to see. A cool breeze rustled the leaves and washed over her cheeks. She shivered.

"Nicole," the slurred voice hissed close by her ear. "Are you awake?"

Kurt. He was the one who'd woken her. But why? Was he in pain? Her body protested that she'd only just started to doze. The effects of the whiskey couldn't have worn off of him yet.

"What do you want, Kurt?" she asked, a thread of leeriness creeping into her tone, countering her exhaustion. "Did your wound open up again? Do you want more whiskey? I think there's . . ." Her voice faced into another yawn. ". . . some left."

Sitting up, she stared at the spot where she knew Kurt to be. His steel-gray eyes were reflected in the dwindling firelight. They looked like those of a wild wolf, momentarily frozen in the reflective light of a lantern.

"I don't want a drink, I want a bath." His whiskey-thickened tone was light when he recognized the concern edging her words. The darkness hid the suspicious grin tugging at one corner of his mouth. "I'm filthy and I can't stand the feel of myself anymore."

"A bath!?" She was fully awake now, and struggling to keep her voice low so she wouldn't wake her sleeping brothers. "You woke me up to tell me you want a bath?!"

"Uh-hmmm. It's a reasonable request, considering."

"Considering I just fell asleep, I'd say it sounds pretty *un*reasonable. Go back to sleep, Kurt."

She started to snuggle back under the blanket, but Kurt put a quick stop to that. "No, baby, you're not going back to sleep on me now. It took me too long to wake you up."

"Me?" Sighing heavily, she shot an indignant glare at the shadows that enveloped him. "You're the one who needs to rebuild strength. I'd say you need the rest more than I do."

"I don't want to sleep, I want a bath," he repeated in no uncertain terms. "And I'll talk your ear off until I get one."

Nikki groaned. If the last two hours were anything to go by, alcohol only loosened his tongue. She wasn't sure how many more "memories" she could stand to rehash. Already she'd heard about the family shipping business his father ruled with an iron hand; his wild mother's even wilder escapades in the California gold mines; his uncle who'd fought in the War Between the States, on the wrong side, and who'd died for the honor; his four brothers, two sisters, four nieces, three cousins . . . the list was endless. Nikki knew she couldn't take much more! If he started talking again she might be tempted to gag him—again—and for some idiotic reason she didn't want to do that.

"Go to sleep," she whispered sharply. "You can have a bath in the morning if you still want one."

"Uh-uh. I want one now."

"Why?" she moaned, fighting the urge to pull the blanket over her head and ignore him. "It can't be too much longer until dawn. Can't you wait?"

Kurt's voice was harsh, uncompromising, and still slurred. "You know, I hate to be the one to remind you, Nicole, but you and your brothers have treated me like dirt for the past twenty-four hours. Now that's fine, I can handle it. I'm even getting used to it. But if I have to sit here in my own blood and sweat for one more minute I swear I'll—"

"Shhh!" she hissed, jerking an index finger he couldn't see to her lips. "You'll wake them up. I won't be held responsible for what they do to you if they go without sleep one more night."

"Then save them the trouble. Give me my bath."

"No," she snapped, yanking the blanket up and adjusting the saddle beneath her head. It made a hard pillow, but she'd ridden on enough cattle drives to be used to the discomfort. "You'll get it in the morning and not one minute before. Now, shush up and *go to sleep!*"

Taking a deep breath, she scrunched her eyes closed and concentrated on the owl hooting plaintively from its perch high above, and Willy's rhythmic snores. The rustle of leaves was a familiar, sweet caress to her ears; a sound that was countered by Kurt's uneven breathing. She heard the twigs crunch beneath him when he shifted his weight. Thankfully, he kept his peace. She was just beginning to doze again when his rich voice shattered her solitude.

"Nicole? Are you still awake?" Pause. "Nikki?"

"Shhh!"

Sighing heavily, he rested his head against the sharp bark. His gray eyes focused on the clouds, and the cottony spot where the moon illuminated them from behind. "Nicole, do you remember the time you decided to take a midnight ride on Stetson? You were seventeen the night I found you bathing nak—"

"Shush up, Kurt," Nikki growled, aggravation riding her hard. "I still remember where I put that gag. Just because I haven't used it tonight, doesn't mean I won't."

Except for a throaty chuckle, and a dry hiccup, he ignored her. "The moon was high and there was a layer of clouds blocking out the moonlight . . . a lot like tonight. You were washing the trail dirt from your hair and humming a song proper young ladies aren't supposed to know about when I found you. Did you know I watched you for a while before I let you know I was there? Watched, and listened." He released a slow, ragged breath. The sound curled up Nikki's spine. "Your hair looked as white and as clean as a new cotton sheet, and even though you were mostly in shadows I could still see enough to know you weren't wearing so much as a stitch of—"

"All right," Nikki exclaimed through gritted teeth. She shoved the blanket off, finding herself suddenly warm. A shiver rippled over her shoulders, though she wasn't entirely sure the cool night air had caused it. "If I give you a bath will you promise to shush your mouth and go to sleep afterward?"

"Of course," he agreed easily. Too easily, Nikki thought. "Give me a bath and I'll be as quiet as a church mouse. You'll never know I'm here. I won't so much as—"

"Escape? You won't try that, will you?"

"You poured so much whiskey down my throat I'll

be lucky if I can stand, let alone run. Besides, it would only open my side again, and you went to so much trouble to close it." He shook his head. "No, Nicole, I won't escape. Not this time."

"You promise? I want your word, Kurt. I won't take you until I have it." Reaching into the saddlebag over her head, she fumbled inside for a washcloth and a bar of soap, which she then shoved inside her pockets. Sitting up, she jerked the blanket around her waist and tied it tight. A towel for later.

"Have I ever lied to you?" he asked, his voice oddly husky.

"As a matter of fact . . ."

"Recently, Nicole," he elaborated with a sigh and a stifled hiccup. "Have I lied to you *recently*."

"I haven't given you the chance," she answered flippantly. "I'll bring my pistol along, just in case you change your mind, or the cold water sobers you up."

Quietly, Nikki approached his shadowy form. Kurt was right; not only did he look awful, he smelled awful. An unsavory combination of whiskey, blood, and sweat. Wrinkling her nose, she squatted down beside him, wondering what the cold mountain water would do to his so-recently-sealed wound. She pulled her trouser leg up and slipped the knife from her boot, deciding that if he wanted a bath so badly *he'd* take responsibility for the consequences. Besides, giving in to his demand was probably the only way she'd ever get any sleep tonight.

"You smell good, Nicole," he said, turning his head toward her. A few silky wisps fell over her shoulder as she cut the rope free. The tips tickled his cheek and jaw. He inhaled deeply, pretending to savor the scent. Wishing he could. The hair grazing his skin reminded him of sultry, sleepless nights.

She glanced down sharply and thought he looked as terrible as he smelled; haggard and tired. She bit back a stab of guilt. "I thought you couldn't smell."

"I can't." He grinned sloppily, his gaze darkened. "I used my imagination. I do that a lot where you're concerned."

"Well, you smell rancid." Tucking the knife away, she unpeeled the cords from around his wrists. She winced at the angry, raw marks the rope left on his flesh.

"There," she said when the binding fell to the leaves his rugged body had crushed flat. She moved to the rope at his ankles. There was no need for the knife here, since she'd made the knot loose enough to work free with her fingers, and positioned it in a place he'd have the devil's own time reaching. Those, too, were tossed onto a clump of dried leaves. "Can you stand, or do you need help?"

Kurt started to say he could stand just fine, then promptly bit the words back. "I still feel shaky," he lied, his fingers wrapping around her wrist. The bones felt fragile in his palm, like one of the sticks that pressed into his back with such regularity. "Do you mind?" he asked, his fingers sliding higher.

The touch, seemingly innocent, kindled a strong flame inside of Nikki. A fiery awareness that was impossible to douse.

"No, of course not," she said with a brisk shake of her head. It couldn't be *her* voice that sounded so high and breathless, she thought. She moistened her suddenly parched lips and searched the ground. Finding a good-sized branch, she picked it up and shoved it into his free hand. "Here, put your arm around my shoulder. Like this." She held her breath against his pungent scent and guided him, wondering where all his strength had gotten off to. "That's right. Now, use your other hand to push on the stick. Good, now . . . My God, you're heavy!" She staggered under his weight, and almost dropped him back to the ground.

"Sorry," he murmured, shifting so more of his weight was supported by the branch. He knew he could have walked quite nicely without any help, but he kept his arm around her shoulders anyway, marveling as they walked at how perfectly she molded into the hardness of his side. Her quicksilver head barely grazed his bristled jaw, and she had to lengthen her own strides to keep pace with his weaker but longer ones.

"Are you all right?" she asked after they'd walked into the woods. His breathing was ragged as it grazed her cheek. "Is your side hurting? We can stop and rest if you want."

"I'm fine," he replied tightly. His lips had thinned to a vibrant white line and he'd tightened his hold on her shoulders when she made to walk away. He may not have needed it back at camp, but right now her supple little body was the only thing between standing and keeling over.

It took twice as long to reach the gurgling river as it normally would have. By the time they neared the sandy banks, both were panting from exertion, and even Nikki had worked up a fine sweat. They collapsed on the hard-packed ground as one.

"After this, *I'll* be the one who needs a bath," she remarked lightly, once her breathing had returned to normal. "I haven't felt this sore since I helped Pop fix the roof."

"And fell off the ladder," he added with a chuckle. That was a memory even he had forgotten—until she'd mentioned it. How long before her aching backside had let her sit down without squirming? At least a week. It was a sight her four brothers had found hilarious. Her cheeks had pinkened at their ribald teasing, and Kurt remembered, vividly, the surge of pity he'd felt at her innocent embarrassment.

"Ready for that bath yet? Or do you want to rest more?"

"Rest. For a few minutes, anyway." He turned his head, letting his gaze rove over each delicately molded line of her profile. The more he looked, the more the razor-sharp pain in his side faded. Her eyes were closed, her features softly relaxed. His fingertips itched to trace her porcelain cheek, just to see if it was still as smooth as he remembered.

"Nicole," Kurt said suddenly, suspiciously. "Why are you being so nice to me? Yesterday you were threatening to kill me—repeatedly—and now you're helping me bathe. Why?"

She shrugged. "That was yesterday."

"And that's no answer."

"It's the only one you're going to get, unless you threaten to talk my ear off again, in which case I'll . . ."

"You'll what?"

"I'll throw you in the river and let you talk to the fish. They might not be able to answer, but they'll have to listen." She grinned impishly, opening her eyes, and was immediately captured by his laughing gaze. "Think about it, Kurt, a captive audience. You can recount your days on the Triple D to them, and they can't tell you to shush up."

He placed a palm on his chest, his expression melting to one of feigned indignation. "Come on, Nicole, I'm not *that* bad."

"Right . . . you're worse. Obviously, you don't listen to yourself. Willy's about ready to shoot you dead the next time you open your mouth, and Mike wants me to use the last of our greenbacks to buy a surplus of gags. I'll let you guess what he wants to use them for."

His voice lowered to a husky pitch when his gaze settled on her naturally pouting mouth. Of its own accord, his thumb reached out and traced the fuller, bottom lip. "And you, Nicole? What do you want?"

She was too shocked by the unexpected contact to

pull away. Confusion shimmered in her eyes when she met his gaze. "I-I want you to take your bath so I can get some sleep," she said finally. Her voice cracked, but only a little.

He gave a clipped nod, his breath catching as he rolled away. Nikki shivered with sudden cold and sat up. Bending her legs, and wrapping her arms around her knees, she watched him. After all, hadn't the sneaky rat admitted to doing much the same thing to her years ago? Turnabout *is* fair play, she reasoned.

Leaning heavily on the branch, Kurt rose to his feet. His stance was shaky, and Nikki half expected him to crash to the ground with each heavy step that brought him closer to the river's twisting currents. He didn't, although once he did come treacherously close to landing on his knees.

She watched him lower himself to the ground and tug at the fancy, ankle-high boots. His attempts were feeble at best, and each one was punctuated with a grunt. She waited for him to ask for help. When he didn't, she realized he wasn't going to.

Cursing his blind stubbornness, she uncurled her body and walked to where he sat. The cool breeze rippled the curtain of hair swaying at her waist. Squatting in front of him, she took his boot in her hand and pulled hard. Again. When she stood, it was to drop his big expensive boots onto the leaves by his side.

"Thanks," he replied tersely. It was the liquor, not the wound, that fogged his senses. Either way, it aggravated the hell out of him. His motions jerky, he began working free the buttons of his bloodstained shirt. "I can do the rest."

Nikki shrugged, retreating to her spot in the grass. "I wasn't offering," she said over her shoulder.

Kurt began slipping the shirt down his brawny arms, and she wasn't sure if he'd heard her. Sighing, she settled back on the grass and prepared to enjoy herself, hoping her prying eyes would cause him more than a little discomfort. Unfortunately, the moon chose that moment to peek from behind the dark layer of clouds. It illuminated the clearing in a soft, silver glow.

Nikki squirmed when her curious gaze was met with firm male sights. A broad back, alive with firmly worked muscles; a lean, taut waist, free for once of its swath of bandages. Sinewy arms rippled in the moonlight as he worked free the belt and unbuttoned his trousers.

So much for embarrassing him! Nikki thought, cursing the blush that warmed her cheeks. She averted her gaze, but raw curiosity pulled it back time and again. It wasn't until she saw him push to his feet—with the aid of the branch—and slip the midnight-black trousers down nicely firm, sun-gold thighs that she diverted her gaze for good. She studied the jutting stalks of grass, tinted a dark shade of gray in the moonlight, with unusual interest. When that no longer fascinated her, she stared at the scuffed toe of her boot. *Anything!*

Her heart was pounding fast and her palms were unusually moist. Her breathing was soft and shallow. She attributed all these nervous signs to lack of sleep coupled with the chill of the night. It made no sense, but then, she didn't try to analyze it, she just accepted it.

A meadowlark screeched high in the branches above at the same time the first splash of water echoed in her ears. Her gaze snapped up, an impulse she immediately regretted as her eyes locked onto Kurt Frazier's naked body. He stood waist-high in the river, cupping his hands and splashing water over his shoulders and back. What she could see of his torso glistened moistly in the moonlight.

Her breath lumped in her throat, and she forced herself to release it in one long, slow exhalation. Her body tingled with awareness when she remembered the feel of his hard chest slipping beneath her palm, pressing intimately against her. The sweet aroma of pine sap and wildflowers was replaced by a whiff of freshly strewn hay. The caw of a bird became the soft baying of her father's prized stallion. And beneath her curious fingertips she could feel the exquisite touch of wonderfully firm, sun-bronzed . . .

Nikki came out of the daydream abruptly when she realized Kurt had said something—and she had no idea what it was. Her flush deepened as her trembling fingers picked at the grass. She stammered, "Wh-what?"

"I said, did you bring any soap?" he repeated, a secretive grin tugging at his lips. He could only guess at where her thoughts had drifted.

"Soap?" she repeated stupidly, shaking her head to clear it. "Oh, *soap*." Reaching into her pocket, she pulled out the soap and washcloth, then untied the blanket from around her waist.

"No, don't throw it," he called when she made ready to toss the pair to him. "The current will take them if they fall in the river, and I'm not strong enough to swim. Just hand them to me, will you?"

Nikki nodded, and reluctantly stood. How was she going to hand him these things and still not look at him? she wondered as she warily approached the riverbank. She kept her gaze trained on the ground passing underfoot, but was excruciatingly aware of the splashes that told her Kurt was moving in the water. Was he moving closer, or farther away? She didn't dare look up to see.

She stopped when she reached the rocky crest leading down to the river. "Here," she said, holding out the soap and cloth in what she hoped was his general direction. She waited patiently for them to be taken. Her toe tapped the dirt when he didn't. "Well? Are you going to take them or are you going to stay dirty? I really don't care either way."

She was about to stuff the soap and cloth back in her pocket and tell him to do without when she heard a croaked gasp, barely decipherable above a frantic splash. "Nico—!"

Her head snapped up in time to see Kurt's dark head disappear beneath the water.

Nikki reacted on gut instinct. She tore her boots from her feet and threw them randomly on the bank in less than one throbbing heartbeat. Her gun and knife quickly followed. Unmindful of her clothes, she plunged into the icy river.

The coldness made her gasp as she dove beneath the surface. Her eyes were open, and they stung from the gritty dirt Kurt had kicked up when he sank. The yawning face of a rainbow trout grazed her cheek. Nikki expelled the air from her burning lungs at the sight of flat eyes, shimmering in the moonlight that played over the water's twisting surface.

She kicked to the top, refilled her lungs, and dove.

This time she found him. His jet-black hair danced with the current as he struggled to free himself from a mud-hole on the river's bottom. His sinewy legs were sunk past the ankles in the shifting dirt. As she watched, he lowered still more.

Nikki kicked herself deeper, until the tip of her nose grazed a muscular calf. Frantically, she clawed at the soft, sandy bottom trapping his legs. Kurt did his best to help, but his reactions were liquor-slow and clumsy.

It took only a few seconds to free him, but it felt like an eternity. They broke the icy surface as one, gasping as they were enveloped in a shimmering blanket of moonlight.

Nikki swiped the curtain of saturated hair from her face and, panting, took his ice-cold, wet arm and draped it around her shoulders. As carefully as possible, she guided him past the rocks and onto the grassy bank.

She lowered him to the prickly grass, noticing the unhealthy gray pallor of his skin despite herself. Whether it was caused by his wound, the cold, or his near brush with death, she didn't know. But one thing was for certain; he was shivering with a vengeance and she'd do best to warm him.

She retrieved the blanket, but not until she was walking back with it dragging from her fingers did she remember he was naked. She didn't break stride, but her eyes widened in alarm as she closed the distance.

He lay on the ground, stretched to his fullest, his sinewy length boldly exposed. One arm was flung over his eyes, concealing the upper portion of his face, while the lower half was cast in enticingly vague shadows. His broad torso and powerful limbs glistened moistly. Drops of water clung to his skin and hair, shimmering like tiny shards of crystal, alive with silvery moonlight. His breathing had slowed to normal, his shivering eased but not abated.

Although she hated herself for the weakness, Nikki couldn't have kept her shocked gaze from straying over his rugged physique if her life depended on it. She reached his side, her heartbeat quickening when, with trembling fingers, she tossed the blanket over his naked body. It was too small, and his wet feet poked from the frayed edge.

"What about you?" he asked through chattering teeth. Moving his arm, he fixed her with a riveting stare. His gaze traveled with deceptive slowness down the drenched clothes that adhered to each tantalizing curve. Her shirttail dripped a wet puddle at her feet. "You're just as wet as I am."

"I'm fine." She forced a shrug, stifling the shudder that threatened to ripple over her shoulders. Ignoring the goosebumps sprouting on her arms and at the nape of her neck wasn't easy, and there was *no* disguising the thin blue line etching her lips. It was there his concerned gaze settled, and settled hard.

"You're not fine," he growled, lifting a corner of the blanket and gesturing her beneath.

Stubbornly, she held her ground, not wanting—or daring—to get that close to him. "I said I'm fine," she insisted, hugging her arms around her for warmth. "I've been wetter before and lived."

He grinned crookedly, still holding the blanket up. "Yeah, like that time on spring roundup when it rained for three days straight. You were wetter than a fish, and still refused to sleep in the mess wagon. Said the other hands would think you soft. You almost got pneumonia for that stunt."

She glared at him, and suppressed a shiver when a cold drop of water wiggled its way down her back. "I survived, didn't I?"

"Just barely. As I recall, we had to sacrifice three good men to ride with you just to make sure you got home all right."

"That wasn't my fault, it was Pete," she sniffed, wiping her nose on the back of her hand. "I could have made it back alone just fine."

"Pete wanted to make sure you went," Kurt added dryly. "He wasn't taking the chance you'd turn back the second you were out of sight."

"See? I told you it was Pete's fault." She shrugged, tugging the curtain of water-darkened hair over one shoulder and twisting out the wetness that made it heavy on her neck. The moisture splashed over the ground, treacherously close to the blanket, and ran like ice over her cold feet.

"Nicole, don't be a fool. Get under the blanket where you at least stand a chance of staying warm."

"No," she repeated stubbornly. Nibbling her full lower lip, she debated what to do. "I'll—um—I'll go back to camp and change into dry clothes. I'll stoke the fire nice and high, and I'm sure after I've had a chance to sit in front of the flames for a while I'll be fine."

"And what are you going to do about me in the meantime?"

"Bring you with me, of course. I wouldn't leave you here."

A slow grin turned his lips. "Hope you're stronger than you look, because I'm not going anywhere right now." His eyes twinkled with a mixture of obstinance and laughter. "Unless you plan to carry me."

Nikki took a deep breath and tried not to let his goading worm under her skin. "You're getting on my nerves, buster," she said. Planting her fists on moist hips, she glared down at him defiantly. "I'm starting to think we'd all be better off if I'd just killed you to begin with."

"Maybe." Kurt closed his eyes, the grin still in place. "Pity you didn't think of that before," he added with a casual shrug, "because it's too late for second thoughts now. Like it or not, you're stuck with me."

"Don't bet on it," she snapped through teeth that were chattering noticeably now.

"Chilly yet? You ready to come under this blanket . . . or are you still trying to prove yourself?"

"I'm not trying to *prove* anything!" If she hadn't been half frozen and drenched Nikki might have given into the temptation to send her bare toes crashing into his arrogant jaw. But all she had the energy to do was shiver.

"No? Then maybe there's something else stopping you from joining me under this blanket." He ran a hand down his bristled jaw, his gray eyes snapping open to study the overcast sky. "Hmmm, wonder what that could be? Don't suppose your reluctance is actually fear, is it?"

"Fear?" she echoed, scowling in confusion. "Why would it be? And what on earth do I have to be afraid of?"

"Me," he answered with animal quickness, his shrewd gaze raking her trembling form. "Or maybe of what two normal, healthy people of the opposite sex would do if they were caught half naked under a blanket together."

"I'm not afraid of you, Kurt," she replied, her voice husky. The image of a moonlit barn she shoved forcefully from her mind.

"No? Then who are you afraid of, Nicole? Yourself?"

"This is ridiculous," she sputtered, turning on her heel and stalking to the place where she'd left her boots, gun, and knife. Her boots were there. So was her knife. The gun was gone.

Rage tightened Nikki's heart as she snatched up the boots. A quick sweep of the area produced no gun. Willing her anger back, she sat down in the tall grass and tugged on her boots, allowing enough time to form a sketchy plan. There was only one place the gun could have gone, although she couldn't for the life of her figure out how he'd have gotten it without her noticing.

She tucked the knife in her boot, rolled the hem of the baggy trousers up to her ankles, then pushed herself to her feet. The metallic click of the gun being cocked from behind was loud against the soft churn of the river current.

Nikki turned, her back ramrod stiff. Then with a calmness Kurt would have thought impossible, she walked toward him.

Chapter Five

A jackrabbit hopped into the clearing, thought better of it, then scurried away. The owl's hoots became more desperate when the bird sensed the snap of tension crackling in the brisk night air. The moon dipped behind an inky black cloud, as though it were afraid a gun was aimed at it.

Nikki advanced steadily, her wet feet squishing in her boots. Her unflinching gaze never strayed from the deadly barrel of the gun aimed skillfully at her chest.

The very last thing Kurt wanted to be thinking about right then was the way the moonlight danced over her saturated hair, turning the tangled mass into shimmering quicksilver. Or the way pale shadows kissed the gentle curve of her cheek, making her skin look richer than the finest bisque. Or the full lower lip, enticingly moist, trembling slightly. Or the indecent way water-drenched clothes clung to large breasts, a tiny waist, and seductively lean hips. No, right now he *should* be concentrating on the way her gaze darkened to furious midnight blue. The way her jaw was set hard with determination. The way her small, capable hands clenched and unclenched at her sopping-wet sides. But oddly enough, all that was secondary to him.

"One of the cardinal rules of the West," she spat with more than a little self-recrimination, and the harshness of her voice pulled him back to vivid awareness, "never, never, *never*, take the word of a wanted man."

Kurt allowed himself a brief grin, still assessing her approach with a keen eye. Anger glinted in her eyes. No fear, no reproach, just plain, undisguised fury. He countered it by keeping his tone light and even. "Isn't it just like a woman to throw honor in a man's face at a time like this?"

She stopped a scant few inches away from his exposed toes, not seeing so much as a trace of humor in his words. "And why wouldn't I?" she asked tightly. "Someone has to remind you of your promise, since you seem to have forgotten it."

He shook his head, clucking his tongue and rising up on one elbow. "Didn't forget a thing." He shrugged. "I'm just not stupid enough to pass up a golden opportunity when I stumble over one—as I did quite literally in this case."

"You've made your point, Kurt. Now shoot me and get it over with. I presume that *is* why you took my gun, isn't it?" The silver brows arched. Pride kept her chin tilted as she looked down her nose as though he'd manifested himself into a form of life more repulsive than a slug.

"Is that what you want?" he asked with deceptive softness. "For me to shoot you?"

"What I want doesn't matter. You're the one with the gun."

He watched as Nikki planted balled fists on her hips and spread her feet wide, in case he decided to rush her with his body instead of a bullet. Apparently she was resigned to her fate—whatever that might be. Only the spark of white-hot purpose in her eyes told him she planned to go down fighting.

"Come here, Nicole," he said, his voice low and

gravelly. The barrel of the gun gestured to the warmth of the blanket.

"No."

"Good God, woman, don't make me shoot you!"

Again, she shook her head. The curtain of soaked hair swayed at her waist, and crystalline droplets of water sprinkled the ground. "Shoot me," she dared him icily. "I'm not moving."

Kurt met and held her gaze, all the while wondering at the lack of fear reflected in those deep blue pools. Most women would be scared witless right now. Oh, hell, who was he kidding? Most women would have fainted long ago—a *man* would be scared witless. But not her. No, this one stood brimming with pride and arrogance, daring him to put a bullet through her heart!

Kurt shook his head. He couldn't figure it. This was *not* the Nicole Dennison he used to know. Raking cold fingers through his damp hair, he lowered the gun until it rested atop his hip. "I'm not going to shoot you, Nicole. That was never my plan."

"No? Then why'd you steal my gun?" she shot back. She pursed her shivering lips as her gaze flickered between Kurt and the pistol. *Her* pistol!

"I told you, I tripped over it." To Kurt, she didn't seem the least bit relieved that the immediate danger had been removed. He was surprised to find how much her lack of fear rankled him. "I figured holding you at gunpoint was the only way I was going to convince you to climb under this blanket before you caught pneumonia. Somehow I didn't think you'd believe me if I offered not to touch you."

"Damn right," she huffed, suddenly leery. She didn't believe his story about tripping over her gun for one minute, but she wasn't going to question it either. "Not after hearing you spout off about what a *normal* man and woman would do under one in these circumstances. I'm not a fool, buster!"

"After the way you just stalked me when I held a gun on you, I'd question that assessment," he muttered angrily. But was he angry at her, he wondered, or himself? "You're going to get yourself killed if you don't start using more common sense. I could have shot you."

"You didn't," she reminded him, a gloating smile tugging at her lips. "Looks to me like my plan worked just fine."

Kurt returned the grin, but it was a cold gesture that didn't touch his steely glare. He waved the gun in her face. "Almost," he conceded with a brisk nod. "But don't chalk up a victory just yet, honey. I still have the gun."

"For now. We'll see how long that lasts." Her good humor evaporated quicker than steam burning off a kettle spout as her expression changed to one of forced dispassion. At least her anger made her forget how cold she was.

"What's the matter? Doesn't your confidence extend to overpowering a wounded man?"

Her eyes narrowed, her gaze spitting ice-blue fire. "I've already proven I can do that. Or don't you remember the night I took you?"

Kurt shrugged and shook his glistening, damp head. "Doesn't count. Mickey and Willy showed up in the nick of time to save your arrogant little hide. Who knows what would have happened if they'd ridden in five minutes later?"

"I had you, Kurt," she replied crossly. "Why can't you just admit it. Five more minutes and I would have had you hog-tied and gagged." He was obviously gleaning an enormous amount of satisfaction from what she considered a travesty of an argument. She was not.

Again, he shook his head. His eyes—narrowed to slits that glistened like cold steel in the shifting moonlight—regarded her intently. "No, Nicole," he said slowly, precisely, "you're wrong. You *never* had me."

His voice suggested he was not talking about the night he had been kidnapped. Nikki felt her cheeks pinken, and she hated herself for it. She looked away, suddenly unable to meet his stare. When she looked back, her gaze was flat, her expression carefully guarded. "If you're going to use the gun, do it now. Otherwise, get dressed and we'll head back to camp. I'm cold and I'm tired and I don't feel like continuing this discussion."

"I'm not going to shoot you," he repeated, his patience severely strained. "I already told you that."

She shivered when a cool breeze wafted over her soaking wet body. "Fine, then get dressed." She snatched up his wrinkled pile of clothes, holding them as she would a disgruntled skunk, in a tight-knuckled grip, at arms' length. She dropped them next to his side by simply uncurling her fingers and letting them fall, watching emotionlessly as the shirt fluttered like a stained dove to the leaf-strewn ground.

Kurt glanced up in surprise when she shoved her hand, palm up, beneath his nose.

"My gun . . . ?" She wiggled her fingers impatiently and waited for the slap of cold metal in her palm. It didn't come. "Come on, Kurt," she pressed, her boot crunching the leaves as she tapped her toe impatiently. "If you aren't going to shoot me, you don't need my gun. And if you don't need my gun, then I want it back."

"Why? So you can jab it in my ribs every time I keel over?" He chuckled harshly, shaking his head. "Not a chance. The gun stays with me until we hit camp. You can have it back then."

"This is ridiculous. I'm not going to stand here arguing with you over *my* gun. Now give it back!"

"At camp."

"Why?!" she demanded, her hand slapping her thigh.

"Don't be so pig-headed, woman," he grumbled, with what might have, on another man, been a sheepish grin. The tiny lines shooting from his eyes crinkled with humor. "I'm trying to prove a point, Nicole. That I can be trusted. That my word is good. That when I say I won't escape, *I won't escape*. I can't very well prove that with you leading me around by gunpoint, now can I?"

"I still have my knife," she reminded him coolly.

"And I still know how to use a pistol," he countered, holding the weapon up. Moonlight bounced off the blue-cast barrel. "Or did you forget who taught you how to shoot this baby when your daddy wouldn't?" His grin broadened. "My arm is faster than your knife. I'd stake my life on it."

"Even after spending the last six years coddling Boston society?" she taunted, and watched his face go hard.

"Even then."

"All right," she agreed grudgingly. "Keep the pistol if you think you have to prove something to me. But I want it back the second we hit camp. And don't fool yourself, Kurt. I won't think any better of you for it come morning." With that, she turned and stalked away.

Plopping down near the riverbank, she focused her attention on *not* listening to the sounds of Kurt Frazier getting dressed behind her. It was agony knowing his warm, dry body was slipping into warm, dry clothes—while she sat shivering, cold, and wet. It didn't help to know she'd gotten soaked by saving *his* miserable life—a fact that still plagued her.

Stifling a yawn, she pulled her knees up, rested her elbows on top of them, and pillowed her chin on her forearms. The sound of the current splashing against the bank was soothing. Leaves rustled in the branches above. The owl continued its insistent calls. Even chilled to the bone, within a few short minutes, Nikki was teetering on the verge of sleep.

That peacefulness was shattered when she felt the blanket being tossed around her trembling shoulders. The cold water, combined with a near drowning, had burned the alcohol from Kurt's system. His movements were more sure, less clumsy. Nikki stiffened, instantly awake. She looked up, and scowled into Kurt's smug grin.

His raven hair shimmered moistly in the moonlight when the clouds parted and bathed them in a soft, silver glow. The curling mane set his features in vague shadows, accentuating the chiseled cheekbones and sculpted hollows beneath. The moonlight also emphasized the endearing cleft that split his chin. He slowly shoved the pistol into his belt, and the polished butt curled against his stomach. He leaned heavily on the stick.

His gray eyes glinted with triumph. "Warmer?" he asked, watching her hug the scrap of cloth closely around her shoulders. He could tell she was reluctant to voice her appreciation—reluctant to even accept the offering! But accept it, she most certainly did. Common sense forbade her to refuse it.

Nikki didn't answer as she returned his gaze. More than a little disgust was mirrored in her eyes. "Ready?" she asked, pushing to her feet. She brushed off the seat of her trousers, noting that her gaze was met with a sinewy shoulder and a thick, sun-bronzed neck. Funny, but she couldn't remember him being so tall before—or so broadly muscular. She swallowed hard and shifted her gaze.

In a gesture that was the epitome of politeness, Kurt held out the crook of his arm for her to take. Nikki's gaze shifted from that arm to the teasing glint in his eyes—twice. She stalked past him with an indignant sniff.

Kurt caught up to her in four long strides, smoothly snatching up the blanket she'd shrugged from her shoulders as he went. Again, he draped it over her shoulders. Again, she shrugged it off. Leaning against the stick, Kurt plucked it up impatiently. Each bend and stand cost him, but he didn't complain. He held the blanket in a tight fist, the frayed hem dragging the ground. This time he didn't try to put it on her. Instead, he grabbed her upper arm and spun her around.

"Don't be a damn fool, Nicole, the wind's picking up," he barked, holding her firm when she would have twisted away.

She glared at him angrily, but stood still. Her lips were lined with blue, her teeth were chattering. The color in her cheeks, plastered with water-darkened hair, was high.

Although she refused to admit it, the silly chit was freezing her ass off, Kurt thought. *Fool!* he swore silently, plowing the fingers of his free hand through his tousled hair. Before he knew what he'd done, Kurt reached out and cupped the delicately pointed chin in his palm. Her skin was ice cold, and the feel brought a fresh curse to his lips.

His thumb caressed her icy jaw. "Pride is a wonderful thing to have, baby, but this time it's misplaced. Why do you keep throwing the blanket off when I know damn well you're half frozen?"

"Because you want it on," she answered honestly. "If I keep that blanket around my shoulders, you'll have won. I'd rather die than let you win."

"This isn't a game, Nicole!" He clamped his fingers hard on her jaw and lowered his face until their noses were touching. The glint of stubbornness in her eyes served only to enflame his anger. "We're talking the difference between getting to Snow Creek in a month and getting there in a year—if at all. You get sick and we may just be burying you in these woods. Is that what you want?"

"You seem pretty anxious to get back to Snow Creek all of a sudden," she drawled evenly. Not an easy feat when one's teeth were rattling like the ground under a herd of longhorns! "If I didn't know better, I'd think you were anxious to see your old friend Sheriff Hardy again—and visit his scaffold."

"When the alternative is Willy's cooking, I'll take my chances." He paused. "All right, I admit I have my own reasons for going back. Reasons I have no intention of sharing with you," he added when she opened her mouth. Her mouth snapped closed. "But that isn't the point. We were talking about a sopping-wet Nicole Dennison and a certain almost-dry blanket. Can't you just swallow that damn pride of yours for one minute and get under the blanket where it's warm?"

She shot the blanket a quick look. *Warm.* The word shot through her mind, tightened around her heart. The temptation was almost too great to resist. Almost. Hugging her arms around her waist, she murmured a curt, "No," and stomped off again.

"Fine," he sneered, stalking after her. This time he made no attempt to cover her with the blanket, but kept a few paces behind her ramrod stiff back.

"I hope you and your stubborn pride freeze," he growled, his eyes straying to her lean hips, and their subtly feminine sway.

He gained on her a step.

"I hope your toes turn to icicles and fall off." The words lacked their former snap when his gaze rose to the gentle curve of her waist, visible beneath the tangled, bouncing curtain of her hair and enhanced by the wet cloth clinging seductively to each tempting inch like a second skin.

He gained another step. Two.

"I hope your skin puckers up like a prune and . . ."

His gaze peeled away the concealing layer of damp fabric and quicksilver hair. His hands itched at the memory of flesh, warm and supple, skimming beneath his searching palm.

He was almost walking up her back now, he was so close on her heels. Peering over her shoulder he saw her large breasts, clearly outlined beneath the shirt plastered over them. Evidence of her chill made his gut tighten. His gaze stripped away the barrier of her shirt and his breath caught in his throat. He released it in one slow exhalation that washed over Nikki's cheek and neck. Her heart skipped a beat, then pounded to frantic life. When she stopped short, Kurt collided into her.

Lightning quick, he reached out to steady her. Though his intent had been to break her fall, Kurt found that the feel of her willowy body enfolded in his arms was too much to bear. Her softly twisting curves wiped all trace of logical thought from his mind, and replaced it with sharply vivid sensation. The cool moistness of her pressing into him was intoxicating.

It had been years since he'd felt like a schoolboy, driven solely by his baser instincts. Nothing mattered except the sumptuous feel of Nicole Dennison, once again enfolded in his arms. Slowly, he turned her around. He couldn't have stopped his lips from lowering to hers if he'd tried. And trying was never a consideration.

At first, Nikki was too stunned to struggle. Yet, when she saw his eyes darken to brilliant turquoise and sensed his reckless intent, she still didn't move. She didn't know why, and when she felt his warm lips cover her trembling cold ones, she didn't care.

Her thick lashes swept down as she lost herself to the bittersweet sensations of his kiss. His lips were like fire against her icy mouth—brushing, teasing—and the warmth of them seeped into her skin, fanning the growing fire in her veins. Beneath her fingertips, splayed over the rigid muscles of his chest, she could feel the racing of his heart. His hands were pillowed atop her hips, spanning the small expanse front to back. When he didn't pull her closer, her body hungrily wondered why.

Warm breath, smelling faintly of whiskey, grazed her cheek. The feel heightened her already dizzying senses. He deepened the kiss and Nikki received her first taste in years of the remembered silkiness of his mouth. His tongue tasted like sweetened honey as it played a provocative hide-and-seek game with her own. His lips, insistent yet gently coaxing, demanded a response she was powerless to deny. Of their own accord her hands inched up, savoring the feel of his broad shoulders, tensed and rippling beneath her open palms, before wrapping urgently around the thick cord of his neck. His damp hair tickled her knuckles as she urged him closer.

With a husky groan, Kurt pulled her close. The smallness of her body complemented the rugged planes and valleys of his to sensuous perfection. He marveled at the way she nestled into each curve and hollow as though she belonged there. And marveled still more at how she returned his hunger with a hot, demanding passion he'd tasted briefly only once before.

He wanted her. Good God, he wanted her! But there was too much standing between them to make taking her in the tall sweet grass, as his body craved to do, a possibility. With a reluctant groan, he sealed the kiss and drew away. But he didn't let her go. He was enjoying the feel of her softness pressing into his hips too much to willingly give up the contact without a fight.

Nikki met his gaze, her cornflower-blue eyes peering out from beneath lids that were thick with desire. Confusion shimmered in her gaze, and not a little self-reproach.

As soon as her senses had stopped spinning, she pushed him away. Her fingers brushed the carved wooden butt tucked under his belt, but she suppressed an urge to yank the weapon away. He wanted to prove himself, and for some stupid reason Nikki needed that proof almost as much as Kurt needed to give it. Dropping her hands to her side, she took a quick step back.

"Don't ever do that again," she hissed weakly. The words were muffled by the back of the hand she swiped across her mouth. Her lips still burned from his kiss and her knees were still liquid, but, she noticed reluctantly, she was no longer cold.

"Why not, Nicole?" he asked, his gaze insolent and probing. "There was a time when you—"

"Don't," she cried on a swift inhalation of breath. She took another quick step back. She was shivering again, but this time it wasn't from the cold. "Don't say it, Kurt. Please. It's over between us. It has been for years."

"Is it? You're sure about that?" he mocked. One raven brow cocked high as he fixed her with a demanding glare. "You didn't kiss me like a woman who's convinced things are over, Nicole."

"As always, you have things backwards. *I* didn't kiss you at all. The kiss was your idea. *I* certainly didn't start it."

His gaze shimmered a frosted steel in the moonlight as it leisurely raked her wet body. "Maybe not, but I didn't feel you fighting me either. You knew what I was going to do and you—"

"I didn't!" she squeaked in her own defense. It was useless to fight the color that warmed her cheeks.

Kurt continued as though she hadn't spoken, "—and you let me. Face facts, Nicole. You responded to me. Whether you wanted to or not, you *did* respond."

He covered the distance between them in two long strides. Nikki gasped when his fingertip drew a slow, hot line down her tightened jaw. Thank God it was the only place he touched her. It was an embarrassing thing to admit, but she knew if he took her in his arms and insisted on pressing the issue, she would surrender again. She wouldn't be able to stop herself.

"It isn't over," he said softly, determinedly. "Not by a long shot."

His touch seared her flesh as well as her mind, leaving her bewildered and confused. Only once before in her life had she had so little control over her emotions. And she hated that lack of control almost as much as she hated the man who caused it. She swatted his hand away.

"You're wrong, Kurt," Nikki said, running a palm over the place where his fingers had been, "it *is* over. You ended whatever was between us the day you put a bullet through my father's heart. M-my response to you just now was a mistake. One I don't intend to repeat. It *won't* happen again."

"You know this for a fact?"

Nikki sucked in a shaky little breath and nodded with more conviction than she felt. "Yes."

"Then you won't mind my testing you . . . just to be sure?" It was not phrased as a question, but a cold, hard challenge. The steely gaze reflected the dogged determination of his words.

Before she could utter a protest, Kurt slipped an arm around her waist and yanked her hard against him. His lips swooped down to swallow her cry of alarm, but he never got that far. A rustle of leaves and twigs from behind sent him spinning on his heel. He hadn't come half circle before the gun was drawn, the hammer fanned, and the barrel deftly aimed at the bushes and trees.

Nikki's gaze scanned the twisting, moonlit shadows. Her ears strained for any sound of the intruder, but she could hear nothing unusual over the flutter of birds and the churning river.

Kurt sent her a look that told her to stay put before creeping silently toward the shadow of trees. For a man of his imposing size and stature, she thought he walked with amazing stealth. Even *she* might not have heard him sneaking up from behind, and her father had trained her well.

Nikki filed the observation away as she bent to retrieve the knife from her boot. She was careful to keep her back to the river, knowing the sound of someone leaving the water would be hard to disguise.

Her gaze flickered between Kurt's rugged back and the forest he was entering. Anyone could be concealed there, with any variety of weapons at his or her disposal. Was he capable of handling the intruder, or, quite possibly, a group of them?

Although the adrenaline was coursing through his veins, Kurt was still weak. Nikki wasn't sure enough time had passed for the whiskey to have left his system. Like Willy, he held his liquor so well it was virtually impossible to tell if he was drunk or sober. In a situation like this, wounded and weak was a bad combination. Wounded, weak, and *drunk* could be deadly.

She snapped to an instant decision and, once made, reacted on it without a thought. Straightening, she brought her knife close to her waist, grasping it so that her wrist was allowed some flexibility. Walking as her father had taught her, on the balls of her feet rather than the heels, she picked her steps carefully, creeping toward the line of trees where Kurt had disappeared. The crunch of leaves under her feet was masked by the peaceful stirrings of the night.

She had almost neared the first tree when a commotion sounded inside the woods. She took a quick step back, barely in time to avoid a collision with the body that was tossed to the ground at her feet. The light-haired man landed with a thud and a groan, rolling onto his back. Nikki looked down into the shocked, somewhat battered face of her brother.

"Mike!" she cried. Sheathing her knife, she knelt beside his inert form at the same time Kurt broke through the trees. She cradled Mike's head and placed it on the soft cushion of her lap, stroking the golden curls off his brow. "Dammit, Mike, what the hell did you think you were doing? He could have killed you."

Mike opened his right eye. The left one remained swollen shut from the fresh purple knot marring his temple, an angry bruise the same size as Kurt Frazier's fist. "This is the thanks I get for helping you?" he chided softly. He started to smile, but winced instead.

"Helping me?" She fixed him with an indignant stare as Kurt settled on the grass a few feet away. "I wouldn't call getting yourself killed a very big help to me, Michael James. Explain yourself, please."

"I woke up and found you two gone. Ouch!" He winced when his fingers gently explored the bruise.

"So you followed me?" she urged.

"Of course he followed you," Kurt cut in. "He's a Dennison, isn't he?"

Mike sent Kurt a silencing glare, then turned his attention back to Nikki. "I saw him with your gun and I figured you needed help. Didn't do much good, though, did I? Now he's got both our guns. Looks like we lost this one, Sis."

"No," she said, shaking her head as her gaze clashed with Kurt's. "We didn't lose anything—yet. He promised to give back our guns once we reach camp."

"And you believed him?" Mike cried in surprise. He squeezed even his swollen eye open, incredulous.

She nodded, glancing down at her brother. "Stupid, huh?"

"Damn stupid," he agreed. "Hell, Nikki, use your head. He fought us bringing him back to Snow Creek tooth and nail. If he's got a brain in his head he'll use those guns, take the horses, and be gone long before we ever make it back to camp."

"He promised," Nikki scolded through clenched teeth.

"Promises don't mean much when death is staring you in the face! Come on, Sis. You've made no bones about wanting to see him hang once we reach Snow Creek. Under those conditions, I'd probably lie, too."

Nikki scowled, watching as Kurt uncurled his long frame and stood. One gun dangled from each powerful hand. In the left was her gun, the one he'd promised to give back when they reached camp. In the right was Mike's, a gun upon which no value had been placed.

"How'd you get so wet? And aren't you cold?" Mike asked, pulling her attention back to him. He fingered the damp silver curl resting atop his lean shoulder.

"Long story and, yes, I'm freezing. Do you think you can stand?" She watched as Mike nodded. "Can you walk, or do you want me to fetch one of the horses?"

"I can walk," he scoffed, shakily rising to his feet and swatting away the hand Nikki placed under his arm. "It's just a bump on the head, Sis. I'm no invalid."

Reluctantly, she nodded. They made the trek back in silence. With each step, Nikki's mind raced. Plan after plan was made, then discarded. How on earth could she get Mike's gun back? She still hadn't formed a plan by the time they hit camp.

The fire had died. The ground was bathed in moonlight. Willy's snores were the only sounds to attest to their presence, the snores and the rustling produced by their feet.

Mike, who was at the head of the single line, continued on when they reached the edge of camp. Nikki, in the middle, stopped short and turned to Kurt to prevent him from following.

"I'd like my guns back now." She held out her hand, her gaze straying to the weapons nestled beneath his belt.

"Of course." Kurt reached down and extracted her gun. He slapped it into her open palm and waited, watching as her expression grew stormy.

Hot fury shot through Nikki's blood as her fingers closed tightly around the handle. Even though she'd known this was going to happen, she couldn't stop her anger. Instead, she fed on it as she extended the other palm. "Both of them, please."

"Un-uh." He shook his dark head, his piercing gaze never leaving her. "I said you'd have your gun back when we got to camp and I kept my promise. You have your gun. As for this one..." He shrugged. "Well, we never said a word about this one."

In a trick Kurt had taught her years before, Nikki let the pistol slide to her fingers. With a flick of the wrist, she had it aimed and ready. "I could shoot you now," she growled, her glare backing up the threat.

To her increasing irritation, Kurt smiled lazily but made no move for his gun. "You could have shot me a lot of times, Nicole. Ever asked yourself why you didn't?"

"I *did* shoot you!" She glared at his wounded side.

"In self-defense," he reminded her coolly. "If you hadn't shot me that night, I would have shot you. But my bullet would have been accurate. What about all the times since then?"

"Give me the gun, Kurt," she demanded, lips tight. "Now!"

"Better do as she says, Frazier," Mike's voice rang out from behind. He jabbed the barrel of Willy's gun between Kurt's shoulder blades. "You can't shoot both of us, and you wouldn't want to shoot just one. Likely to make the survivor mad enough to take it out on your hide."

"You're going to hang me anyway, so what's the difference? At least this way, I'll bring one of you down with me. I just can't decide which one." His gaze trailed suggestively down Nikki's front, stopping at the generous swell of her breasts. "Then again . . ."

"Go to hell," she spat.

"Oh, I will. But not alone." Steel gray clashed defiantly with cornflower blue. "I hear the place gets damn lonely, Nicole. What do you say we go together?"

"I don't think we'd end up in the same place." Nikki returned his gaze unflinchingly.

Kurt cursed her rigid composure. He had to get away from her. He couldn't think straight when this girl was around him. Apparently, some things never changed, no matter how much time one gave them.

"I'm leaving, Nicole," he informed her coldly, then sent a heated glance over his shoulder. "I kept my promise to give you back your gun. Now I'm leaving."

"You won't make it past the first tree," she pointed out, her mouth suddenly as dry as a wad of fresh-picked cotton. "If Mike doesn't shoot you, I will."

"Maybe," he shrugged, plowing his fingers through tousled curls that glistened to dark silver in the moonlight. "But a bullet's about the only thing that's going to stop me at this point. I won't be trussed up like a chicken ready for slaughter again. And I won't sleep for days on end in clothes soaked with dirt and sweat. Shoot me if you have to, but I'm still leaving."

Nikki weighed his words carefully. Although she had been the one to put the lead in his side, the shot had been meant to wound, not kill. This time it was clear that if another shot from her gun sank into his flesh, it would mean the end of his life.

An image of Beth flashed through her mind, and though she quickly pushed it away, it tarried long enough. Whether Kurt knew it or not, he was Beth's father. Could she fire the bullet that would bring her daughter's father down? And was hanging him a whole lot different? Yes, she thought, hanging was legal.

Mike, sensing Nikki's hesitation, made ready to bring the butt of his gun down on Kurt's head. Kurt, hearing the crack of twigs behind him, made a swift sidestep. The gun missed his temple by less than an inch. Kurt's arm snaked out, wrapping around Nikki's waist and knocking the gun from her hands. He groaned when she was brought up hard against his wounded side.

The moon glinted off the blue-cast barrel of the gun Kurt pressed against Nikki's neck. Mike, in the process of lifting his own gun, froze. There was no fear in his sister's eyes, but then, he hadn't expected there to be. The terror pumping through his own blood made up for it.

"Drop your gun, Mickey," Kurt growled, his hold on Nikki tightening. She squirmed, but didn't cry out.

The cold gray eyes left no doubt in Mike's mind that Kurt was capable of ending his sister's life here and now. He dropped his gun, raising his hands to where Kurt could see them.

"Good boy. Now go wake Willy, then both of you go sit next to that tree. I want your backs as close to the bark as they can get. Closer."

Mike mumbled a curse, but did as he was told. His gaze strayed to his sister's emotionless gaze as he woke a grumpy, oblivious Willy and shoved him over to a tree.

Kurt shook his head, a hard grin turning his lips

when the two settled back against the trunk. "Not that one." He nodded to the tree he had been tied to. "Over there." The boys shared an angry glare, but did as they were told. Kurt shoved Nikki toward them, bending to collect stray weapons as he followed. His strength had come back with alarming swiftness, she thought.

"Tie them up, Nicole, and make the knots good and tight. I'll be checking your handiwork."

"You won't get away with this, Frazier," Willy growled. "Nikki will find you. You can't hide anywhere that she won't find you eventually."

"Who said I was going to hide?" Kurt mocked. He watched Nikki pick up the rope she had used on him, and now used to secure her brothers to the tree.

"You'd better hide," Mike warned, flinching when the rope around his wrists was yanked taut, "because if she doesn't find you, I will."

"Point duly noted. Nicole, get the scarves," he said, nodding to the two bits of black silk resting atop the bed of leaves. "I think you know what to do with them."

She sent an angry glare over her shoulder, then shoved the first gag in Willy's mouth. His light-blue eyes glistened indignantly when she shoved it in a little too far.

Once they were gagged, she stood and turned toward Kurt. "Anything else, *sir?*"

"Nope," he chirped, as though he'd just declined her offer to accompany him on an afternoon stroll. He made a quick check of the rope and, satisfied the knots were tight enough to hold the two for a while, cleared the distance separating him from Nikki. "That should do it. Come on, I want to be out of here by sunup."

He grabbed her arm and started dragging her from the clearing, but she jerked away. "I'm not leaving them here."

His eyes narrowed to angry slits. "You don't have a choice. Like you said before, when I have the gun, I call the shots. And my shot says you're coming with me."

"No." She took a step back when he reached for her again. Swiping back the damp curtain of hair, she glared at him.

"You see this gun?" he asked, shoving the weapon under her nose.

She didn't look at it, just continued to glare at him.

"Unless I've underestimated Mickey, it has six fresh bullets in it. The first one is for him. The second one is Willy's."

"You wouldn't," she gasped. Her cheeks whitened at the thought of her own stubbornness being the cause of her brothers' deaths. A prick of fear nipped at her, but she pushed it away.

"Try me." Turning his back on her, Kurt leveled the gun at Mike's head. "You've got to the count of five—and I start counting at three."

Nikki watched Mike's eyes widen, his gaze flickering between the deadly weapon and his sister.

"Three . . ."

She searched the clearing for a weapon, any weapon. Except for assorted tree limbs and her empty rifle, there was none. None that she could get to quick enough, anyway.

"Four . . ."

She thought about smashing his head with a branch, but the larger ones had been used for the fire. Besides, she didn't want to take the chance his gun would accidentally go off.

"Fi—"

"All right!" she screamed, "I'll go."

Kurt turned slowly while Nikki wrestled with the urge to slap the arrogant grin off his face. Spinning on her heel, she stalked from the clearing, toting the heavy saddle Kurt barked for her to bring. The sound of her brother's muffled protests rang in her ears. She didn't slow down until they reached the horses, resting beside the swift currents of the twisting river.

"Saddle the black," Kurt ordered, leaning hard against a maple trunk.

"Do it yourself." She dumped the saddle on the ground. Crossing her arms over her chest, she stepped to the riverbank and plopped down in the grass. She didn't know he'd followed her until she heard his words, close over her shoulder.

"You never did take orders well, did you, Nicole?"

"No," she said, pulling her knees up and resting her chin on top of them. She wrapped her arms around her shins and stared at the cloud-strewn sky. "I'm not going with you."

"I never asked you to."

She scowled, glancing at Kurt from over her shoulder. He was a tall, rugged silhouette, encased in shadows, the moon glistening at his back. "But you said—"

"I know what I said, and how it sounded, but I never planned to take you with me." He bent and drew her to a stand. She was too stunned to protest. "I had to make sure one of you was free to untie the ropes." His gaze darkened, dropping to her mouth, caressing her full lower lip. Her flesh burned. "And I also found I had an urgent need to finish what Mickey had so rudely interrupted. Any objections?"

Before she could answer, his hand slipped possessively around her waist. His lips swallowed any protest she might have made. His mouth was warm, oddly gentle, and away from her much too soon. Though the contact was brief, it seared Nikki to the core.

"This isn't over yet, buster," she said finally, her voice a husky, quivering whisper. She didn't realize she was clinging to him until she felt his muscles flex beneath her fingers. She loosened her grip, but didn't have the strength to pull away. Not yet. Her trembling knees would never support her weight. "M-Mike was right. I *will* find you again."

A slow grin curved his lips when his thumb trailed the soft line of her jaw. His sweet breath fanned her face, igniting a fire in her veins that was hard to ignore; and harder to deny.

"You do that, baby," he sighed. "I'll be waiting for you."

"I'm not joking, Kurt." She pulled away from him. It was difficult to think with the hard warmth of his body penetrating the dampness of her clothes. "This isn't a game. I intend to see my father's killer pay . . . with his life."

Kurt didn't answer. Again, she thought, she had given him the chance to defend himself, to explain what had happened the day her father had been killed. And again, he had not. Not that it would have mattered. He could deny it until the cows came home, but she had her witness. Still, it would have been nice if he'd tried. Instead he sent her a long, piercing look, then strode away.

Since he didn't have the strength to throw the saddle over Stetson, Kurt mounted the horse bareback. His rugged body swung onto the sinewy back with incredible ease. He guided the horse to a stop a few feet away from where Nikki stood. The moon was at his back, his face was cast in twisting shadows. She didn't have to see his expression to know it was intent, each hollowed valley and curve alive with promise.

"We *will* meet again, Nicole Dennison," he said, his voice so soft it might have been the breeze that had spoken. "And when we do I'll see you finish what you've started here with me."

Nikki didn't reply.

Kurt turned, sinking his heels into the stallion's flanks. Horse and rider disappeared past the line of trees.

Nikki watched him ride away in silence, knowing he took all of her sweet dreams for justice with him. Deep down, she knew he was right. It would be a long time before Kurt Frazier was out of her life for good. A very, very long time.

Chapter Six

Summer, 1886
Snow Creek, Dakota Territory

The scent of roasted venison hung in the air as Nikki guided the dapple gray through a narrow coulee. High banks flanked her as the horse's hooves slapped into ankle-deep water, running cool and clear in the shallow stream. Behind her, Mike and Willy rode in silence, although both seemed equally glad to be on home soil.

A prairie dog howled in the distance, causing the restless herd of longhorns to snort in annoyance. The familiar sound brought the first smile in weeks to Nikki's lips. Tugging on the reins, she inched through a break in the coulee, toward a line of cottonwoods that spread into the distance. The horse, sensing her excitement, hastened its pace. In minutes the scraggly trio were clopping over a well-trodden bridle path.

Nikki reined the gray in and stared in fascination at the Triple D, spreading out before her in all its glory. No matter how many times she saw the house, split-rail corrals and grassy bluffs that stretched up front and rear, it was never enough.

She took a long, slow breath of the hot summer air

and yanked off her hat. Sweat dotted her brow. She wiped her forehead with her sleeve and turned to Mike. He guided his squat brown filly next to her.

For the first time in months, Mike was treated to Nikki's brilliant smile. To him, the sight was a welcome change. "Happy to be home?" he asked, returning the grin. Willy grumbled from behind, obviously not as thrilled. His surliness won him only neglect.

"Happy?" She settled the hat back on her head. "I'm thrilled. Maybe even ecstatic."

"Maybe?" Mike laughed. His gaze strayed from his sister to the ranch, then back again. "Only maybe?"

Her grin broadened and her eyes sparkled in the midday sun. "Well, aside from the obvious, I'd be happier if I knew Dally saved us some dinner. God, it smells so good I can taste it already. What about you, Willy?" she asked over her shoulder. "Are you sick of jerked pork yet? Ready for some *real* food?"

The mention of food, real or otherwise, brought an eager grin to the boy's face. Now when he looked at the ranch his Dennison-blue eyes were bright with hunger. Nikki thought what a pity it was that only the thought of Dolores's venison steaks and mouth-watering apple cobbler made home an appealing prospect for him. His attitude would change soon enough, she decided as Willy murmured something unintelligible, then sank his heels deep in the horse's flanks and shot off toward the ranch and "real" food. The food his thinning body said he'd been deprived of.

Nikki sighed, reaffirming her vow to give Willy a first-hand taste of what ranching life was really like. If he thought the last few months had been bad . . . he should just wait! Of course, if she knew Willy, he'd fight her every step of the way.

"Are you going to tell them?" Mike asked, drawing

Nikki's attention away from Willy's retreating back. When she frowned, he added, "About Kurt. Are you going to tell them what really happened or do you want to keep it between the three of us?"

"That would be tough to do, since Willy's already gone. Knowing him, the whole story will be common knowledge by the time our trail dust settles." She shrugged, crossing her hands over the saddle horn. Her gaze caressed every familiar inch of the ranch. "I suppose it won't matter if they know. I did my best to bring Kurt back and see justice served. My best just wasn't good enough . . . this time."

"So you *are* going after him again?" Mike sighed. His horse shifted restlessly when it caught the scent of others penned in the corral. "Are you sure you want to do that, Sis? I mean, real sure?"

"Of course I am," she snapped, then grudgingly softened her tone. "I've been waiting a long time to see that murderer pay. I had him once, I'll have him again. Even Kurt Frazier isn't that good at hiding." She shook her head in a stubborn gesture that was hers alone, and that set the fringe of the thick silver braid swaying at her waist. The top of her head was already warm from the summer sun beating through her hat, and it was barely past noon. "I won't give up. Not now."

"I didn't ask you to. I was just thinking about Beth, and wondering if what you're doing is really for the best. . . ."

His voice trailed off. She didn't encourage him to continue. Mike sent his sister a long, hard look, noting the way her features relaxed and a smile of pure delight crossed her face. Something at the ranch had caught her eye and he didn't have to look to know what it was. Only one person was capable of putting *that* look on Nikki's face.

"Don't look now, but I think she heard you." She nodded to the dark-haired child who came tumbling out of the ranch house, catapulting herself into Willy's arms as he crossed the yard. A high-pitched squeal of delight cut the air. Without breaking stride Willy scooped the squirming bundle up and continued on, tickling Beth all the way.

Nikki watched as the pair disappeared inside, then turned back to Mike. Her grin was broad. "He may not be good for much, but he can sure keep Beth entertained. Maybe I won't send him on fall roundup after all."

"Ah, send him. He won't like it, of course, but I think it'd be good for him. Just what he needs." He sighed, pushing the hat back on his brow. His eyes sparkled a clear Dennison blue under the shadowy brim. "Besides, I think we could all do with a rest from his nightly poetry readings. Face it, Sis, the kid is boring as hell. Even Pete can't stand to be around him for long before getting the urge to string him up and pull his toenails out, and Pete likes everybody! A good, rowdy cow-hunt will be just the thing to give the fat little brat a touch of character. God knows, he could use it."

Nikki fixed her brother with a reproachful glare, but the laughter in her eyes, and her impish grin, made her reprimand lack severity. "First of all, we'll have to work on the 'rowdy' part. Those things are usually pretty tame." Her voice hardened. "Secondly, that 'fat little brat' is *your* brother, Michael James. You should show more respect for your own flesh and blood."

"Why? He doesn't deserve a drop." Mike shrugged, flashing Nikki his most charming grin.

Oh God, not that grin! "You're awful hard on him, Mike," she said, her tone degrees lighter. "If you eased up, there's a chance you two might get along. He looks up to you, you know."

"Nope. If Willy wants my respect, he can earn it the way everyone else does. Just cause he's family doesn't make him any different as far as I'm concerned." The grin faded as he peeled the hat from his head and covered his breast with it. With his chin tucked in and his eyebrows drawn down hard, he looked a lot like their father, which was his intent. His voice lowered. "'Earn respect or go without.' That's what Pop always said."

"That's between the two of you. I won't get involved." She sighed, lifting the reins and preparing to move. "Come on, I want to see my daughter. Two months is too long for a mom to go without a hug. And I want to see how the spring cow-hunt went without us. You coming?" she added when he hesitated.

His gaze flickered between the ranch and the well-trodden bridle path. Apparently the lure of roasted venison and steamy apple cobbler didn't have the same effect on him as it had had on Willy. "You go ahead. I'm going for a ride, see what's been happening on the ranch while we were away."

"The Triple D? *Our* ranch? You're sure about that?" Nikki almost laughed at the guilty flush staining her brother's suntanned cheeks. She wagged a finger under his nose, and this time managed to keep her voice low and stern. "I don't want any trouble, Michael James. We just got home. I want at least one day's rest and some time with Beth before I have to go traipsing all over the Territory explaining to angry fathers exactly what it was you were doing with their daughters out behind the barn. Am I making myself clear?"

"Yeees, Momma," he recited in a perfect imitation of his niece. He settled the hat back on his head, his eyes sparkling.

Mike took the gentle scolding with ease, made Nikki a pack of promises he probably wouldn't keep, kissed her lightly on the cheek, then turned his mount and kicked it sharply.

"And you keep that damn smile to yourself, brother dear!" she yelled at his retreating back. His answer was to pluck his hat off and swing it in the air. It was his only response.

Brothers! she thought as she kicked the gray on, her eyes and ears soaking up the sights and sounds around her. It was lulling, this place, soothing to frazzled nerves. Even with the ruckus of ranch hands milling about the yard under a beating midday sun, and the snort of horses being worked through their paces, Nikki knew there was nowhere on earth she would rather be.

By the time she'd dropped her mount off at the stable and started across the yard, she felt more tranquil than she had in weeks. It was good to be home. So good, in fact, that she found herself wondering if making another attempt to round up Kurt Frazier wasn't foolish after all.

Maybe Mike was right. Maybe she should leave well enough alone. Let God wreak His own form of Almighty Justice and leave her out of it, as Brian would so eloquently put it. Pete would simply think the whole idea stupid. Willy wouldn't care whatever she decided, so long as he didn't have to go with her again. Out of all of Hugh Dennison's children, Nikki was the only one hell-bent on seeing their father's death avenged. And for the life of her, she couldn't understand why.

She called a greeting to a group of passing cowboys. She noticed a few new faces among them as she started to climb the three short steps leading to the long, wraparound porch. She hadn't placed her foot on the porch before the door was thrown wide and Beth came bounding from the house. As she'd done with Willy, the girl launched herself at her mother with the energy of a speeding cannonball.

Nikki stumbled back from the force of the collision, but steadied her balance by grabbing onto the wooden railing with one hand while hugging Beth close with the other. The small body wiggled happily, and Nikki drank deeply of her daughter's scent; rose soap and bread flour. God, how she'd missed it.

"Momma, Momma, Momma!" Beth cried, twisting in Nikki's arms and pressing her face into her mother's hair. The wiry arms circled Nikki's neck and held on for dear life. "I knew you'd come back. I just knew it. Kristen Jenkins said you wouldn't, but I *told* her you would."

"Of course I came back, sweetheart," Nikki murmured. She climbed the last step, then collapsed onto a squeaky rocker. She settled Beth on her lap, enjoyed the feel of the small body squirming against her. "Don't I always?"

The smile Beth sent her reminded Nikki of Kurt. Pushing the similarity away, she forced a grin and ran a hand over silky black hair—Kurt's hair—and slender shoulders. A thick fringe of raven lashes batted saucily over piercing, blue-gray eyes.

Beth's small hands rearranged the green cotton skirt over her legs in a gesture usually reserved for those much older than a mere five summers. "I told Kristen so," she said proudly, "but she said I was a liar."

"You didn't lie, sweetheart."

Grinning with enthusiasm, Beth nuzzled Nikki's shoulder. "I know. But she didn't believe me." A mischievous grin made her round cheeks rounder. "So I pulled her ugly brown pigtails until her eyes watered and told her you said it wasn't nice to call people names. Are you proud of me, Momma?"

"Proud? Oh yes, very proud," Nikki replied, smothering a laugh. How could she yell at Beth when there were times when *she* would have liked to pull Kristen Jenkins's pigtails until her eyes watered? With a push of her toe, she set the rocker to swaying.

"What else happened while I was away?"

Beth lifted her head. Her smooth brow furrowed as she scowled up at her mother. "Before or after *he* showed up?"

"He?" Nikki glanced down sharply, her body abruptly stiff. "Who, exactly, is 'he'?"

"The man who rode in on your horse," Beth informed her with a sigh, as though her mother should have known. "Geeze, you haven't been gone *that* long, Momma."

Nikki's breath caught and her heart started to hammer. Beth squirmed when her grip tightened. "Sweetheart, tell me about the man on my horse," she instructed flatly, a sinking feeling in the pit of her stomach. She knew what Beth was going to say, but she needed to hear it anyway.

The small lips puckered, the babyish scowl deepened thoughtfully. "Well, he's *very* nice, and Kristen says he's *very* handsome, and Uncle Pete said he could go to hell, and—Kurt!"

Beth smiled at a point past her mother's shoulder. The smile broadened as she scrambled off Nikki's lap, and threw herself into Kurt Frazier's outstretched arms.

Over the darkness of her daughter's head, cornflower blue clashed with steel gray. The striking image of father and daughter hit Nikki like a fist. They both sported the same shaggy dark hair, the same high cheekbones, and the same laughing eyes. Her heart tightened.

And then there was Kurt himself. The aroma of soap drifted to her. It was a sharp contrast to the odor of leather and sweat that attacked her from other sides. The sunlight danced over his damp hair. His color had returned, and deepened. No whiskers shadowed his granite-hard jaw. His face was no longer drawn and tired, but alert and healthy. Any weight that had been lost as a result of their backhanded treatment of him had been replaced, as was attested to by the clean cotton shirt he wore, the way it stretched over his broad shoulders, the light-blue material giving definition to his solid frame.

And he was clinging to her daughter as though he owned her!

Swallowing hard, she tried to overlook the way Beth clung back, the way her child's eyes shimmered with youthful trust. Despite herself, Nikki felt a stab of jealousy.

"Beth," Nikki said, her voice tight, "do you smell what I smell? Yup, that's Dally's apple cobbler, all right. Go inside and have her cut you a piece while I speak to your friend here."

Scowling, Beth disentangled her arms from Kurt's neck and stamped her foot in childish vexation. She seemed unaware of the tense undercurrents running thick and heavy between the two adults as she wrinkled her pert little nose and whined, "Awe, Momma, you know I can't smell a thing."

Nikki felt her blood run cold as her gaze shot to Kurt. His eyes were dark with mockery. *Does he know? How could he not?* Sucking in a shaky breath, she sent Beth a stern glare. "Trust me on this. Now go on. Tell Dolores I said it's all right."

"But I don't want any—"

"Elizabeth Ann Dennison!"

Thrusting out her lower lip in a moist pout, Beth went, stamping her feet to show her displeasure.

"How did you get here?" Nikki demanded when she had gone, avoiding the question that burned in her throbbing heart. *Does he know?*

"Stetson," he replied evenly. A rakishly patient grin curved his lips. "Fine horse, but spirited. I had a devil of a time keeping him under control. Maybe you should think of finding yourself a nice, calm filly. Or an old gray like the one you saddled me with."

"I'll choose my own mount, thank you," she snapped, not fooled for a minute. Kurt was the best broncobuster the Triple D had ever had. Her father had said so often. Make that *constantly*, she thought. "Why'd you come back, Kurt? What do you want?"

Kurt ignored the question. Running a palm down his smooth jaw, his gaze strayed to the door. The sound of banging pots and pans, and murmured voices, drifted out on the hot, dry air. An occasional Spanish phrase also wafted out. Inside the house Beth giggled, her anger forgotten. "Nice kid you've got there, Nicole. A real joy. How old is she?" His voice lowered. "And where's her father?"

Nikki's mind raced. The topic was potentially explosive. One slip and she wouldn't have to *guess* if Kurt knew about Beth. She decided that a quick change of subject was in order. "Considering the circumstanaces, I'll presume you didn't come all this way just to ask me about my daughter. Save me the trouble of an argument and spit out what you really want."

Kurt lowered his hand to his side, his gaze shifting back to Nikki. Except for the hair, he thought, the resemblance between mother and child was stunning. But there were differences too. Beth had her mother's finely chiseled features, true, but where the daughter's eyes were filled with youthful enthusiasm, the mother's were guarded, opaque. He knew there was a full range of emotions playing behind those light-blue pools, but her feelings were concealed by a sweetly innocent gaze and elusively young features.

"You know, I would have thought you'd be happy to come back and find me waiting," he said lazily, eyeing her. "This *is* where you were bringing me, isn't it? You wanted me back in Snow Creek for your 'trial,' didn't you? So what's the problem?"

"W-well, yes," she stammered, taken off guard. Her short, blunt fingernails cut crescents into the sensitive heels of her palms when her fists tightened still more. "But you left. I'd have thought you would be halfway to Mexico by now."

"Can't. I don't speak Spanish. Canada was an option. I can hold my own there." Shrugging, he moved to lean a shoulder against one of the whitewashed porch posts. "Then again, I figured if you could hunt me all the way to Boston, you'd have no trouble finding me in Mexico." He shook his head, his dark hair sparkling with moisture. "I'm not a coward, Nicole. I'm not going to run away now that I know what you want me for. I can't live looking over my shoulder every two minutes, always wondering when you and your brothers are going to show up next."

"I'd think running would be preferable to hanging," she snapped.

"Who says I'm going to hang?"

"I do. You killed my father. I have enough proof to see them slip a noose around your neck and pull it tight. You were a fool to come back here."

One raven eyebrow rose as he rested an elbow on top of the porch railing. He cocked his hip out arrogantly. The position accentuated the coiled power of his body, which was dormant, for now. He turned his lips up in a confident grin. "Why, Nicole, is that concern I hear in your voice?" He clucked his tongue. "Nah, couldn't be."

"Damn right it isn't. Stay if you want, Kurt. With my blessings. But don't expect a grand welcome, because you won't get it." She clapped her hands together, as though trying to remove any dirt that was there, and added, "I think I'll go find Pete and spend some time with my daughter. I've been gone longer than I'd like, thanks to you, and I miss her." She headed for the door, then stopped with one foot on the threshold. She sent him a quick glance from over her shoulder. "Don't get too comfortable. I'll be fetching the sheriff before nightfall."

Once inside the shadowy interior of the house, she leaned against the wall beside the door. Her breath caught and her heart hammered when she heard Kurt pacing over the porch floor indecisively. She could feel his thoughts as though they were her own. She knew he was debating the wisdom of following her, of demanding she finish the conversation she'd abruptly terminated.

After what seemed like hours, he descended the porch steps. Low voices hollered a greeting, and in her mind's eye Nikki pictured him nearing the corral in the center of the yard. Oh, how easily his self-confident swagger came to mind! A hoot of approval rumbled through the cowpunchers, and Nikki knew Kurt had agreed to show the new hands the talent that had earned him his reputation. Good, Nikki thought. With any luck, he'd break his fool neck!

Relieved, she let her mind fix on the problem at hand. Beth. Her relief was short-lived.

Except for the look he'd shot her when Beth blurted out her lack of any sense of smell, Nikki had no reason to think Kurt knew he was the child's father. Oh, there was the physical resemblance, true, but that could be explained by citing all of the dark-haired, light-eyed cowpokes in the area. Any one of them could be Beth's father, and more than one wished he was. *But does Kurt know?* she wondered. How could he? Or was the question, How could he *not?*

And then her thoughts lit on still another problem. Pete. Why hadn't he sent for Sheriff Hardy the second Kurt Frazier took his first arrogant step onto Triple D soil? And why on earth wasn't Kurt in jail, where he belonged?!

These thoughts continued to nag at Nikki as she went in search of a free man to send into town for Hardy. This accomplished, she was determined to have it out with Pete—just as soon as she'd washed the dust and sweat from her body.

An hour later, feeling clean and refreshed, she entered what had once been her father's study. It now belonged to Pete. She hadn't bothered to knock, but then, Pete had long since forgotten he deserved the courtesy since no one had ever respected it.

He was, as always, behind a desk that was as imposing in size as their father had been. The light-blond head, with its unconventionally short, prematurely thin hair, was bent over ledgers. A squint marred his brow. The constantly smudged half-spectacles he used only for book work were perched so far down on his long, narrow nose that Nikki half expected them to plop onto the jumble of papers scattering the desktop. He didn't look up when she moved farther into the room.

"Whoever you are, whatever you want, don't distract me. I'm almost done," he said, holding up a hand as she slipped into the red leather chair in front of the scuffed oak desk.

Peter Dennison was the oldest of five children, and it showed. He wore his responsibility in the permanent creases carved deep in his brow, and in slender shoulders that hunched forward as though the weight of the world rested there. Looking at him now, at the constantly dour expression on his face, Nikki wondered if perhaps it did.

She rearranged the plain brown-and-yellow calico skirt around her knees and leaned toward her brother. His index finger trailed down a long column of barely readable figures while he hissed the numbers under his breath. She tapped her fingers on her thigh and waited for him to finish.

"Six hundred and seventy-three. Good, good, I love it when I add wrong." He picked up his pen, drew a quick line through a previously written total, dipped the pen into the inkwell, then scribbled the new figure. "Now what can I do for—Nikki!" he exclaimed upon looking up. Slamming the ledger closed he yanked the glasses from his nose, tossed them aside, and sprang from behind the desk with more energy than his lean body looked capable of possessing. He swept his sister out of the chair and into a tight bear hug. "If I'd known you were riding in today I would've been there to greet you," he said, pulling back but not letting her go. "Oh, don't look at me like that. I knew when I told you not to go that you'd go anyway. You would have disappointed me if you hadn't. Now *that* I wouldn't have expected. So? When did you get back? How was your trip? Did you—? Uh-oh," he gulped, grinning skittishly, "that's your 'Hello, I'm Nicole Dennison and I'm mad as hell' look. What did I do?"

"It's what you *didn't* do, you wart-faced toad," she replied with a deceptively sweet smile and bat of her thick lashes. The place where the glasses had pinched his nose stood out bright red on his suddenly pale face. "Why hasn't Sheriff Hardy been called? And don't you dare tell me you've been too busy, because I swear I'll take that big ledger book and swat you aside your too-thick skull with it. That should rattle some sense loose."

He ran his hands down the length of her arms. "Now, Nikki, calm down. I can explain—"

"Calm down?" she raged, taking a step away from him and approaching the cold, dry hearth. Cold, dry hearths were one of the things she hated most about summer. Nikki turned her back on the empty fireplace and glared at her brother. "How dare you tell me to calm down? Or did you think I'd be pleased as punch to find out you'd invited Pop's murderer to live under our roof the second my back was turned?!" She laced her arms over her chest, the toe of her boot tapping an impatient rhythm on the gold rug. "Well? I'm listening. You have some explaining to do, Peter Aaron. *A lot* of explaining. And I'm not budging from this spot until you tell me what's going on."

"I'd be happy to explain if you'd just give me the chance." Pete massaged his craggy temple, shook his head, and leaned his gaunt hip against the desk. "Nikki, I sent word to Hardy when your friend showed up here last week. He wouldn't arrest Kurt."

"Of course he'll arrest him," she replied. "Don't be ridiculous. We've finally caught the man who killed Pop. The sheriff *has* to arrest him. That's his job. That's what Snow Creek pays him to do."

Pete shrugged, looking as though there were a thousand places he'd rather be. "Yup, that's Hardy's job all right. *If* he thinks the guy's guilty, which he doesn't."

"Not guilty?!" Nikki stared at her brother incredulously and leaned her back against the rough stone fireplace. Her breath left her in a rush. "Not . . . but what about . . . ?"

Pete shook his head, his voice softening to a tone that bordered on patronization. "Hardy already talked to Ben. Didn't do any good." He sighed, crossing his booted feet at the ankles. "Six years is a long time, Nikki. Even at his best, Ben could only give a vague description. You know as well as I do that vague descriptions won't get a man hanged. Not in these parts, anyway. What you need is more proof."

Her head snapped up and she glared at Pete like the traitor she thought he was for saying such things. "What *I* need? What about what *we* need, Pete? I'm doing this for the family. For all of us."

"Really? And what good will stringing Frazier up do for the 'family' at this late date?" His lips pursed. The scowl that constantly marred his brow furrowed into deeper crevasses. "Face it, Nikki, you're doing this for yourself. No one else."

"That isn't true!"

"Isn't it? Then maybe you can explain to me how—" The door to the study opened, stopping him short. Pete glared at the doorway, his Dennison-blue eyes sparkling with annoyance. *"Now* what? Doesn't anyone around here know what the word *privacy* means? Well, don't just stand there eavesdropping, come in!"

Willy shuffled lazily into the room. In one hand was a thick slab of venison stuck between two equally thick slices of bread, with gravy threatening to gush out the sides. Obviously, he was well on his way to regaining the weight he'd lost on the trail. In the other hand was a worn, leather-bound book. "Nikki said to tell her when the sheriff got here," he explained around a mouthful of food.

"And?" she prodded, glancing over his shoulder at the empty hall. She ignored Pete's raised eyebrow and indignant glare.

He shrugged lazily. "And I saw his horse coming up the bridle path. He'll be here in a few minutes, if the boys don't stop him for something. Want me to stay and help?"

"No, thank you," she said, "I can handle it. Where's Beth? I looked for her after my bath and couldn't find her."

"I brought her to the stables to see Sombrero's new foal. She's in the kitchen with Dally, eating lunch."

Nikki heaved a sigh. "Good. As soon as she's done I want you to take her to the river. Bring her fishing, or show her the birds. Just keep her busy until the sheriff leaves. And watch her close, Willy. You tend to forget she's only five."

Scowling, he fingered the worn volume of verse. "Ben's bringing in a band of strays in a while. How about I get Andy to bring her out to watch. She'd like that."

"I'm sure she would," Nikki snapped. *"I* would

not. I don't want my daughter in the middle of a herd of wild horses while I'm trying to talk to the sheriff. I'd be too worried to concentrate on what I was saying." She reached up and massaged her suddenly throbbing temples. "William Andrew, just do what I asked."

"Why don't you bring her over to the Jenkins' place?" Pete suggested. The comment won him a horrified glare from his brother as Willy almost choked on the last bite of his sandwich. "She hasn't seen Kristen in a couple of days, and Mrs. Jenkins has been asking for you."

"Yeah, right. I can spend the day worrying about Laura throwing herself at me again," he huffed indignantly.

Nikki struggled with a giggle and swallowed it back with great difficulty. *"Laura Jenkins* throws herself at *you?* Oh, Willy, you don't honestly expect us to believe that!"

Willy's cheeks reddened as he watched his brother collapse into peals of laughter. Unlike Nikki, Pete made no attempt to hide his mirth. "It ain't funny!" he sputtered. "It ain't. She throws herself at me, I tell you. She hangs all over me from the second I step foot in that house to the second I leave. 'Have some lemonade, William,'" he whined in a voice that sounded remarkably like Laura Jenkins's. "'Isn't it a lovely *day*, William,' 'My, but don't you look *fine*, William.'"

"And she whispers sweet nothings in your ear too, I'll bet." Pete wiped tears of laughter from his eyes. "She hasn't suggested you meet her out behind the barn yet, has she?"

Willy sent his brother a blank look. "'Course not. Why would she?"

"Ask Mike," Nikki interrupted. "Or Bri. They'll be happy to tell you. And speaking of Brian . . ." Her eyebrows rose suggestively. "I haven't seen him around. Where is he? I want to talk to him later."

"Dolores said Pete sent him to Snow Creek for supplies," Willy chirped in, fixing his suddenly flushed brother with a superior glare.

"Oh, Pete," Nikki groaned, "tell me you didn't."

"I did," he answered guiltily.

"And how long's he been gone?" Willy prodded gleefully. "Tell her how long Bri's been gone, Pete. If you don't, I will."

"Six weeks," Pete grumbled between gritted teeth. His jaw hardened and his gaze clashed with his brother's.

"Six weeks?!" Nikki cried. "You sent him to Snow Creek six weeks ago and he hasn't come back yet? What did you send him for, railroad tracks?"

"Oh, come on, Nikki, it isn't that bad," Pete defended weakly. "Besides, it's not like this is the first time. He's gone off before, but he always comes back . . . eventually."

"'Eventually' can mean anything from a few weeks to a year, where Bri is concerned. Lord, last time we sent him for supplies he took off and we didn't see him again until October. As I recall, he came back just in time for fall roundup."

"*After* roundup," Willy added condescendingly.

"Don't you have something to do?" she shot back. "If you don't want to go visiting, fine. Get a pole for you and a small one for Beth. There are fish out in that river just screaming to be caught, William Andrew. I can hear them from here."

"Awe, Nikki," he whined, fingering his book and casting her a wide-eyed, plaintive stare.

"Don't 'Awe, Nikki' me." She settled one fist on her hip and jabbed a finger at the door. "Now, go!"

He went, a pout as long as the Little Missouri, which flowed past the house, tugging at his lower lip.

"Going to have to do something about that boy,"

Pete said after his brother had disappeared around the corner.

"I know. He's fifteen years old, and he acts like he's twelve. I was thinking of that when we were out in the middle of, oh, I don't know, some mountainous eastern place."

Nikki outlined her plans for Willy come fall. Pete didn't look pleased, but she was saved from hearing his lecture when Glen Hardy let himself into the study. Retreating behind his desk, Pete watched the huge bear of a man pump his sister's hand, welcoming Nikki back with a hearty slap on her slender back.

Her teeth rattled from the blow. "Sheriff," she greeted through a strained smile, and gestured him to one of the chairs. "Thank you for coming over on such short notice. Have a seat."

"Don't mind if I do," Hardy said, lowering his bulk onto the chair. Dust billowed up from his clothes. "Can't stay long, mind you. Promised Horace Winfield I'd be by this aft. He's got a few horses missing. Probably strays, but the Delhoussey Gang's been raising Holy Hell 'round here. Promised I'd ride by, check it out. So what's on your mind, young lady?"

Nikki slipped into the other chair, glad to be as far away from the sheriff as she could get. While his stance reeked of authority, his body reeked of something a little more base. Arranging her skirt around her legs, she kept her back straight and tried her best to look feminine and demure. "I wanted to speak with you about Kurt Frazier," she stated bluntly. "You do know he's back in Snow Creek, don't you?"

"'Course I know. Split up a mob egging to lynch him just yesterday." His gaze shifted to Pete, who squirmed anxiously. "Didn't you tell her we already talked about this?"

"Yup," Pete replied with a helpless shrug. "She wanted to talk to you anyway."

"Well, since I'm already here, s'pose that'll be fine." Hardy slapped his thick thigh, rubbing his palm down his leg and mixing the dirt on his trousers with the sweat on his hand. "What do you want to know, honey?"

Keeping a stiff smile firmly in place, she said, "For starters, Sheriff, you can tell me why Kurt isn't in jail. Then you can tell me when you plan to put him there."

Hardy sent Pete a crafty grin; a grin that wasn't returned. "She gets right to the point, don't she?"

"Always has," Pete replied, plucking up his pen and tapping the tip of it on a pile of papers. "Nikki, why don't you offer the sheriff a glass of Dally's fresh-squeezed lemonade before you back him into a corner?"

The thought of a nice, refreshing drink made Hardy's watery eyes sparkle. Nikki decided he would have to wait until she had her answers. "Well, Sheriff? Why isn't he in jail?" Her voice lowered, but stayed sugary. "He isn't free just because he happens to be a friend of yours, I hope. I mean, you are a *sheriff*, after all. A man of the badge. People look up to you. Why, some even respect you. You have a duty to the good people of Snow Creek to dispense justice, and I'm sure you'd never let friendship stand in the way of that . . . *would you?*"

"I think I resent that." The green eyes narrowed as he pushed the wide-brimmed hat back on his brow until it sat on the crown of his big, thinning, gray-haired head. "Young lady, I'm doing the best I can, under the circumstances, to keep law and order in this town. While you, on the other hand, seem to be doing your best to kick up trouble."

Nikki picked at a small, three-cornered tear in the leather chair arm. "All I want is to see my father's killer swing. I *don't* think that's a lot to ask from the county sheriff."

"Maybe. Maybe not. Now, if you had more proof . . ."

"More proof?!" She almost jumped out of the chair, but at the last minute restrained herself. This was the second time today those words had been slapped in her face. She was getting sick of hearing them. "What more do I need? Ben Rollison was there. He *saw* Kurt put a bullet in my father. He said he'd testify to it if he had to."

"That's all well and good, honey, but it's been *six years*. A man's memory ain't to be trusted after so much time's gone by. Especially if that man's Ben."

"What about Kurt leaving the ranch the same day my father died—*before* the body was found? That's certainly damning."

The sheriff nodded slowly. "Damning? Sure. Convicting? Heck, no." He shrugged his large, heavy shoulders. "Could'a been just poor timing on Kurt's part. Won't really know his reasons unless we ask him."

Nikki fixed the sheriff with a reproving glare. "Ask him?! Why bother? He'd lie just as sure as he'd breathe. No man is going to admit he left town in such a rush because he'd just killed his boss and was afraid of being found out, Sheriff. Asking for honesty from an accused murderer would be asking a bit too much, don't you think?"

"No, I don't," a strong, powerful voice intruded. Three pairs of eyes snapped to the open doorway.

Chapter Seven

Kurt Frazier leaned lazily against the doorjamb. His clothes were covered in a fine layer of dust, and his denim trousers were torn at the knee. No hat graced his head. The crop of raven curls clung to his scalp, which glistened with perspiration. He wiped his sweat-moistened brow on his sleeve. To an impartial observer, it would have been hard to believe that the fate of his life hung in the balance of the argument going on inside the small room.

"Kurt! Didn't see you standing there," Pete said, trying to smooth the rough edges from the tension crackling in the air. "Come on in, pull up a seat." He waved a hand at one of the ladder-back chairs lining the wall. "You might as well stay, since this involves you."

Kurt pushed from the door frame and strode to the center of the room. He exchanged a quick, friendly greeting with the sheriff—who slapped him heartily on the back and told him not to be a stranger—then pulled up one of the chairs and, turning it backward, straddled it. His large body dwarfed the small chair, not to mention the *room*, and Nikki found herself waiting for the rickety, creaking seat to crumble under his weight.

Even though she diverted her gaze, refusing to look

at him, she could feel the heat of his eyes caressing her. She also noticed how he'd placed himself right between herself and the sheriff, as though his body could somehow block any accusations she might hurl.

"Well?" the sheriff said with a sideways glance at Kurt. "You've been pretty tight-lipped about this whole thing since you rode back into town, but you better start talkin' soon or this perty little filly here"—and he nodded at Nikki—"is gonna see your neck stretched longer'n you can spit. So? What've you got to say for yourself, son? You kill her pa or not?"

Kurt leaned forward and pillowed his arms on the back of the chair. He sent the sheriff a long, hard look. "What do you think, Glen? You think I'm guilty?"

"Hell no," Hardy boomed, then chuckled. "If I thought you were guilty, I'd'a thrown your hide in a cell the second I heard your spurs jangling on the boardwalk."

Kurt nodded and turned to Pete. "What about you? You think I killed your father?"

Pete, not expecting the blunt inquiry, paled. The pen he'd been fiddling with dropped to the desk unnoticed as he clasped his hands tightly together. "Me?" he squeaked. Clearing his throat, he sent a sharp glance at his sister. A trickle of sweat twisted down his temple. He swiped it away. "I-I'll hold my opinion until the verdict comes back."

"Coward," Kurt said, his teasing lilt taking the sting out of the insult. He turned to Nikki. "Do I even have to ask what you think?"

"Guilty," she spat as she met and held his gaze. "As sin."

The sheriff sat forward in his chair and glanced across Kurt. "See what I mean, young lady? Four people, one room, three answers. Don't seem like you can even get your family to agree on this one. Gonna be a lot tougher to convince the town." He sliced a hand through the air. "Snow Creek's split right down the middle when it comes to figurin' out if Kurt's guilty or not. He's got as many people backing him as he's got against him. Either way, they're all perty uppity in their beliefs. I don't think we could give the boy a fair trail now if we tried."

"How would you know?" she snarled, her fingers tightening on the chair arm. "You *haven't* tried."

"Give me more evidence, honey, and I'll be glad to give it a go. Until then . . ." He shrugged. "My hands are tied."

Nikki lapsed into angry silence as the men picked up the threads of the conversation. Talk turned to the Delhoussey Gang and what could be done to stop their raiding, then tentative plans for the fall roundup. She was too busy brooding to pay much attention, until she heard her brother mention Kurt's name in relation to the ranch.

"—has agreed to stay on through roundup. After that? Well, I'm hoping we can convince him to stay and lead the trail drive come fall. Doubt we'll be that lucky, though."

Hardy puckered his fleshy lips and nodded. "Yup. Good hands're always appreciated. 'Specially a seasoned broncobuster like this boy. I'd say you did yourself right proud when you signed him up again. Surprised another ranch didn't steal him out from under you."

"Clarkson tried," Pete answered, glancing at Kurt. "Offered him quite a bit, too, if there's any weight to the rumor. Kurt decided to stay with us. Lord only knows why. We can't pay him much until after the drive."

Nikki's shocked gaze was drawn to Kurt. He was watching her carefully, gauging her reaction. If the reddening of her cheeks was anything to go by, he knew she was madder than a wet hen.

Sheriff Hardy must have sensed Nikki's outrage, for he chose that moment to make his departure. He heaved himself from the chair, straightened the garish yellow bandanna around his flabby throat, and extended his hand to Pete. "Well, son, sorry I couldn't be more help."

"And I'm sorry we wasted your time," Pete replied, shaking the meaty hand. As inconspicuously as possible, he wiped the moisture of the fat man's palms off on his trousers when the sheriff turned to Kurt.

"You take care now, boy," he said, slapping Kurt on the back with one hand and vigorously pumping the other. "And don't you be a stranger in town. Give it a few weeks, things'll die down. Then you mosey on out and visit me and Meg. She'll be happier than a steer in ruttin' season to see you again."

"I'll do that, Glen," Kurt promised. "And you be sure to tell her I've been thinking of her apple pies for the last six years. I won't be leaving Snow Creek until I've had a taste of one. Are they still as good as I remember?"

"Better," Hardy beamed proudly. The watery gaze drifted over Kurt's shoulder, fixing on Nikki. "And you remember what I said, young lady. Give me more proof and I'll slam this wildcat in the county jail. Until then . . . ?"

"I know, you tried. Thank you anyway, Sheriff." She nodded tightly, watching as the large man made his final round of good-byes, then left. The thud of his retreating footsteps was echoing down the hall when she turned accusatory eyes on her brother. "'I'll hold my opinion'? Are you crazy?! That's as good as saying this killer is innocent!"

Pete flushed to the roots of his thinning blond hair. He opened his mouth to defend himself, but it was Kurt's voice that cut through the study. "Maybe he thinks I didn't do it, Nicole. Or didn't that thought ever occur to you?"

The full skirt rustled around her ankles when Nikki whirled on him. She settled angry fists on her hips, her eyes spitting fire. "No," she hissed, "it never did. I'm not that stupid and neither is Pete." She puckered her lips and sent a quelling glare over her shoulder. The silver braid bobbed at her waist, the ragged edge brushing her hip. "At least he never used to be. Now I'm not so sure."

Kurt's eyes narrowed. For a second, Nikki suspected he was struggling with the urge to strangle her. If so, he was robbed of the opportunity when the study door burst open and a soaking wet Beth rushed in. A glistening ribbon of water trailed behind her.

"Momma!" she cried, flinging herself into Nikki's outstretched arms. She nuzzled her moist face into her mother's neck, sobs shaking her small, trembling body.

Nikki's anger vanished as she knelt down to comfort her daughter. "What is it, sweetheart?" she asked, her throat tightening when she looked over Beth's shoulder and saw a perfectly dry Willy framed in the doorway. "What happened?" she demanded. "Dammit, you were supposed to take her fishing, Willy. How'd she get so wet—and why the *hell* are you so dry?!"

"Answer your sister!" Kurt bellowed, surprising them all. His booming voice managed to shock the sobs from Beth, who peeked at him with sudden curiosity from the safety of Nikki's arms.

Willy's eyes widened at the sight of Kurt, and the anger that reddened his chiseled cheeks. He instinctively took a step back, then stopped retreating when it became clear that Kurt intended to stalk him into the hall. "I didn't d-do anything!" he whined. A childish pout pulled at his lips as his gaze flickered between Nikki and Kurt. Both were equally furious, so he turned his soulful eyes on his brother. "I didn't!"

"He did too," Beth insisted, wiping the tears from her eyes with the back of her fist. "He pushed me into the river, Momma. And then he wouldn't help me get out."

"I didn't! I was reaching for her. When I tried to get her away from the riverbank, she fell in. Honest! You believe me, don't you, Pete?"

"It doesn't matter what he believes," Nikki said, her voice as sharp as a finely honed razor as she hugged her squirming, wet daughter close. "It's *me* you've got to convince. And you'd better do it quick because I'm about two seconds away from—"

"I'm telling the truth," Willy sniffled. His eyes were moist with the tears that threatened to pour down his cheeks. He bit down hard on the fleshy inside of his cheek to hold them back. "I didn't push her, Nikki. I wouldn't do that."

Tightening her arms around Beth, Nikki stumbled awkwardly to her feet, the child's wet legs encircling her waist. She closed the distance between herself and Willy in three angry strides, but had her answer long before then. "How much have you had to drink, Willy? Come on, I'm no fool. I can smell it on your breath. How much?"

A tear ran down his cheek, splashing on his boot as his gaze dropped. "Not much. A glass of gin," he shrugged, "or two."

"That's it?" A silver brow cocked with angry skepticism.

"I don't know," he wailed. "It might'a been three or four. I-I don't remember."

Tears were flowing freely down his face now, but the sight didn't move Nikki one wit. "Get out of my sight!" she yelled. Her arms tightened protectively around Beth. "Now! Before I strangle you where you stand."

With a sob, Willy spun on his heel and raced from the room. Pete sped after him. Two sets of boots clomped loudly on the stairs, then raced down the upstairs hall. Nikki barely heard the noise as she hugged Beth tight and returned to her chair.

Kurt watched the two closely. His urge to reach out and touch the wet raven head as it passed shook him to the core. He resisted by stuffing his fists deep in the pockets of his trousers, but even then his fingers itched to touch the smooth, babyish cheek, if only to reassure himself that Beth was all right.

"It's okay, sweetheart," Nikki whispered into her daughter's sopping wet hair as she rocked Beth back and forth. "Uncle Willy didn't mean to push you into the water. It was an accident."

"I know," Beth said with an exaggerated sigh as she exchanged a sly wink with Kurt. Her chubby fingers played with the buttons under Nikki's chin. "He didn't mean it. Uncle Willy would never hurt me on purpose." She wiggled in her mother's arms. Picking her head up from Nikki's shoulder, she sent Kurt a wide smile, her fear and anger evaporated. "Hi, Kurt. Wanna go fishing with me? I don't think Willy wants to anymore."

As though he'd been waiting for the opportunity, Kurt crossed the room and hunkered down beside the chair. He lifted Beth's small hand from Nikki's dress, taking it into his own. Nikki tried not to notice the way his fingers lingered over the warm flesh of her neck.

Kurt sent the child his most charming smile, which was readily returned. "You, little girl, are too wet to be going anywhere except up to your room and into a nice, dry dress."

"But I don't want to. I'd rather go fishing." She turned soulful eyes on Nikki. "Momma?"

Nikki sighed. "As much as I hate to admit it, Mr. Frazier's right." Beth scowled, obviously not sure who this "Mr. Frazier" was. "Go upstairs and get into some dry clothes, and then we'll talk about fishing. Go on," she urged, nudging Beth toward the door when the small feet shuffled reluctantly over the floorboards. *"Elizabeth A—"*

"Yes, Momma." On impulse Beth went from her mother to Kurt, throwing her arms around his neck. She delivered a moist kiss to his rugged cheek before she pulled back and smiled brightly. "You'll wait for me, won't you, Kurt? Just in case Momma says we can go?"

"I won't go anywhere until she decides, kitten," he said, hugging her tightly and looking at Nikki from over the small head. He saw that Nikki's lips were tight, her eyes hard and unreadable as she watched him hug her daughter. "Now go change that dress before you catch a cold. I'll wait for you right here. I promise."

Beth giggled, nodded, then disappeared through the doorway. Nikki watched her go, a frown of concern marring her brow.

Does he know? she wondered as she sneaked a glance at Kurt, who stared at the empty doorway. His gray eyes were soft, his expression oddly clear. The residual effects of gazing at Beth, she thought. *But does he know?!*

With Beth gone, Kurt knew he had no reason to linger beside Nikki, but linger he did. Leaning an elbow on the arm of her chair, he shifted his gaze, letting his eyes drink in each delicate line of her profile. For a split second he thought he saw moonlight skimming over her quicksilver hair. He blinked hard, and the pale silver glow melted to vibrant gold sunshine. He felt the same urge to reach out as he had with Beth. This time it was not easily ignored.

Cursing inwardly, he shoved to his feet and crossed the room. Putting distance between himself and

Nicole Dennison was the only way he could keep his wits about him. By the time he'd plopped onto the opposite chair, he felt almost normal again. *Almost*. Stroking a palm along his clean-shaven jaw, he met Nikki's gaze. "How old is Willy now?" he asked suddenly. Ah, now this was a good, safe topic. He mentally commended himself. "Fifteen? Sixteen?"

"Fifteen," she answered cautiously. "Why?"

"Hmph! Is that all? He looks older. Either way, he's still a little young to be breaking into the liquor cabinet this early in the day, wouldn't you say?"

"We don't give him permission to drink, if that's what you're implying. If anything, we try to stop him."

"Yeah, and I can see you've done a mighty fine job. So fine, in fact, he came painfully close to getting your kid drowned."

Nikki's face paled, her eyes widened. For the first time since she'd kidnapped him, Kurt saw actual fear floating behind her rich blue gaze. Oh, she tried like hell to hide it, but he had enough practice concealing his own emotions to recognize hers for what they were. He smiled, realizing he'd just found Nicole Dennison's only weak spot.

"My child, Kurt. *Mine*." She pushed to her feet and glared down at him. "I am perfectly capable of taking care of Beth myself. I've done it for years, and I'll continue to do it."

"Like you did today?" he growled. "God, Nicole, what's wrong with you? Something could have happened to her. Why the hell did you send her off with Willy, knowing he's a drunkard?"

"Because today is the exception, not the rule. This has never happened before. Willy has always taken very good care of Beth. He never drinks when she's around, and after today I don't think he ever will."

Kurt thrust himself to his feet, forcing Nikki to crane her neck to look up at him. The urge to

135

throttle her stubborn neck was strong, but he leashed it. "And you'd take that chance? Even knowing you'd be risking your daughter's life?"

"*My* daughter, Kurt," she repeated hotly. "And that's none of your business."

She turned to leave, but Kurt reached out and grabbed her arms, spinning her harshly around. "I'm *making* it my business. I want to know, Nicole. Will you let her go out alone with Willy again?"

"Why?" she demanded angrily. "Why do you care?"

Kurt hesitated. "It doesn't matter why," he growled, his grip loosening as a scowl furrowed his brow, "I just do."

Nikki looked deeply into his eyes. She saw confusion in their steely depths, but if paternal concern was there it was buried so deeply that even *she* couldn't see it. *He doesn't know Beth is his daughter!* Nikki was caught between the urge to laugh with joy and the urge to slap his face for his obvious stupidity.

"Come on, Nicole," Kurt pressed, his voice strained, "you're killing me here. I need to know. Just tell me if you'd let her go with Willy again, then I'll let you go."

Nikki returned his gaze with an intensity that surprised him. Her voice was hard, and very sincere as she said, "If I've loved no one else in my life, I love my daughter, Kurt. I'd never do anything I thought would put her in danger. Today was a mistake that won't happen again. There. Does that put your mind at ease?"

"Yes, I believe it does." He dropped his hands, and felt a surge of relief he told himself he had no right to feel. He thought himself foolish for jumping down her throat that way, yet when it came to Beth he felt, well, something primitive... fiercely protective. These were emotions Kurt wasn't used to feeling, and he didn't much like feeling them now.

To cover the uncomfortable emotions pumping through his veins, Kurt dropped his gaze. He groaned when his vision filled with Nikki's large breasts, straining against the damp calico of her dress. Lord, he wished he'd held on to the sight of those enticing blue eyes instead. It was safer.

"Why is it every time I see you, you're wet?" he asked, his voice low. "Years ago in the pond, then the river, and now," his voice cracked, "and now . . ."

He couldn't resist. Before he could stop himself, his hands had reached out to span her tantalizingly nipped waist. The damp cloth slipped beneath his open palms as he circled the tiny expanse with both hands and drew her close.

Nikki's heart skipped when she saw his eyes darken to fiery turquoise. His intent was clear; it sparkled raw in his eyes. Her senses were engulfed with the tangy scent of leather and sweat. The way his masculine aroma mixed with the soft, fresh fragrance of herself was downright indecent!

She felt his hard body pressing against her, forcing all lucid thoughts from her mind as she was engulfed with bittersweet memories. Her eyelids thickened. Instinctively, her chin tilted up. Her moist lips parted, ready for his kiss.

It was all the invitation Kurt needed. His mouth dipped, claiming her fiercely, possessively. "Oh, baby," he rasped against her lips. "You taste like sweetened wine. No, make that, *better*. Much, much better."

Nikki's arms stole around his neck when his tongue pried open the barrier of her teeth. The moist tip teased her palate, sipped at her quivering lips. He thrusted and retreated, coaxing her to do the same. One hand nestled snugly in the small of her back, holding her firmly against him. The other ascended the narrow line of her back. She shivered beneath his palm, capturing his groan of pleasure with her mouth.

She wanted him. Right or wrong, good God how she wanted him! With a small whimper, her hands tightened around his neck. She pulled him lower, clinging to him as she deepened the kiss to a frenzied pitch.

"Kurt, what does sweet-nut wine taste like?" an innocent voice asked from the doorway. Beth scowled when the two adults wrenched guiltily apart. "Does it taste like Momma? And why are Momma's cheeks so red? Are all our cups dirty? Is that why you were drinking from each other's mouths?"

"Beth!" Nikki cried. Her fingers fluttered to the high-buttoned collar of her dress as she sent her daughter a weak smile. "How long have you been standing there?" Her voice was strained. It came humiliatingly close to a squeak. "And why didn't you let us know you were there sooner, dear?"

Beth shrugged, leaning against the door frame. "Not long. I just wanted to see if you'd slap Kurt's face the way you slap Mark Winfield's every time he tries to drink sweet-nut wine out of your mouth. How come you didn't, Momma?"

Nikki, hearing Kurt chuckle, sent him an angry glare. "I don't know," she said through clenched teeth, "but there's still time. I'll tell you what, sweetheart. Kurt can explain it to you on the way to the river. How does that sound?"

"Coward," Kurt scolded lightly. He could barely be heard over Beth's wild hoots of delight.

In no time at all, Beth managed to drag Kurt from the room. Nikki listened to silence, but her ears were filled with the rush of Kurt's breath. Her palms still tingled with the beat of his heart beneath them. If she listened close, she could hear their ragged breathing, feel his body straining against hers.

"Damn, damn, *damn!*" she swore, and stalked into

the hall. Her footsteps led her to the front door. It didn't take a great deal of thinking to know where she wanted to go, and who she wanted to see. Unfortunately, her visit would have to wait. Ben Rollison had been out since sunup mending fences on the eastern part of the ranch where they kept the horses. He wouldn't be back until after dusk.

"Damn!" The hem of her skirt slapped her ankles as she spun away from the door. Marching toward the kitchen, she vowed to seek Ben out first thing in the morning. Maybe a nice long talk would jog the man's memory. If he could recall even a sliver of information, it might be enough to put Kurt Frazier behind bars. And behind bars was the safest place for Kurt to be. For *both* their sakes.

She *had* to get that man out of her life. Out of Beth's life, before the child became too attached to him. As it was, it looked like she might be too late for that, but she had to try. The sooner she could arrange a trial, and find a nice loop of rope to coil around his neck, the sooner she could get her own life back in order.

She'd start tomorrow.

Chapter Eight

"It's about time. I was beginning to think you'd planned to spend the whole day in there."

Nikki stood outside the Rollisons' cabin, trying to adjust her eyes to the glare of scalding sunshine. She'd spent the afternoon sequestered in the too-neat-for-comfort cabin . . . and for what? A single name that would probably lead to nothing, and an even stronger dislike for Abigail Rollison. It did nothing to improve her temper. Scowling, she glanced in the direction Kurt's voice had come from.

She ground the heel of her palms over tightly closed eyes and growled, "I hate that woman. I really *hate* that woman! I don't know what Ben sees in her. She's so . . . so . . . oh, I don't know, but whatever it is, I don't like it."

"What, did Abigail refuse to help you?"

The crunch of dirt whispered in Nikki's ears as he moved to her side. She forced her burning eyes to focus on the light and dark silhouette that was Kurt Frazier. "No, she didn't." Anger rode her words hard. "As a matter of fact, she was quite helpful. She gave me a—" Nikki stopped short, deciding it would be smart to keep Josh Cleagan's name to herself. Talking to Josh might lead nowhere, but it would *definitely* lead nowhere if Kurt talked to him first.

"So what's the problem?"

"I told you," she snapped, "I hate her. She's smug... *manly.*" Nikki paused, glancing over her shoulder. A curtain moved in one of the windows and Nikki felt Abigail Rollison's eyes boring into her. Shivering, she rubbed her hands up and down her arms. "When she looks at me, my skin crawls. It's like, well, like those beady eyes of hers are always lording something over my head. Like she knows something I don't. It's unnerving!"

Kurt could have argued. Right now, *unnerving* was Nicole Dennison's lithe little body, only a handbreadth away, and the warmth of it seeping through his sleeve. Unnerving was her voice tightening his gut. Unnerving was the remembered feel of soft, moist...

"And Beth spends entirely too much time there," she added hotly. "I've mentioned my concern to Abigail, but the woman does nothing! You know, I saw Abigail slip one of Beth's bracelets off the table and into her pocket. Imagine the nerve! It was the one I gave her last year for—" She scowled. "Speaking of Beth..."

Nikki's senses tuned to a fine pitch. The aggravation she'd felt on leaving the Rollisons' cabin shifted, flowing into quite another channel. Her mouth went dry when she felt a deliciously slow heat curling up one side of her body—the side *he* stood on. Her heart lurched as the fiercy spark ignited her blood. How had he gotten her body to respond like this without even touching her?!

She took a quick step away.

He took a counterstep forward. "Last I saw, Beth was in the kitchen helping Dolores bake cornbread."

"Cornbread, hmmm?" Nikki started walking, and noticed the way Kurt fell into step beside her. Her hands clenched at her sides. "Sounds good. I think I'll go lend a hand."

"I don't think so."

She stopped cold. "I beg your pardon?"

"I said, I don't think so."

"I didn't ask for your permission, Kurt. I'm going to—"

"Talk to me," he finished for her, his voice as gritty and hard as the dirt underfoot. "It's long past time you and I had a chat, Nicole, and I for one intend to see that we do. Whether you like it or not." His fingers coiled like a steel trap sprung shut around her slender forearm. With a flick of his wrist, he was dragging her behind him.

"Let me go, Kurt!" Her skirt wrapped around her legs as she lurched forward. She would have fallen had his grip not been so sure, but then, he didn't allow her room enough to fall. "If I yell now I'll bring the whole ranch down on your head."

"You won't yell," he announced calmly, still walking with what Nikki felt to be arrogant strides that made her run to keep up. She didn't doubt he'd drag her kicking and screaming through the dirt before he'd let her go.

"Wanna bet?" She dug her heels in the parched ground and tried to wrench her arm free, only to be brought up hard against him. Her free hand shot out to steady herself. Lightning quick, her hand came away from the firm cushion of his upper arm. "I'm not kidding. I *will* scream. *That* should put your arrogant hide in jail for a while. Where it belongs!"

His boots crunched in the dirt when he stopped. Nikki, unprepared for a sudden halt, smashed full force into his rock-solid arm and shoulder. The breath left her lungs in a hiss and she stumbled back. Her gaze narrowed when she saw him pull something dark and billowy from the back pocket of his denims.

"Recognize this?" he growled, waving the black silk scarf under her nose. The rolled hem slapped her chin, and he smiled cockily when her gaze widened.

"Thought you might. I saved it. A memento of our—ahem—*memorable* days together." His eyes glinted dangerously. "You can have it back now, if you want, but I don't think you'll like the way I plan to put it on you . . . if you catch my drift."

Her angry gaze shifted between the scarf and the man who taunted her with it. "Are you threatening me?!"

His grin broadened. "Oh, Nicole, that's very astute. Now, come on. If you're a good girl, and don't scream I won't have to use this. But if you aren't . . . ?" His voice trailed away.

He thrust a corner of the scarf into his back pocket. The black silk fluttered as it slapped against his lean hip. Before she could stop him, he'd reached out and grabbed her hand. His fingers were warm and tight as they entwined around hers. She found the strength of his grasp oddly exhilarating.

He started off at a brisk pace, dragging her behind. Her feet still felt encased in lead, but this time it was for quite another reason. Her heart pounded with awareness. She couldn't stop it, or control it—she didn't want to. Her fingers warmed in his palm. A hot tingling feeling slipped up her wrist, her arm, her shoulders. Her blood boiled as it raced in her veins, splashing her cheeks with healthy color.

Kurt's feet kicked up a cloud of dust, and Nikki coughed in annoyance as it gritted between her teeth. Her skirt billowed, almost tripping her, but she hoisted it out of the way with trembling fingers. She was half tempted to scream, just to defy him, but thought better of it. She wouldn't give him a reason to shove her own scarf down her throat! Not when she knew how much satisfaction he'd get out of doing it.

"The barn," she stated flatly when she noted the building she was being dragged toward. She tried to wrench her arm free. With a flick of his wrist, he yanked her back into step. "No, Kurt, please," she panted, the exertion of keeping up with his hectic pace stealing her breath. Her free hand clawed at the fingers that held hers tight.

Kurt sent a smirk over his shoulder and quickened his pace. It was almost supper time. The few hands who worked in or around the barn would be busy getting ready for the evening meal. Good, he thought. There would be no interruptions.

His strides as he crossed the apron leading into the barn were the strides of a man with a purpose. His face was set hard, his eyes darkly determined as they adjusted to the lack of light. Dragging a kicking and clawing Nikki behind him, he approached the narrow ladder that led to the hayloft above.

"Up," he ordered, and pushed her toward it. He let her go when she squirmed around to face him.

Nikki planted her feet firmly in the hay-strewn dirt. Her stormy gaze swept the murky interior, to assure her they were alone. "No. If you have something to say to me, you can say it right here. I'm not going up there."

"Why, Nicole? Are you afraid?" he taunted, leaning close.

Cornflower blue clashed with silver steel. "Of what?" she countered coldly. "A little dirt on my dress? Hay in my hair? I don't think so."

His rakish grin forced her back a step and her spine drew up hard against the ladder. The squared-off wooden steps bit into her back.

Kurt reached up and drew a slow finger down her jaw. His gray eyes burned when he noticed the tremor she tried hard to conceal. "I'm not talking about hay or dirt, baby, I'm talking about memories," he said, his tone husky. "Don't you have any memories of this place?"

She jerked her chin away from the heat of his finger, startled by the reaction his fleeting touch aroused. "No, I don't," she answered breathlessly. "Not fond ones."

One raven brow shot up mockingly high. "Ouch! that hurt. Hasn't anyone ever told you that fiddling with a man's pride can be dangerous? We put a lot of stock in our reputations, you know."

"As far as I'm concerned, you can take your reputation and—"

He slashed an index finger across her soft lips. "Be nice, Nicole, or I won't feel I have to be nice in return."

He let her pull away. He saw how her lips trembled where his finger had been. Her lower lip—oh, so moist—thrust out in an endearing pout. For a split second, Kurt was reminded of the Nicole Dennison he used to know. Then his gaze dipped and he was brought up hard by the sight of "Nikki," the woman.

"I don't feel like being nice," she snapped, "I feel like making cornbread with my daughter. And the sooner you tell me why you brought me here, the sooner I can leave."

His dimpled chin jerked to the ladder at her back. "Up there. You want to know what I've got to say, you climb that ladder and find out. Otherwise," he shrugged, "I'm not talking."

"Or letting me leave?" Nikki hesitated, her fingers running over the jagged edge of the step pressing into her back. "Talk?" she asked thoughtfully. "That's all you want to do? Just talk?"

"On my mother's grave, I swear that's all I want," he lied. His eyes sparkled when he wondered what Hope Frazier—alive and well—would do if she'd heard her son say *that!* "Unless, of course, *you* want to do something else, in which case . . ."

"Go to hell, Kurt."

Clamping her jaw tight, Nikki spun on her heel. Hoisting her skirt, and seemingly oblivious to the display she was making of her own shapely ankles and calves, she climbed the ladder.

Kurt sucked in a breath as his gaze was met with creamy flesh and well-turned limbs. A perfectly shaped bottom, firm and round, was molded enticingly by the skirt she held out of the way. His hands tingled, remembering all too well the feel of her naked flesh searing his palm. His gut wrenched.

Mumbling a cuss, and clenching his fingers into white-knuckled fists, he tried to will his body to relax. But the luscious sight of her swaying backside foiled every attempt. Releasing a ragged sigh, he followed her up the ladder.

She was waiting, standing in the knee-deep hay with feet apart, fists on hips, glaring daggers at him as he shoved himself over the ladder. Her color was high, her jaw tight, but otherwise Kurt observed that she looked composed.

Nikki would have been shocked to hear it. Her insides were churning. In the last six years, she'd done her best to stay away from the barn, the hayloft in particular. She needed no reminders of the night her daughter had been conceived, they were with her constantly. More so now, with the scent of fresh hay stinging her nostrils, and Kurt Frazier's dark head towering over her. She found herself caught up in a painful rush of memories—she was shocked to realize that not all of them were unpleasant. Rubbing her hands together, she backed up as far as the slanted roof would allow. "All right, I'm here. Say what's on your mind and make it quick. I won't be staying."

Kurt shrugged, and plopped down on the thick blanket of hay. It crinkled nicely beneath him. A few prickly tips poked through his trousers, but he ignored them as he plucked up a long yellow stalk and clamped it between his teeth. "How's Ben's memory faring?" he asked suddenly. "He remember anything new yet?"

"No," she answered crossly, lips tight, eyes

sparkling. She locked her arms over her chest and glared at him. "Did you bring me all the way up here just to ask me that?"

His smile made her heart flutter, and would have made Mike pea-green with envy. "Hell, no. I brought you up here to watch you squirm. And I figured as long as we're here, I'd see how close you've come to throwing my a—er—me in jail."

"Not close enough, obviously."

"Tsk, tsk," he wagged his finger at her. "That temper always did get you into trouble, Nicole. I thought you would have learned to control it by now."

"Well you thought wrong," she huffed, her gaze sharp with annoyance as she marched toward the ladder. "And if all you brought me up here for was to watch me squirm, then—"

"Oh, no you don't."

Lightning quick, Kurt uncurled from his seemingly relaxed position and grabbed her silky calf when she would have scooted down the ladder. He reeled her in, but she yanked free of his grasp before he reached her knee. Pity, he thought, as he thrust himself to his feet.

"Let me go," she hissed as he forcefully seated her atop the prickly hay.

Planting one hand on each slender shoulder, Kurt pushed her back down when she tried to stand—twice. "One more time and I swear to God I'll sit on you," he warned. "*I* won't mind, but *you* might."

"You wouldn't dare."

His eyes sparkled—with challenge, she wondered, or desire? "Try me."

Nikki clamped her jaw shut and tugged her skirt primly into place. She didn't try to stand again, though she did almost scream in frustration when Kurt settled himself on the bed of hay next to her. His firm leg pressed against her outer thigh, setting the flesh beneath the calico on fire. She groaned and, shifting, put a few of what she knew to be much-needed inches between them.

Kurt waited half of a heartbeat, then stretched languidly. When he was done, he'd again brought his thigh up against hers.

"Stop that," Nikki snapped, maneuvering away again. A few more feet and she'd topple out the open haydoor to her right—the one that let in a flood of golden sunlight to caress every plane of Kurt Frazier's ruggedly handsome face.

"Stop what?" he asked with boyish innocence. But there was nothing boyish in the way his leg remolded itself to hers.

"Stop touching me, dammit!"

A raven brow cocked teasingly high. "Am I touching you? Really? Sorry, I hadn't noticed."

Nikki had noticed. How could she not? Her body warmed and tingled at being in such close proximity with each masculine inch of him. Her breath lumped in her throat and her heart thudded to life with every deliciously warm rush of his breath against her cheek.

With a jerky, self-conscious movement, she shifted away again. This time, thankfully, he let her go. Good. With distance between them, no matter how small, she could think straight. Well, she reckoned, as straight as she would ever be able to think when she was in this arrogant man's presence!

She averted her attention out the haydoor. From Nikki's vantage point the activity on the whole northern quarter of the ranch was visible. At another time, with another person, she would have enjoyed the view. Right now she barely saw it. Her body and mind were too distracted by Kurt to enjoy anything.

"So Ben told you nothing new?" he asked rolling the stalk of hay over his tongue.

"I already told you he didn't. Not yet. He promised

to think about it and let me know, though. That's a good sign."

"Hmmm, great sign," he agreed with marked sarcasm. His finger traced the tapered line of her neck before slipping beneath the collar.

Nikki shivered, batting his hand away. "Stop it, Kurt, this is serious."

"You're telling me? It's my neck we're talking about here, Nicole. I don't take stretching it lightly."

The heat of a blush kissed her cheeks. She rearranged the skirt around her ankles. The hem whispered over the hay as she sighed, "I guess."

Kurt plucked the stalk of hay from his lips and tossed it away. His gaze seared the opposite wall. "What took you so long to talk to him? Seeing Ben should have been the first item on your list of things to do once you got back."

"I wanted to talk to the sheriff first. I thought I might be able to convince Hardy to arrest you where Pete had failed."

"And my showing up when I did ruined your plans?" he asked, intuitively guessing the turn of her thoughts. He turned his head and looked at her. Unconsciously, his index finger drew a hot line down her arm.

"It would've gone better if you hadn't," she admitted. "But I don't think it made that big a difference. Hardy isn't one to change his mind. If he's decided he won't arrest you until I have more proof, then he won't." A quick glance saw Kurt watching her closely. His finger paused on the indentation of her elbow. Her breath caught. Awareness rippled hotly up her spine. "Can I go now?" she asked weakly. "Do you think I've squirmed enough?"

"Depends on where you're going," he replied with deceptive ease. The finger rose. He felt her flesh quiver beneath the calico. "Are you going to gather more evidence against me?"

"No, that can wait until tomorrow." She sent a pointed glare at the hand that so ably worked against her concentration. "I don't think the delay will hurt. You don't look ready to kill anyone any time soon." *Except maybe me,* she thought. Then again, murderous intentions were not what she saw sparkling in his darkened gaze. She took a deep breath. "Actually, I thought I'd find my daughter and help her bake cornbread. Why?"

He shrugged noncommittally. His hand had reached her shoulder. "And then what?"

"And then I plan to eat supper, same as you. Why?"

"Just curious." He smiled crookedly as his hand cupped her shoulder. The bones felt small beneath his palm. Fragile. Enticing. "Don't go yet, Nicole. We have to talk."

"Isn't that what we're doing?" She tried to slip away from him but his fingers tightened their grip.

"What we were just doing is called pussyfooting around. I don't want to play that game, I want to talk to you . . . about Beth." His eyes narrowed when he noticed her cheeks flame with color.

Nikki swallowed hard, averting her gaze. *Does he know?* And how many times could she ask the question without driving herself mad? "Do I have a choice?"

"No."

Her heart fluttered like a wild bird against her ribs. Her thoughts whirled. Yesterday she had been so sure he hadn't made the connection. But that was yesterday. Anything could have happened between now and then.

You put Beth and Frazier in the same room together and the whole town's going to know who the kid's father is. Mike's words, spoken that day by the riverbank, came back to haunt her. It was true. Side by side, the resemblance between father and daughter was striking. So striking it scared her. How could he have missed noticing? Was it possible he didn't know?

Nikki stole a quick glance at Kurt from beneath her thick silver lashes. His gaze was sharp but unreadable, his expression closely guarded. She had to distract him. She had to get his mind off Beth and she had to do it quickly. But how?

The answer, fueled by the hand burning into her shoulder, stunned Nikki. There was no mistaking her tremor of desire, or the reflection of it mirrored in Kurt's passion-darkened dyes. Eyes that bored into her very soul.

Now that the thought of seduction had been planted, it took root, refusing to be dislodged. Deep down, she knew this was not the answer. But it would prevent Kurt from asking questions about Beth, and aside from that, his lips were oh, so close; his body oh, so firm and inviting.

Chapter Nine

"Kurt," Nikki breathed, his name a bittersweet sigh on her lips. She watched him tense, and felt his coiled strength in the hand she rested hesitantly on his forearm. The muscles strained beneath her palm, and her fingertips itched to feel more.

"Oh, God, Nicole," Kurt groaned, his voice husky and strained. "Don't do this to me. Not again. I don't have the strength to fight you a second time. Not when I know it's a fight I can't win."

His palm cupped her cheek. Nikki closed her eyes, losing herself to the feel of his warm, rough flesh. The smell of hay surrounded her, engulfed her, enveloped her in a blanket of desire.

Nikki's resistance—if she'd ever really offered any—drained away in a hot rush when his hand slipped past her temple and his fingers buried themselves in her hair. She couldn't deny it anymore. She wanted Kurt now as much as she'd wanted him six years ago. No, she wanted him more . . . consequences be damned!

The spicy scent of his skin stung her nostrils. The ironwork of his chest beneath soft cotton was alive with rippling promise. His hard, square jaw hovered mere inches away, and she longed to reach out and touch it. *Was it still wonderfully firm and smooth?*

she wondered, *or had six years changed even that?*

Her breath caught in her throat as thick silver lashes fluttered up to meet his gaze. His steely eyes smoldered. His attention lowered to the tempting, creamy shadows only hinted at by her unbuttoned collar. Her flesh tingled with every inch his hungry gaze explored.

His perfectly turned lips loomed close. Yet, even though she tilted her chin up expectantly and closed her eyes, he did not kiss her. She opened her eyes, and what she saw was a man tormented; a man split between the desire to abandon the fight and surrender to blinding passion, and the fear of what would happen if he did.

Nikki could see how much self-inflicted restraint contributed to his resistance. She, however, harbored no such self-control. For six years his mouth had tortured her dreams, and though she'd often thought of it bathed in moonlight, she found the golden shadows now flickering in through the haydoor, playing over a face that had matured from simply appealing to recklessly handsome, had the same dizzying effect on her senses.

On a soft bed of hay, bathed in moonlight, Nikki had been a willing seductress. Now on a soft bed of hay, bathed in sunlight, she would be again. The need to touch and *be* touched was too strong to deny. Not now. Not when his touch felt so good!

A shiver of desire shot up her spine as she cupped his jaw—*ah, it was as smooth!*—in her trembling hands. Leaning into him, she drew his lips to hers.

His jaw was warm, his lips warmer. Her mouth brushed his hesitantly, his lips gradually yielding to her kiss. When his hands encircled her waist, pulling her hard against his side, she allowed herself a tiny, triumphant smile before deepening their pleasure.

Kurt's palm stroked the slender line of her back, roved over her small shoulders, then blazed a path over her upper arms before returning to the gently nipped waist. Warm breath kissed his cheek—it felt like the touch of a butterfly: delicate, fluttering wings branding flesh that flamed hotly with the first quickening of her tongue in his mouth.

She tasted warm, sweet, intoxicatingly wonderful as he drank deeply of what he'd been for so long denied—he drank now, drank greedily. Like a man drying of thirst, he drank. *She* was his sustenance.

Nikki instigated the moist parrying of their tongues as her hand slid down his tightly muscled chest, over his quivering stomach, up. His shoulders were familiar territory to her searing palms, but she reacquainted herself with them anyway. She greeted his upper arms like long lost friends. Turning her palms inward, she let the sleeve covering his forearms tease her sensitive knuckles, then wrapped her fingers around his wrists. His kiss hesitated for one throbbing pulsebeat when she insistently tugged his hands upward.

Kurt's palms smoldered over soft, generous breasts, the outline of which had been branded into his flesh and mind. It wasn't enough. The barrier of fabric, while scant, was too thick. He wanted, *needed,* to feel the hot flesh that teased him from beneath the wisp of calico.

With a husky groan, captured by her soft, moist, tantalizingly skillful lips, he pulled her onto his lap. His fingers worked the tiny buttons, begging for release that trailed from her collarbone like a beaded ribbon. Under his expert guidance, one by one the buttons gave way. The length of a sigh saw him parting the high neckline. In another, his calloused fingertips brushed against her warm, satiny flesh. His breath came long and hard as he tore his lips from hers and rained a path of hot, moist kisses over her cheek and jaw. His teeth nibbled a tasty earlobe as his palm possessively claimed a straining breast.

Nikki trembled and buried her face in the cotton-covered hollow between Kurt's wonderfully thick neck and sensuously firm shoulder. Her own inquisitive fingers were quick to push aside the barrier. Her fingertips glided over hot flesh. The raven pelt of hair curling on his chest tickled her sensitive palms. With a breathless sigh, she feasted on the place where taut skin cushioned the pulse beating wildly at the base of his sun-kissed throat. His flesh tasted warm, salty, wonderful. The feel of his heartbeat, fluttering frantically against the tip of her tongue, was electric.

Of their own accord, her fingers found the place on his body corresponding to the one he was torturing on hers. Her own tongue restlessly stroked a damp path up his neck, worshipped the dent in his chin, strayed higher. She sipped at his lips, then drew the lower one into her mouth. She nibbled on it, savoring the faint taste of coffee as her fingers teased each masculine nub to erection.

"Oh, baby," Kurt growled against her, his breath hot and scorching. "I hope you know what you're doing."

Nikki's response was to slip her hands lower still. His stomach felt like pulsating iron beneath her palms, but she didn't tarry there. The buckle of his belt captured her attention. She wiggled her hips to the side for better access and felt his lightning quick response throb beneath her.

Kurt tipped his head back and moaned deep in his throat. He didn't know how much more sweet torture he could stand. Her lips tasted smoother than sweetened wine and her flesh felt like spun satin. Any minute, he felt that his rigidly leashed restraint was going to snap. But restraint didn't count for much when a velvety moist tongue was licking his hard male nipple the way Nicole's was doing now.

Nikki's fingers dipped beneath the loosened waistband of his trousers as her tongue and teeth gently teased him. Her sensitive fingertips were met with a thinning of the silky curls coating his taut abdomen. Her breath quickened and a shock of pleasure rippled up her arm, tightening around her heart until she could hear the frantic pounding of it drumming in her ears. A deliciously decadent warmth settled like a raw whiskey in her stomach, stayed for a throbbing heartbeat, then seeped lower, heating the junction of her thighs like a branding iron.

She tilted her head to the side. A small whimper escaped her when Kurt buried his face against the tingling flesh of her neck and shoulder. His teeth nibbled, his tongue stroked. And as wonderful as it all felt, her attention was abruptly diverted by the work-roughened fingertips lightly teasing her stomach, loosening more buttons as they went.

She shuddered against his searching palm. Her back arched. The center of her soul was locked on the hand sliding beneath the hem of her skirt, caressing her aching flesh, and on the male hardness throbbing beneath her. Her blood simmered as it rushed through her veins.

Somehow her lips found his again. She kissed him deeply, like a woman who knew what she wanted and wasn't afraid to get it. Her hands seared his stomach, her palms slowly ascended. She allowed a few precious seconds to tease a pink nub, beaded hard amidst raven curls. Her breath caught his moan and her hands moved higher. With trembling fingers, she eased his shirt over wonderfully firm shoulders, down rippling arms that glowed a deep bronze in the flickering sunlight, over hands powerful enough to snap her in two—or make her crazy with desire. By the time she'd tossed the limp cloth to a wrinkled heap in the hay, she was burning and breathless.

"What if someone comes in?" he rasped against her lips.

"I don't care," she sighed.

"Neither do I, baby." His fingers left what they were doing to cup her face. "Neither do I."

His mouth crashed down on hers in a hungry, possessive kiss. He buried his tongue in the honeyed recesses of her mouth, and gasped when she sucked and nibbled the tip.

Holding her as close to his body as he could without melting her willing softness into him, he lowered her to the hay. His only regret was that there was no moonlight pouring in through the hay door to bathe her naked body—when he got to her naked body—and he intended to get to it very, very slowly.

His fingers were trembling with tightly checked desire as he loosened the leather thong securing the thick, quicksilver braid. He coaxed the silky tresses free, fluffed them around her oval face and slender shoulders until they framed her like a soft, sensuous cloud. Ah, here was the moonlight he'd been searching for! Spellbound, he lifted a silky curl from the hay and watched it coil around his finger. He rubbed the strand between his thumb and index finger as though trying to melt the satiny texture of it into his flesh.

"So soft," he groaned, bringing the back of his hand to her flushed cheek. In languorous strokes, he brushed the glistening strand against her skin. Her sharply indrawn breath brought a twitch of a smile to his lips as her hands crept up his back.

"And so hard," she murmured appreciatively as her fingers curled into the rigid muscles of his shoulders. Nikki had felt wisps of her own hair brush her cheek before but, dear Lord, it had never felt like *this!* Her head arched back as the ragged fringe fell slowly over her jaw. It teased her earlobe until she gasped, then slipped down the length of her neck.

"Hmmm," he murmured, his mouth skimming over her parted lips, "so very hard."

The strand slipped lower. Nikki groaned. Kurt guided the silver lock between the cloth that parted invitingly over her breasts. The silky strand slipped beneath. It was soon teasing the swollen, aching nipple that peeked around the calico placket.

With a plaintive whimper, Nikki stretched out her arms and coiled them tightly around Kurt's neck. Her tongue flicked over the mouth that had teased her so unmercifully. The hay beneath them crunched as she tugged him down on top of her. His hand was trapped between their bodies, but his powerful fingers were never still. Nikki twisted against him, her body begging for what her mind and lips would not. He molded himself against her willingly, still managing to whisper some words of resistance in her ear.

"Not a chance, buster," she growled with a husky laugh. What had begun as a way to protect Beth had changed somehow, had raged into a physical need that was so strong she ached from it. The purpose behind her seduction had been lost to the seduction itself. The game had been turned on her, but Nikki felt no urge to defy it. What she railed against was Kurt's taking his own sweet time in satisfying her. She couldn't wait. She wanted him too much.

Positioning her palms against his sinewy shoulders, she rolled him onto his back. Kurt opened his mouth to protest, but she never gave him the chance. Her finger raked over his lips, and the flush kissing Nikki's cheeks deepened when his tongue flicked out to leisurely taste every slender inch of it.

He drew her fingertip into his mouth and nibbled gently on the tip. Nikki shivered and withdrew it to leisurely stroke the moisture over the sensuous turn of his lips. A husky sigh rumbled in his throat as the fingertip caressed the dent in his chin, brushed lightly over the column of his throat, teased his collarbone, ran a searing path between his hard nipples, dipped teasingly into his navel, then descended. She hesitated for no more than a sigh before slipping hungrily beneath the coarse, gaping waistband.

His breath caught when she boldly caressed his throbbing flesh in the torturous manner he'd taught her to a dozen lifetimes ago. His body, rigidly alert, responded to her skilled touch in a way that told him she'd been an apt pupil.

Nikki delighted in the way Kurt's ragged breaths rushed over her shoulder like the kiss of the summer sun beating down on the hot ranges. She teased him unmercifully, and when he tried to push her back to the rustling hay, she laughingly prevented him from doing so. She had the upper hand, so to speak, and she intended to keep it.

With a sly grin, she divested him of the rest of his clothes, accepting help from him only when necessary. Her hungry gaze reacquainted itself with muscle that was harder than she remembered it being, and flesh that was much, much hotter.

She reclined with uncommon grace at his side. Elbow bent, she rested her cheek in one hand and ignored the way the hay prickled at her skin. Even that felt delightfully provocative. The other hand she used to torture him. Very, very slowly.

Remembering the breathless rush of pleasure his actions had caused, she decided to employ the same excruciating tactics on him. Lifting a soft silver curl from her waist, she drew the ragged fringe up his rippling stomach, circled it around a proud male nipple, then blazed it down the same fiery path.

Kurt groaned. His palms were moist, his brow beaded with sweat as he reached out to pull her on top of his aching length. She swatted him away even as he strained toward her. She giggled saucily, using the curl to tease the exposed firmness visible in the parted wedge of his trousers.

This time Kurt took her by surprise. His fingers curled around her wrists, pinning them beside her head as he flipped her onto her back, pushing her hard into the hay. Her meager protest was swallowed by his demanding mouth as his hand moved fervidly down her arms. His calloused palms settled over her breasts. His tongue was quick to follow. He teased each nipple to erectness, until it was Nikki's turn to groan in tormented pleasure.

The husky sound ignited his passion to a dizzying pitch. Short work was made of her dress and undergarments. They fell where they landed, forgotten before the soft cloth could form a wrinkled heap. The warm, dry air caressed her naked flesh, enhanced by the hands that greedily, expertly roved her body.

Kurt's insistent palms slipped over her waist. The tip of a roughened finger tickled her navel. Feeling her skin ripple beneath his touch, he slipped lower.

What had begun as a spark now kindled into a raging inferno. Nikki's blood boiled when Kurt found her need, then stroked her to such desperation that she thought she would go crazy with the want of him. She arched against him, groaning in torment as her fingers dug into the solid bands of his arms. But he refused to let the she-devil who had teased him so unmercifully off lightly. He waited until he knew she could take no more before easing his body onto hers.

Nikki needed no provocation to wrap her silky legs around his hips. His warm flesh felt like rippling steel beneath her palms when she stroked his back. The tangy scent of sweat and hay curled around her, inflaming her spiraling senses.

Her back arched high as she met his first insistent thrust. Pain was a thing of the past. Now there was only pleasure. Sweet, exquisite pleasure that cut through her like a knife.

Their bodies fused together, thrusting forward and

back, both seeking, both receiving. The burning of her thighs fired through her blood and built like a spark of kindling catching to flame. The inferno was close. So wonderfully, torturously close.

He couldn't wait. It had been too long, and she felt too good. He'd intended to prolong both their agonies, but his body had other ideas. So did Nikki's. She whimpered against his shoulder, her teeth nibbling the tight, salty flesh there. Kurt tensed, sensing her urgency, unable to control his own. Restraint was forgotten. Restraint did not exist.

Of its own accord, his hips increased the already frantic pace. It took him only a second to lower his weight to his elbows and bury his face in her neck. Her hair was like satin against his cheek, her skin like velvet. His tongue teased her sensitive flesh as a passionate groan filled the air. His, or hers? It didn't matter. All that mattered was the delicious, moist, shuddering warmth that drove him so close to the breaking point, he thought he would die.

Her chin went up. Her back arched. It started as a tiny shudder, a small, insignificant vibration that soon crashed in the junction of her thighs and shattered into a thousand glorious spasms. Lightning shot through her veins, setting her blood on fire. Her fingers curled inward, clutching hot flesh as her nails dug ribbons into his skin. She pulled him closer, as though trying to merge with his sinewy chest.

With a strangled cry, Nikki buried her face against his neck, letting herself be swept away by the glorious tremors that ripped through her. She nibbled and sucked at his salty flesh as each thrust of Kurt's driving need extended her own pleasure. Much too soon he gave a low, feral grunt and collapsed on top of her. His passion was spent, but he'd in no way had enough of her.

The weight of his body pinned her to the crisp bed of hay. Instead of feeling crushed, Nikki felt light as air. She thought that nothing had ever felt so good as the hay beneath her, or the hard muscles on top of her. She had achieved perfection.

Reality returned in slow, languid waves. Try though she did to push the elements away, her ears slowly hearkened beyond the ragged breath singeing her ear and cheek, stirring the silver wisps clinging to her sweat-moistened brow. Over the echo of her calming heart she heard the early evening thrushes calling in the thicket outside. The whicker of a horse floated up the ladder.

Kurt shifted, easing himself to her side. When his strong arm wrapped around her waist and pulled her close, Nikki went without question. Not once had it occurred to her to deny them both the sweet need that fused their contented flesh together.

His lips grazed the top of her head, making her scalp feel warm and tingly. The hand that cupped her waist slipped lower, his palm tenderly stroking the gentle curve of her hip. The tip of a hot, moist tongue darted out to taste her temple, and Nikki felt a shiver of delicious contentment ripple through her. She closed her eyes and sighed, nuzzling close.

"Baby, you can 'talk' to me this way any time you like," Kurt said, his voice still husky and breathless.

"Talk," she echoed flatly, her spine stiffening. The warm glow of contentment burned away as her reason for being in Kurt Frazier's arms came back to her in a guilty rush. Dear Lord, what had she done?! "Kurt, I have to go."

"Go? Now? Nicole, come back!"

But it was too late. Nikki had already slipped away from him and was tugging on her clothes. His eyes narrowed as he watched her. The quicksilver hair fell in mad disarray to her waist. Her flesh, what he could see of it, was still flushed a becoming pink from their lovemaking. Her fingers were trembling badly, her breasts rising and falling with unnatural quickness beneath the calico she nervously smoothed into place.

Although Kurt was tempted to bolt off his soft bed and drag her back to his side, he didn't. Force would get him nowhere with Nicole Dennison. And after what they'd just shared, it wouldn't be wise to push her. No, better to let her simmer in the memories of their passion instead of causing her to look back on this day with regret, which, now that he thought of it, she would probably do anyway. But she would remember the steamy pleasure of it too. She wouldn't be able to help herself. And if she forgot . . . he'd be there to remind her.

Nikki scooped up her boots from a pile of hay. With as much decorum as she could muster—working against the hay that slowed her footsteps and a skirt that insisted on wrapping itself around her ankles—she stalked to the ladder. She hesitated when Kurt made no move to stop her.

A quick glance found him reclined in the hay, his hands clasped behind his head. He'd made no attempt to dress, and his gloriously naked body glistened in the dwindling sunlight. One ankle swung lazily from atop its perch on the other bent knee. A piece of hay was clamped between his teeth. He chewed on it absently while staring at the roughly planked ceiling.

For all intents and purposes, Nikki had been dismissed. The thought would have rankled, had she not felt so relieved. She needed to get away from him. Needed to think, to sort things out. Not only about what had happened between them, but about what might happen in the future, with Beth. She had to figure out what she would tell Kurt if he'd somehow stumbled on the truth.

Hoisting her skirt, she descended the ladder. It wasn't until her feet were planted on firm ground that she let out a slow sigh of relief. A sound that was countered by the rustling of hay behind her.

Spinning on her heel, Nikki caught a glimpse of a stacked-heel boot and a black-clad leg disappearing around the corner of the barn's back door. Stetson, in the far right stall, snorted nervously. Nikki would have sworn she heard a whimper of fright.

Seizing any excuse not to think of Kurt and what they had done, she stepped away from the ladder and walked swiftly down the center passage separating the stalls. The sun was warm on her head as she stepped outside, the air uncommonly hot as it slapped her cheeks like dry heat pouring from an open oven.

Shielding her eyes with her hand, she scanned the area. Spurs jangled on the few ranch hands milling about, but none of them was wearing black trousers.

"Looking for me?"

Her hand dropped as her gaze snapped over her shoulder. The frown melted. "No, actually, I was . . . never mind, it's probably nothing. You just getting back from the Winfields'?"

A flush kissed Mike's cheeks as he grinned secretively and chuckled. "Yup. What gave me away?"

"Oh, I don't know." Eyes sparkling, she fingered the tail of the scarf around his neck. "Unless it has something to do with those nicely pressed trousers, new shirt, and *perfectly* tied scarf. And that blush is absolutely wicked, Michael James."

His grin deepened as he swatted her hand away. "Speaking of blushes, Sis, you've got a pretty good one going yourself. Should I ask where you've been? Or, more correctly, with *whom?*"

"Nope," she said with forced lightness. She slipped a hand into the crook of his arm, while the other tightened on the boots she carried. She sent him her most charming smile. "Come on, Dally will skin us alive if we're late for supper. And on the way you can tell me how Shelly's doing." He coughed nervously at that, and fidgeted. "And Josh Cleagan. You remember Josh, don't you, Mike? He used to work here, oh, let's say about six years ago."

"Yeah, I remember," Mike replied, eyeing his sister cautiously. "He works for Winfield now. What of him?"

"Oh, nothing. I was just wondering how good old Josh is doing. Abigail Rollison told me he got hitched to Sue Martin this spring past." She smiled up at her brother, her spirits lighter already. *Proof, Nikki. You just need a little more proof.* "I think I'll mosey on over to the Winfields' tomorrow afternoon. Pay Josh a call . . . just for old time's sake, mind you."

Chapter Ten

The barn was a moonlit silhouette, a solid contrast to the velvet sky and its smattering of stars. Nikki hesitated as she approached the large red doors. Except for the gentle snort of horses and an occasional stomping hoof, no noise came from inside. If there was another noise, it was lost to the thrushes, singing loudly from their hiding place in the cottonwoods.

Pressing her ear to the door, she listened. Nothing unusual. Her thoughts turned to the letter now burning a hole in her pocket, the one she'd found waiting on her pillow after supper. It was a summons from Kurt. He wanted to resume their conversation about Beth. He would come, she knew, if only to "make her squirm."

Nikki pushed the door open. The smell of horses and hay was strong. Stetson rumbled about in his stall. He stomped his hoof when he caught Nikki's scent.

The ladder loomed closer, and with each step Nikki felt her heart's rhythm increase. She didn't want to go up there. Not with the silver rays of a full moon pouring in through the open haydoor, not with the sweet scent of hay filling her senses, and definitely not with Kurt Frazier. Not after this afternoon.

Nikki flushed hotly. Her lips warmed with the searing memory of his kisses. That Kurt had responded to her was not surprising. That she had responded to him, on a base, physical level that she had no control over, stunned her to the core. Her body still tingled, her lips still burned, and she knew, deep down, that she wanted Kurt Frazier again. The afternoon had been wonderful, but it wasn't enough. Not by a long shot.

Nikki rubbed her hands together, surprised to find her palms clammy. *Is he up there?* There was one way to find out. "Kurt?" she called out hesitantly, taking small, precise steps as she neared the ladder. "Kurt, are you here?"

The slight crunching of hay behind her made her heart stop, then lurch frantically. She spun around, but the center passage was emtpy. A horse whickered nervously. She caught a scent of something—a sweet, cloying scent that was vaguely familiar, where had she smelled it before?—but it vanished so suddenly she thought she must have imagined it. Nikki berated herself—she was startling at nothing! She reached the ladder and started to climb, her thoughts on Beth, on getting through the inevitable confrontation with Kurt and putting it behind her.

Her foot had barely settled on the middle step of the ladder when she heard the wood beneath her crack. She lunged for the top step, her fingers coiling around the thick wood as the rung beneath her feet snapped neatly in two.

With nothing to support her, she swung forward. Her head came up hard against the corner of a step and she groaned when pain exploded in her temple. A dull throb cut through her right shoulder, another through her left leg. The lower one could be ignored; it was the pain in her shoulder that could mean the difference between reaching the loft, or falling to the floor.

"Kurt!" she gasped. She tried to pull herself up, but her arms were stretched to full length. Pain shot through her shoulder at the slightest movement. "Damn! *Kurt Frazier, where are you?!*"

Her fingers started to throb. Splinters pierced the skin. She knew she couldn't hold on for long. She glanced at the hard-packed ground below. She reasoned that a fall from this distance wouldn't be fatal—a broken leg or arm, a few cuts and scrapes; nothing she couldn't live through. But Nikki wasn't about to take that chance. Again she tried to pull herself up. She winced at the shooting pain, but refused to give in to it. Her legs flailed as she tried to fling them over the closest step. The calico skirt twisted around her legs, making the attempt feeble at best.

Her grip was starting to slacken. There was no telling when her fingers would give out. Supporting most of her weight with her left arm, she forced her fingers to keep hold of the step. Using the last of her energy, she screamed, "Help me! I'm in the barn! Somebody *heeelp meeeee!*"

An eternity seemed to pass before the barn door crashed open and a man stepped inside. "Sis? Is that you?"

"Mike," she breathed in relief. "Thank God! I'm up here, on the ladder."

"You're whe—? Nikki, what are you doing?"

She bit down hard on her lower lip to keep from screaming. "Later," she snapped through gritted teeth. "I'm starting to slip. Come on, Mike, *hur-ry!*"

Mike bolted for the ladder, testing the few steps left before trusting his weight to the weathered wood. He climbed as far as he could, then leaned a hip against the rail and reached for her. His breath caught when he felt his sister's waist slip beneath his arm. "Okay, Sis, I've got you. Let go of the step, then turn toward me. But do it *slow!* You go fast and we'll both go flying."

Nikki pried her fingers from the step. They ached from supporting her hanging weight, and from where the hard corner of the wood had bitten into her tender flesh. As soon as her hands were free, she felt herself fall.

Mike was fast. Already he'd threaded one arm through the side rail, securely anchoring himself to the rigid wood. When Nikki's weight shifted toward him, his lean body accepted the burden with ease. Very carefully he twisted, lowering Nikki to the first solid step as he guided her hands to the rail. He didn't release her fingers until he saw her nod to him curtly.

The hard ground cushioned Nikki's feet. Her muscles protested as she collapsed in a breathless heap, aching from where she had stretched and yanked sensitive tendons; ones she didn't even know existed.

Mike scrambled down the ladder. "Are you all right?"

"Fine," she lied softly.

His shrewd gaze was quick to catch a delicate shiver pass over her shoulders. He sank to the ground beside her and drew her into a sideways hug, surprised at how easily she came to him.

"What happened?" he asked when her trembling had subsided. She pushed away from him, and he let her go gently, his eyes never leaving her. "Better yet, what are you doing here? You never come to the barn. Never." His gaze drifted to the broken step. "Why tonight? And what the hell happened to that ladder?"

Nikki took a deep breath. "Kurt asked me to meet him. He wanted to talk about Beth. As for the ladder . . ." She shrugged. "I guess it broke. It *is* old, Mike."

"Just like that?"

"Just like that." If she didn't believe a word she'd just spoken, how could she expect Mike to? "You don't think it broke, do you? *Do you?*" she pressed when he looked guiltily away.

"No," he answered finally, "I don't. If that thing broke, it's the queerest break I've ever seen." His eyes flashed with suspicion as he met her confused gaze. "That step was sliced clean with a saw. Not all the way, mind you, but enough so a little weight would make it give."

Nikki drew her knees up to her chest and crossed her arms over her shins. She focused on the shadowy wall, her mind churning with suspicion. "If it didn't break, Mike, then—"

"Who knew you were coming here tonight?"

"Nobody. Kurt, of course, but that's it. I didn't tell anyone, and I doubt he did." Reaching into her pocket, she extracted Kurt's note and passed it to her brother, watching him carefully as he read it. "I can see that mind working, Michael James, and you're wrong. You said yourself I never come to the barn. Everyone on the ranch knows that. *If* someone rigged that ladder to break, they weren't doing it to hurt *me*."

Mike's jaw tightened and he shook his head. "I'm not so sure."

Nudging his arm, she pointed to the broken ladder. "Look at that. Even if I had fallen, the most I'd have gotten would have been a broken arm or leg. If the fall wouldn't kill a body, why bother?"

"Lord, I don't know. Maybe whoever did it wasn't too smart. Or maybe they wanted to hurt and scare, not kill." His eyes narrowed as he raked his long fingers through his tousled blond hair. "Wait a minute, you said you were meeting Kurt, right?"

"Um-hum," she answered cautiously. "What of it?"

He grinned—Oh God, she thought, not *that* grin!—obviously proud of his deductive reasoning. "Maybe whoever cut the stairs wanted *him* to fall.

Maybe they thought *he* would get here first and go up the ladder, and when he did . . ." His open palms slapped together.

"And maybe, just maybe, it was Kurt who cut the steps," Nikki said slowly, dryly. Her memories of the afternoon, spent in Kurt Frazier's arms, abruptly soured.

Mike's grin vanished. "Yeah, maybe. It makes sense. You have been coming down on him pretty hard, Sis. And you're always reminding him that you'd rather see him with a rope necktie. I'd say that's a pretty good reason for a man to want to kill you."

"Kill me?" she corrected softly, "or warn me? The fall wouldn't have killed me. But if someone was trying to warn me to leave things alone, this would be a good way to do it."

"A real good way," he agreed tightly. "You think it was him?"

Nikki swiped a silver curl back from her brow and sighed. "I'd like to say no, but everything points that way. He had reason, opportunity, and the fact that he isn't here right now is certainly condemning. Who else could it be?"

"The man who killed your father," a husky voice inserted from over their shoulders. "Or did you forget about him?"

She stiffened as Kurt's voice ripped up her spine, prickling the hair at her nape. She hadn't heard his approach. She realized she shouldn't be so surprised. Hadn't he already demonstrated how stealthy he could be if he wanted to?

It took a few seconds longer for recognition to flicker in Mike's eyes. When it did, it was mixed with an anger bordering on cold fury. "What do you want, Frazier?" he growled, pushing to a stand. He stood glaring, his feet spread and his balled fists planted firmly atop his lean hips. "Haven't you done enough damage? Or did you come back here to finish the job?"

"I came here to talk to Nicole," Kurt answered smoothly. His icy gaze flickered between brother, sister, and broken ladder. "No more, no less."

"Yeah, right," Mike scoffed, jabbing a thumb over his shoulder. "If that's your idea of 'talk,' then my sister doesn't want to speak to you."

Kurt's gaze shifted to Nikki, who was visibly pale even in the shadows. His jaw hardened. "You're wrong, Mickey, I didn't do that. It's not my style."

"No?" Nikki asked coldly. "What is your style, Kurt? Wait for me to take one of the horses out, then use me for target practice? Or would you rather kill me with your bare hands?"

He ran a palm down his freshly shaven jaw. "If I wanted you dead, Nicole, I could have killed you a thousand times over. I've had plenty of chances . . . as you well know."

"So you're saying you didn't do it?" Mike pressed.

"What I'm saying is that if I was going to kill your sister, I'd think of a better way to do it. The chances of her dying from a fall like that are small. Me, now I'd pick a way that would kill her quick and sure. No maybe's."

"And what if you weren't trying to kill me?" Nikki demanded. "What if you only wanted to scare me? Or warn me that if I kept digging for proof against you, *then* you'd kill me? How would you do that, Kurt? Would this be your style then?"

"Hurting women has never been my style, Nicole," he replied, his voice as thick and as ragged as the dark hair scraping the cotton collar of his shirt. His eyes shimmered in the moonlight that filtered in through the slats in the barn wall.

"If it wasn't you, then who'd I see hurrying away from the barn when I heard Nikki scream?" Mike countered hotly.

Crossing his arms over his chest, Kurt shook his head. "I don't know, but I'm damn sure it wasn't me."

"No?" Mike scowled. "Funny, it *looked* like you."

"It wasn't."

"Then who—?"

Nikki cut her brother short. "Where have you been, Kurt? What took you so long to show up?"

"You did," he replied bluntly. "I got your note, and, well, I think you *know* the reaction I had to it." Reaching under his black leather vest, he withdrew a scrap of paper from the pocket of his shirt. The page crackled as he unfolded it and read: "'Kurt. Beth's sick. Meet me in the barn at midnight. We have to talk. N.' When I went to the house to see how the kid was feeling, you weren't there. I asked Dolores, and she looked at me like I'd just asked for the moon. Pete did the same thing. No one knew what I was talking about."

Nikki stood, her eyes wide. Kurt handed her the note when she reached for it. She scanned the page, her scowl deepening. "I didn't write this," she hissed, shaking her head and gesturing to the bold, crisp, thoroughly unfamiliar script. "It isn't my handwriting."

Mike leaned over his sister's shoulder, his gaze running down the paper. "She's right," he seconded. "I'd recognize my sister's handwriting anywhere. Sloppy, illegible. This is too precise, too neat. If you can make out the words, Nikki didn't write it."

"What do you mean she didn't write it?" Kurt growled, snatching the paper from Nikki's hands. As his gaze devoured the page, his cheeks drained of color.

Nikki looked at Kurt sharply, confused by his reaction. "Just what he said. I didn't write it, someone else did. Someone who knew we were meeting. Someone who Mike thinks wanted to hurt me, warn me, or get me out of the way. Who'd you tell about our meeting tonight?"

"No one." He sent her a hard look. "We didn't have one."

"Kurt, I—" Nikki stopped short, remembering the letter she had given to Mike. She snatched the note from her brother and handed it to Kurt.

He read it quickly, his cheeks paling further. "I didn't write this," he stated flatly. His gaze shot to the steps. "And I didn't do that. Whoever sent this note knew I'd be delayed when I went to check on Beth. But why?" The scowl deepened when he folded both letters and stuffed them into his pocket. He gestured to the broken ladder. "Who hates you enough to do that?"

She shook her head. "You're the only one I can think of."

"You have a good reason to," Mike added gruffly.

"But I was at the house," Kurt reminded them. "Ask Dolores or Pete. They'll tell you."

Nikki pursed her lips and tapped a finger against them thoughtfully. "All right, suppose you were at the house. I know I was in here. So who did Mike see leaving the barn?"

"Good question," her brother agreed. "When I saw the guy, I thought it was him," he nodded at Kurt. "Now I'm not so sure. He hid in the shadows before I could get a look at his face."

"Why the hell didn't you follow him?" Kurt demanded. "Especially someone who looked as suspicious as this guy sounds?"

"Yeah, he looked suspicious," Mike agreed. "And I was going to chase him, find out what he was up to, but I heard Nikki scream so I rushed in here instead. Judging from the way I found her, it's a good thing I did."

Kurt's gaze drifted to Nikki. His eyes smoldered to

rich turquoise when he noted the bruise marring her brow. His fingers itched to stroke the swollen, purple flesh. "You didn't see anyone?" he asked her.

Nikki shook her head. "No, but . . ." she scowled, remembering the sound of hay that had rustled behind her.

"But what?" Kurt and Mike asked in unison.

"Nicole," Kurt continued, "if you saw something, it won't do any good to keep it to yourself. The sooner we find out what happened, the safer you'll be. What did you see?"

"Nothing," she answered honestly, her gaze drifting past his shoulder to the shadowy center passage. "I didn't *see* a thing. But just before I started up the ladder I could have sworn I heard something move behind me." She shrugged and sent Kurt a sharp glance. "I don't know, it could have been my imagination. Or the wind. Or the horses."

"Not the wind," Mike informed her. "It's dead still out there. Has been all week."

"I'll check," Kurt growled, his jaw hardening. "The guy who did this might have left something behind. I wouldn't count on it, but if he did, I intend to find out."

Nikki spun around, following close on Kurt's heel when he stalked past her. Mike fell into step.

She saw nothing unusual in the shadowy center passage. Certainly nothing incriminating. She was quite surprised when she heard Kurt's "Gotcha!"

He stopped beside Stetson's stall. The stallion's black nose peeked over the half-door when Kurt reached to pick something up from the hay-strewn floor. "Either of you ever see anything like this before?" he asked, extending his hand, the object dead center in his calloused palm.

"What is it?" Nikki asked when Mike plucked up the chunk of dull metal. She looked at the thing, dangling from her brother's narrow fingers. "A spur?

A spur? Is this supposed to *mean* something? All of the hands wear spurs, Kurt."

"This isn't just any kind of spur, Nicole, it's a *Cal-i-forn-i-a* spur."

"A Cal-i-forn-i-a spur," she echoed. "Right. Mind telling me exactly what a 'California spur' is? Besides ugly." She wrinkled her nose at the garishly carved heel band. On closer inspection she noticed that the thing had more sharp metal spikes protruding from the circular rowel wheel than the spurs most of the men on the Triple D favored. The spikes were longer than the three-inch ones fixed to her own work boots. "How the hell can anyone walk in those things?"

Mike tossed the spur to Kurt. "In California they must take their spurs *off* to walk."

"Or they wear them higher up the leg," Kurt said, tossing the spur in the air. Nikki watched, mesmerized, as it slapped into his palm time and again. "Know anybody around here who has the match to this one? Because unless I miss my guess, when we find the guy who favors California spurs, we find the guy who's out to get you."

"This is ridiculous," Nikki scoffed, turning away. "No one is out to get me, Kurt. Who would want to?"

"Good question," he replied solemnly, stuffing the spur into his trouser pocket. As his gaze locked with Mike's he gestured toward the barn door. Mike hesitated, glanced at Nikki, then nodded. "As a matter of fact, I've been wondering the same thing myself. Except for me, I'm drawing a blank."

Mike shifted uncomfortably. "Look, Sis, I-I've gotta go."

"Go?" Nikki spun on him. "What do you mean you've got to go? We've got to find out who—" Her gaze narrowed. "Come here, brother dear," she purred, gesturing him forward with a wagging finger. Mike took a cautious step toward her.

"Closer." Crossing her arms over her chest, she sniffed the air. "I thought so! That's perfume I smell clinging to your collar, isn't it, Michael James? Well?"

He flashed her a grin. "Yeah, I guess it is. Like it? I'll buy you a bottle for Christmas if you want."

"What I want," she said, "is to strangle you. And so help me, God, I think I might. Should I ask her name? Or don't you remember it? Maybe I should tell Shelly about—?"

"Uh-oh, I hear Pete calling. Better see what he wants." Mike gave her a quick peck on the cheek, sent Kurt a helpless shrug, then left before Nikki could make good on her threat.

"What are *you* laughing at?" she snapped, noting the grin that tugged at Kurt's lips. "For God's sake don't encourage him, Kurt. Shelly loves him, but he's too damn reckless to care. He's going to get himself into trouble one of these days. And where will you and your laughter be then?"

"Dead," he answered, suddenly sober, "if you have your way."

"Is that why you tried to kill me?" she shot back.

"Nicole, if I'd wanted you dead I'd have killed you long ago. God knows, you've tempted me often enough."

"So you've said." Nikki paced an angry circle around him. "I'll ask you again. What if you only wanted to warn me?"

"What if I did?" Eyes narrow, he watched her pass him, then reappear on the other side.

She jerked her chin in the direction of the ladder. "Well, is this your work or isn't it?"

"I already told you."

"Wrong. You *avoided* telling me. You skirted around the issue like it was a walking case of cholera."

"Stop that," he growled when she started her third

circle of agitated pacing. Grabbing her arms, he dragged her roughly against him.

She brought her chin up. He lowered his. Their cheeks grazed.

His breath caught at the tension their contact exposed. *Silk and sandpaper,* he thought before his attention was consumed by her generous breasts molded enticingly to his side. She felt good. Too good!

"Let me go," she ordered through clenched teeth. Twisting to the side, she tried to pry his fingers from her arms. His grip held painfully firm.

Kurt kept his expression stern, but he couldn't deny the sizzle of desire that heated his blood, the way it always did when Nikki's supple body wiggled against him. Her curves were warm and generous, filled with a promise only hours old. Why had he vowed not to repeat the afternoon's mistake?! He wanted to repeat it. Here. Now.

Kurt turned his head until the tips of their noses met. Warm, rapid breath seared his cheek and neck as his steely gaze clashed with her stormy blue one.

"What do you want from me, Nicole Dennison?" he demanded huskily. "Do you want to hear me say again that I didn't try to hurt you? Is that it?" With a groan of self-reproach, he pushed her away. She stumbled back, but quickly caught her balance. "Well, you'll get nothing from me."

"Then you admit it?" she gasped, shocked despite herself. The two notes had almost convinced her of his innocence. Now she wasn't so sure. Why did it hurt so much to think it had been him?!

"No, I don't admit it," he snapped, raking his fingers angrily through his tousled raven hair. "And even if I did, what difference would it make? You've already played judge and jury. I'm convicted before I'm accused in your eyes. How's that for a fair and unprejudiced judicial system? All that's left now is the hanging," his gaze narrowed, "and I'd bet my saddle you can't wait for that part. Can you, Nicole? *Can you?!*"

Nikki pressed back against the stall door. The hard ledge bit into her back, but she hardly noticed the pain. "That isn't fair," she argued. "All I want is justice. I want Pop's killer brought to trial. If you didn't do it, Kurt, then why not have the trial and be done with it? If you're innocent, you have nothing to fear."

He approached her slowly, like a cougar stalking its prey. He rested one sinewy forearm on the door frame beside her head. He arched his back slightly, until his chest was almost against hers. He was close enough to feel the raw heat of her body, and resolved enough to ignore it. "Nothing to fear?" he said mockingly.

She raised her chin. "Nothing... *if* you're innocent."

He cocked one raven brow high. His strong fingers captured the thick plait draping her slender shoulder. With slow precision, he coiled the silky, quicksilver rope around his hand, stopping only when his knuckles grazed her tapered neck.

Nikki met his gaze. Defiance shimmered in her eyes.

"Baby, do you remember a kid by the name of Jim Hanson?" he asked, his voice low. A cold grin touched his lips when she nodded. "Do you remember what they did to Jim back in seventy-nine?"

"Of course I do. They hung him for rustling. Why?"

"Just curious," he said. "Lately I've found myself wondering what you would have done with Jim... if the decision had been yours. Would you have seen him hanged? Or would you have believed him when he said he didn't do it?"

"There was evidence, Kurt," she scoffed, "and lots

of it. Three men saw him near Winfield's stolen cattle. One of them was Winfield's own son. You can't dispute evidence like that."

"I'm not 'disputing' anything. Just tell me what you would have done with Jim."

Nikki scowled. Gritting her teeth, she looked away. "I don't know. Probably the same thing. Hanson was caught red-handed. I wouldn't have let him walk away scot-free. He should have thought of the penalty before committing the crime."

His steely gaze darkened, his expression inscrutable as he searched her face. "So you would have hanged him?"

"Yes," she replied impatiently. Stetson whickered in his stall as though sensing her confusion. "Why are you asking me this? What does Jim Hanson have to do with my father's murder?"

"Jim?" Kurt shook his head, his lips pursed. "Not a thing."

He pushed away from the door frame and strode to the barn door. The moonlight glistened over his raven hair, turning each strand to dark silver. He stopped on the threshold and looked out at the dry, still night. The pale light bathed him in a soft glow as he glanced back at her. "You might be interested to know that I met up with a guy from Dakota a few years back. Went by the name of Fromont. Dan Fromont. Said he lived in Snow Creek for a year, maybe two, before he moved East. Ever heard of him?"

Nikki couldn't see his eyes, but she could feel them. "I don't think so. Look, Kurt, if you're trying to—"

"Poor Dan," he sighed. Shaking his head, he planted balled fists on his hips. "Died in my arms. He was shot robbing a train. Knew he was a goner, but he didn't seem to care. Anyway, while poor Dan was lying there spilling his blood on my lap, he decided it was time to make some confessions. Lots of them.

Tons of them. One had to do with the summer of seventy-nine and a few of Old Man Winfield's prime head."

Nikki's blood ran cold, her cheeks drained of color. "But they hung Jim Hanson for that," she cried. "Are you saying he was innocent? Are you saying that that stupid vigilante committee hung the wrong man?"

He turned back to the door. "I'm not saying that."

"Then what *are* you saying?!"

"That a dying man has about as much reason to lie as one on his way to the hangman's noose." With that, he strode into the moonlight.

Nikki collapsed against the stall door. Her rigid back grazed the wood as she slid, breathless, to the floor. She felt as if she had been soundly punched.

Half an hour later Kurt sat behind Pete's desk in the study. The soft orange glow of a single candle saw him methodically opening and closing drawers. A satisfied grin curled his lips as he opened the bottom one.

"Okay, baby, come to Papa." He rubbed his hands together and blew on them for luck. Unless he missed his guess, this was Nikki's territory.

He extracted the ledger of household accounts and placed it on top of a small stack of folders. He flipped open the worn leather cover, then took the note he'd received, the one supposedly sent by Nikki, out of his pocket. Unfolding the crisp sheet of paper, he rested it on top of the open ledger.

"Well, I'll be damned." His stunned gaze flickered between the letter and the ledger. "She really didn't write it."

His heart raced as his thoughts flew to a third letter. In six years, the once-white sheet had aged to faded yellow, the crisp paper now limp and torn from being opened, read, and refolded many times over. It was stashed in a bureau drawer at his parents' house in Cambridge. But Kurt didn't need the letter in front of him to know which sample of handwriting it would match. He'd read the thing so many times that now all he had to do was close his eyes and see the words seared into his mind, and his heart.

That letter had the same crisp strokes as the one staring back at him now. He was positive. But Nikki hadn't written the six-year-old letter, he realized, as his gaze snapped open and greedily devoured the sloppy journal entries. If he needed more proof, all he had to do was glance at the top of the page where her name was scribbled in the same scratchy hand. Her *N* looked like a flat line with a hump dead center. It didn't come close to matching the *N* of the second letter; three precise slashes of even length and spacing.

Kurt's palms were uncomfortably moist as he slammed the ledger closed and returned it to the drawer. He didn't realize his fingers were trembling until he folded the letter and returned it to his pocket. It nestled beside the letter that had been sent to Nikki. A letter *he* hadn't written. A letter that, he knew without looking, would match the others.

But if Nicole didn't write the letter that ruined my life six years ago, then who did? Kurt pushed himself from the chair and blew out the candle. *Who would want me out of Snow Creek so badly they'd send me a note like that and sign Nicole's name to it?*

Hugh Dennison's murderer, of course. But who, exactly, was that? More importantly, why had he now, whoever he was, turned his sights on Nikki? And how close was she to discovering the truth about her father's death?

Chapter Eleven

"Where have you been?!"

The familiar voice shot out from the blinding midday sun to race up Nikki's spine. She was riding bareback, not by choice. Tugging on the horse's mane, she guided her mount to a stop. Shielding her eyes with her hand, she scowled, scanning the hot, dry, hilly terrain. Her eyes rested on Kurt, who stood beside the wagon she had hoped would have taken her to the Winfields' four hours earlier. The wagon had broken down at the midway point between the two ranches.

Kicking the workhorse to a trot, she neared the disabled wagon. The closer she drew, the more she could see of him, and the more she wished she'd stayed on the Winfields' porch sipping lemonade with Mark—as detestable as the idea was to her.

"Well?" Kurt barked when she stopped the horse beside him. "I asked you a question. *Where have you been?!*"

His gruff tone made the horse's ears flatten. Hooves shuffled nervously in the parched dirt. Reaching down, Nikki ran a palm over the thick brown mane. Her condescending glare never left Kurt. Even the shadows beneath his hat, riding arrogantly low on his brow, couldn't conceal the furious glint in his eyes.

"What are you doing here, Kurt?" she snapped. "Pete pays you good money to do ranch work, *not* to follow his sister."

"Don't flatter yourself, Nicole. I'm not following you . . . but someone is. Look at this."

Nikki didn't see the long chunk of wood in his hands until she found the dirty thing shoved beneath her nose. It was the broken shaft that had caused her to abandon her wagon, and to travel the rest of the way to the Winfields' ranch on the workhorse. Scowling, she asked, "What are you doing with that?"

"Worrying myself sick mostly." A thick bronze fingertip picked at the jagged edges of the shaft. "See this?" he turned the wood and pointed to the other side. Scowling darkly, he jabbed a finger at the spot where it had broken. "Nice cut, isn't it? Almost looks like it was sliced clean with a saw. Remind you of anything?" His smile was confidently cold as he watched her gaze narrow.

"No, Kurt, it doesn't. This was an accident," she protested, a bit too emphatically. Her gaze wavered between the broken shaft and Kurt.

"Yeah, right, and I'm Abe Lincoln." With an angry growl, he tossed the chunk of wood into the dirt. When it didn't land far enough away, he kicked it. "Good God, woman, are you so thick-skulled and blind you can't see the truth when it's sitting smack-dab on the end of your great big nose?!"

"I think I resent that," Nikki said, balling her hands into tight fists.

"What? What I said about your nose?"

"No," she snapped, "what you said about my being stupid and blind. I'm not. I think you're reading something into this that isn't there." She heard his grunt of disgust. Her patience, already strained, broke. "Accidents *do* happen, you know!"

"And this was one of them, was it? Just another unlucky coincidence, like the step that *accidentally* broke in the barn last night." His tone was lethal.

Nikki's gaze narrowed. Her fingers, moist from the sun's oppressive heat, tightened on the mane. "It could be."

"But it isn't."

"But it *could* be."

Although she'd braced herself for his reaction, there was no time to protest the steely fingers that wrapped around her upper arm and hauled her from the horse.

"Let me go!" she yelled, fighting him to no avail. Her riding skirt twisted around her legs, the thick folds conspiring to trip her as Kurt dragged her to where he'd thrown the shaft. Not breaking stride, Kurt reached down and snatched up the chunk of wood. For the second time, Nikki found it thrust beneath her nose.

"Does this thing look like it broke all by its lonesome?" he demanded. His cheeks were red with rage. "Well? Does it?!"

Nikki swallowed hard, her gaze flickering over the shaft. On close inspection it was obvious the wood had been cut. Like the step, one side was jagged, the other smooth to the touch. Slowly, she met Kurt's gaze; stubbornly, she held her tongue.

Kurt dropped her arm as though he couldn't stand to touch her. "You scared yet, Nicole? You damn well should be."

"I'm not," she answered honestly, absently. At the same time, she knew that the sudden churning in her gut was caused by Kurt Frazier's proximity. It had no foundation in fear.

Kurt dragged the hat from his head, plowed his fingers through his hair angrily, then settled the worn leather back into place. With supreme effort he resisted the urge to reach out and shake her until her pearly teeth rattled. "What is it going to take to get it through your thick little skull that *someone is trying to kill you?*"

"So what?" she scoffed. "Even if someone is, and I'm still not convinced of that, at the rate they're going it could take years."

"Not if I help them," he muttered under his breath. Louder, he said, "Where have you been?"

Nikki became immediately defensive. "I needed air, so I went for a ride." Crossing her arms over her chest, she shot him a defiant glare. "Not that it's any of your business."

"Wrong. Everything you do is my business." His hand reached up and the tip of his thumb grazed her proudly lifted chin. The contact surprised them both. His hand quickly dropped to his side, but his flesh continued to smolder from the touch. "Until we find out who's trying to kill you."

The feel of his calloused finger grazing her flesh bothered Nikki more than she'd ever admit. In an attempt to work off her frustration, she began pacing the dirt in front of him. "All right, suppose what you're saying is true. Suppose someone *is* trying to kill me. What do you propose I do? Run home and hide under the bed covers until I find out who it is?" She shook her head and snickered dryly. "I don't think so. Hiding has never been my style. Neither has running."

"Do what you normally do, just keep low. Try not to stir up any more trouble." Kurt laughed the second the words spilled off his tongue. It was a low, rumbling sound that emanated from deep in his chest. He watched as Nikki's pace quickened. "Forget I suggested it," he added, his tone degrees lighter. "I'd have more luck asking a skunk not to spray."

His laughter was the last straw. In less than twenty-four hours she'd had two attempts made on her life—or so everyone kept telling her—and if that wasn't bad enough, she now had one devilishly handsome and equally unmannered lout laughing at her! And for what? She hadn't been able to worm so much as a smidgen of information out of Josh Cleagan about her father's murder.

"You may think this is funny," Nikki hissed, "but I do not. And if you knew what kind of a day I've been having, you'd think twice about laughing at me."

"What's the matter, Nicole? Things not going the way you'd planned?" His eyes glinted with a wicked, secretive light. "What happened at the Winfields' place to get you so moody? Didn't Josh have the answers you wanted?"

"That's part of it," she answered tightly, not surprised he knew where she'd gone and why. She would have been disappointed if he hadn't guessed. "Add to it the embarrassment of having to ride in there wearing this"—she pinched a fold of her skirt—"on that"—she jerked a thumb in the direction of the horse waiting patiently behind her—"and you've got the makings of one miserable day. Oh yes, and you can top it all off with Mark Winfield telling me why Brian hasn't been home in weeks." Her gaze sharpened. "Did you know Bri got married?"

Kurt turned his attention away. It was answer enough.

"Thanks for telling me. He's only my brother. Why should I care?" Thrusting her chin high, Nikki spun on her heel and stalked back to her horse. The coarse skirt rustled around her legs, the hem releasing billowing clouds of dust with each angry stride.

Kurt's mood darkened when his gaze lit upon her softly swaying hips, and the ragged fringe of her silver braid as it slapped against a waist so small, his tingling palms said he could span it blindfolded. His gut tightened. His smile faded.

Logically, Kurt couldn't blame Nicole for being angry. If any of his brothers had gotten married, he'd want to know about it, too. Kurt pulled himself up quick. What was wrong with him? Hadn't he learned months ago that *logic* and *Nikki Dennison* didn't mix?

Grumbling to himself, Kurt turned back just in time to see Nikki's heel sink into the horse's flanks. He sucked in a ragged breath.

She was riding bareback, with an ease just shy of sinful. Her ugly brown skirt was hoisted well above creamy knees and well-turned ankles. Her hair, loosened from its braid, bounced like a tempting silver waterfall down her back. Her fingers gripped the silky mane as she leaned low over the horse's back. Large, full breasts strained against her coarse bodice, their firm tips brushing the mare's sinewy flesh with each sure stride.

Kurt clenched his fists in an attempt to fight back the fire the sight of her induced. No doubt the cowpunchers would react much the same way when she rode into the Triple D looking like that. His lips thinned, his jaw hardened. The thought of other men looking at her that way almost sent him into a rage.

His gaze was hotter than the sun beating down upon his head as he rounded the wagon. In three long strides he reached the horse he'd tethered there.

Cursing under his breath, he vaulted onto the stallion's back. His fingers clenched and unclenched the reins, and he was hard pressed not to imagine Nicole Dennison's temptingly long throat within his grasp.

"Nobody's going to have to kill her. When I get my hands on her there won't be anything left!" he muttered before planting his spurs in the stallion's flanks.

* * *

Kurt would have hunted Nicole down immediately, but was waylaid by Pete and plans for the upcoming cow hunt and trail drive. And if Kurt had thought himself angry with her before, he was furious when he found out that Nicole planned to be on the drive.

He walked away from Pete mid-sentence, combing the house for Nicole. He found her in the dining room with Mike. Without offering an explanation, he grabbed her roughly by the arm and dragged her into the study, where he slammed her hard into one of the red leather chairs.

Towering over her, hands on his hips, he bellowed, "You're *not* going on that trail drive!"

His angry words rushed through the open study door, echoing down the hall.

If she was surprised by his outburst, she didn't show it. Instead, she stiffened and yelled just as loudly, "I *am!*" With an indignant toss of her head, she met his angry gaze measure for furious measure. Her jaw was set hard. Her Dennison-blue eyes shot him daggers as she shouted, "If you don't believe me, just sit and watch!"

"I won't have to. *You're not going!*" His outraged glare darkened. "I don't care if I have to lock you in your room until snowdrifts pile up so high you can't pry open the window. I'll do whatever it takes to keep you safe!"

"Why should you care if I'm safe?!" She shoved from the chair and commenced pacing furiously in front of the hearth. Her arms flew up, then fell against her thighs. "You should be glad to get rid of me. I *am* the one who's been trying to slip your neck in a noose. Or did you forget about that?"

"How could I? You remind me of it every two minutes!"

"I *have* to remind you. It's the only way I can be sure you don't get too settled, don't start thinking of this place as *home*. I don't want you getting too

191

attached to any of the people here. You won't be staying long enough, and I don't want to see any long faces when you're gone."

Kurt's gaze hardened to shards of turquoise and cold gray steel. Crossing his arms over his chest, he leaned one hip against the desk and glared at her. "You mean Beth."

"Who *else* would I mean?" Her pacing increased as she spun, stalking to the other side of the room. The skirt billowed like a cloud of trail dust, then settled in thick folds around her ankles. Her boots thumped over the gold rug. Her arms were knotted over her stomach, her fingers digging painfully into her waist. "My brothers won't care when you go. And Dolores certainly won't miss you. You've made such a pest out of yourself in the kitchen that she's about ready to kiss your skull with the broad end of a skillet!"

Kurt shrugged. "I don't like Mexican food."

Her furious pace never broke as she jabbed a finger at the door. "Then get on your horse and ride into Snow Creek for your meals if you don't like what's being served here. Your rudeness is making everyone in this house suffer. Last night Dally was so upset she put a cup of salt in the cornbread. *We* took turns sneaking out to the river for a drink of water half the night because *we* ate the damn stuff. *We* didn't insult her—unlike *you*, who couldn't give a good fig! A little inconvenience on your part is a lot better than insulting someone who's always been very nice to you, buster. Or is that asking too much?"

"She wasn't insulted," he argued hotly.

"She was! She didn't tell you because"—Nikki paused long enough to send a poignant glance at the shiny new six-shooter strapped to his thigh—"she was afraid to. But she told me. And she told my brothers, who also told me. Do you think I have nothing better to do with my day than listen to Dally complain about you invading her kitchen? That's private domain. I don't even go in there!"

Kurt swallowed hard and resisted a very powerful urge to throttle her. Schooling his features to rigid composure, he watched her pace. Her angry strides did nothing to ease his own simmering anger. His tone dipped to one of carefully leashed fury. "All right, Nicole, what does Dolores have to do with Beth? Or aren't we discussing your daughter anymore?"

"What we're 'discussing' is the fall trail drive," she snapped. "And I'll thank you not to change the subject again."

"Nothing to talk about. You're not going."

"I am!"

"By God, you're the most stubborn woman I've ever had the *mis*fortune to meet!" He plopped himself into one of the red leather chairs and stretched to his full, imposing length; booted feet crossed at the ankles; large, powerful hands clasped with deceptive lightness atop a taut stomach. The hat covering his raven curls was pushed low on his brow by the cushion pillowing his head. His eyes were cloaked in the orange shadows beneath the wide brim, and although she couldn't actually see it, she could feel his determined glare rake her head to toe.

"I am going," she repeated when she couldn't stand the silence. "You can't stop me."

One corner of his mouth turned up in an arrogant grin that accentuated the cleft in his chin. "Watch me."

Nikki thought he took great pleasure in hurling her own words back in her face. "I'd love to, Kurt, but I won't have time," she sniffed. "I'll be too busy getting ready for the trail drive."

The hem of her skirt rustled as she made ready to sweep past him. What would have been a grand exit was spoiled by the strong fingers that wrapped around her wrist and stopped her short.

Cornflower blue clashed like lightning with hard steel gray. She was close enough to see his gaze fix with interest on the buttons she'd loosened at her collar, in deference to the scorching summer heat. Her neck, and the wedge of exposed flesh, burned as though it was his calloused fingers caressing her skin, not just his gaze.

"I don't make idle threats, Nicole. Push me on this, and you'll live to regret it."

"Excuse me if I'm not intimidated," she answered tightly. She glared down her nose at the fingers coiled around her wrist, as though the crackling blue fire in her gaze could melt the shackle away. "Growing up with four brothers underfoot made me somewhat immune to masculine threats. Silly me."

"*Dead* you, more likely. Someone out there is trying to kill you. Or did you forget about that?"

"How could I? You keep throwing it in my face every two minutes!"

With a growl and a flick of his wrist, Kurt yanked a stunned Nikki onto his lap. The length of his jaw smoldered with the feel of her breast grazing it. His growl became predatory when she landed hard, and he felt her soft bottom pillowed nicely atop the firm cushion of his thighs.

Nikki struggled to retain the anger that threatened to dissolve within her. She tried to hold in check the tumultuous emotions that suddenly crashed to the fore. Tried to ignore the heat raging within her, tried not to notice the way the heart beneath her fingertips, splayed over his oh, so warm chest, began to hammer in time to her own heart's wild tempo. Tried, and failed. Her mind locked on masculine firmness, focused on his hard warmth pressed against her. White-hot fury swiftly channeled itself elsewhere, settling in her blood like a flame.

She wanted him again. Here. Now. Desire sliced

through her, cutting away the long, sleepless night she'd spent telling herself that what they had done in the barn was wrong. Suddenly it didn't feel wrong. In fact, it felt like heaven.

Kurt felt the air charge with an excitement he was powerless to ignore. It ripped through him, demanding immediate response. The hand that had dragged her onto his lap with the intent to punish, loosened. She felt warm and soft pillowed atop his lap. Her breath was a torturously sweet caress on his face. And when her lips rose to meet his, Kurt knew he didn't have the strength to deny her. To deny himself.

His vow not to touch her again evaporated as he drank deeply of her lips. His mouth was hard and punishing, demandingly thorough. When he lifted his head, just enough to speak, he felt her whimper of protest rush warmly over him.

"The door," he rasped against her sweet, sweet mouth.

"I don't care," she sighed.

Although his own sentiments echoed hers to perfection, he couldn't stop his thoughts from straying to Beth. As much as he wanted, needed, craved, what Nicole offered, he didn't want Beth straying in to find her mother lost to the searing ecstasy of passion. And she *would* be lost to it. If he knew nothing else, Kurt knew that.

Slipping a hand beneath her knees, and another under her arms, he cradled her close and pushed from the chair, crossing the room determinedly.

His mouth crashed down on hers as his long strides carried them to the door. He promptly kicked it shut with his foot. Hunkering down until his thighs screamed at the weight of his soft, willing burden, he threw the latch and spun on his heel. At the same time, his tongue pillaged her mouth.

The urge to take her where he stood was strong. It ripped through him like a knife, leaving him shredded, panting, crazed with the need to be buried deeply in her moist softness. Now. Cursing, he strode to the rug spread in front of the hearth. He spanned the distance to it in record time.

After their rapturous afternoon in the barn, he'd found his thirst for her only whetted. He wanted her again, hard and fierce this time. He wanted her writhing beneath him, her nails digging ribbons in his back, her body meeting each hungry thrust, until the problems separating them no longer existed. He wanted to possess her—fully, deeply—the way a man possessed a woman.

His body drove him hard, fueled by his arduous thoughts. His fingers didn't fumble as they quickly loosened her buttons, then tossed her cotton frock into a corner. Her underthings were quick to follow. There was no need to remove his own clothes—Nikki fairly tore them from his body, her need equally fierce and as driving as his.

When they were both naked, she pushed him to the floor. Her mouth settled hotly on the hard plane of his stomach, her tongue moistly teasing his navel. Kurt groaned when her velvet fingers splayed his thighs and began a breathtaking ascent. He died a thousand sweet, agonizing deaths when her lips trailed lower.

"Oh, baby," he groaned at the feel of her supple little body wiggling against him, stroking him, enflaming him. "I don't think I can stand this."

"You'll survive . . . somehow," she countered hotly, huskily, her warm breath branding his flesh. Her head turned and the silver lashes flickered up, hooding eyes that sparkled with midnight-blue hunger.

She bent her head and drew the tip of her tongue through the narrow band of raven curls pelting his stomach. His skin tasted salty-sweet on her tongue. It tasted wonderful. It tasted like Kurt. Her heart raced and the blood throbbed in her ears, sounding very much like the hesitant approach of footsteps. Her attention strayed greedily lower.

Nikki's eyes snapped open and she stiffened. She brought her head up fast, her ears perked.

Footsteps!

Her hands, which were busy tormenting Kurt's enflamed flesh, froze. The masculine body she now knew every intimate inch of hardened to granite as a metallic jingle sounded just outside the door. A muffled curse slipped through the slats as the doorknob turned, stopped, turned, then rattled.

With lightning speed, Kurt rolled from beneath her and to the side. He landed on the balls of his feet in a predatory crouch. Grabbing his shirt as he went, he tossed it to a stunned Nikki. Her reactions were slowed from dread, shock, and an abrupt dousing of passion, but she managed to catch the thick swatch of cotton midair. She was slipping her arms into the baggy sleeves when the door to the study burst open.

"God, it's quiet in here. And dark. Did you two make up, or did you finally kill each . . . other . . . ?"

Mike's lanky body filled the doorway, blocking out the hall light as it flickered around his ramrod stiff back. His gaze narrowed cynically, and his sharp blue eyes seemed to sparkle out of the shadows as he quickly assessed the room. His mouth was open . . . the words he would have spoken had withered on his tongue.

Nikki's eyes rounded, shimmering with guilt as her attention shot up from the buttons her trembling fingers refused to work closed. She swallowed hard and her cheeks flooded a hot shade of crimson when she met and held her brother's accusing glare.

Chapter Twelve

For two hours Nikki endured a lecture on morality, delivered by a brother who didn't begin to understand what the word meant. That Mike thought nothing of sleeping in every bed from here to Abilene didn't seem to matter, nor did it take the sting from the angry accusations he hurled at his sister's head.

Kurt, Nikki thought, had the right idea. He had suffered no more than fifteen minutes of her brother's ranting before abruptly getting up to leave. Though she was tempted to follow, Mike's stern glare convinced Nikki to remain and listen to a lecture he would probably have followed her to the grave to give.

All right, maybe she didn't *listen*, but she pretended to. That wasn't easy. Not when her gaze strayed to the gold rug and her mind pictured a certain bronze body lying in sweet repose atop it. A long, slow breath brought Kurt's tangy aroma back to her. Closing her eyes was a torture unto itself. When she blinked she saw the passion-darkened gaze that had seared itself into her memory forever.

The guilt took longer to come than she expected. But what it lacked in urgency it made up for in force. Like the destructive gusts of a hurricane, the image of her father's body circled in her mind. And the realization that she had slept with his killer made her blood pump like ice water in her veins. It was hard to admit the intimacy had been shared at her own urgings—*again!*

The guilt grew in intensity over the two miserable hours she sat listening to Mike's heated attack. When he was done, he swept from the room with the force of the storm he'd brought on with his unexpected arrival.

Nikki stared at the empty doorway and thought the room, indeed the entire house, seemed unusually quiet. The silence pressed in on her. The *lack* of sound was deafening.

Feeling weak and slightly defeated, she rose from the chair and retrieved her skirt from where it lay in a crumpled heap near the hearth. The cool night air kissed her calves and thighs as she tugged it over her hips and tucked Kurt's too-long shirttail under the waistband.

The hem rustled around her ankles as she took slow, unsteady steps toward the door. The paneled hall was empty, the only sound to reach her ears that of the hardwood floor creaking beneath her bare feet. She passed the stairway leading up to the second floor and let herself out the front door. Her feet dragged as they took her wherever they cared to go. She had no destination in mind. She just walked.

It was going to be a hard winter, Nikki thought, glad of any diversion that would keep her mind off her guilt, off of Kurt. Hard and cold. Every six or seven years it happened, usually after a summer that had been as uncommonly long and dry as this one was turning out to be. They were due one—the last bad winter Snow Creek had seen was almost seven years ago. When her father was still alive.

Nikki, paying no attention to where she was going, stopped short a split second before colliding with the closed barn door. *Oh, great,* she thought as she regarded the wood with a glare just shy of loathing. Of all the places to get to, her feet had landed her here. Not exactly the place she wanted to be right now. But then, solitude was solitude. If nothing else, Mike would have the devil's own time finding her should he think of another caustic remark to fling at her spinning head.

With a resigned sigh, she pushed open the door and let herself in. The sweet smell of hay invaded her nostrils at the same time the gentle whicker of horses whispered in her ears.

The door creaked as she pushed it closed behind her and crossed to the new ladder leading up to the hayloft. This time she was careful to test each step before trusting any part of her weight to it. She made it to the top without incident, but was stopped short by the sight of Kurt sitting in the hay, his rugged shoulder resting against the open haydoor's frame.

Moonlight poured in through the square portal. The light accentuated each hard muscle that rippled beneath his sun-kissed flesh. Pale silver danced over the lines of his face, softening the hardness and adding an extra sparkle to the steely gaze that turned on her full force.

"Pull up some hay and have a seat," he invited coolly. His gaze lowered, darkening when he saw that it was *his* shirt that still covered the large breasts his mouth had delighted in tasting just a few short hours before. He moistened his lips, and thought he could still taste the honeyed sweetness of her on his tongue.

Nikki turned back to the ladder. She tilted her chin proudly, struggling to regain her composure. "I'd rather not, thank you," she declined, her tone unnaturally stiff.

"Haughtiness doesn't become you, Nicole." He shifted his weight and patted the blanket of hay next to his thigh. It crinkled invitingly under his palm. "Come sit down. We need to talk, and . . ." his eyes sparkled devilishly in the moonlight, "I promise not to bite unless you ask me nicely."

Nikki glared at him. Though she made no attempt to descend the ladder, neither did she take a step forward. "We have nothing to talk about," she said. "I thought that was obvious."

Kurt's expression clouded. "The only thing that's obvious is your stubbornness. What happened to the sweet little thing who seduced me—three times? I'd like to see more of *her*."

"I'll just bet you would!" Lacing her arms over her chest, she continued to glare at him. "Well, don't get your hopes up, buster, because I don't plan to repeat that mistake again."

"Is that what you call it now," he demanded, "a mistake?"

"Of course. What would you call it?"

"The same thing everybody else does . . . making love," he growled. "Call me strange, but I don't see anything wrong with making love to the woman who bore my child." He paused, fixing her with his gaze. "Or weren't you going to tell me about that?"

Nikki gasped. Her heart slammed against her ribs and she stumbled back as though he'd just punched her hard in the gut. Her bare heel slammed against the edge of the ladder, she would have fallen to the floor below if Kurt hadn't uncoiled and lunged for her. He yanked her close to his chest a split second before she would have tumbled over the edge.

"Let me go," she cried, even as she clung to his warmth and strength. Her fingers dug into his back as she buried her face into the warmth of his bare shoulder. The strong arms that held her close made her feel safe and protected, and it was security that she suddenly realized she had been craving.

"Go ahead and cry, baby," he whispered huskily

into the soft silver cloud of her hair. His palms stroked her slender back in a feather-light caress. "No one deserves to more than you do."

"I don't want to cry," she muttered miserably as the first dewy tear kissed her cheek. It was followed by another, and another, and soon she was sobbing uncontrollably in his arms.

Nestling her head against his shoulder, Kurt bent over and slipped a hand beneath her knees. Lifting her took no more effort than it would take to lift a scrawny kitten. His long strides crunched as he carried her to the haydoor. Cradling her sobbing body close, he lowered them as one to the prickly carpet.

Her tears moistened his shoulder, then twisted a warm path down his naked back. The silver curls that floated over her shoulders tickled his chest and waist. Her small body felt warm, supple, infinitely right as it settled closer to him. Was she trying to draw on his strength, he wondered, or fuse their bodies together?

"I don't want to l-like you, K-Kurt," she sobbed. She tightened one arm around him as she dashed a fist over her wet, silver lashes.

"I know," he soothed. His hand moved in steady strokes over her arm, her back, her hip. "You're fighting me harder now than you did when I saved you from that tornado. I just don't know why. We have a lot to share, but you keep pushing me away."

Nikki drew in a ragged sniff, wiped her nose on her sleeve—*his* sleeve!—then picked up her head to look at him. His eyes glistened a rich turquoise in the moonlight as he returned her stare. "I have to," she confided, her voice small as she nuzzled her head back into his shoulder. "I can't start depending on you. Not now. You aren't going to be here long enough."

He pillowed his cheek atop her head as his gaze drifted out the open haydoor. "Ah, back to that again, are we?"

"As long as you are alive and my father is dead, things will always come back to that between us."

He raked a hand through his tousled raven hair. "It doesn't have to be that way." He slapped his open palm into the hay. The sound echoed through the loft. "Good God, Nicole, we share a child! Can't we at least try to get along . . . for her sake?"

"No!" Nikki cried. Shaking her head, she pushed away from him. She felt his muscles ripple beneath her fingertips as he forced her to stay within the circle of his embrace. But though the arms around her waist held firm, he did permit her a little distance. "You don't understand," she said. Her eyes narrowed with determination when their gazes locked. "Beth is *not* your daughter, Kurt. She never was and she never will be."

For a split second Nikki saw confusion mirrored in his penetrating eyes. Then it was gone, flickering out like the flame of a candle. "I don't understand," he said, his jaw twitching slightly. "Are you saying you seduced another man at the same time you seduced me? Don't look away from me, woman, I have the right to know. Did you sleep with another man?" His hand roughly forced her attention back when she would have looked away. *"Did you?!* Answer me! Whose daughter is she?!"

"Mine," she spat, trying to squirm away from his anger. His fingers bit into her upper arm as he dragged her up his body. Their noses were inches apart and she could feel his hot, rapid breath grazing the flesh beneath her unbuttoned collar.

"And who else's?"

"No one's!" A fresh supply of tears moistened her lashes, but this time Nikki refused to give in to them. She wasn't proud of the way her voice cracked when she said, "She's mine, Kurt. Just mine."

"Sorry, Nicole," he sneered, "but that's not good

enough." When she started to struggle again, he shifted his weight and threw her back on the hay. His heavy body pinned her easily as his face loomed above. His steely gaze was hard with fury. "I want to know who her father is and I want to know now. If you won't tell me, I'll find someone else who will."

To the best of Nikki's knowledge, the only person who knew with any certainty that Kurt was Beth's father was Mike—and no matter how angry he was with her, he'd never tell. Her fingers tightened as she dug them deep into his iron-hard biceps. It was like trying to crush a stone.

"Go ahead then," she taunted, proud that her voice didn't waver. "No one knows. You can ask around Snow Creek until you're old and gray and still never have an answer."

"Wrong, baby. Someone had to attend the birth." When her face paled, Kurt knew he'd hit a weak spot. He pounced. "It won't take long to find out who that someone is."

"So what? A name isn't going to tell you anything." She tried to make her words ring with conviction. "I didn't cry out the father's name between pains, Kurt."

"You didn't have to. All I need is a date. I'm sure if I try I can figure out the rest. Even us dirt-poor cowpokes can count, Nicole," he snarled viciously, "or didn't you know that?"

She struggled to get up. He pushed her back. With a swift, nimble movement he managed to cover most of her body with his heavy frame. The elbows positioned at her sides allowed her to breathe, but only just barely.

"The date," he pressed. "When was she born? You aren't getting up until you tell me, so you might as well make it easy on yourself and spit it out." She glared at him, her mouth stubbornly clenched shut. His eyes hardened to chips of ice as his hips ground against her. She could feel the raw masculinity pressing hard into her pelvis as surely as she could feel the warm stain flooding her cheeks. "Looks like we're going to be here awhile." His voice rumbled with a sardonic lilt. "Care to know how I plan to pass the time?"

"Even if I told you her birthday, it wouldn't matter," she argued, frustrated. She turned her head, hoping he wouldn't see the desperation in her eyes; or the passion his movements stirred. "You'd still have to remember the date we—"

"August first, 1880. You want the time, too, or do you remember that part?" A cold smile lifted the corners of his mouth as her shocked gaze snapped back to him. His probing stare pierced her to the core. "You know, that's something I've always wondered, Nicole. Just how much of that night do you remember?"

"Too much," she spat. "Let me up, Kurt. I don't want to scream and wake up the entire ranch, but I will."

"Do it," he shrugged, "if you think it will do any good. Of course, the second you open that sweet little mouth I'll take it as an open invitation to shut you up." His gaze sparkled, but it lacked the warmth of a few hours ago. "Any ideas?"

Nikki held her tongue, letting her furious gaze do the talking for her.

"All right," he said as he slowly rolled his weight onto her chest. Not enough to crush her, but enough so her heaving breasts were trapped firmly beneath him. "I wasn't lying when I said I planned to keep us both—ahem—*occupied* until you tell me what I want to hear. You know me well enough to know I mean every word."

She swallowed hard and stubbornly kept her unspoken vow of silence. It wasn't easy. Not when she saw his eyes darken with turquoise promise, saw his lips dip ever so slowly to claim her own. A shiver curled up her spine when his mouth detoured, landing in a hot caress on her sensitive neck.

"Hello, neck," he whispered hungrily. His breath warmed her flesh a split second before his tongue darted out to moisten her throbbing, porcelain throat.

Nikki sucked in a ragged gasp as his mouth strayed lower. His nose nudged the shirt collar aside. His tongue flicked at the curve of her shoulder. He licked and nibbled the tender flesh until she thought she would scream.

"Please, don't," she pleaded huskily. Her heart skipped as she planted the heels of her palms against his shoulders and shoved. He didn't even acknowledge her struggle. "You don't want to do this, Kurt. Really you don't."

Kurt lifted his head and fixed her with a stare that would have made a lesser woman cringe. "You're wrong, Nicole. I want this more than I've ever wanted anything in my life."

"No. No, you don't. Not . . . like this. Not by force."

"Are we talking about what *I* want, or what *you* want? There is a difference, Nicole. A *big* one." He shifted until his weight was balanced on one elbow. Warm fingers brushed the curls from her brow. "Are you going to tell me? I wouldn't advise you to stall too long. A man gets to the point where he can't stop even if he wants to," he paused succulently, his gaze devouring her, "and I'm not sure I'd ever want to."

"April twenty-third," she said suddenly, finally. She looked away so he wouldn't see the tears in her eyes. "Her birthday is April twenty-third, damn you! There, are you happy?"

"No," he said, careful not to move in a way that would suggest he was going to let her up. "I've known that for weeks. Some things are just too juicy to be kept a secret . . . no matter how hard you try."

"Then why—?"

"I needed to hear you say it." His gaze hooded. "Say it, Nicole. Tell me Beth is my daughter."

Nikki shook her head. "She isn't yours, Kurt, she's mine. Only mine. She was from the day she was born and she will be until the day I die. You have no claim on her and you have no claim on me. I won't allow it."

"You have no choice. She's my daughter and I plan on being a part of her life for as long as I'm around." He left that statement hanging in the air as his fingers reached out and gripped her chin, pulling her gaze back to his. "You have no say in the matter. *I* won't allow it."

A tear threatened to spill from the corner of her eye. Nikki angrily swiped it away. "Why are you doing this? Why won't you just let it drop? We were happy before you came back to the ranch and stirred things up."

"Oh, no you don't. You're the one who wanted me back here," he reminded her coldly. "I would've been perfectly content to stay in Boston and never know I had a child, so don't you turn this back on me. I may not have started this war between us but, make no mistake, Nicole, I intend to finish it."

"Leave," she said suddenly, her gaze wide and pleading. "Take Stetson, he likes you. He's mine, but you can have him. Consider it a gift. Please, just take the horse and leave. Now. Tonight."

Kurt shook his head slowly. His assessing gaze never left her. "Sorry, but you can't get rid of me that easily. I'm staying here until my daughter *knows* she's my daughter." His eyes narrowed. "And there's also that nasty business about me having murdered your father. Or did you forget about that in your haste to get rid of me?"

"I didn't forget. I just don't want to see you hanged

at the expense of *my* daughter."

"You should have thought of that before. And she's *our* daughter," he corrected darkly. "Say it! *Our* daughter. Not yours. Not mine. *Ours!*"

Nikki clamped her teeth shut and refused to answer. If he was waiting for her to admit his parentage he had a long wait. A slow, torturous death at the hands of bloody savages would be preferable to giving Kurt any claim over her life—or Beth's.

Kurt was torn between the urge to throttle her, and the urge to kiss her soundly. The latter won out. It wasn't a pleasant experience, for him or Nikki, and when he raised his head to look in her eyes he felt a pang of guilt at the reproach shimmering in her deep blue gaze. In his own peculiar manner of compensation, he rolled off of her.

Nikki wasted no time in scrambling to her feet. She wiped the taste of him off her lips with the back of her hand and glared at him with a look that adequately conveyed her outrage. "Leave, Kurt. If you ever had feelings for me, you'll be gone by sunup."

Kurt turned his attention out to the moonswept night. He didn't look at her when he answered. "She's my daughter, Nicole. I won't leave until she knows that."

"She won't ever know that, Kurt," Nikki swore. She clenched her hands into tight fists, which were hidden in the folds of her skirt. "I'll deny it. I'll deny ever having known you if that's what it takes, but as long as there's a breath left in my body, Beth will never know about you."

She spun on her heel, her back rigidly straight. The hay pricked at her bare feet as she picked her way to the ladder. As she was about to descend it, she sent a final glance at Kurt, only to find him watching her closely.

"And if I tell her?"

It was a question she didn't have to think about.

"I'll kill you. I'll do whatever it takes to protect her. From you, or anyone else."

A lot of things had changed in the six years Kurt had been gone from the Triple D, but the one thing that hadn't changed was the texture of Nicole Dennison's flesh.

Kurt sighed and leaned back against the hayloft wall, his ankles crossed. Hay clung to his denim trousers and bare chest, clung to his raven hair. One stalk protruded from his tightly compressed lips. The hard line of his jaw tightened and released with each thoughtful chew.

His thoughts burned, occupied by the Nicole Dennison he had known six years ago, and the insufferable, irresistible "Nikki" she had become.

It was like meeting two separate people who coincidentally looked alike. The same Nicole Dennison who had driven him to distraction with her buoyancy and innocence as a girl had matured into Nikki, the silver-haired temptress who taunted, teased, and returned his passion with such hot intensity, her boldness quashed all logical thought in the way an ant hill is pulverized under a rolling wagon wheel.

He hadn't planned what had happened that first afternoon. And he hadn't planned to repeat the mistake again tonight. He should have known better. He should have guessed that things would get out of hand between them. He remembered the battle that had raged within him at seeing her years ago in the lake, nude, and he had a sinking feeling that that's how he would feel around her always. Lust. Driving, insatiable lust.

Kurt's jaw clamped down hard on the sweet-tasting stalk of hay. He rolled it over his tongue, and in a last-ditch attempt to rid his thoughts of Nicole, he concentrated on her daughter.

His daughter, not that Nicole would ever admit to it. Her parting shot had been as close as she would come to a confession. Although she'd never actually said Beth was his child, what she hadn't said was a hell of a lot more convincing. And if that wasn't proof enough, one look at Beth could confirm any doubts. The child didn't get that dark, wavy hair, cleft chin, and *lack of a sense of smell* from her mother's side of the family!

"How could she not have told me?" he asked himself, his voice thick with emotion as he stared out the haydoor and into the cool, dark night.

From his first glimpse of Beth, Kurt had known with a certainty whose daughter she was. Her birthday was an extra piece of proof, easily attained, but unnecessary. Self-assured, he'd bided his time thinking Nicole was only waiting for the right time to tell him the truth. Only now he realized that she had no intention of telling him anything. Not now. Not ever. If she'd had her way, he would have walked to the gallows and never known about Beth.

The Nicole Dennison he used to know would never have been so deceptive. That girl had been honest and practical, as if God had taken the best of both her parents, molded it together, then wrapped it in a neat, pretty little package. Add hair the color of moonlight skimming over an icy winter lake, and eyes that sparkled like the sea after a summer storm, and you had a masterpiece. Add a fiery temper and a streak of bitterness longer than the Mississippi, and you had a stubborn, headstrong, conniving shrew.

The "Nikki" who'd seduced him in the spot where he now sat—twice!—was not a woman he recognized. It was hard to believe she was the twenty-four year old version of the shy girl who had seduced him six years before. What had changed that guileless girl, burgeoning with the promise of womanhood, into the fearless, tempestuous witch who was now trying her hardest to get him hanged?

That's something I've always wondered. Just how much do you remember about that night, Nicole?

Too much.

It wasn't an answer, it wasn't an answer at all. Now he wondered those same thoughts again. How much did she remember? How much of that night, or of any other time they had been together? It was a question he'd asked himself a thousand times over. And every time he asked it, he came up with a different answer.

Kurt spit the hay to the ground, suddenly loosing his taste for it. The mystery that was Nicole Dennison continued to plague him, and when it didn't intrude on his waking thoughts, it followed him to bed and burrowed itself into his dreams.

Chapter Thirteen

Nikki's first instinct as she walked from the barn to the house was to grab Beth and get as far away from the Triple D as Stetson could carry them. Not from the ranch itself, of course, but from the one person on it who had the power to turn her perfectly structured world upside-down. Just his presence was enough to send her senses whirling. And the thought of *anyone* having so much control over her emotions—especially if that anyone was her father's murderer—did not sit well. Not well at all.

The next day, Nikki awoke to find Kurt gone. Her sour mood darkened. For the next two weeks she snapped at anyone who was stupid enough to come within shouting distance. A stalwart few made the attempt, but only when necessary.

The first week of September found her moody and glum. Only Beth was able to break the bonds of bitterness that seemed to hold her mother captive, and the child had dozens of opportunities since Nikki refused to let Beth out of her sight. It didn't matter that she hadn't seen Kurt once since the night in the barn. She didn't trust him. And she didn't want him near Beth.

Three weeks later Nikki sat atop a conspicuously empty wooden bench beneath a hot mid-September sun, and concluded that she hated weddings almost as much as she hated Kurt Frazier.

The dry, still air was thick with the smoke of a dozen or so cigars. The pungent odor of burning tobacco mixed with the aroma of roasted beef, baked bread, and hot apple pie. Music and laughter echoed around her, but she listened with only half an ear. She sipped at the glass of punch that was cradled in her hands, and wished she'd listened to her instincts and stayed home. Instead, she'd let Pete convince her to attend a boring nuptial party.

So she sat, drank punch that tasted like weak paint thinner, smiled stiffly, and pretended not to notice the way the rest of the guests ignored her. She wished she could just go home.

Why had she let Pete convince her to come today when every instinct in her body screamed to stay at home?! Kurt was due back any day. She learned that he'd ridden out to inspect the damage done in the latest Delhoussey Gang cattle raid. He'd been gone three weeks, but he wouldn't be gone forever. She wasn't that lucky.

Nikki squirmed atop the bench that suddenly felt too hard. Kurt's threat to be an active part of Beth's life still plagued her. What would he do if he returned to find Dolores alone in the ranch house with Beth? Logic said Kurt wouldn't "do" anything. Still, the urge to run home and check on her daughter was as strong as it was illogical. It pumped through her blood with an urgency that would not be denied.

Cupping a hand over her eyes, she scanned the crowd. Bodies pressed against bodies endlessly. Some danced in time to the music of a single fiddle. Others mingled, their muffled voices blending together in an undistinguishable rumble that buzzed in her ears and made her temples throb. The smell of sweat and flowery perfume was as cloying and pungent as the hot, dry air.

Her decision was made. Wrinkling her nose, she set her glass on the ground and stood, her gaze sweeping the crowd in search of Mike's golden head. As always, he was easily found. One had only to look for a group of giggling young females and one had found Michael James Dennison.

Nikki thrust herself up on tiptoe, waving her hands to attract her brother's attention. Getting a dead heifer to sit up and do tricks would have been easier than catching Mike's eye when he was surrounded by a circle of attractive women.

Deciding she would leave a message for her brothers in the stable, Nikki headed away from the crowd. She hadn't gotten far when Shelly Winfield cornered her. Because the girl said she needed desperately to talk about Mike, Nikki postponed her departure. She was in the middle of a heated conversation with Shelly when an intrusive third voice cut in from behind.

"Hello, Nicole."

Nikki didn't turn around. There was no need. She could feel the warm breath kissing the back of her neck, exposed beneath the tight silver chignon. And if her ears didn't recognize Kurt Frazier's voice, her body was having a hell of a time forgetting him. Her flesh tingled wherever his steely gaze roamed. The dark muslin of her Sunday Best was a poor barrier to separate the intensity of his gaze from her suddenly too-warm flesh.

Shelly's inquisitive gaze narrowed. Her attention snapped over Nikki's shoulder, her brown eyes darkening with approval. With a toss of her chestnut head, she raked the intruder head to toe and purred, "Well, well, as I live and breathe. If it isn't Kurt Frazier, in the flesh. To what do we owe the honor?"

"No honor," Kurt shrugged, lazily leaning a shoulder against the porch railing. Although his words were aimed at Shelly, his gaze was fixed on

Nikki's rigid back, and showed no signs of budging. "I was on my way to the Triple D when I heard the music. Figured I'd stop and see what all the fuss was about."

"Um-hum, that's my theory, too," Shelly teased, her gaze shifting to Nikki. Nikki's cheeks had flooded a deep crimson at the first sound of Frazier's voice. They were now deathly pale. Smiling secretively, Shelly reached out and clasped Nikki's hand. "Thank you for the advice, Nikki. I'll let you know what I decide."

Nikki smiled tightly, but her mind was no longer on Shelly Winfield. "Mike's the one you should be talking to, not me."

"Hmmm, maybe." Shelly shrugged, swaying back and forth and seeming to enjoy the way the crisp cotton skirt rustled around her ankles. "Maybe not. We'll have to wait and see, won't we?" The dark gaze shifted to the man standing poised at Nikki's back. "Nice to see you again, Kurt. Don't be a stranger now."

"What was that all about?" he asked when Shelly twirled and made her way back into the crowd. She was immediately surrounded by a small gathering of chattering females.

Nikki watched her go, watched the speculative glances cast in her direction. She was accustomed to the uncomplimentary stares and her eyes didn't register the sight. She sent Kurt a quick glance over her shoulder and said bluntly, "She's pregnant . . . with Mike's baby. Apparently, when Pete found out, he decided to propose, since Mike refused to. She didn't know what to do, so she asked me. *I* didn't know what to tell her."

A low whistle shot through Kurt's teeth as raven brows rose in speculation. "That would explain Mike's lecture that night. I thought he was acting a little too proprietary. Not like him." Sighing, he loosened the dark blue bandanna knotted at his throat. "So which one gets stuck with the coy little Miss Winfield?"

"Neither. Mike won't marry her, and she turned Pete down. She said she didn't want one brother taking responsibility for the other one's mistakes. I guess I can see her point. I wouldn't marry a man just to give my baby a name, either."

"Don't I know it!" he stormed. His gaze bored holes into her rigid shoulder blades and Nikki's flesh singed with his glare. "Stubborn little Nicole Dennison," he chided derisively, "heaven forbid she comes down off her damn pedestal long enough to admit she made a mistake, or ask for help."

"We aren't talking about me," she spat, "we're talking about Shelly."

"Right. Shelly and Mike, or Shelly and Pete. Either way, one of them has to marry the chit. She can't have a baby without a husband, not in a town as small as Snow Creek. The old biddies will be all over her for years to come."

"She'll live!" Nikki's gaze focused on the parched dirt underfoot, but her voice echoed with pride. *"I did."*

"I know. But at what price?" he demanded as he stepped briskly around her stiff, unyielding form.

Nikki groaned and fought to hold on to her anger when it threatened to slip away. The first thing to come into view was the toe of his scuffed boots. *Large* boots. The leather was well-tooled and weathered. The stacked heels added an extra three inches to his six-foot frame.

Her gaze ascended as desire chiseled away at fury. With each snug inch of denim she felt her heart quicken. By the time her gaze reached his lean hips, her breathing came in shallow gasps. She let her attention linger on the core of his masculinity, even if her boldness did bring the kiss of a blush to her cheeks.

His taut waist came under her careful scrutiny next. Then the solid wedge of his chest, and his enticingly broad shoulders. Against her will, her fingertips itched with the remembered feel of his firm flesh, now dormant beneath the dusty, plaid flannel shirt. Her palms stung from the memory, and she clasped her hands tightly together, if only to give her whirling mind something else to concentrate on.

Her gaze drifted up. She felt a stab of disappointment at the coat of stubble concealing the indentation of his chin. Her disappointment faded when she noted how the bristled shadow also lent him a reckless air. The illusion was enhanced by the deep raven brows, furrowed in a V. The scowl reminded her too much of Beth for it to have its proper sting.

A confident grin turned Kurt's lips as he took an equal amount of time to measure her up. The dress she wore, while dreary in color and form, fit her like a glove. Every curve was outlined and enhanced to perfection. Her hair shimmered like captured rays of moonlight, and the heat of the day gave her cheeks a healthy glow. Kurt swallowed hard. His hands clenched into tight-knuckled fists. He liked what he saw. Too much.

With effort, he tore his gaze from her breasts, which were straining against the dingy gray fabric. He met her gaze, but only by exerting a tremendous amount of self-control. "Either I look like hell or I've startled you speechless. Since I've never known you to be at a loss for words, I'll assume it's the former."

Her lips tightened. "Go away."

"Now?" he countered with feigned indignation. His eyes twinkled as he hungrily searched her face. "But I just got back. Don't tell me you didn't miss me."

"I don't intend to. You know how much I hate a liar." Her full skirt billowed around her ankles, the pitch-black trim stirring the dirt as she made to sweep past him.

"Oh, no you don't!" He reached out and yanked her back when she would have stomped away. "Don't I even rate a kiss hello? I'm sure the other hands are getting one right about now. I feel—er—left out."

His gaze dark, he started to tug Nikki into the circle of his arms. The heel of her palms shoving at his shoulders nipped that idea in the bud.

His body seared her hands and she snatched them back as though she'd been burned. "If it's kisses you want then I suggest you find a nice woman to wife and build yourself a cabin in the woods."

"What's the matter, Nicole?" he taunted. "Afraid someone will see us together and put two and two together? Afraid they might figure out how things are between us?"

"There is no 'us,' Kurt." She took a step back, retreating as much from the caustic remarks as from the man who made them. It was hard to think straight with her foolish body responding in ways it shouldn't to his nearness. And the way his whiskey-scented breath caressed her cheek was simply indecent! She forced her voice to remain calm and repeated, "There is no 'us.' There never has been, and there never will be. You saw to that."

"By killing your father?" he asked tightly. A muscle stood out in his stubble-coated jaw, twitching in rhythmic fury.

"So you finally admit it!"

"That was a question, Nicole, not a confession. No need to run off screaming for the sheriff. Last time I saw Hardy, he was passed out drunk on the porch swing." He chuckled dryly, and dragged a hand down his jaw. "Even if I was making a confession—and I'm not—he's in no shape to take it."

"Maybe." She squinted against the blinding sun at his back. "You've done a nice job skirting the issue so far, Kurt, but you can't avoid it forever. When I get my evidence—and I will—you'll have to answer the accusation. Only this time it won't be coming from me, it'll be coming from a judge."

"You seem pretty sure of yourself. What happens if you find your evidence, and it points to someone else?"

"Will it?" she demanded sharply.

"Un-uh, I don't want to spoil the surprise." His smile was as slowly tantalizing as the finger he drew down her nose. The calloused tip edged her lips then stroked the delicate line of her jaw. "You'll find out soon enough. And when you do, I want to be there. I want to see your face when you're finally told the truth. One way," he shrugged, "or the other."

"Do you?" she countered, pulling back from the disturbance of his touch. "As badly as I want to see your lifeless body strung up at Hanging Oaks?"

"Worse."

Nikki felt a surge of doubt she would rather not have felt, and decided it was time to change the subject, to explore an area that had been eating at her all day. "Have you been back to the house yet?" she asked nonchalantly.

"Do I look like I have?" She followed his glance down to his sweaty, dusty clothes. "But that isn't what you wanted to know, is it, Nicole? To answer the question you didn't ask but wanted to, no, I haven't seen my daughter yet."

"*My* daughter, Kurt," she hissed, and hugged her arms tightly around her waist when she noticed more than one curious glance shift their way. Reluctantly, she lowered her tone. "*Mine*, not yours. And keep your voice down. Someone might hear."

"So? Would that be so bad?" Reaching out, he

retraced her jaw. The tip of his finger was calloused and rough, scraping against her quivering flesh like a strip of sandpaper.

Drawing in a shaky breath, she swatted his hand away. "Yes, it would. But not for the reasons you think."

One raven brow cocked high. "For Beth?"

"Yes, for Beth." She scowled, wondering how he had been able to guess her thoughts so easily. What else had he guessed about her? And did she truly want to know if he could read her as easily as he could read a label of Arbuckle Coffee?

Kurt stared at her long and hard. For a split second, Nikki thought he was going to say something. He changed his mind, his attention diverted over her shoulder by a boisterous shout.

Nikki glanced back in time to see the happy couple being lifted high onto liquor-lightened shoulders. They were carried, laughing, toward the house. Her gaze returned to Kurt. "If you came to congratulate the bride and groom you'd better hurry. Once inside they may not come out for months. Not if this winter's as bad as the old folks are predicting."

Kurt planted his fists on lean hips and shook his head. "I didn't come to see them. As a matter of fact, I don't even know them. You?"

"Barely." Now that they'd moved on to a safer topic, Nikki felt more comfortable. "I came because Pete hounded me to, and because my father did business with her father way back when."

"And that's the only reason?"

She glared at him suspiciously. "Of course it is. What other reason could there be?"

"You tell me. And while you're at it, you can answer my first question. What price did you pay for having Beth without a husband, Nicole? And how'd the God-fearing Christians of Snow Creek treat you because of it?" Her eyes narrowed, her jaw tightened. The change was duly noted by Kurt.

Nikki's hand swept the area. "Do you see anyone around me now?" she asked tightly. He shook his head, pushing the hat back as he eyed her. "Shelly was the first person not related to me who has spoken to me all day, with the possible exception of the bride and groom. Aside from sly glances, and slyer whispers, they leave me alone. There's your answer, if you really want it. There are some things this town can't forgive or forget. Beth is one of them."

He gave a brisk nod, his expression unreadable. "I'm sorry. I didn't know."

His words could be taken two ways. Nikki didn't bother to take them at all. "Save it for someone who cares what you think. God knows, I don't anymore."

Turning on her heel, she stalked toward the stable. She'd taken less than a dozen steps when it dawned on her that the need to go home had evaporated with Kurt's arrival. Dammit, she'd stay and enjoy herself if it killed her. She wouldn't give him the satisfaction of seeing her run. Taking a sharp detour, Nikki returned to the milling crowd.

Kurt watched her through hooded lashes. At first he let his gaze feast on the gentle sway of her hips, until his attention was abruptly directed elsewhere. He watched as the invited guests parted like the Red Sea wherever Nicole Dennison walked. More than one person stepped back farther than was necessary, as though afraid she might brush against them and spread some sort of contamination. A few properly dressed women sent haughty glares in her direction, then turned their backs and walked purposefully away. The men settled for snickers and lurid remarks that went ignored by all but Kurt.

Kurt's gut tightened as though it was him they had turned their backs on, not Nicole. He didn't try to understand the outrage that hammered at his heart. He didn't *want* to understand it. It was just there, gnawing at his gut and pulling at his emotions in a way they hadn't been pulled on in years.

"Nicole!" he growled, and set out after her, only to see her brought up short by Ben Rollison.

Chapter Fourteen

That Ben had sought her out was a good sign, Nikki thought. That he seemed reluctant to talk, was not.

With tightly leashed patience, Nikki watched his tongue dart out to moisten parched, fleshy lips. His brow was beaded with sweat. He gripped a dusty black bandanna in his large fist, and used it occasionally to mop the sweat from his brow. It didn't help. No sooner would one coat of perspiration be wiped away than another would sprout to take its place. Thin brown curls were plastered to his head, his sharp green eyes watery from the sting of sunshine and the amount of whiskey he'd consumed. His gaze anxiously returned time and again to the wedding guests.

"At this point *anything* you could tell me would help," Nikki coaxed when he said nothing. Her hand reached out to touch his arm. It stopped in midair, hesitated, then dropped back to her side. "Anything at all, Ben."

"What I'm thinkin' of ain't much," he sighed. His voice was gravelly and slow. Plucking off his hat, he dragged his thick fingers through his sweaty hair, then settled the worn leather back atop his scalp. Doubt shimmered in his eyes. "You'll pro'bly think

I'm crazy, honey, and maybe I am, but—"

"But what?" Nikki asked, agitated. She felt a sudden urge to reach down his throat and pull out the words he was trying to say. "Tell me, please. No matter what you say, I promise I won't think you're crazy."

"It ain't gonna hold up in front of a circuit judge, mind you." He eyed her, only marginally relieved when she gave a tight nod. "And I didn't mention it b'fore cause, well, it just didn't seem important. But that day your daddy died, well, I remember standin' there watchin' the guy who shot him walk away and I remember thinkin' to myself 'Ben, that guy looks like Frazier all right, and he dresses like Frazier, *but* . . .'" He paused, scowling thoughtfully. "Heck, honey, it's not like the guy who shot your daddy walked away from the body as slow as molasses in January. But I saw him, all right. And he was walkin'. Just . . . walkin'."

"Walking," she echoed, eyeing him intently as her spirits plummeted. This was it? This was *all* Ben could remember?

"Yeah, walkin'. You know how a guy who spends most of his hours warmin' a saddle walks, don't you?"

At her skeptically raised brows, he proceeded to enact the most elaborate—and wretched—imitation of a bow-legged strut Nikki had ever seen. He looked like an ape—arms arched, legs bent, hips swaying cockily.

"That's the way most of the hands walk, if'n you've got a mind to notice. But this guy, he didn't walk that way. Nope, he walked nice and even as you please. No strut, no swagger, just walked. At the time I thought . . . well, I don't rightly know what I thought, 'cept'n it was a mite peculiar. Don't mean much to you, does it?"

Nikki nibbled her lower lip, turning his version of

a cowpoke's swagger over in her mind. "That depends," she answered slowly, cautiously.

"Yeah? On what?"

"On whether you'd recognize that walk if you saw it again."

His gaze drifted past her shoulder to the dancers who were kicking up dust beneath their heels and billowing hemlines. "Well now, I might. Ain't guaranteein' nothin', honey, but I s'pose if you was to dress the guy up in the same clothes, put him in the same spot, same distance and all . . ." He shrugged noncommittally. "I might."

She shook her head. "'Might' isn't good enough, Ben. You have to be so sure you'd swear a month's backpay on it or Hardy won't listen. Worse, it might shadow what you've already said and make it look like you don't know what you're talking about."

Ben scratched his paunchy stomach and shook his head. His toe tapped in time to the tune creaking out of the fiddle. "Wouldn't say either way unless I was sure, honey. Last thing I want on my conscience is the hangin' of an innocent man. 'Specially after what happened to Jim Hanson. Somethin' like that don't get forgot too easy. Or happen again too fast."

Nikki's gaze took in the meaty hand dabbing the black bandanna to his sweaty brow. "How do you know about that?"

"Hell, everyone 'round these parts knows."

She looked at him doubtfully. "I didn't," she said.

He started shuffling his big feet again as he jammed the bandanna deep into his back pocket. "Yep, well, s'pose you could say there's a lot goes on 'round here you Dennisons don't know about."

He didn't have to mention Brian Dennison's marriage for Nikki to know exactly what he meant.

Nikki thanked him for his help as he turned back toward the group of dancers. Her gaze strayed to his hips, and darkened when she noticed the bow-legged strut. Not cockily arrogant like Kurt's, but a cowpoke's swagger nonetheless. Her gaze lowered. The spurs attached to his boots drew her attention. On the left was a jangle-bob that looked much the same as one any of the ranch hands wore. On the right, and worn higher so as not to trip him, was the match to the one Kurt had found in the barn. A California spur, he had called it.

Her shock-filled gaze lifted as she watched Ben disappear. *Ben? Was he the one who had rigged the ladder? The one who tampered with my wagon shaft? The one who tried to kill me?!* Nikki shook her head and hugged her arms around her waist. No, he couldn't be, Nikki thought. If Ben was the culprit, then he was also the man who'd killed her father. But Ben had been Hugh Dennison's friend. He had no reason to want her father dead!

Or did he? She didn't know, but she was determined not to mention anything about Ben to anyone—not to Kurt, not to anyone. Not until she figured out what it all meant.

From the corner of her eye, Nikki spotted Abigail Rollison standing near the circle of dancers. Tall, dark, almost masculine in her appearance, the woman had a tucked-in chin and puckered lips that made her look like nothing so much as a reproving schoolmaster. Her eyes were dark as her hair, and in the hot afternoon sun, they looked somewhat glazed.

Was it only two years ago that she had actually felt pity for this woman, Nikki wondered, returning Abigail's stare? It was hard to believe, for pity was the last thing she felt for Abigail now. It was bad enough that Beth spent entirely too much time in the woman's company. But Abigail Rollison encouraged Beth in ways that Nikki did not approve of, and had at times even provoked Beth to disobey her mother. Nikki feared that Abigail was in some way *obsessed* with Beth, that she looked to Beth as though she were the child long since laid to rest beneath the Triple D's parched soil.

In her pity for Abigail, Nikki had, at first, allowed it. She'd thought it would help Abigail get over the grief she experienced at losing her own child, to have another child around. Now, she wasn't sure that that had been a very wise decision. In fact, she was beginning to think it had been the biggest mistake of her life.

Nikki focused on Abigail again, and tensed when she noticed how intently the woman eyed her. Her skin tingled when she realized Abigail had been staring at her for quite some time. A chill ran down her spine when she also realized that Abigail had overheard every word she had said to Ben.

A half an hour past dusk saw most of the remaining guests drunker than river rats and having the time of their lives. The gay laughter and uproarious shouts had coaxed even the bride and groom into delaying their honeymoon—for a little while anyway. Changed into calico and cotton, the happy pair now kicked up their heels with the best of them. And when their guests insisted the couple share a passionate kiss every once in a while . . . well, who were they to refuse?

Another fiddle, in need of tuning, had joined the first. Lanterns were lit, the flickering orange glow bathing the dancing couples as well as the laughing onlookers.

Nikki's toe tapped out a beat in time with the music. Someone had placed a glass of something in her hand, and she was in the process of raising the glass to her lips when she saw him.

Kurt stood on the outskirts of the crowd. His satiny hair glistened in the lamplight. One broad shoulder rested against the corner of the latticework porch.

His feet were crossed at the ankle, causing his hips to tilt at a cocky angle. A green plaid shirt hugged the knotted muscles of his shoulders, while his denim trousers molded to lean hips and thighs. His thick eyelids were lowered to half mast, making his steely gaze appear somewhat insolent.

People meandered about him, and though he struck up a few conversations, he wasn't taking an active part in the festivities. The dark whiskers shadowing his jaw, combined with his dirty attire, made him look as out of place as Nikki felt.

She brought the cool glass up to her lips. The smell of the strong punch assaulted her—suddenly, the drink held no appeal, not when she had Kurt's piercing gaze to contend with.

She watched him raise his glass in mock salute before draining the contents in one fiery gulp.

It was as she stooped to set her own glass on a nearby table that she noticed how badly her fingers were trembling. The object of her discomfort leaned scarcely a few dozen feet away, and as she sent a quick glance in his direction, she saw a smile sensuously lift one corner of his mouth. Apparently she wasn't the only one who'd noticed her nervousness.

Arrogant fool! she thought, turning away and letting the heat of a steely gaze warm her back. A throbbing heartbeat later, her thoughts welcomed the intrusion of the boy who stepped close to her side. She summed her brother up with a sidelong glance, her gaze resting on the nearly empty glass in his hand.

For the last few weeks, Willy had avoided her at every turn. Nikki thought that was just as well, since she would have yelled at him the way she yelled at anyone who came within shouting distance. The incident with Beth at the river hadn't been forgotten—by either of them. Guilt shimmered in his eyes, tempered by an equal dose of embarrassment.

"Hello, Willy," she greeted coolly, her gaze never straying from his hand. His fingers tightened guiltily around the glass. "I hope for your sake that's water."

She took the glass from him before he could answer and lifted it suspiciously to her nose. Her gaze hardened with fury as the gin fumes stung her nostrils. Straight and neat.

With a flick of her wrist she tossed the contents onto the boots that Willy had begun to contemplate with a fierce intensity. A foamy puddle gathered in the dirt around his soles.

"Haven't you learned yet?" she hissed, thrusting the empty glass into his slackened grasp. "No, I guess not."

"Nikki, I'm sorry. I—"

She slashed a hand in the air to cut short his plaintive whine. "Don't! Until you can tell me you've stopped drinking—*for good*—I have nothing to say to you. And until then, you stay away from my daughter."

Willy's hurt look gave her pause. But the memory of Beth, and what could have happened to her in the river, strengthened Nikki's resolve. Straightening her shoulders, she turned her back on her brother and walked away.

The fiddles squeaked out a gay country dance, while the fiddlers themselves encouraged the remaining guests to join in the frantic merriness. The gathering thinned with the dusk. The revelers who remained were none the worse for the glasses in their hands. Well, the festive group was about to be depleted in the manner of one more head, Nikki thought as she marched angrily toward the stables.

She was halfway through the crowd when an insistent hand wrapped around her forearm. The way her skin responded to the touch was a good indication of who belonged to those strong, thick fingers.

A wild hoot went up beside her as a man doing a clumsy jig crashed into Nikki's back. No apology was made as, with legs kicking high, he sent Nikki a lecherous wink then danced his way back to his voluptuous partner.

Kurt's eyes darkened, and he looked ready to go after the drunk and drag an apology from the man, with his fist.

"I thought you'd left," she said, as much to distract him from the drunk as to distract herself from the wild sensations of his touch. Each word was clipped, precise. She glanced at the offending hand, but he didn't let her go.

"I plan to." A hint of a smile lurked at one corner of his sensuously thin mouth. "But I found something I'd like a whole lot better than a long, hot bath."

His suggestive tone traveled the length of Nikki's spine, leaving her warm and in no doubt of what that "something" was.

She considered wrestling her arm from his grasp, but decided not to make a scene. It was bad enough her name was already linked with Kurt's—in a less than flattering way. The last thing she needed was to fuel the gossip. And, of course, there was the fact that she liked the feel of his possessive hand on her arm almost as much as she liked the hot, tingling sensations his touch evoked.

Dangerous thoughts, she silently admonished. "Let me go, Kurt. I'm tired and I'm hot and I want to go home."

"What? Now? Before I've had the pleasure of dancing with the mother of my child?"

Nikki glared into his laughing gray eyes. She tried to yank away, but his grip held firm. "Shhh! Will you please keep your voice down? Someone might hear."

"Everyone's going to hear if you're not careful,

Nicole. I plan on exercising my lungs on anyone who'll listen if you don't give me the next dance." He ran his free palm down his bristly jaw. "Want to know what I'm going to tell them? It's juicy enough to keep the Quilting Bee jabbering for weeks."

"You're drunk!"

"Could be. I repeat, do you want to know?"

Nikki clamped her jaw tight and swallowed the curse that sprang to her lips. The fire in her eyes seared him. "I'm getting sick of being blackmailed by you, buster."

"Dance with me and I'll stop."

This time when she yanked, her arm came away. Crossing it tightly over her stomach, she lifted her chin. "No."

"Okay fine, but don't blame me for what happens next because it's your own fault." Kurt grabbed the arm of the first person to stumble by. Dumb luck made it the drunk who'd rudely crashed into her. A smile of vengeful delight twisted Kurt's lips as his gaze feasted on familiar features. "Well, well, well, if it isn't Maxwell Potter himself. You weren't planning to bang into the lady again, were you, Max?"

"I—uh—again?" The lump in Potter's throat bobbed nervously as his beady gaze traveled to Nikki. He may have been drunk a minute ago, but right now he was stone cold sober. "Did I bang into you, *ma'am*?" The watery blue eyes said he knew perfectly well that he had. "Why, I surely am sorry, *ma'am*. Guess I didn't see you standin' there." With a weak smile, he turned his attention to Kurt. "Haven't seen you 'round much, Kurt. Been a mite—ahem—*busy* since you got back, huh?"

Kurt's free hand balled into a tight fist at his side. The steel gaze hardened. He didn't like the suggestive tone dripping off Potter's tongue. He liked even less the lewd glint in the man's beady eyes when they shifted to Nikki.

His finger's tightened around Potter's arm. Kurt felt a surge of perverse delight in the way the fat man sucked in a fearful gasp through femininely full, moist lips.

Kurt's hand dipped. He returned the beady gaze. "Well now, Max, I've been pulling some long hours out at the Triple D these days. I don't have time to visit Rosie with your regularity . . . much as I'd like to."

Max's fury-darkened gaze swept the people around him. His fleshy mouth opened and closed like a fish short on air.

"And speaking of that pretty wife of yours," Kurt continued, even though he had been talking about Rosie, Snow Creek's lone prostitute, "where is Mazie? She still keeping time with Rag Duffrey while you're down at Rosie's, or did she find someone else to satisfy her, where you so obviously failed?"

If anybody but Kurt Frazier had said that, he'd be picking himself up out of the dirt and nursing a bloody lip. But Max Potter was no fool. He knew when a man was spoiling for a fight, and Kurt Frazier looked to be spoiling for a dozen. With a nervous little laugh, he wiped away the spittle wetting his lips before it could drip down his chin. "Always did have a sense of humor, didn't you, Kurt?"

"I'm not laughing."

"Uh, no I guess you're not." Potter scanned the crowd as though willing one of them to come to his rescue. "Well, I—uh—gee, it's been good talkin' to you again, Kurt. Yup, real good, but I—uh—"

A feminine scream ripped the air, snatching away whatever else the fat man would have said. Nikki's gaze snapped to the people gathering behind Kurt, just in time to see a Dennison-blond head dip from view. Her blood ran cold.

Kurt shoved Potter away, his gaze turning on Nikki. Her eyes were wide, unblinking, her skin a deathly shade of white. "What—"

"Willy!" The single word tore from her lips at the same time she gained control of her feet. She rushed past Kurt and started clawing at shoulders and arms, shoving people out of the way. She didn't see Kurt hot on her heels, or the way his tight jaw and determined glare made the close press of spectators step back to allow Nikki an easy path.

Willy lay on the ground, eyes closed as though sleeping, his head cradled in Mike's lap. His face was ashen, his full lips slack and lined a sickly blue.

With a stifled sob, Nikki collapsed to the ground by his side. Her shaking fingers soothed back the blond wisps clinging to his clammy brow as her gaze met Mike's. "What happened?"

Mike shook his head numbly. "I don't know. I was standing here talking to him one minute, and the next thing I know he starts wheezing and falls to the ground. God, Nikki, *I don't think he's breathing!*"

A murmur went through the crowd, but Nikki's heart was pounding too loudly to hear it.

Kurt's fingers gripped her arms in no pretense of gentleness as he shoved her aside. He dropped hard on his knees in the spot where she had been kneeling. His strong fingers gripped the open collar of Willy's shirt and ripped it open from neck to waist. Buttons popped, scattering everywhere.

Nikki scrambled to her feet. Cold, gripping fear made her knees all but useless. She leaned weakly against whoever stood next to her, but took little comfort in the arm that coiled tightly around her shoulder. Her trembling fingers covered her lips as her eyes fixed on her unconscious brother. Tears blurred her eyes but she quickly blinked them away. She barely noticed when Pete skidded to his knees at Mike's side.

Kurt lowered his ear to the bare, hairless chest. There wasn't even a faint rush of breath to disguise the weak, fluttering heartbeat.

Tilting Willy's head back, he pried the limp mouth open with his fingers and lowered his lips to Willy's. The boy's mouth was cold beneath him as Kurt blew his own breath into Willy's dormant lungs. And again. The third time, Kurt lifted his head and looked harshly down at the pale, lifeless face.

"Breathe, Willy! *Breathe!*" he barked before renewing his efforts with a vengeance. Every few breaths he would stop, lower his head to Willy's chest, and listen. Then the procedure would begin again.

Nikki's heart stopped and her brow beaded with cold sweat each time Kurt bent over her prone brother. Her breath would catch in her throat and the arm around her would tighten when he would again cover Willy's mouth with his own. She chanted a silent prayer each time his head descended.

She didn't know how long Kurt had worked on her brother when her gaze fell on the two glasses sitting atop a nearby table. As though in a daze, she remembered setting her own untouched glass there. She presumed the glass sitting next to it was the one she had poured over her brother's boots. But her glass had been full, and both of these were empty!

Her memory whirled with the pungent tang of alcohol stinging her nostrils. Gin. The odor was gin and gin was Willy's favorite. The punch hadn't smelled right, but at the time she'd thought it was the heat, and Kurt Frazier's gaze. In rapid succession the broken barn ladder flashed in her mind, then the sawed wagon shaft. Her heart stopped, then thudded to furious life.

"Poison!" she screamed as her mind instantly pieced the puzzle together. "Kurt, he's been poisoned!"

Two minutes passed at an agonizing crawl before

Willy drew in a fast, ragged gasp. The boy arched his back, which then thudded to the ground. A cloud of dirt puckered up from his sides and a muffled groan rushed through his lips.

Kurt wasted no time. He flipped Willy onto his side as though the pudgy boy was no heavier than a rag doll. Once again he pried the mouth open. Without a thought, he stuck his finger down Willy's throat, forcing the boy to gag. Nikki winced and turned away when her brother heaved the sour contents of his stomach onto the ground.

It was a good thing the arms around her were strong and tight because Nikki came perilously close to collapsing. She recognized Mark Winfield's voice whispering encouragement in her ear, but she ignored the meaningless words. The choked gags echoing in her ears made her own stomach convulse. *That poison was meant for me, not Willy!* her mind told her over and over until she wanted to scream and make it stop.

And then it was done. When Willy stopped vomiting, and began to cry, Kurt rolled him onto his back. The wet blue eyes flickered open, and regarded the man looming above him with a mixture of fear, surprise, and respect.

Nikki's body flooded with relief. She heard Kurt mumble something to Mike and Pete before thrusting himself to his feet. In the time it took him to close the distance between himself and Nikki, every muscle in her body had begun to visibly shake.

Kurt opened his arms, and Nikki rushed into the sweet haven of his embrace. It wasn't until his strong arms had wrapped around her, fusing his firm body close, that she released the torrent of tears she could no longer hold back. Her fingers dug into his back and she clung to him desperately, drinking of his spicy scent as she buried her face in his shoulder and surrendered to the sobs that racked her body.

Chapter Fifteen

There was only one thing Nikki hated more than whiskey. But right now she was too drunk to remember what it was. Oh yes, she remembered. *Kurt Frazier.* She hated Kurt Frazier more than she hated whiskey. In fact, she hated Kurt more than anything. Didn't she? That's funny—*hiccup!*—she couldn't remember anymore.

Lifting the bottle shakily to her lips, she gulped down another fiery shot. Her throat didn't burn this time—it had been chafed raw from swallowing almost a quarter of the bottle. For that matter, so had her stomach; chafed raw, but warm and tingly.

She lowered the bottle clumsily to her lap, the glass cold and smooth as it rested against the inside of her thigh.

Inside of my thigh? Nikki scowled exaggeratedly. Glancing down, she saw the skirt of her Sunday Best indecently hoisted to mid-thigh. Her petticoats were a rumpled cloud of white linen, tossed atop the hay near the opposite wall. The soft gray folds of her dress shimmered in the moonlight pouring through the open hayloft door, the muslin hopelessly wrinkled from where she'd bunched the bulk of the skirt between her legs. Her cuffs were unbuttoned, her sleeves rolled sloppily up her arms, one below the elbow, one above. The stiff collar had been loosened, exposing a generous portion of creamy flesh. Cool night air snuck in through the gaping placket. To Nikki, it felt sinfully delicious.

Closing her eyes, Nikki rested her head against the wall, at once dismissing her state of dress—or undress. Who cared how brazenly exposed she was? The cool night air caressing her skin did not require that she be demure. Besides, she was alone in the hayloft. Everyone else was in bed. Everyone, that is, except whoever it was that was now clambering up the hayloft ladder with all the stealth of a rutting grizzly bear. Good God, whoever it was, was making enough noise to wake the dead!

Kurt Frazier topped the ladder, the expression on his face cornering the market in the surprise department. Settling his fists on enticingly lean, denim-clad hips, he regarded Nikki as though she'd just sprouted a second head.

"Howdy, par'ner," she slurred, waving the bottle to greet him. Looking him over, she patted the hay beside her. She looked down in confusion when she didn't feel any hay—she was patting her naked thigh! Funny, she didn't feel that either.

"You're drunk!" He countered the sting of his words with a pleasantly thick chuckle. His gaze darkened when it was met with creamy flesh—*everywhere*. The laughter faded from his voice and his eyes. "You're also half naked."

Hiccup! "Could be."

His feet crunched over the hay as he cleared the distance between them. The floor supporting her bottom vibrated with his weight as Kurt dropped to her side.

"How's Willy?"

"Good question." She stifled a hiccup and shrugged. "Beats me."

Kurt was close enough for their arms to touch, but

Nikki didn't move away. Why should she? She liked the feel of his firm muscles pressing against her, not to mention the sweet breath stirring the curls at her cheek. Lord, when it came to raw sensation, the whiskey had nothing over the warm tingle this man's touch sent rushing through her blood!

With a hesitant smile, she offered him the bottle. Her gaze fixed on the strong fingers that brushed against her own.

"Whiskey?" he asked, one raven eyebrow cocked high.

"Smell it"—*hiccup!*—"and find . . . oops!" She giggled, belatedly remembering he lacked that particular sense. Her gaze raked him. Kurt Frazier may lack one sense, but he more than made up for it in other ways. Her eyes darkened to cornflower blue swirled with midnight sapphire. "It's whiskey."

Kurt kept his eyes on Nikki as he raised the bottle and tossed back a mouthful of the potent brew. He didn't cough or sputter the way she had with her first sip, and Nikki gazed at him admiringly.

"Kurt, does that wall over there look like it's breathing to you?" Dead serious, she pointed to the far wall. She sent him a quick glance when he made small, choking sounds. "Don't laugh at me, I'm serious."

"I know. That's what worries me."

She slapped his arm and sent him a stern glare—except she'd forgotten how to work her eyebrows. She settled for a lopsided squint, which only made him laugh harder. Oooh, how she liked that laugh. "Well? Does it? I've been"—*hiccup!*—"sitting here for—um—a while, watching, and I can't decide."

"And that's all you've been thinking about?" he asked, handing the bottle back.

She sighed thoughtfully. "No. I've been thinking of Willy, and what happened . . . and my nose."

He tipped back his head and let out a throaty

chuckle. "Your nose? You've been sitting here, drunk as a boiled owl, thinking about your nose?"

Blinking, Nikki tried to touch the tip of her index finger to her nose. It grazed her ear, until Kurt's hand guided it. "Um-hmmm," she sighed heavily, "my nose. You said I had a great big nose and I was wondering if"—*hiccup*—"you were right."

"If I said that, I must have been mad," he replied. His hand trailed slowly down her wrist, down the thin taper of her arm. "Your nose isn't *that* big, baby." He reached up and drew the tip of his finger in a slow, hot path down the body part in question. "In fact, it's very nice . . . if you like noses."

"Do you? I mean, do you like *my* nose?"

"Do you care?"

Nikki managed a scowl. "Yes," she answered honestly, nodding. "I do care. In fact, I care very much what you think about me."—*hiccup!*—"God only knows why."

Clumsily, she lifted the bottle to her lips and took another sip. Her senses were whirling, her head felt light. She couldn't decide if the reaction was caused by the liquor, or Kurt. Wiping the mouth of the bottle, she passed it, all the while wondering at the companionable silence they'd suddenly slipped into.

He tilted his head back and took another long swallow. Like before, his gaze never left her. That was all right, too, she decided. Somehow she would find the strength to endure the hot caress of his eyes— if she absolutely *haaad* to. She felt like a proper martyr.

Her gaze drifted out the haydoor, sweeping the moonswept darkness that shadowed most of the ranch. The house was dark. Not a single lamp burned in its windows. The other buildings looked deserted. Only the plaintive baying of a prairie dog could be heard in the distance.

"You saved my brother's life," she said, then

foggily wondered if she'd only thought the words as they skittered across her brain, or uttered them aloud. A quick glance at Kurt found him staring at her.

"I know."

"Why? After everything that's happened I would have thought you'd enjoy seeing us Dennison's push up roses."

"Willy's a good kid. Screwed up, but good. I have nothing against him." Kurt shrugged and placed the bottle between Nikki's legs.

Nikki shivered at the feel of cold glass resting against her skin, a contrast to the warm fingers that grazed her smoldering flesh. She moved neither the bottle nor the hand that had settled lightly on her naked thigh.

Again, they lapsed into silence, but this time it was tight, strained, electrically charged, slicing through Nikki's liquor-induced lethargy. She told herself it was the liquor she'd consumed that was making her feel so restless. But her thoughts shifted to the palm searing her flesh, and the roughened fingertip that was tracing a pattern of tiny circles a few inches above her knee.

"I think Willy had the right idea," she slurred, plucking the half empty bottle from her lap. "Being drunk isn't so bad. It helps you forget."

The bottle was halfway to her lips when Kurt snatched it away. "It also makes your problems worse," he told her as he nestled it in the hay on his other side, out of Nikki's reach. His voice softened to a silken caress, punctuated by the calloused fingertip that scraped down her jaw. "What are you trying to forget, Nicole? What happened to Willy tonight, or what *could* have happened to you?"

Nikki heaved a sigh and leaned her head against the wall. The rough planks made a hard pillow, but she was too far gone with whiskey to care. "If you must know, I was trying to forget about you. Trying, and failing miserably . . . as always." She closed her eyes, shutting out the sight of his piercing gray eyes. She saw them in her mind anyway; they haunted her.

"Is thinking about me really so bad?"

"Worse. When I think about you, dream about you, I feel like I'm betraying Pop. I'm betraying his memory by thinking the way I do about his killer." She gave a derisive chuckle. "Do you know that when I lie in bed at night, staring at the ceiling, my body aches to feel your arms around me?" Her fingers trembled against the dewy moistness of her mouth. "My lips tingle when I think about how you kiss me. My cheek burns when I remember how your breath tickles my skin. Do you know about any of that?"

His eyes darkened to turquoise fire as his gaze seared her delicately relaxed profile. "No, I didn't."

"Of course not. How could you? I've never told you. I've never told anyone. I'd be too embarrassed." The silver brows furrowed in a clumsy scowl as she tried to purse her lips. The attempt made her giggle. "I'm only telling you now because the whiskey's greased my tongue. I won't remember a word come morning." She opened one eye a crack and sent him a mischievous glance. "If there's something you want to ask me, Kurt, do it now. I get brutally honest when I'm snookered."

"Anything?" he asked. His voice was seductively low and husky as his hand returned to her thigh. The roughened thumb stroked her bare flesh. The feather-light touch sent a shock of excitement pumping through her blood.

She pouted thoughtfully, then grinned and shrugged. "Sure. Why not?"

Kurt sucked in a deep breath when her cool flesh slipped smoothly beneath his palm. "All right, I'm game. Why'd you come tonight, Nicole? Why here?"

She stifled a hiccup and a laugh with the back of her hand, trying to mold her features into seriousness. "To be alone."

"Un-uh. It's a big ranch, Nicole. There are dozens of other places to go if all you wanted was a little privacy."

"True. But I didn't want to be interrupted, in case anyone woke up and came searching for me. They wouldn't look for me here because this is the one place I don't usually go."

"And you didn't expect to see me?"

"You still want the truth?"

"Yes."

She opened her eyes and met his hard, penetrating stare. "I expected to see you. I hoped to see you. I *wanted* to see you. I told myself I shouldn't ever want to see you again. That you killed my father and that I should, by all rights, hate you to the bone. But as much as I want to, as much as I've tried, I don't. I just can't seem to hate you, Kurt Frazier." Her open palm smacked her naked thigh. The sound was loud as it shot through the moonlit loft. "Why can't I hate you?" she muttered under whiskey-soaked breath.

"You tell me." His hand rose boldly on her thigh, pushing away the cumbersome folds of wrinkled muslin. Her hip was a gentle curve beneath his palm. Soft, smooth, and inviting. Turning his hand in, he let his knuckles glide slowly down the inside of her right thigh. He cupped her knee in his hand and began another torturous ascent. His palm burned with each inch of flesh that slipped like spun silk beneath his work-roughened skin.

"I w-wish I knew."

With a groan, Kurt lowered his head, surrendering to the urge to taste her temptingly long, creamy throat. His tongue moistened the hollow where her pulse quickened with desire. Her skin tasted warm, salty, wonderful.

"You're taking advantage of a woman who's snookered," she warned with a giggle, tilting her chin to allow him better access. A soft moan escaped her when he teased her earlobe. The scent of fresh hay in her nostrils was sweetly pungent.

"It's my turn, wouldn't you say?" he rasped in her ear. His hand blazed a hot trail over her quivering stomach. "Six years ago, here, you were the seductress. Again, here, *you* were the seductress. Then in the study. As appealing as that is to a man—and, baby, it's appealing—it's about time *you* learned what it feels like to be seduced."

"Are you going to seduce me, Kurt?" she asked, her eyelids fluttering contentedly shut. One hand strayed to his shoulder, and she felt a hot rush of excitement when his muscles flexed beneath her open palm.

She opened her eyes when he lifted his head and cupped her chin in his palms. Moonlight danced off his raven hair. His eyes shimmered a stormy turquoise. For once Nikki could read his emotions clearly. He was raw with desire, and that desire was for her. His voice was thick. "Baby, if I have my way I'm going to seduce you until you can't think."

Nikki had only enough time to suck in a ragged gasp before his lips crashed down on hers. He tasted warm, a sizzling combination of coffee and whiskey. He tasted delicious.

Her mouth opened under the demand of his lips. Her hands slipped up his rippling arms, then wrapped around the thick cord of his neck. She entwined her fingers in the silky black strands of his hair. Her breath caught as she pulled him closer.

The kiss intensified. Their tongues engaged in a moist, parrying battle where the only loser was time; the winner, sinfully rapturous sensation.

Warm breath grazed her cheek. Roughened fingers sent waves of dizzying awareness through her as his hands caressed her chin and jaw. He rubbed her small earlobe between thumb and forefinger as his tongue ran along the pearly line of her teeth. The insistent fingers slipped farther back, burying themselves in the moonlit cloud of hair tied loosely at her nape.

With deft fingers he coaxed away her black ribbon, then flung it aside. She caught Kurt's moan with her lips as he tunneled his fingers in the silky waterfall of her hair.

Shifting his weight, he held her close, as though trying to fuse his body into hers. A few feathery strands of quicksilver were tossed over his broad shoulders, trickling down his back. He tore his lips from hers and buried his face in the soft hollow between her shoulder and neck.

"You feel good," he groaned against her flesh. "Too good."

As if to prove it, he twisted her to the side and lowered her to the soft bed of hay. In an instant he was covering her. Hungrily. Possessively.

Nikki accepted his weight. He was deliciously firm, she thought, as her hands roved his back, down the sides of his taut waist, over his hips. Feeling his shiver of desire, she smiled.

Leaning on one elbow, Kurt slowly drew his hand up the length of her thigh. He dragged the wrinkled skirt with him until it was wrapped askew somewhere around her hips. Her skin felt warm beneath his palm, warm and sensuous.

"I want you," he sighed hotly in her ear. "I want you so bad I can taste it."

His warm breath grazed her neck and shoulder, blending with the raw huskiness of his voice to create a throbbing, undeniable need deep in the pit of her stomach. The feel boiled in her blood and honed each sensitive nerve ending until she felt nothing but the pulsating awareness of the man pressed against her.

Kurt's tongue dotted a hot, moist path down her neck, over the throbbing pulse in her throat, lower. A groan tore from him at the feel of large, creamy breasts grazing his chin. "Sweet-nut wine," he murmured against her flesh. "Sweeter. Tell me you want me, Nikki." His breath seared her.

She strained up until her breasts were crushed against him. The evidence of his desire, long and hard, pressed into her. Nikki's breath caught. She dug her fingers into the solid muscle of his arms. Clamping her teeth together, she bit back the honeyed words that threatened to slip from her tongue.

"Say it," he coaxed as she arched. His tongue dipped, licking a path to the creamy base of her breast. The hand that had been exploring every excruciating detail of her thigh now slid up her stomach, hesitated for a delicious heartbeat over her breasts, then made short work of the buttons trailing a wrinkled path to her waist. The cloth parted beneath his fingers like golden leaves tumbling from an autumn tree.

Nikki gasped when his hand passed beneath the cloth. His palm was hot, searching, insistent. A wonderful ripple of sensation sliced through her, robbing her of any surprise she might have felt. His thumb teased a rosy nipple to a sensuously firm erection. Again, she arched. Hungrily. Beseechingly.

"Please," she whispered on a ragged sigh. The voice that echoed low in her ears was not her own. It was too thick with passion, husky as it begged for release.

"Say you want me," he urged, his voice muffled as he nuzzled his head between her breasts. He arched his hips against her. She tightened with want. With demand. "Come on, baby, tell me you want me. Tell me your body aches for me. That you'll die if you don't feel me touch you here . . . and here . . . and here. Say you want me to fill you. Say you need to feel me inside you as much as I need to feel myself there. I need to hear you say it."

His head turned to the side. His lips closed around

an achingly alert nipple as his fingers paid special attention to its mate. The fiery yearning that throbbed in her stomach now crashed in the junction of her thighs. More than anything in her life, Nikki wanted him, desired him, craved him. Her body demanded him. And her body never considered denial.

"Say it," he rasped between the hot kisses he lavished on her breast. "This is your last chance. I can stop now if I have to. I won't seduce a woman who doesn't want me." One hand slipped under the hem of her skirt. His thick, roughened fingers stroked her stomach. Lower. *"Say it, Nicole!"*

"Yesss!" she cried, her voice slurred with passion as his fingers slipped inside her moist warmth. "I want you, Kurt. I want this, and I want you. Now!"

Nikki knew a second of intense embarrassment—and boiling hot rage—when he pushed away and rose shakily to his feet. But then he extended his strong hand, and she saw his eyes darken with silky promise in the moonlight. She tucked her hand in his, the gesture unwittingly trusting.

The meaning of it knifed through Kurt, fired him beyond reason. "Come on," he growled. His fingers closed around hers, tugging her in his wake.

Their feet crunched over the hay. Nikki hesitated, then followed him down the ladder. Her body stung with the heat of him as she stood trembling before him. Dennison-blue eyes shimmered with a mixture of curiosity and pent-up desire.

"Where are we going?" she panted when he again snatched her hand and pulled her urgently toward the door.

Kurt spared a brief glance over his broad shoulder, his gaze one of passionate determination. "To make new memories. I won't have the ghost of old ones hanging over my shoulder. Not tonight."

Instinctively, she knew where they were headed.

Silver moonlight skimmed the gentle currents of the Little Missouri River. The crisp water licked the bank. A prairie dog howled. Crickets chirped in the underbrush that served as a barrier between house and river. The scent of crinkling leaves and sap filled the air.

The ground was a hard bed that he swiftly lowered her to, spreading himself beside her. His body was half on the ground, half on Nikki. It was the half that was on Nikki that was vibrantly, pulsatingly alive.

He kissed her hungrily, his mouth devouring the intoxicating sweetness of her lips as his hands hungrily searched and caressed her body. His breaths were harsh and ragged against her skin as he stripped away the last of her clothes.

"*I'm* doing the seducing this time," Kurt growled huskily when she tried to reciprocate. He brushed her hands away and loosened his own clothes with fingers that trembled with desire.

What seemed like a lifetime later, he hunkered down and scooped her lithe, naked body into his arms. He cradled her yielding flesh to his chest with all the warmth and protectiveness of a parent. Only parents didn't lick one's neck the way Kurt was now licking and nibbling at hers, Nikki thought.

Moonlight bathed them as Kurt took long, purposeful strides into the brisk water. He slipped his hand from beneath her knees and let her small body slide with tantalizing leisure down the length of his. Her feet had barely touched the giving softness of the river's slippery bottom when insistent fingers cupped the firmness of her bottom and pulled her roughly against his hips.

The brisk water lapped at her skin. It was a heady contrast to the hotness of male flesh. His leathery scent filled her nostrils as she buried her face in his shoulder and nibbled on the warm, salty flesh. The drunk of liquor had long since given way to the drunk of passion.

She wanted him, ached for him. Water-lightened legs encircled wonderfully lean hips. She tightened around him when his hands skillfully positioned her hips and he made his first, breathtaking thrust.

A throaty groan bubbled in her throat as she ground her hips against him and pulled him closer. Deeper. Her fingers dug into his forearms and she arched her back, her water-darkened hair floating like a quicksilver cloud atop the water.

Kurt sucked in his breath as he bent to capture a moist, peaked nipple. He teased the aching flesh with his tongue and teeth until Nikki whimpered and writhed beneath him. Pulling her up and holding her firmly to his chest, he moved urgently within her. Each demanding thrust and retreat was greedily matched.

Earth-shattering sensation ripped through Nikki's stomach, tingling in her blood with hot, throbbing urgency. She burrowed her fingers into the firmness of his back, quickening the pace. It was silkily sensuous, the way his damp curls tickled her breasts, the way the water splashed against their naked, straining bodies.

Their coupling was fierce and urgent, hard and fast. Moist flesh teased and fired moist flesh. The sheer wantonness of it all made the act sinfully delicious. Impatiently quick. Desire flamed to an incredible pitch. The spasms started in slow, pulsationg waves of fire that soon fanned and spread until an inferno of satisfaction sang through her blood.

Kurt slipped his hands over her waist, up her back, hooking over her shoulders and pulling her down as he felt her moist, tight warmth shudder around him. He fused their bodies together, driving his own need home in long, slippery, glorious thrusts.

Nikki clung to him as surge after surge of delicious release crashed through her, carrying her away on the twisting, pulsating currents. Their groans, throaty and long, shattered the night, melting together until one could not be separated from the other.

When she felt herself being pressed onto her back, Nikki wondered fleetingly when and how they'd gotten to solid ground. Then Kurt's body was stretched out beside her, warm and hard, and she let herself be scooped against his side. She decided she didn't care how she'd gotten there, just that she was there.

Kurt pillowed her damp head on his shoulder and Nikki snuggled against the warmth. His hand rode the curve of her hip, possessively seared her flesh. Stifling a yawn, she flung a leg over his thighs and closed her eyes. Lulled by the whiskey, her own slaked passion, the rhythmic beat of his heart, and the gentle rush of his breath, she slept.

Kurt glanced down at the sleeping woman in his arms and wondered how she could lie there in sweet oblivion while, hours later, he was still tortured by memories of their lovemaking. His flesh was alive with the satiny softness pressing into him. Curled wisps of her hair tickled his cheek. Her shallow, rhythmic breaths quickened in his ear and he could feel the steady beat of her heart against his chest.

His gaze fixed sightlessly on the inky sky stretching above, and its smattering of stars. With a sigh, he closed his eyes and let his mind carry him back.

Kurt never knew what had drawn him West, only that his body and mind demanded he go. Drifting from one ranch to the next, he'd polished his skill at busting mustangs and breaking hearts before landing a job on the Triple D. His friends in Boston had snickered about that when he'd return for quick visits. Imagine, the son of Drake Frazier, a man who owned a veritable shipping empire—the biggest and richest in the East—turning his back on it all for the meager wages of a lowly cowpoke. Which only went to prove that even a Frazier wasn't immune to "frontier fever."

He'd worked on the Triple D for almost a year before noticing the way Hugh's daughter followed him around like a lost pup. At the time, he was too restless to see Nicole as anything more than a nuisance, but in the space of a year she'd managed to worm her way under his skin. Soon he found he even enjoyed her tagging behind him, begging for attention, asking him questions and learning anything he would teach her. He'd complained about it, sure—couldn't let the other hands think he'd gone soft over a scrappy kid—but he'd enjoyed it. It was the first time in his life anyone had ever admired him. Respect, he'd learned early on, was something usually reserved for his brothers, not him.

Kurt shifted on the cold, hard ground. From behind his lashes he saw Nicole, the girl. Long silver hair fell from a center part, gathered on each side of her neck in twin braids that bobbed down to her nonexistent waist. A sprinkle of freckles smattered a nose that was, at the time, still childishly pert. Her cheeks were rounded in a perpetual grin, her Dennison-blue eyes wide with trust. Boys' clothes hung unflatteringly from her lean frame.

He'd taught her to shoot, to hunt, and to track like a Dakota Indian, the way Drake Frazier had taught all his sons. She'd learned it greedily, earning his respect with her lightning-quick mind and easy grasp of things. And her laughter.

The friendship flourished until the night he'd stumbled upon her bathing and realized she wasn't a child anymore, but a girl teetering on the edge of womanhood.

His gut tightened when he remembered the way the moonlight danced over her wet, quicksilver curls.

Her breasts were smaller then, the nipples perkily tipped and thrusting. Her flesh glowed with dewy moisture that, even concealed behind trees, he could see. Lord, how he remembered his body's fervent, white-hot reaction to *that* sight!

His intention had been a quick midnight swim to wash away the layers of trail dust. But when he saw the river already taken, and recognized the occupant, he'd stayed behind the cloak of trees and watched. He'd told himself his reason was to offer Nicole protection if she needed it.

He didn't make his presence known for fear his strange, gut-wrenching desire would override his normally good sense. But there was no such thing as good sense where Nicole Dennison was concerned. From that moment on, there was only lust, passion, and an insatiable need to make her his woman.

He'd watched her bathe, and his palms had itched to follow the washcloth that slipped rich suds over her porcelain flesh. His breath had caught in a painful lump in his throat as he watched her body emerge from the sparkling water. At the time her hips had been lean, her thighs tight from long hours spent straddling a saddle. For a scrappy kid, she'd moved with uncommon grace. Even at seventeen, her face had looked younger than her years. It was her body that did not.

He'd waited until she was fully dressed and securing the buttons of her frock before letting her know he was there. If someone had put a gun to his head and demanded it, he could not recall the words they had exchanged that night. What he did remember was the way her cornflower-blue eyes had darkened with desire. The memory had haunted him, spawning more than one sultry dream since.

How long had he wanted Nicole Dennison? It seemed forever, but his first memory of desire was that night at the lake. The moonlit night of passion in the hayloft had increased his need to feverish desperation. Kurt hadn't dared to want her then, but she'd given him no choice. When she'd told him she would find another man to fulfill her "need to know" if he refused, well, he'd gone crazy. What good would denial do if she'd only seek out someone else to take his place? And why had that threat stung so much? Couldn't he see that it was a weak threat, not meant? Yes, he could, in retrospect. But at the time...

When it was over, when she'd snuggled in his arms the way she did now, Kurt knew he couldn't take her innocence and just leave her. It wasn't his style. It wasn't what he wanted.

After she'd returned to a bed he craved desperately to share, Kurt made his decision. He would talk to Hugh Dennison come dawn and beg for Nicole's hand in marriage. And if his friend refused, he would admit the night's indiscretion. Whatever it took to make Nicole his wife.

He'd never gotten the chance. Hugh was dead by the time the second sun of August streaked a fiery path across the sky, but Kurt wouldn't find that out for months. He woke before sunup, alone in the hayloft, a note from Nikki imbedded in the wall over his head with an oak-hilted bowie knife. The knife and letter were now tucked in a bureau drawer in Boston. But the contents of the letter, he carried in his heart.

Her venomous words had shattered his world. "A dirt poor cowpoke," the note had said. "Not near good enough for me. Fun for one night, but never for more... You're too arrogant. Womanizer... I don't even like you." For the first time in his life, Kurt Frazier had tasted what it was like to love and lose, and for a man used to getting what he wanted, this failure did not sit well. Not when his heart was so deeply involved.

Hurt and angry, he'd suppressed the urge to confront her. Instead, packing the belongings he could cram into his saddlebag, he'd left. When he'd heard about Hugh's death a few months later he'd grieved, but by then he'd hardened himself. By then he didn't care about anyone he'd left behind on the Triple D. He just wanted to forget. To hide. To find some place where he could lick his wounds and get on with the rest of his life.

Nikki murmured, shifting against him, but Kurt kept his eyes trained on the sky. The pale glow reminded him of the silver hair tickling his cheek.

For six years he'd hated Nicole Dennison more than he'd ever hated anyone in his life. But he'd never forgotten her. He couldn't, no matter how hard he'd tried.

His thoughts shifted to that night in the woods when he'd found out who his kidnapper was, and why she'd taken him.

Realization had ripped through him with a force to make the gunshot wound in his side feel like a mosquito bite. The emotions he'd thought long dead were rekindled by bewitching silver hair and hard blue eyes. He hadn't expected to react that way. What he'd expected, and didn't get, was a hatred as strong and as sure as the one he'd nursed for six long years.

But the kidnapper wasn't his sweet, sensible Nicole anymore. The enticing girl who'd tortured his sleep and made his life a living hell had matured into "Nikki". Hard, cold, and vengeful.

As much as he wanted to deny his feelings for her—run from them—tonight proved they were still very much alive. He'd loved this girl for as long as he could remember. Most of his adult life had been spent waiting for her to grow up and return his love. Losing that hope had shattered every dream for happiness Kurt had ever had. The other half of his life had been spent making sure he never felt that pain again.

It didn't matter that *she* hadn't written the letter that had destroyed his life. Six years of hurt, founded or unfounded, was not easily banished. No matter how hard he tried to push the residual pain away, it wouldn't go. There were some things that rational thought couldn't override. This was one of them. The hurt ran too deep, and getting rid of it just wasn't that simple.

Something else made Kurt reluctant to turn his carefully guarded heart over to the temptress in his arms. He wasn't sure he wanted the little spitfire who called herself "Nikki," over his lifelong love "Nicole." He had loved "Nicole." With all his heart, he'd loved her—still did. But he didn't even like "Nikki."

Then, there was the matter of Hugh Dennison's untimely death. How could he fully give himself over to a woman who believed he'd committed unprovoked, cold-blooded murder? A woman who didn't believe in him? Who didn't even trust him?

The answer was simple. He couldn't. Never.

Kurt closed his eyes on the night, and on the searing pain that tightened like icy fingers around his heart. He would *not* be hurt again!

Chapter Sixteen

The new day washed over Nikki in slow, languid waves. She was alone. She was in her own room, tucked in her own bed. And beneath the covers, she was barer than a baby's bottom. The crisp sheet covering her felt wonderful, reminded her of the feel of cold water lapping at her skin.

Stifling a groan, she pulled the sheet higher. She didn't know whether she'd made it to bed under her own power or Kurt's.

A cool breeze tossed the curtain at the window. Through the billowing lace she glimpsed a gaggle of wild geese, honking as they sliced through the cloudless sky in symmetrical form. They were heading south late this year, she thought, and snuggled beneath the covers. Most years the waterfowl migrated in early September. But then, thought Nikki, summer had given way this year to Indian summer, with no frost to separate them.

The voices of shouting cowpokes drifted in through the open window. Although the sound itself wasn't unusual, the excitement that laced the commotion was.

Realization hit hard. The long-postponed cow-hunt—the precursor to the expressly forbidden trail drive—started today. Since Brian hadn't returned and Willy was too sick to join them, the ranch would be shorthanded. Nikki's skills would be needed.

She threw the sheet off and jumped out of bed. Her stomach lurched in protest, and she thanked God queasiness would be the only effects of the liquor she'd have to fight. A perverse grin tugged at her lips as she rifled through her bureau drawers. She doubted Kurt would be so lucky.

In ten minutes she was ready. She worked her hair into a long, thick plait. Baggy brown trousers hung from her hips, secured with a rope belt. Over them was a pair of altered chaps. A thin, faded flannel shirt hung from her shoulders, the tails purposely left untucked. She hastily knotted a brown bandanna at her throat, and a tan leather hat completed the outfit. She grabbed cracked leather gauntlets off the top of her bureau, tucking them under her arm on the way out.

A brief check on Willy found him up and about, although tired and more than a bit sore. His face was still pale, but he was improving. *Thank God!* She teased him that he had probably poisoned himself to avoid going on the roundup, kissed his cool forehead, then went in search of Beth. When she couldn't find her in the house, Nikki knew where to look.

The yard was in a state of confusion. Dust curled thick clouds in the air as men barked orders. Dusty, sweaty cowpunchers darted back and forth on summer-lean mavericks, between the branding corral and the temporary pen used to keep the unbranded calves. Cows balked as they were dragged to be branded.

Nikki found Beth in Abigail's cabin. Dragging her daughter out, she gathered a group of various of the cowhands' children and settled them in the hayloft to watch the commotion.

Once assured that her daughter was safely out of

harm's way, Nikki went to the corral and roped out her workhorse. As always, Brero was eager. The brown-and-white maverick bucked in agitation once the saddle was cinched and she'd mounted, but in a few short minutes her trained hand brought him under control.

She didn't see Kurt, but then, she wasn't necessarily looking for him. It wasn't until midday that she spotted him dragging a balking calf to the branding corral. He was mounted atop a sinewy gray, so self-assured it seemed he had been born in a saddle.

There was much to envy in his skill with a horse, Nikki thought, and more to envy in his skill with the men. The few orders he gave went unquestioned, although he was careful never to countermand any given by Ben. Ben was foreman; his word was law. Any hand who couldn't adhere to that hard and fast rule was shown the property markers in no uncertain terms. Kurt respected that.

Nikki lost sight of Kurt in the crowd of men and the dense fog of kicked-up dust. She didn't see him again until the noon meal. He ignored her, as though the previous night had never happened. Her pride stung, but she nursed it in silence. It wouldn't do to rehash the night's events, or to question the motives that had thrown them into each other's arms. What had happened, had happened. It was best forgotten— for both their sakes. And never, never, *never*, would it be repeated.

At least, that's what Nikki told herself. Unfortunately, her body and her mind weren't in total agreement on that score. It galled her to realize she spent the rest of the day with her ears perked to catch the sound of Kurt's voice, her gaze alert for a fleeting glimpse of his enticingly dark head.

So it went for the rest of that day . . . and the next . . . and the day after that . . .

And then it happened. When she'd least expected it, two attempts on her life were made in the very same morning. Both coincided with her decision to talk to Ben about his missing spur. Ben's heated denial of being in the barn the night she had fallen from the ladder was still ringing in her ears when she discovered that her saddle cinch had been cut. Since she always made a point of saddling her own mount, Nikki found the broken cinch herself. The only inconvenience caused was Nikki's having to ferret out another saddle—she ended up with one that was molded to a man's lean hips, instead of her own gentle curves.

It was the shots aimed directly at her head when she had joined the other men in the roundup that had taken her off guard. The quick reaction of the man riding by her side had saved her life—even though he had almost broken her neck when he shoved her from her saddle!

It was this second, bolder attempt that required her presence in the study, squirming uncomfortably in a red leather chair as she dodged angry glares from Pete and Kurt.

"Someone's been trying to kill you and you didn't have the decency to tell me?!" Pete shouted in an uncharacteristically shrill tone. He pounded his fist on the paper-cluttered desktop. "Didn't you think I'd care?!"

Nikki smiled weakly and stifled the urge to tear Kurt apart with her bare hands. If not for his big mouth, Pete wouldn't have been dragged into this, she thought. But no, Kurt's bellowing voice had made sure the entire ranch knew someone was trying to kill her. He really did deserve to hang, she thought as she sent him a sidelong glance.

Calm and cool, Kurt stretched out in his chair as though he was about to fall asleep in it. Nikki knew better than to be fooled by his tranquil demeanor. He may *seem* to be taking this quite casually, but Nikki knew that, like a sleeping wildcat, every muscle in his body was alert and ready for action.

"I'm sorry," she offered obligingly, entwining her fingers in her lap. "I know I should have told you, but you've been so busy and, well, it just didn't seem important enough to bother you with."

"Not . . . Why didn't . . . *Not important?!*" Pete sputtered. Snatching the spectacles from his nose, he threw them on the desk and fixed her with an incredulous glare. Then, with a huff, he collapsed back into his chair. "And what's *your* excuse, Frazier? Why didn't *you* tell me? Or were you going to wait until she was dead before you took these threats seriously?"

Kurt's lips turned up in an insolent grin. The gray flannel shirt stretched out over his broad shoulders. The muscle working in his jaw was the only indication of his anger, and Nikki was the only one to see it. "I only work here, Pete. You hired me to break horses and help on the drive. You're not paying me good money to spy on your sister."

"I'm not paying you good money to bed her, either."

Nikki immediately shot out of her chair, her fist slamming onto the desk with bone-jarring force. "And what would that make me if you were?" she shouted. "Better yet, what would it make *you?*" She swiped back a silver curl, her gaze spitting angry blue fire. "What's the matter, Pete? No answer? You seemed to have plenty to say a minute ago."

Pete's jaw hung open. He snapped it shut. It was just as well, because Nikki had been about to do the job for him.

"Nikki, I—um—" Pete stammered, "I didn't mean it that way." His cheeks were ashen as he pushed up the imaginary glasses that had fallen down his nose.

"No?" she asked tightly. "Then just how did you

mean it?! Forget it. I don't want to know." She spun on her heel, unaware that the tip of her braid had slapped her brother's cheek. Her glare settled on Kurt, who seemed cautious, but not overly concerned by the exchange. "What's the matter? Can't find it in your heart to jump to your lover's defense?"

His steely gaze narrowed. The entwined fingers tightened over the hard plane of his stomach. "You're not my lover, baby."

"That's right, *baby*."

Slowly, precisely, Nikki approached him. She brought her hand up and struck him swiftly across the cheek.

"You wouldn't know a lover if one came up and slapped you in the face!" she snarled before spinning on her heel and stalking out of the room. She came within inches of crashing into Willy in the hall. She barely noticed him. Her eyes were too flooded with tears for her to be able to see much of anything!

"Nikki, wait, I've gotta . . ." Willy scowled, staring at the corner around which his sister swiftly disappeared. He glanced inside the study.

Pete looked madder than when Brian had told him about his wife. He was staring at Kurt as though he expected the dark-haired man to reach out and throttle him. As for Kurt, well, his jaw was harder than a mound of granite, the imprint of Nikki's hand standing out in vibrant red on his suntanned cheek.

Willy gulped and backed slowly into the hall, praying he hadn't been noticed. If the two men were about to come to blows, he didn't want to be around when it happened. He doubted either noticed when he eased the study door closed.

Kurt reached up and ran a palm down his stinging cheek. His steely gaze never left Pete. "You have something to say, say it now. I'll be gone come morning."

"You move even a toenail off this ranch—

tomorrow or any other day—and I'll hunt you down like the rabid dog you are!"

A lazy grin pulled at Kurt's lips. "Oh, really? And what are you going to do when you find me? *If* you find me. Remember, it took Nicole six years. And *I* taught *her* how to track."

Pete's fingers curled around a pen as if it were a dagger. He was half in, half out of the chair, leaning threateningly across the desk. His cheeks flooded with fury. "Oh, I'll find you, all right. And when I do, I'll blow your arrogant head off."

"Aim improved that much, Dennison?"

Pete made to clamber across the desk. Kurt's next words stopped him.

"I don't appreciate being slapped once in a day. I'd get downright testy if you made it twice." His eyes slitted dangerously. There was enough warning in his glare for Pete to ease slowly back into his chair.

"You're not leaving," Pete repeated, his voice still tinged with fury. "Not until I find out if my sister's carrying another one of your bastards."

This time Kurt was brought up out of his chair—like a pouncing wildcat. Balling his fists, he rested the tight white knuckles on the desk and leaned angrily across it. "Don't you *ever* refer to my daughter that way again, Dennison." He brought his hand out, the fingers twisting in Pete's collar. A flick of the wrist and their noses were touching. "Do it again and I'll bury my fist halfway down your throat—for starters."

Pete slammed into the chair when Kurt shoved him away as if Pete were a piece of dirt he didn't want soiling his hands. He recovered quickly. "Oh, you're admitting to Beth these days, are you, Frazier? Real big of you." His fist slammed the desktop. "Isn't it a little late? Where were you six years ago when Nikki needed you, huh? Where were you then?"

"I didn't know!" Kurt spun on his heel and headed

for the door.

"Because you weren't here," Pete snarled. "If you'd stuck it out, maybe you'd have found out. But you didn't. You took what you wanted from my sister, then left." He shook his head, a sneer of disgust puckering his lips. "Nikki was right. You wouldn't know *decency* if it smacked you in the face."

Kurt stood stock still, then turned and crossed again to the chair in front of the desk. "Things would have been different if I'd known about Beth. I would have . . ." He fell abruptly silent. What would he have done? he wondered. He was accused of killing his daughter's grandfather. If he'd stayed, he'd be dead right now. Ironically, the only thing keeping the noose at bay was the amount of time he'd been away. Time that had dulled some of his memories, and most of his anger—except where Nicole was concerned.

Pete watched each emotion flicker across Kurt's face. The confusion shimmering in his steely eyes grabbed at his heart. It shouldn't have, by all rights, but it did. His own anger dissolved.

"I don't want Nikki going on the drive tomorrow," he said, dragging his fingers through his short, thinning brown hair. "If someone's trying to kill her, the trail would give whoever it is the perfect chance to get the job done right. I won't risk it."

"And what do you propose *I* do about that?" Kurt gave a dry chuckle. It didn't help to remember the results of his last "talk" with Nicole Dennison. His gaze strayed to the gold rug. His gut tightened. Letting out his breath in a long sigh, he shrugged. "She won't listen to me, if that's what you're thinking. After today, I doubt she'll even *talk* to me."

Pete rested his elbows on the desk, clasped his hands tight, and pillowed his chin on entwined knuckles. "Don't talk to her. Don't say a word to her." One narrow shoulder lifted and fell. "I know

I'll live to regret this, but I want you to do whatever it takes to make sure she doesn't leave with us tomorrow."

Kurt's jaw tightened. "Get one of the other guys to do it."

Pete shook his head. "Un-uh. We're already short half a dozen men. As it is, it's going to take every last one of them to drive the herd. The cattle are already half starved from this damn drought. The herd's bound to get restless once we hit the trail. I could use your help, no lying there, but since I didn't plan on you going in the first place, you're expendable. I can't say that for any of the other men . . . and even if I could, they'd never be able to handle Nikki when she's mad. She'd either kill them, or have them wrapped around her little finger inside of an hour. She can't do that with you."

"Is that the only reason you're asking me?"

"No." Weighing his words carefully, he added, "It might interest you to know that the only reason you aren't warming a jail cell right now is because *I* convinced Hardy not to arrest you. *I* convinced him there wasn't enough proof."

Thick raven brows shot high on Kurt's forehead. "Now why would you do a thing like that, Dennison?"

"I don't really know," Pete said. "But I'm not the only one with doubts. Mike has his share. So does Bri. We know Pop trusted you, respected you. You must have earned that trust somehow. For some reason, he put a lot of stock in you. I'd always thought the feeling was mutual." He paused when Kurt didn't respond. "If ever there was a time I prayed my father's trust was well-founded, it's now. Will you do it?"

"She'll follow you the first chance she gets."

"Not if you don't let her."

Steel gray clashed with determined blue. "She won't like it."

"I don't care what she likes, so long as she lives long enough to be angry." Pete sighed, twirling a pen end to end. "I don't know who's trying to kill her, Kurt, but I do know I can't take the chance of posting her murderer as her guard."

"So you trust me not to kill her?" Kurt snickered dryly.

"At least you have a vested interest here—your daughter and her mother. Because of that, I know you'll take good care of Nikki and Beth while I'm gone. Again, will you do it?"

Kurt sucked in a long, slow breath. He didn't answer Pete right away, but there was never a doubt in his mind as to what he would do.

Chapter Seventeen

For the first time in months, Nikki woke to the sound of rain pattering on the rooftop. The fresh scent wafted in through the window, which had been propped open with a gnarled tree branch. The steady drizzle dampened the fluttering curtains and puddled on the hardwood floor, but Nikki reasoned that the mess was worth it. The cool breeze had felt too wonderful the previous night to shut out.

Dawn would be breaking over the horizon in less than an hour. For now there was only the cool October breeze, the gentle sound of rain, and the rumble of the waking house below, echoing up through the slats in the floorboards.

She dressed quickly, then used an old sheet to mop up the mess the rain had made. She knocked the tree limb out of the open window, and it dropped, splashing in the mud outside as she lowered the casing. Drizzle streamed down the outside of the glass in icy rivulets. Nikki found herself anxious to get outside. It had been a long time since she'd felt brisk raindrops splattering against her face, dampening her head and shoulders.

Cracked leather chaps rustled around her legs as she tucked the damp sheet under her arm and grabbed her gauntlets from atop the bureau. Settling her hat on her head, she reached for the doorknob.

It rattled, but didn't turn. Again. Nothing. The lazy yawn that had been building in her throat vanished like dew under a broiling summer sun.

"Damn, damn, *damn!*" She slammed the balled-up sheet to the floor, where it lodged between the door and her bureau. Using both hands, she wrenched on the knob. It jiggled, but refused to budge.

"Dammit!" she yelled at the top of her lungs, the word punctuated by her fist slamming into the wood above the knob. "Open it! Do you hear me? I said *open this door!*"

Using both fists, she pounded again. Nothing. Pressing her ear to the door, she found the hallway beyond quiet. The sounds floating up through the floorboards had stopped. Muffled footsteps were followed by the low rumble of voices. Somewhere, a door slammed.

Cursing, she ran to the window and shoved the casing up. Cold rain sprinkled her face as, relieved, she caught sight of her brothers, about to round the corner of the house.

"Pete! Mike! Willy! Up here!" she called, waving a hand over her head to attract their attention. Her other hand gripped the window frame, steadying her so she wouldn't tumble onto the wet earth two stories below. It was a straight, deadly drop.

Willy continued around the house, a bit too quickly, she thought. Mike and Pete stopped, conferred, and turned. Slowly. Cautiously. Nikki's gut hardened when she saw their faces; both set for a confrontation.

"Pete?" she asked suspiciously, her stomach fluttering. "You aren't planning to go without me, are you?" Her gaze shifted. "Mike? You wouldn't let him leave me behind, would you? *Would you?!*"

"Told you she was going to be mad," Mike

informed his brother, while sending Nikki a weak smile and a shrug.

"Mad!" she screeched as the full impact of what was going on began to sink in. "If what I think is happening *is happening*, then *mad* doesn't even begin to cover it. This isn't funny! Now get up here and unlock my door!"

Pete took off his hat, smoothed back his rain-slickened hair, and glanced up at Nikki. He settled the hat back on his head. "Now, Nikki, don't get all riled up. When you calm down you'll see that what we're doing is for your own good."

"My own—" Her lips pinched with anger, the fingers clutching the window frame tightened. "Peter Aaron Dennison, you unlock my door this instant!"

"Afraid I can't do that, Nikki."

Her jaw hardened. "Wrong. You can and you will. *Now!*"

When Pete merely shook his head, she fixed her angry glare on Mike. His feet shuffled in dirt that was quickly turning to mud. "Sorry, Sis. Got my orders."

"Orders? *Orders!* I'll give you orders you little . . . !"

Nikki was half-in, half-out of the window. Her legs straddled the sill; no easy task since she needed one hand to keep the window from crashing down on her head. Her position was precarious, yet neither man below looked eager to catch her if she fell . . . if only for fear she would live through the drop and vent her wrath on them.

She sent an angry glare down her nose. "If you don't unlock this door, and I mean *now*, I'll jump. I swear it. Do either of you want my death on your conscience?"

"Nikki, I couldn't unlock it even if I wanted to," Pete argued, his hands spread wide. "I don't have the key."

That gave her a moment's pause. "Mike?" He shook his head, lifting empty hands. "Willy?" she gulped, her bravado dwindling. "Then who—?"

Her answer came in the form of strong, rough hands. They wrapped around her waist and dragged her into the room. It was all Nikki could do to keep the window from falling on her skull, let alone fight the firm chest pressing into her back.

The second her feet hit the floor, the window came down. The sound of splintering wood shot through the air as Nikki was spun roughly around to face him. One strong arm was wrapped around her waist—a bit tighter than was necessary—and the front of her body pressed intimately against his side. It galled her to think he could pin her so easily, and still have one hand to spare. Her furious gaze swept up, clashing with laughing gray.

"Any questions?" Kurt asked with a lightness that made her want to smack him good. He didn't wait for an answer, but tugged her back to the window and raised the pane with one hand. "You two go ahead. I'll take care of everything from here."

Nikki's angry response drowned out her brother's reply. "No! Pete! Mike! Don't leave me with him!" she yelled. She twisted until her back was brought up hard against his firm chest, and was just in time to see her brothers disappear around the corner where Willy had vanished just moments before.

"I don't believe this," she sputtered as, wiggling, she turned back to Kurt.

He sent her a sarcastic glance. "What? That they'd leave you behind, or that they'd leave you with me?"

"Both. Last time I saw Pete he was itching to kill you."

"Could say the same about yourself, Nicole. Sorry you didn't get the chance?"

"Sorry doesn't even begin to cover it," she snapped.

Curling her hands into tight fists, Nikki cushioned them atop his solid shoulder and arched her back. She gave a brutal shove, trying to break the circle of his embrace. Instead, she managed only to grind their hips provocatively together. At the first bolt of awareness to course through her, her hands dropped. She settled for glaring at him, hoping the white-hot anger in her eyes would intimidate him into releasing her. He didn't even flinch.

"It won't work, you know," she informed him through clenched teeth. Her back was still slightly arched, as though to put as much distance between them as she could. "You can't watch me twenty-four hours a day. I *will* get away from you. Or I'll kill you. With any luck I'll manage both."

Kurt's eyes sparkled as his gaze dipped to her heaving breasts. A wicked grin tugged at his lips as he brushed his free palm down his smooth-shaven jaw. "Twenty-four hours a day? That wouldn't happen to be an invitation by any chance?"

"What it is is a promise," Nikki growled, ignoring his sarcasm, "a statement of fact. You have to sleep sometime, buster, and the first time you do, I'll be gone."

A dry chuckle rumbled in his throat as the roughened tip of his thumb grazed her lips. Nikki almost jumped out of her skin. She tried to ignore the way her heart skipped, but she couldn't. Not when the touch was combined with the husky promise in his voice. "Not if I'm with you twenty-four hours a day, Nicole. The very last thing I think about when I'm near you is sleep—*if* you get my meaning."

"I'm sure the whole Dakota Territory got your meaning."

With an indignant jerk, Nikki pulled away from him. Rubbing her bruised arm, she backed to the window and glanced over her shoulder, out the wet pane. The rain was coming down hard. The large drops pounded against the glass, distorting the view. A jagged bolt of lightning cut a path from the clouds like a snapping whip. The thunder to follow crashed deafeningly across the range, vibrating up from the floor beneath her feet.

"Where's Beth?" she gasped, at the same time spinning to face him.

He scowled, the gray eyes lit with sudden caution. "Still sleeping. Why?"

"Why?!" she cried, racing for the door only to find it locked. She punched it with her fist and glared at Kurt over her shoulder. "Because she's afraid of thunder, that's why!" Her face drained white and her eyes widened as another clap of thunder reverberated through the room. *"And you locked my door!* God, she couldn't have gotten to me if she tried. Open it, Kurt. Hurry!"

Kurt didn't waste a second. Before she could draw a breath he had the door flung wide, his long strides spanning the corridor. The door crashed into the wall and he was immediately swallowed up by the shadows of Beth's room.

Nikki lost her hat in the hall, but didn't stop to retrieve it. She was so close on Kurt's heels that she slammed into his back when he stopped beside her daughter's bed. His hand shot out to steady her. Without thinking, Nikki clung to it as her gaze roved over the rumpled sheets. The bed was empty.

Another clap of thunder drowned out Nikki's strangled gasp. Her gaze lifted and locked with Kurt's. His features were set with alarm. To see that emotion etched so plainly on his face made her heart lurch. Her fingers curled into his sleeve.

"Where would she go?" he demanded, his voice strained with urgency. His jaw was tense and his grip, as he covered her hand with his, tightened until it was unbearably firm.

Nikki noticed the pain as her ears alerted her to a

soft, plaintive whimper. Her gaze shifted to the bed. Lower.

Kurt let her go, dropping hard on his knees as the room was lit by a bolt of lightning. Thunder crashed around them.

Kurt's muffled voice reached her as the thunder faded. She almost wept with relief when he stood, a frightened Beth in his arms, clinging to his neck as she sobbed into his shoulder. For a split second Nikki remembered another time, a tornado instead of thunder, and her heart tightened. Her fingers trembled as she reached out and hesitantly stroked her daughter's rumpled head.

Her arms ached to enfold Beth in the safety of her embrace, yet she found a surprising pleasure in watching father and daughter cling to each other. Although she wanted to desperately, Nikki couldn't bring herself to tear Beth from Kurt's arms.

Kurt shifted, then lowered them both to the bed. The mattress creaked and sagged with his weight. He rocked her back and forth, whispering reassurances against her soft raven hair. A crash of thunder cut the air, and his arms protectively hugged the wiggling body. He held her close, as though trying to melt her tiny body into his, as though he never wanted to let her go.

Over the quivering shoulder, Kurt's head lifted. His gaze met Nikki's and held. Her breath caught when she saw the raw emotion in his eyes. Concern and helplessness glistened there in equal proportions, as though the crying child in his arms had somehow split his soul wide open, unmanned him, left him defenseless and confused.

Despite logic, Nikki softened. Seeing him cradle Beth, hearing his tender words as the sobs receded under his paternal touch, was too much for her. The wall of vengeance she had constructed, and clung to for dear life, was blown to ashes by the vulnerability reflected in Kurt's eyes.

She lowered herself to her knees and encircled father and daughter with her arms. Kurt's hard, vibrant flesh was a strong contrast to her daughter's giving curves. Nikki drank deeply of both, as though her life depended on drawing the best from father and child.

Clinging to each other, they saw the storm through.

Nikki didn't remember falling asleep. All she knew was that one minute she was wide awake, the next her cheek was being cushioned by Kurt's rock-hard thigh. The sound of Beth's shallow breathing mixed sweetly with the rain pattering against the window.

She rubbed the sleep from her eyes and slowly lifted her head from the warmth of Kurt's leg. Glancing up, she saw he had moved backward. His shoulders were propped against the wall beside the bed, his back curved awkwardly to make his chest a more even pillow for the child cradled protectively against it.

Nikki clenched her fist and fought an unreasonable urge to smooth back the tempting wisp of black that curled over his sun-bronzed forehead. Swallowing hard, her gaze lowered.

Like her father, Beth slept soundly, a water-wrinkled thumb hanging droopily from her mouth. Her gentle snores were timed to coincide with each of Kurt's shallow breaths.

Masculine fingers twitched over the shock of black curls cascading down a slender back as Nikki moved cautiously away. She caught the movement from the corner of her eye and stopped. Her breath caught as she waited for the fringe of sooty lashes to sweep up. Instead his chin sleepily nuzzled the small head.

Releasing her breath in a long, slow hiss, she straightened. The chaps crinkled around her legs as she inched toward the door. Only the rain trickling down the glass saw her creep stealthily into the hall. She left the door ajar, afraid the click of the lock would awaken Kurt and she would have to forfeit her escape.

Her pace increased once she reached the hall. She didn't break stride as she plucked up her hat from the floor and plopped it onto her head.

Adrenaline born of victory pumped through her veins as she raced down the stairs and out of the house. She ran through the deserted yard, toward the barn. Her boots squished in the mud. The sound was countered by the heavy rain still pelting the ground. The cool drops felt liberating. She rubbed the refreshing moisture into her skin.

Like the yard, the barn was deserted. Except for Stetson, the other horses had been taken by her brothers. Nikki felt a split second of surprise that they'd chance leaving her favorite mount behind, then decided to be thankful as she raced down the hay-strewn center corridor.

The stallion snorted a greeting as she led him through the half-door and into the corridor. Her feet crunched over the hay as she retrieved the only saddle remaining. She flung the heavy saddle onto the horse's back and was in the process of working the cinch tight when she heard the barn door open behind her.

Nikki froze, her mind racing as she tried to remember who, besides Dolores and a few of the older ranch hands, had remained on the ranch. The only person who came to mind was Kurt Frazier. A pang of dread sliced through her as her worst suspicions were confirmed.

"Going somewhere?"

She turned to find him leaning against the

doorframe. A damp shirt clung to his muscular shoulders. His hair glistened wetly around his angrily set face. The furious glint in his eyes, and the way he clenched and unclenched his fists, told Nikki he was madder than a bull caught in a patch of bumblebees.

"Yes," she answered tightly, turning her attention back to the cinch. "As a matter of fact, I have a trail drive to get to and I'm already late."

Although she hadn't heard his approach, Nikki wasn't surprised to feel his large hand close over her shoulder.

He tugged her a safe distance from the horse and spun her around. "You're not going, Nicole. When are you going to figure that out?"

Her jaw hardened as she returned his gaze measure for intimidating measure. "You're wrong. I don't care how I get there, or when, but I'm going on that drive. I will not let you decide where I go or do not go. You have no control over me, Kurt. When are *you* going to figure *that* out?"

His lips curled in an arrogant grin. "Already done—long since—but it doesn't change a thing. Pete asked me to keep you here and *here* is where you're staying. Like it or not."

"Pete?!" Her eyes darkened. "He wouldn't dare." *Would he?* Kurt's expression said Pete most certainly had dared. "He had no right. I can take care of myse—Eeek!—What are you doing?"

A firm shoulder smashed into her stomach as Kurt crouched, tossing her up and over his shoulder as if she were a sack of potatoes.

"Put . . . me . . . down!" The air whooshed from her lungs with each long, purposeful stride that carried them to the barn door, which Kurt opened with a well-placed kick. Her ribs felt like they were going to snap. She beat on his broad back and hips with her fists. Trying to flail her feet was useless, his grip around her knees was much too tight.

Only once was she lucky enough to get in a sound blow, managing to box his ear. His grunt of surprise was a hollow victory since his retaliation took the form of a sharp slap to her wiggling bottom.

"Stop struggling," he growled over his shoulder to the head that bobbed upside-down at his waist. "The only good it'll do will be to get me angry. What I just gave you was a tap. How'd you like to know what it feels like when I *really* slap back?"

Nikki hesitated. She didn't think he'd make good on the threat, but she wasn't sure. She hadn't seen Kurt angry enough times to know just how far she could push him—and she didn't want to find out now, when no one was around to help her if he got violent. Her bottom, still stinging from his "tap," was the deciding factor in her rethinking her strategy.

Pursing her lips, she let her hands dangle limply over her head and feigned resignation. To pacify her outrage at such humiliating treatment, she toyed with various ways she could kill him. Slowly. Torturously. That lifted her spirits somewhat.

Her hat had fallen to the ground. The rain now beat against her scalp in cold, relentless drops. It didn't feel good anymore, she decided. The tip of her braid dragged across the mud.

Kurt's boots clomped over the porch. He opened the house door in the same manner he had opened the barn. The door crashed against the wall and slammed shut on the rebound. By that time Kurt was already halfway up the stairs.

"Whachya doing, Kurt?" Beth asked sweetly. She stood framed in her doorway, her too-big white nightgown puffed around her legs as she rubbed the sleep from her eyes. Her mouth opened for a gigantic yawn, which was promptly stifled with her fist. "Why're you carrying Momma like that?" Scowling, she tilted her head from side to side, as though trying to look Nikki in the eye. "Can't she walk?"

"She can walk just fine, honey. It's where she's walking *to* that we're arguing about."

Out of respect for Beth, Kurt did not kick Nikki's door open. Instead, he hunched down and turned the knob with his hand. So what if it was thrown open with a bit more force than was needed? He deposited Nikki in the middle of the room.

The blood rushed from her head in a dizzying surge that made her reach for the bedpost in order to keep herself from keeling over. Her gaze met Kurt's and her fury mounted as she watched his steely eyes sharpen with cocky self-assurance.

Without a word to her, he turned to Beth, who was watching the adults curiously from the doorway. "All right, kitten, what say you and I go downstairs and rustle up some breakfast? I'm hungry enough to eat the—" He stopped abruptly and frowned.

Beth grinned and bluntly finished the off-color saying for him, "behind out of a dead skunk."

"Beth!" Nikki gasped.

Kurt's incredulous look regarded his giggling daughter, then a proud grin turned his lips. "Something like that. You ready to eat yet?"

"Yeah!" Beth nodded eagerly, her gaze straying past him. "Is Momma coming?"

"Nope." He moved to Beth and, planting a large hand between her shoulders, ushered the child into the hall. She dragged her small feet, reluctant to leave her mother behind. Guessing the reason behind her hesitation, he added, "Momma's tired. We'll lock her door behind us, just to make sure she gets a good rest."

"Kurt," Nikki growled when the door started to

swing shut. "Don't you dare lock me in here again. Kurt!"

Kurt stuck his dark head back inside and sent Nikki a bright grin.

Did Mike teach him how to do that? she wondered.

"Hungry, Nicole?" he asked. "I'll bring you back some breakfast if you want. Of course, you'll have to promise to behave yourself, first."

I would as soon make a pact with the devil, Nikki thought. She sent him an exaggerated smile, her narrowed eyes spitting angry blue fire. "I'd rather die, thank you very much," she replied.

He shrugged. The door inched closed. "Suit yourself. You're bound to get hungry sooner or later. Let me know when you do. I'm sure we can arrange *some* sort of deal."

"That's blackmail!" she gasped, stepping toward the door. Her fingers itched to wrap around his arrogant throat, and she thought that if she got the chance, she just might let them.

"Maybe, but it'll keep you alive," his gaze hardened, "which is more than you'd be if you went on that trail drive. Now, when you're ready to give me your word that you'll stay behind like a good girl, I'll feed you and let you out. Until then," he grinned, "get used to this room. You won't be leaving it."

"I'll throw myself out the window," she warned angrily.

His insolent grin broadened into another breathtaking smile. "Feel free. Just don't expect me to catch you. Push you, maybe. Keep aggravating me, that's a definite possibility." His lids lowered to half mast as he raked her head to toe. "Lady, if you're stupid enough to go out that window, you deserve what you get." His shoulders rose and fell. "I'll decide whether or not to patch you up when I find you face down in the mud. But I wouldn't count on my help. Any patience I ever had where you're concerned burned off a long time ago."

The door slammed shut, cutting off Nikki's angry outburst. Kurt was halfway down the stairs, with Beth's hand tucked in his own, when he heard something crash into the door. Whatever it was, it shattered to splinters, then rained to the floor.

"Your mother has one heck of a temper," he said as they reached the downstairs hall. "She always throw things like that?"

Beth nodded seriously. "Last year she broke the vase Uncle Pete gave her for Christmas. He told her she couldn't ride Stetson anymore because he was getting too wild. Momma said she'd do what she wanted, and hit him upside the head with the vase to prove it."

Kurt grinned. He couldn't imagine proper little Nicole Dennison giving in to such raw emotion. But he could see Nikki doing it. All that and more.

Tipping his head back, he laughed. The deep, pleasant, husky sound floated up the stairwell, drifting under the door to curl up Nikki's spine. She'd been in the process of cleaning up the broken porcelain pitcher, the sharp shards of which were now strewn all over her floor. At the sound of Kurt's laughter, she threw the pieces back into the corner.

Her gaze shifted to the window. No escape route there, no matter what she'd threatened. If the fall didn't kill her outright, it would injure her. What good would she be on the drive with two broken legs—or worse? No, she'd have to think of another way out of the room, out of the house, and away from Kurt Frazier. A way that would not put her in slings and bandages.

Pursing her lips, she tapped her finger against them and crossed to the window. The pane was foggy, impossible to see through. No immediate plan sprang to mind, but she was sure that, given time, she'd think of something. And she had no doubt Kurt would give her plenty of time to think. He hadn't looked ready to unlock her door any time in the near future.

"Oh, shush up!" she spat at her grumbling stomach. With a sigh, she flung herself onto the bed and started to plan.

Chapter Eighteen

"Nicole?" *Knock, knock, knock.* "Nicole, are you awake?" Pause. *Bang, bang.* Kurt's voice lowered. It was threaded with concern, and more than a little fury. "Are you in there?" *Pound, pound, pound!* "So help me God, Nicole, if you went out that window I swear I'll . . ."

He fumbled in his pocket and yanked out the key. It slipped into the lock. The metallic click of tumblers smoothly turning in place echoed down the eerily silent hall.

Kurt's heart throbbed as he pictured Nikki's lifeless body crumpled and sprawled in the mud two stories below. He told himself not to be concerned. He told himself that if she had done as he suspected, she'd gotten what she deserved. But if that was the case, then why did his mouth feel like bone-thirsty dirt in a dry Texas desert? Why did his heart slam against his ribs like it was threatening to break free? Why did his palms turn suddenly moist and shaky?

He hated the feeling that ate at his gut, the feeling that only *she* was able to create. His jaw hardened to granite and he made a mental vow to kill the stubborn little witch himself—if the fall hadn't already stolen the pleasure from him.

When the key turned as far as it could, he gave the

door a shove and took a step forward. But the door didn't open. In fact, it didn't budge. Stormy realization dawned.

Kurt stopped short, his nose coming treacherously close to kissing solid pine. Blinking stupidly, he glared at the door as though the fierceness of his gaze could send it crashing to the floor in shards of broken wood. Had any innocent bystanders been watching, they would have been surprised when the door didn't do exactly that.

But no one saw him. No one witnessed the dangerous glint in his eyes, or the muscle of anger throbbing in his jaw. No one saw his powerful fingers clench and unclench at his sides, in time with each sharp breath he took. The key bit into his tender palm, cutting grooves into his skin. He barely noticed.

His fist collided with the door with enough force to make the wood groan, and Kurt wince. White-hot pain exploded in his knuckles. He neither ignored it nor gave into it. Instead, he let it fuel his anger as if he were a vulture feeding on its half-dead prey. He pounded a second time. A third. His fist lifted for the fourth assault when a fledgling giggle floated from the other side of the thick panel. It tickled his ears; lightly muffled, devilishly mocking.

Any relief he might have felt at knowing Nikki was safe was lost to the wave of anger that splashed over him. "Open this door or so help me I'll break it down!" The command was punctuated with another thundering blow. "Did you hear me, Nicole?" he stormed. "I said—"

"'Open this door or so help me I'll break it down,'" Nikki mimicked from inside. The laughter was gone, replaced by guarded indifference. "I heard you just fine, Kurt."

Kurt's fingers itched to wrap around her long, creamy, stubborn throat. "Then do it!" he bellowed.

His fist dropped to his side, but stayed clenched. What had she done to the door?!

"Sorry, no can do," a soft voice sighed. "Somehow the thunder must have caused my bureau to slide in front of the door and..."—heavy, *heavy* sigh—"I can't seem to budge it. I've been trying half the day, but it just won't move."

"The thunder stopped at least an hour before I threw you in there, Nikki," he stormed, lips tight. *I called her Nikki,* he realized absently, then, *Of course I did. She's acting like a spoiled little brat. She's acting like "Nikki"!*

"Did it? Hmmm, I hadn't noticed."

"Open the door, Nikki."

"Not on your life, Kurt."

"You'll starve."

"That's my problem, isn't it?"

"You're being childish. What am I going to tell Beth?"

"The truth leaps to mind."

Kurt snarled at the door. "I see. You want me to tell a five-year-old child that her mother is having a fit of temper—exactly what that same mother tells her daughter *not* to do—and won't leave her room. Somehow, I don't think she'll understand." As he talked, his hand reached out and wrapped around the doorknob. It was a wonder the thing didn't snap off under the pressure of his grip.

"Tell her I'm sick. Tell her I'm tired. Honestly, I don't give a hoot what you tell her, Kurt. I'm not leaving this room. Not unless it's to go on the trail drive."

Kurt's fist slammed into the door. The collision added to the pain already throbbing in his fingers. "What is wrong with you? When are you going to get it through your thick little skull that *someone is trying to kill you?!*"

He heard her impatient snort over the click of her

boot heels pacing the floor. "About the same time you get it through *your* thick little skull that *I already know that!* And *I don't care*. I'm not going to rearrange my life for this killer! I'm not going to hide in corners and jump at shadows!"

"Well, you had better start wanting to!" he raged at the barrier between them. Like Nikki was doing inside her room, Kurt started pacing the hall. But instead of providing an outlet for his fury, the sharp, rhythmic steps only fed it.

What's wrong with her? he raged. Why didn't she react to danger the way any other woman would? With fear. With caution. *That* would be normal. This abundant lack of concern was *not normal*—and Kurt didn't have a clue how to deal with it.

He jammed his hands in his pocket and stalked back to the door, stopping in front of it and glowering at the inanimate wood as though expecting it to gaze hatefully back. "This isn't a joke, Nikki," he growled menacingly, "and it isn't a game. Whoever is doing this might be successful next time."

"Let him try. He hasn't done too great a job so far, and chances are he won't improve."

"Not only is your logic lacking—*severely*—but you're taking a pretty big risk here. A stupid one. Whoever this killer is, he's getting desperate. The last two attempts prove that."

"My risk to take, don't you think?"

His voice lowered to a gravelly purr. "No, I don't. What *I* think is that you've got to be the biggest fool I've ever met. They don't need you on the drive, Nikki. They wouldn't have gone without you if they did."

"Not *on* the drive," she corrected tersely. Her rigid tone said he'd hit a weak spot. The aggravation lacing her words made him smile. *"After* the drive. It's my job to see the cattle get in the proper pens without getting mixed with other herds. Then *I* arrange the final sales. Pete can do it," she paused proudly, "but I can do it better."

"You can't do anything if you're dead."

"I can't do anything locked in my room."

Kurt's brows drew down in a sardonic scowl. Had he ever loved this stubborn-to-the-point-of-stupid woman? he wondered. No, it wasn't possible. He had better sense than that. Or did he?

Kurt snatched some consolation from the fact that his original attraction to Nicole Dennison had struck when he was young and senseless. He would never have fallen in love with such a headstrong, foolish girl. He preferred common sense and wisdom to stubborn recklessness. He was almost sure of it. Yet his love for "Nicole" was years strong, his attraction to "Nikki" as undeniable as it was exasperating.

Why wouldn't the woman listen to reason?!

Kurt opened his mouth, then snapped it shut again. Talking sense to Nikki when her mind was set was like talking to wool. He resumed pacing. "What happens to Beth when you're dead? How do you think she'll feel when she finds out her mother died because she refused to take precautions—even though she knew someone was hell-bent on killing her?"

"How can I take precautions when I'm locked in my room? I've told you before I can take care of myself, but you won't give me a chance to prove it."

"You don't have to! What do you think *I'm* here for?"

"To hang for killing my father," was the immediate, angry response.

Dead silence. Silence so electric it crackled like sizzling bolts of lightning.

"When you're ready to talk sense, call me and I'll bring you food. Until then, you can eat your pride."

Kurt relocked the door, almost breaking the key off

in the lock when he wrenched it free. He spun on his heel and stomped down the hall. The house echoed with the staccato click of his boot heels as he stalked through the halls.

By the next morning, Nikki was hungry. By the next afternoon, she was famished. She'd taken Kurt's advice about eating her pride and came up wanting. Now she wanted food. Real food. *A lot* of food!

The smell of Kurt and Beth's breakfast still lingered in the air. Each waft of the tantalizing aroma triggered her salivary glands and made her stomach grumble and ache with emptiness.

Nikki refused to give in to it. She told herself she was stronger than that. That food should not, *would* not, be her sole reason for capitulating to Kurt's dictates. She was positive that if she told herself this enough times she was bound to believe it.

She spent the remainder of the day in restless agitation. She paced, she sat, she made the bed and unmade the bed. She swept the floor, dusted the bureau with an old petticoat, and stared out the window. She found a dog-eared western about Billy the Kid buried in the dust under her bed and read it— four times. She read the short references to food slowly, repeatedly, savoring each delectable word until her mouth watered and her stomach growled.

When she was busy, she thought of food. When she sat and did nothing, she thought of food. She imagined herself cooking every tidbit of Christmas dinner, then eating each tender morsel while Kurt looked hungrily on. Of course, in her dreams she never gave him a crumb.

Everything from Dolores's light, flaky apple cobbler to her mouth-wateringly fresh cornbread skittered through her mind. She hated the taste of steamed carrots, but right now she would have given her horse for one tender, juicy root.

She did fine until the sun started to set. That's when the weakness set in. She ignored it. It got worse. A half an hour after she'd lit the lamp on her bedside table she'd noticed her knees were trembling. Then her hands. Soon she was trembling all over and she felt as weak as a kitten. If she didn't eat soon, she knew she would faint. The ultimate humiliation!

Nikki hated herself with each inch of the floor she weakly covered as she shoved the bureau back into place. She despised the physical weaknesses that forced her to admit defeat.

The bureau scraped across the hardwood floor, the sound grating on her nerves like the clap of a stick whacking against the slats of a fence. By the time it was in position, her skin was slick with a layer of perspiration that made the bodice of her dress cling provocatively to her heaving breasts. The silver curls plastered to her sweat-beaded brow were dark with moisture.

After she ate, she told herself, she wanted a bath. Then, she wanted to kill Kurt Frazier, very, *very* slowly. Perferably with her bare hands.

Nikki reached up to bang on the door and noticed how badly her fingers were shaking. Her knees felt like liquid. Her mouth opened, but remained silent. Her hand halted in midair.

Beth's voice echoed sweetly beneath the door. "In the hall? We're eating in the hall? I don't think Momma will like it."

"I don't think Momma can do anything about it. Have a seat, kitten."

The sound of bodies settling down in front of the door was followed by the sound of a fork clattering against a plate. The succulent smell of roast duck, baked apples, and fresh bread wafted beneath the one-and-a-half-inch crack beneath the door.

Nikki groaned. She mumbled a curse under her

breath as her hand dropped to her side. Only an idiot, or a child, wouldn't know what Kurt was doing. Beth was a child, but Nikki was no idiot.

"Hmmm, this is good, Kurt. Better than Uncle Pete makes. He always burns the carrots, but yours are nice and soft."

Kurt? *Kurt* had cooked dinner? Where was Dolores? At her cousin's, Nikki remembered belatedly. Dolores had asked for time off during the trail drive to visit her sick cousin in Missouri. She was supposed to bring Beth with her. Of course, the Dennisons had agreed. Dally gave a lot to the family, but she rarely asked for much in return. Little was denied her when she did.

Nikki's spirits sank. So much for any plans of escape that included the housekeeper's help!

"The gravy's good, too. Better than Dally's."

"Want more, kitten?" He raised his voice as he added, "There's plenty."

Nikki turned and leaned heavily against the door. She slid her back down the thick panel until her bottom slapped the floor. Her stomach felt as big and as empty as the Grand Canyon. Her throat was as dry as a patch of prairie grass scorched by a broiling summer sun.

They ate for what seemed like hours. Nikki found herself chewing and swallowing with them. When they drank, she did that, too. The only difference was that, where they were slaking their body's cravings, she was increasing her own.

"That was great, Kurt. What's for dessert?"

Dessert? Nikki swallowed hard. She didn't think she could stand listening to them eat dessert, let alone having to smell the tantalizing scent slipping under her door. But she doubted Kurt would give her a choice.

"Biscuits with some of Dally's peach jam." *Oh,*

God, not peach jam. Not her favorite peach jam!
"Sound good?"

"Hmmm!" Beth's fork clattered to the plate. Nikki's stomach echoed agreement. It sounded heavenly, but then, she thought, fried dirt would sound heavenly right about now.

"All right, kitten. Pass your plate over and you can finish your bread while I run downstairs and fetch dessert."

"Can I have two biscuits?" Beth asked shyly.

"You can have *three* if you want." Again he raised his voice. "Why not? Nobody else is eating them—and they sure are good."

Beth giggled when Kurt mumbled something Nikki couldn't hear under his breath. His footsteps receded down the hall.

Nikki was on her knees, facing the door in an instant. Her heart hammered and her mouth watered when she thought about what she was doing. Starvation had put her conscience on a diet; it was excruciatingly light.

"Beth," she hissed, her face pressed against the slat between door and frame. "Beth, can you hear me?"

"Momma?"

"Yes, sweetheart, it's Momma. Beth, do you still have that piece of bread?" *Please, God, don't let this be the one time she eats all her bread. Not tonight!* Nikki's voice lowered with impatience. "Beth? Do you?"

"Yeees," came the small, hesitant reply.

"Good. Pass it under the door, sweetheart. Momma will help you finish it so Kurt doesn't get angry and eat all the biscuits himself. Just pass it under the door."

"But you always say I have to eat all my—"

"I know what I say, *dear*," she snapped, "But tonight's different." She ground her teeth. "Beth, just pass me the bread. *Please.* I promise I won't be angry."

"Kurt won't like it."

And since when do you care what Kurt does or does not like? Nikki thought. It didn't matter. Food was the only thing that mattered right now. She softened her voice to a coaxing purr. "We won't tell him, sweetheart. It'll be our little secret."

"Well . . ." she said, weighing the punishment of Kurt finding out against the urge to obey her mother.

The slab of bread was hesitantly shoved beneath the door. It grazed the top, causing flaky crumbs to speckle the floor.

"Thank you, honey," Nikki murmured as she grabbed the bread, and at the same time pressed as many crumbs as she could against her index finger. The tender morsels were immediately licked away. She wrinkled her nose as a flake of dirt gritted between her teeth, but she was too hungry to be picky. Who was she kidding? Even the flake of dirt tasted good.

"Momma," Beth said as Nikki cupped the bread in her hand and regarded it as though it was something holy. "Why don't you come out and eat with us? Kurt said he made plenty, just in case you changed your mule-headed, pig-stubborn mind."

"Momma doesn't like to eat with Kurt," she explained around her first bite of the wonderfully yeasty bread. It was good. Very good. And not just because she was starving, either. The crunchy crust fell apart on her tongue, teasing her deprived tastebuds. She took another bite, this one smaller. She intended to savor each delectable morsel for as long as she possibly could.

"Momma, why did Kurt say you don't like him very much?"

Her daughter's innocent honesty made Nikki

choke. Coughing, she swallowed hard, licked her lips, then shrugged—forgetting for a moment that Beth couldn't see the gesture. "Because I don't," she answered bluntly.

"Not at all?"

"Not at all."

"Can I like him if I want to?"

Nikki opened her mouth, then snapped it shut before uttering the instant, hot reply. "Yes, if you want to," she said as she turned and sat with her back propped against the door. She rested the half-eaten bread atop her bent knees, focusing all her attention on Beth. "Do you like him, sweetheart?" Her breath caught as she waited for the child's answer.

"He's very nice." She heard Beth squirm against the other side of the door. "And he plays Ranchman better than Kristen does. She always wants to be the Momma, but Kurt lets me."

"Is that the only reason you like him?" she pressed. *Beth will hate you for it. The only thing she'll ever understand is that her mother hated her father enough to put a rope around his neck. No kid will understand why.* Mike's words returned without warning to haunt her. Her heart raced.

"Not the only one. I don't know, I just like him I guess. I don't know why."

It's because he's your father, Nikki thought but didn't say. She didn't want Beth to know that crucial fact. Not now. Well, if she had her way, not ever. She shifted uncomfortably. "It's okay to like him, sweetheart, just try not to like him too much. He—he won't be here much longer." The sound of footsteps climbing the stairs made Nikki stiffen. She shifted quickly, pressing her face against the door. "Beth, don't tell Kurt you gave me the bread. Please. Don't even tell him you talked to me. That's our secret. Yours and mine."

"Okay, Momma," Beth murmured slowly.

But then Kurt was back and Beth's thoughts were distracted by biscuits smothered in peach jam. Nikki groaned, nibbling on her dwindling morsel of bread as she listened to their chatter. Her ears perked when he asked Beth about the missing bread.

"You said I had to eat it, Kurt," Beth answered sweetly, skillfully avoiding the question.

Pretty clever for a five year old! Nikki made a mental note to talk with Willy about that, since he would be the only one Beth could have learned such sneakiness from—aside from Abigail Rollison.

She popped the last sliver of bread into her mouth with more than a little regret. Leaning heavily against the door, she chewed it until there was nothing left to chew, then licked her palm clean of crumbs. Her stomach still grumbled, but at least her fingers had stopped shaking.

And then it happened. While complimenting Kurt on his tasty biscuits, Beth let slip that she'd snuck a piece of bread under the door. Nikki could feel Kurt's sudden alertness seep through the wood and race up her spine.

"When, kitten?" he asked with deceptive ease.

Nikki leapt to her feet before she heard Beth's answer. She was at the bureau, pushing for all she was worth, in a matter of seconds. The heavy thing had only just creaked and started to move when she heard the key slide into the lock.

A strangled cry whispered through Nikki's lips as she planted her bare feet and pushed harder. Thick wooden legs scraped the floor, but not fast enough. Before she had moved the bureau more than a few inches, the door crashed open, slamming into the side of the bureau.

Nikki gasped, jumping guiltily back. Her gaze flew to the open door . . . and to Kurt Frazier.

Balled fists were pillowed firmly atop his lean

hips. The crop of messy raven curls shadowed dark eyes that sparkled with a blend of fury and bitter determination. His thick brows were drawn in a pinched *V* that made her catch her breath.

To Nikki, he looked like a demon spit from the fires of hell. A demon who had arrived, hungry for vengeance.

Chapter Nineteen

Nikki watched as Kurt bent to whisper something in Beth's ear. The child looked at Nikki, smiled, then turned and skipped gleefully down the hall, giggling as she went.

Kurt walked forward, kicking the door shut behind him. It closed with a deafening crash that left Nikki waiting for it to fall off its hinges.

He took a slow, deliberate step toward her. The room vibrated with his presence. Any previous thoughts she had entertained about giving in to him died a quick, painless death.

"Get out!" she yelled.

He took a step closer.

"I mean it, buster, I want you out of my room!"

Another step. And another.

His heels clicked ominously over the hardwood floor until he stopped close enough to her that they both felt the heat of the other's body. His lips curled angrily. "Not on your life, baby."

Nikki tipped her chin up proudly, returning his angry glare.

"I'm surprised moving that thing didn't kill you," he growled, his gaze flickering to the bureau and back.

"It would have been worth the effort."

A rough hand snaked out to clamp over her jaw. Like a vice, the powerful fingers closed around her fragile bones. He yanked her close. "Would it have been? Are you sure?"

Her hands splayed his chest for balance. The wonderfully firm muscles beneath his faded flannel shirt seared her open palms, scorched her fingertips as though there was no barrier of fabric to separate flesh from hungry flesh. Nikki's gaze shimmered with confusion as his breath kissed her upturned cheek. Ignoring the fiery sensations Kurt Frazier kindled in her blood was like trying to ignore the hunger churning in her stomach. While both could be overlooked temporarily, neither could be denied.

"Are you hungry yet, Nicole?" Kurt asked gruffly. His gaze devoured her lips.

It was a double-edged question, one Nikki refused to answer. The sharp reply that tickled the tip of her tongue evaporated at the feel of his heart hammering beneath her fingertips. She gave a brisk nod, then wondered which hunger she'd just acknowledged; the starvation that left her dizzy and breathless, or the desire for him, which also left her dizzy and breathless.

"You don't have to be," he said, his searing gaze never leaving her lips. Her mouth burned with the remembered taste of him. Her body fired until it was hot, tingly, and very much alive. "Tell me what I want to hear and I'll feed you."

Nikki sucked in a ragged gasp when his hand slipped around her waist. Her heart throbbed in time to his as he drew her up hard against his sinewy length, her hand trapped between his chest and hers. There was something undeniably arousing in the feel that greeted her knuckles; pressed on the one side by his rigid masculinity, on the other by her own feminine softness.

"Tell me," he demanded as his head lowered with

excruciating promise. "Say it, Nicole. Say it."

Her lips tingled with anticipation as his mouth drew near. "I . . . Oh, God . . . Kurt, I can't."

"Wrong. You can, and you will."

Her lips parted, ready for his kiss. Eager for it. Her lids lowered. A soft whimper left her throat when she felt the warmth of his mouth brush her own. It was a brief, teasing contact, but jarring nonetheless.

He turned his head. His lips nuzzled her ear, her neck, her jaw. His hair grazed her cheek and it smelled of fresh soap and river water. The raven tips were still damp, as was the hot tongue that lapped a moist, sizzling path from slender shoulder to sensitive earlobe. Her flesh quivered.

"P-please, don't," she begged. Her hands pushed against his chest, but it was a weak, meaningless gesture. They both knew it. She didn't want him to let her go. Her body said so in the way it gently arched toward him. She wanted more. Much more. She wanted him to touch her, everywhere, and she wanted to touch him. *Needed* to touch him. Urgently. Desperately.

As much to herself as to Kurt, she appeased her conscience and stammered, "S-stop." The word came out as a breathless sigh.

"I can't," he rasped in her ear. His words tingled up her spine and dizzied her already spiraling senses. "I don't want to. *You* don't want me to."

"Yes, I do," she lied in a rush of warm breath that kissed his cheek and made him shiver. As she spoke, her hands inched up the wonderful firmness of his chest and laced around his neck. The action gave proof to the lie. She rubbed against him, hating herself for the weakness that demanded she feel his body pressed against hers.

He felt good; solid, warm, invitingly firm. He smelled like heaven; spicy and soapy clean. He would taste wonderful; hot and tangy. She knew it, her tongue told her so, and she craved the satisfaction of being proven right.

Her fingers tunneled in the silky raven curls tickling her palms. His head lifted, his sensuously thin lips hovered a mere inch away. Her gaze fixed on them hungrily.

Right and wrong blended smoothly into want and need. They were inseparable now, and Nikki found she no longer cared where one left off and the other began. If he'd asked for the moon, she would have agreed to get it for him. Anything he wanted, if only he would end the bittersweet torture and kiss her hard!

She stood on tiptoe, her arms tightening around the thick cord of his neck as she tugged him down. A soft sigh escaped her as she fused their lips together.

Except for the hands cupping the gentle curve of her hips, grinding her against him, Kurt let Nikki take the lead. She accepted this familiar responsibility gladly. Her fingers plowed through his hair, slipped lower, stroked a luxuriously slow path down his firm shoulders and hard back. She slipped her aching palms beneath his collar as her darting tongue plunged forward for a bold, insistent taste of his lips.

She swallowed his groan of pleasure as his thrusting tongue ravished her mouth. He tasted of spiced duck and sweet, juicy peaches. An oddly enticing combination. The heady taste was honed by her own insatiable hunger. She clung to him, deepening the kiss to a desperate pitch.

Kurt tore his lips away only long enough to scoop her small, complacent body into his arms. He cleared the space between themselves and the bed in three long, determined strides.

The mattress groaned as it cradled Nikki's back in the same instant Kurt blanketed her front. The contrasting hard and soft textures pressing in against her from everywhere was provocative, glorious, headily seductive.

His mouth possessed hers as his hands greedily reacquainted themselves with her feminine curves and valleys. He touched her, loosening and peeling layers of clothes as he went until she lay naked and hungry beneath him. His strokes softened, became more intimate, more insistent, as though he were trying to absorb her flesh through his palms and couldn't touch enough of her.

In response, she increased her own strokes and caresses until they matched his in both brazenness and urgency. She managed to rob him of his shirt and belt, accepting his help only when he offered to remove his own boots, which crashed to the floor like echoing reports of thunder. Nikki let his trousers remain. The rough denim felt too wonderful as it scraped against her flesh to dispense with just yet. She *did* unbutton them, though.

He stretched beside her, pulling her hard against his side. Nikki curled into him, nuzzling his hot firmness as though she belonged there. Her hands refused to be still. They roved his body, stopping to explore a hidden hollow or span of silky-warm flesh. Kurt did the same, with expert skill. She moaned when she felt a calloused palm mold over her aching breast, and arched off the bed when the proof of his desire throbbed against her thigh.

"Beth," she whispered against his shoulder. Her voice was a ragged, tortured sigh when she realized the exquisite torture she was experiencing would have to end if there was a chance her daughter would walk in on them now, discover them like this. "Where is she?"

"Downstairs"—his lips grazed her cheek—"eating"—he tasted her neck—"dessert"—then devoured the hollow in her throat where her pulse leapt. His teeth nibbled, his tongue licked, his lips made little sucking motions that made her melt beneath him.

"Food," Nikki groaned throatily, her tone wistful—but not as urgent as it might have been. She needed nourishment, to be sure, but not of that nature.

Her voice turned abruptly demanding when she felt a sudden burst of cold air wash over her naked body. "Kurt? Where are you going?" The disappointment that crashed over her as he left the bed was tempered when she saw the devilish twinkle in his eyes.

"Don't move," he growled, disappearing out the bedroom door—only to reappear seconds later. His bare feet slapped the floor and the lamplight cast his magnificent body a wonderful shade of bronze as he approached the bed. Cradled in his large hand was a biscuit smothered in globs of gooey, sticky peach jam.

"Hungry?" His voice, as well as his gaze, was filled with husky, lurid suggestion, Nikki's stomach growled in a vehement response that manifested itself in the sudden flush of her skin.

Kurt smiled wickedly. The mattress sagged as he rested his weight on his right knee atop it. The rough, faded denim encasing his thighs rubbed against her waist. The sun-kissed flesh beneath was vibrantly warm, pulsatingly hard. It seared her, scorched her, set her blood on fire.

The steely gaze locked with and held eyes that had darkened to midnight blue. Exquisite promise shimmered in his gray gaze—promise and desire. The sight registered in Nikki's spine and wove a hot thread of urgency through her pounding blood.

He held the biscuit a scant few inches from her nose. The sweet, tantalizing aroma surrounded her. Engulfed her. Mixed with the soapy scent of the man who held it, and her own musky scent. Her hunger intensified.

"Are you hungry?" he repeated, his index finger dipping into the peachy jam. Nikki watched, mesmerized as he tipped his head back and stroked the sticky substance in a twisting ribbon from the top of his shoulder, down amidst the rich pelt of his raven hair, and lower. The jam made the hairs on his chest glisten a soft shade of amber in the glow of the lamplight.

Nikki swallowed hard and gave a short, barely perceptible nod. It was all she was capable of. The thought of tasting the fruity delicacy, mixed with salty male flesh, was enough to make her dizzy. Hunger and desire were one in the same. And both washed over her in hot, urgent waves.

His lids were thick, lazily lowered as he watched her gaze cloud over with sexual hunger. That she was starving, and he knew it, made his next question decadently erotic. "Want a taste?" he offered on a husky sigh.

Nikki groaned. A taste of what? The jam . . . or raw, hot passion? Again she nodded. She wanted both. Badly.

The mattress creaked when Kurt shifted his weight, straddling her. The heavy firmness of him riding her hips was a luxury unto itself. Nikki's back arched as she pressed her own hips insistently beneath him. His throaty moan made her smile.

Kurt deposited the biscuit on the pillow beside her head. As soon as his hands were empty, he cupped her small, sweet, youthful face in his palms and drew her up.

Nikki clung to him as she greedily licked the sticky sweetness from his shoulder. Salty skin and sugary jam blended on her tongue. The taste inspired her tastebuds, and fed her desire. She devoured every juicy drop from his flesh, then hungrily searched for more. Kurt was quick to comply.

He eased her away long enough to snatch up

another mound of jam. This one he applied to the spot where his heart pulsed frantically against his breastbone, then stroked slowly downward.

Nikki's tongue followed that trail of its own accord. Kurt's warm breath seared her scalp when he buried his face in her hair. She sucked in a shaky breath when she felt his heart throb beneath her flickering tongue. She paid special attention to the scar puckered at his waist; the scar *she* had given him.

The provocative meal was immediately, sensuously, devoured.

When she had licked off every drop, she collapsed onto the bed. Kurt reached for the biscuit. Her fingers wrapped around his wrist, drawing it back. She brushed his warm palm down her cheek, then settled his hand on the gentle curve of her hip. The nail of her index finger scraped teasingly up his arm, tickled the hollow of his elbow, then left him to reach for the biscuit.

The steely gaze looked down in askance, but Nikki only smiled and scooped up a generous portion of the jam. Kurt's eyes darkened and he watched, intrigued, when she smeared two globs of the amber jam on the tips of her breasts.

"Hungry?" she rasped, their gazes locking.

A low growl rumbled in the back of Kurt's throat as his head dipped with passionate determination. He needed no more urgings to enjoy the sumptuous delights of his dessert.

The knees that straddled her hips tightened as he hunched his back and lowered his head. His hair scraped her skin. His tongue darted over her breasts, teasing each nipple to rigid peaks. His teeth nibbled, his mouth suckled. Nikki buried her fingers in his hair, arching back as she savored the delicious sensations his mouth created.

Slowly, he lowered himself atop her slender body, nuzzling only one leg between her knees. His hand blazed hot paths up her sides until a swell of sticky flesh was nestled in his palm. He pinched the rosy bud gently, smiling when she whimpered.

Nikki squirmed beneath him. Her lips found his neck and she nibbled and sucked the salty flesh in turn. Her nails burrowed into the flesh of his back, making him gasp. In response, his own strokes became bolder, hotter, filled with the promise of satisfaction. She died a sweet, agonizing death when his fingers slipped over her quivering stomach, then parted her thighs.

"I need you, Kurt," she groaned huskily against his skin. Her hips thrust upward when his fingers slipped inside her dewy warmth. Her tongue tasted the raven hairs on his chest, hairs that still held the sting of jam. "I'm hungry . . . starving . . . for you." Her chin tilted as his mouth ravished her neck. His fingers plunged deeper. She gripped his arms, her hips arching with rhythmic desperation. "Only . . . you."

"I want your hunger, Nicole," he murmured against her throat. Nikki shivered at the implication of his words, as well as the assault his hot breath had on her spiraling senses. "Oh, God, do I ever want it," he groaned hoarsely. Lifting his head, he lost himself in the pools of her eyes. He removed the hand buried in her moist, shuddering warmth and tenderly cupped her cheek. "My body craves it, but my mind wants more. I need so much more than that from you."

The raw desire she saw in his gaze made her voice lodge in her throat. She did without it, instead mouthing the single, sweet-tasting word of surrendered, body and soul: Anything.

Kurt swallowed hard as his lips lowered by slow degrees. "I want what you tried to give me six years ago. What I was a fool to leave without taking." His mouth, tasting provocatively of peaches and salty flesh, brushed her lips, teasing her as she searched for a fuller, deeper kiss. His gaze continued to devour her. "I want you, baby. *All* of you. No restraints."

"And no commitments?" she whispered hoarsely. It was a question that shouldn't have been asked. Not now. But it was too late to bite the words back. Her heart throbbed and her breath held as she awaited his reply.

"You never asked for one."

"You never offered."

His eyes clouded, but only for a second. She was never sure if the expression was one of pent-up emotion or pent-up passion, for her body chose that moment to wriggle demandingly beneath him. The leg between her knees rose. He stroked her with his thigh, slowly, hotly. The feel of rough denim rubbing against her intimate softness was almost her undoing.

Kurt groaned, a deep, rumbling sound that seemed to issue from the depths of his soul. "And if I had?" he sighed, smoothing a silky, quicksilver curl from her sweat-dampened brow. "If I'd offered?"

She smiled sadly as her hands slipped up his back and her thigh tightened around his leg. Her hips arched in time to his movements. "I would've told you to go to hell," she admitted.

"And now?" His body tensed beneath her fingertips, his gaze grew hard, guarded. "What would you tell me now?"

Thick silver lashes lowered in a feeble attempt to mask her churning confusion. "To go to hell."

"Come on then," he said, "we'll go to hell together."

His mouth crashed down, capturing hers in an all-consuming, primitively possessive kiss. They clung to each other with frenzied intensity.

Nikki was only half aware when Kurt shifted to the side and peeled off his trousers with lightning speed.

But she was excruciatingly aware when he stretched out beside her, hot and naked. His flesh, sensuously hard, drove her crazy with desire.

Her hands were everywhere, but she couldn't feel enough of him. His spicy, masculine smell filled her nostrils and she took long, slow breaths of it as though trying to absorb him in every conceivable way. Their bodies strained, their lips entwined. They pressed into each other, seeking, searching, desperate for blinding, white-hot release.

Kurt pressed her urgently onto her back. In a heartbeat, his body covered hers. Nikki sucked in a sigh of anticipation as his fingers wrapped around her wrists, drawing them up. A flicker of residual, physical hunger sparkled in her eyes when her hand brushed what remained of the biscuit.

The steely gaze shimmered with wicked amusement as Kurt released her wrist and plucked the crusty thing up. "Still hungry?" he asked huskily, seductively.

Nikki didn't answer. She couldn't. She was too consumed by the feel of raw masculinity nestled between her thighs to spare much thought for anything else.

When the flaky biscuit was pressed to her lips, Nikki nibbled at it. It was hard to concentrate on chewing and swallowing when all she could feel was Kurt's hardness pressing with infinite promise against her.

He fed her slowly, all the while stroking her achingly hard nipples with his chest. His hips moved, his need stroking her thigh. He came close—tantalizingly close—to fulfilling the promise, but with a groan of denial he would stop short, only to start the rapturous torture anew.

When all that was left of the biscuit was a small, crumbly handful, he held it poised above her. A rakish grin curled his lips as he crushed what was left in his fist, then sprinkled the crumbs over her stomach, peppering the tangle of curls below.

Nikki felt the tiny morsels rain over her. She whimpered when his head dipped. Her body burned with the first velvet stroke of his tongue. The second left her hot and breathless, and he'd only just begun.

Kurt took his time devouring the crumbs from their plate of quivering porcelain flesh. He refused to be rushed, even when Nikki physically and verbally demanded it. Not until he had nibbled up every last crumb did his lips return to hers.

Nikki licked the crumbs from his mouth as her hands strayed down to cup his hips. Lean and hard. She tried to twist him on top of her, but he refused to budge.

"Un-uh. Open for me, Nicole," he rasped against her neck, his breath a hot desert breeze scorching her skin. His hands moved to the inside of her upper thighs. His palms seared her flesh as he nudged her, showing her what he wanted her to do.

Kurt's head lifted. He looked down into her passion-darkened eyes as his palms strayed up to cup each side of her hips. "Open for me, baby. Show me how much you want me."

She did. Without thinking, only feeling, she did. "Now, show me how much you want me," she whispered huskily, holding his gaze. "Now, Kurt. Show me."

Her hands wrapped around his neck, pulling him down as his body covered her fully. She hooked her legs around his thighs and shivered when the coarse raven curls there teased her tingling skin. Stifling a moan she arched, initiating and meeting Kurt's first hard thrust.

He pierced her to the core, and strained to fill her still more. His demanding, sliding strokes awakening a new wave of raw sensation. It lapped over her in hot, steamy waves that built in urgency until the next hard thrust and retreat.

He moved, almost withdrew, then plunged into quivery wet velvet time and again. His thrusts were slow, almost lazy, as though he could prolong indefinitely the exhilarating agony. They were also very deep. Sweet agony tore Nikki apart. He felt good, wonderful, hard and long as he buried himself inside her time and again. But it wasn't enough. Nothing was enough—no matter how exquisite it felt. She wanted more. She *craved* more. Craved it and demanded it. Her body quickened with urgency.

When her arching hips increased the tempo, Kurt accepted her insistence without complaint. Over and over he withdrew, then resheathed himself inside her warm, tight softness. Each time was a little deeper, a little longer. Each time Nikki could feel a little more of her self-control slip away, replaced by hard male promise. She left reason behind and abandoned herself to magnificent sensation without regret.

The pillow cradled her head. The cotton brushed her cheeks as her head twisted from side to side. The fire was building, boiling in her blood, searing down her spine. Each time she arched toward him, his chest hairs tickled her nipples to firm peaks. She groaned, and the sound was swallowed by his mouth.

His tongue set a rhythm to match the urgent driving of their bodies. Nikki felt the first spasm of release tighten her thighs, spread like fire in her stomach, fan through her blood. She wimpered, not being able to remember ever having felt such exquisite, pulsating pleasure.

Kurt, sensing her climax, increased the tempo to a nerve-shattering pitch. He filled her, ground his hips against her. He groaned, trying to hold back, knowing he couldn't.

The spark of desire kindled to searing flame. In waves of throbbing sensation, it crashed around her. She clung to Kurt, trembling with each glorious spasm that ripped through her; each piercing shudder made more intense by his own feverish thrusts.

Tearing his lips from hers, he buried his face in her silken neck. He thrust—deeply, repeatedly—until he was consumed by the same fire that burned in Nikki. His groan shattered the air as he spilled himself into her moist, tight, yielding body. Hot ripples of completion surged through them both, carrying them together to unknown peaks of perfection.

"Oh, God," Kurt panted against her earlobe as he collapsed, quivering, atop her. His ragged breath stirred the curls clinging to her brow as Nikki signed in contentment. "You feel so good. So soft and warm. I could stay like this forever."

"So could I," she replied softly against his neck, her voice trembling with awe. Her heart was beginning to slow, but her body was still very much aware of the man on top of her, inside of her. Excruciatingly aware of him.

He shifted his weight to look down at her, and the feel of him quickening inside her made Nikki gasp. Her lashes swept up and she was immediately captured by eyes that were darkly devouring. "Any regrets, baby?" he panted. "Any misgivings?"

"None. You?" She tried to ignore the way her very life hung in the balance of his answer.

The tip of a roughened finger stroked her jaw, her cheek, her brow. His touch was warm, as soothing as his steely gaze was penetrating. "I've never had any regrets where you're concerned," he replied softly. "Never have, never will."

"You never regretted leaving me, then?" she asked weakly. She hadn't meant to voice the question that had haunted her for the last six years. Searching his expression, she found it suddenly alert, guarded.

His hand dropped from her brow. Shifting, he withdrew from her to stretch at her side. He threw one sun-bronzed forearm over his eyes, as though to shield his gaze from a summer sun.

He weighed his words carefully before giving his tongue permission to murmur them. When they came, they were torn from a place deep in his soul. "I left because that's what I thought you wanted." His thoughts drifted to the letter, and he sucked in a ragged breath as a wave of pain knifed through him. "Dammit, Nicole, I didn't want to go!"

"But you did."

"Yes." He nodded slowly, reluctantly.

She shivered, hugging her arms around her waist. "You left me behind." She bit hard on her lower lip, hating the tears that blurred her vision. "You left me to face the humiliation of bearing a child alone." Her jaw hardened as bitter emories washed over her. "Do you have any idea how they laughed at me? Ridiculed me?" She shook her head, averting her gaze before he could see the hurt in her eyes. "They were right, you know. I couldn't defend myself because, deep down, I always knew they were right. I was a whore."

Kurt's arm lifted and he rolled lithely onto his side. Supporting his weight on one elbow, he reached out, cupped her jaw, and pulled her gaze back. His calloused fingers scraped her skin, but the feel was somehow reassuring. "Is that why you act so tough, baby? So fearless? Is this all an act?"

"No. I *am* harder now. I'd have to be, wouldn't I?" she scoffed, sniffing loudly. "You know this town, Kurt. You know what they're capable of. I wasn't lying when I said the last six years have been rough. They were sheer hell."

"Because of me?"

Moist silver lashes flickered up. Their gazes locked. No reproach shimmered in her eyes, no condemnation in his. "Yes, because of you."

In one swift motion he collected her against his side and held her tight. He was afraid to let her go, afraid she wouldn't be there if he closed his eyes for even a second. She trembled in his arms, and the feel of it ate at him. "I didn't know," he whispered against her hair. "If I'd known you were carrying my child . . . If you'd told me . . ."

"I know," she nodded and shrugged with false ease. "It doesn't matter, and it doesn't help, but I do know."

Kurt sighed, nuzzling his cheek against her head. "I know it's a little late for this, but I can make things right now . . . if you'll let me." His arm tightened and she could hear his heart drumming the ear she'd cushioned atop the firm pillow of his chest. "Marry me, Nicole. Now. Tonight. Let me take care of you and Beth the way I should have from the beginning."

She smiled sadly as her lips grazed a hard male nipple. "It's a little late for that, don't you think? If you'd asked me after that first night, I would have said yes. But not now. There's too much between us now. Too many differences."

"Because of your father?"

"That's one reason." Feeling him stiffen, she glanced up. His eyelids were hooded, the steely gaze masked with apathy. "You've never denied it. I've asked you a dozen times, but you never have. Your silence just makes me more sure you're guilty."

She felt rather than saw Kurt withdraw from her. Nikki let him go, thinking it would probably be better this way, better to put their relationship aside—for good—here and now.

Pillowing his jaw atop her head, he sighed huskily, "I'll always be condemned in your eyes, won't I?" He didn't give her time to answer. "Yet you lay with me anyway. Why? If you're so damned sure I'm guilty, why don't you deny me? Deny yourself."

"I can't," she answered honestly. "Believe me, I've condemned myself a thousand times for what we've done. But it doesn't make me want you less." She sucked in a breath, searching for the right words.

"There's something about you that, well, I don't know. I can't think straight when you t-touch me. It's always been that way." Kurt watched her as her fingernails flicked the sticky curls on his chest. "You feel it, too, don't you?"

"I must," he answered, his voice thick as he took her hand and tugged it low. Her heart skipped when he guided her hand over his renewed need. Slowly, he stroked her fingertips up the long, hard shaft before curling her fingers around him. "I want you again, baby," he groaned, his hand tightened around her fist as he guided it down. "Badly. But even if I take you now, I know it won't be enough. I'll just want you again after that. And again. No matter how many times I have you, it isn't enough. It's never, never enough."

With a groan, Kurt released her, then brushed her hand away. Raising up on an elbow, he pressed her back on the bed. His mouth dipped, his tongue flicked away a crumb that had found its way onto her kiss-swollen lips. "Oh God, I want so much more."

"Then take it," she invited huskily, "because, God help me, I want it, too."

Her lashes swept shut and her arms inched up, savoring each firm inch of his sweaty flesh. Encircling his neck, she pulled him down. Her aching breasts rubbed his chest; she strained to fuse their bodies together in an age-old dance of love.

They took each other slowly, and found that without the throbbing urgency to drive them hard, their bodies held untold possibilities. Greedily, they explored each one.

By the time Beth had eaten her dessert, finished her chores, and wandered up to her mother's bedroom, Nikki and Kurt were nestled in each other's arms. Passion spent, they slept on, unaware when their daughter scrambled onto the bed and snuggled up between them.

Chapter Twenty

Autumn, which had offered a welcome reprieve to the ravages of a long, dry summer, quickly succumbed to the ravages of winter.

Trying to avoid Kurt Frazier, Nikki thought, was like standing naked in a blizzard and avoiding the snow.

Everywhere Nikki turned, Kurt was there. His eyes burned holes in her when he thought she wasn't looking, and when their gazes clashed—as they did, *constantly*—Nikki caught sparks of desire shimmering in the shadowy depths of his eyes. She knew the emotion was reflected in her own, but steadfastly refused to acknowledge it.

She was careful to keep Beth with her at all times. She was no longer afraid Kurt would steal the child; she had gone past that. Instead, she used her daughter as a shield. At least with Beth in the room Kurt was aware of the inappropriateness of bringing up the subject she knew lingered on the tip of his tongue: *them*.

During the day she did fine. She was calm, she was cool, she was excruciatingly collected. She talked to Kurt when she had to, knowing it would ignite Beth's curiosity if she didn't, but tried to keep her eyes off of him. Not easily done since her gaze had a tendency to stray to his rugged frame. It was something she had no control over and, truthfully, she wasn't entirely sure control was what she wanted. She liked to look at Kurt. She liked the warm pool of awareness that curled in her stomach at the sight of his hard planes and angles running beneath her gaze. It wasn't the same as feeling his sun-kissed flesh gliding beneath her palms, true, but it ran a close second.

During the day she coped just fine. But at night . . . ah, that was a different story. At night her body betrayed her. At night she hungered for the man who'd taken up residence in her brother's room two doors away. At night she lay in bed, with the cool breeze washing over her skin, and her tortured mind would lock onto the door down the hall. She would conjure up images of Kurt's wonderfully tanned body laying amidst crisp cotton sheets. Then, groaning, she would turn and bury her face in her pillow, willing forth a sleep that refused to come. Once she had even locked herself in her room, after waking up from a particularly vivid dream and finding herself in the hall outside Kurt's door. She did not trust herself, and with good reason.

Her mind was her own worst enemy. When she wasn't remembering Kurt's hands on her flesh, she was dreaming of them. And, if that wasn't bad enough, every time she looked Kurt in the eye she saw his gaze sparkle with open invitation. His bed was her bed, those steely eyes said. She had only to ask.

That was the hardest part. She *wanted* to ask. The words trembled on the tip of her tongue and they tasted like sweet peach jam. Only pride stood between her and the bedroom door down the hall. But her pride was Dennison-fierce, and she avoided that portion of the house at all costs.

Two weeks passed. At the end of them, Nikki was harboring so much furious energy that she thought she would burst. And if she had to eat one more breakfast of warm biscuits and sweet peach jam she would scream! It seemed like that was all Kurt was willing to serve her, much to Beth's delight.

No more attempts were made on Nikki's life, which lulled her into a blissful security. She was in unspoken agreement with Kurt that whoever was trying to kill her had gone on the trail drive. Nikki reveled in the freedom of not having to look over her shoulder every two minutes to see if she was being followed or shot at. She began riding out to the outlying camps in the afternoon, checking and feeding the few head of cattle she could find. She enjoyed the feel of the horse moving beneath her and the cold wind fingering her hair. Her ears basked in the sound of hooves crunching over the snow that now covered the ranges in abundance. Her rides became a much-needed outlet for leashed energy, and so long as she took one of the hands who had remained on the ranch with her, Kurt let her go. Only once in a while would he remind her of her promise to stay behind on the ranch.

It was as she was drawing close to the house on her return from one of these rides that Nikki noticed a tall, broad woman being let in the front door. She recognized Abigail Rollison immediately, and just as quickly slowed Stetson to a trot. Her lungs were panting from exertion, stinging from the brisk December air. It was snowing again. The delicate flakes clung to her hat and coat. Her cheeks were red and cold, her body aching from hours in the saddle. She wanted nothing so much as to curl up in front of a crackling fire with Beth, a good book, and a steaming cup of hot, spiced tea.

Her curiosity as to what Abigail wanted at the main house was countered by her intense dislike of the woman and her desire to avoid her at all costs. With a tug on the reins, she turned Stetson toward the barn, stretching out the time it took to rub the stallion down and see him bedded.

By the time she was wearily climbing the porch steps, Nikki was sure Abigail was gone. She was wrong. Abigail's shrill voice snapped through her like the biting end of a whip before she had closed the door behind her.

"I don't know what you're talking about," a high, nasally, feminine voice sneered.

"The hell you don't!" Kurt bellowed. Papers crinkled. The sound of his fist punching the top of Pete's desk was loud. Nikki jumped, startled, and imagined the broad-framed Abigail doing the same.

Despite her resolve, Nikki snuck down the hall and molded her back against the wall flanking the door. The woolly chaps encasing her legs crinkled. The heat of a fire crackling inside the hearth crept out the open doorway to engulf her in warm, comforting fingers. Her tiredness gave way to curiosity.

"I'm not stupid, lady," Kurt barked, punctuating his words with another blow to the desk. "Or did you think I wouldn't find out? Did you think I was some kind of *fool?*"

"I said I don't—"

"And I say you're a liar!"

"I don't have to listen to this," Abigail huffed.

A chair scraped against wood. Angry footsteps were followed by the sound of more, angrier footsteps. They neared the door, then receded in a rush. Nikki guessed Kurt had just shown Abigail what he thought about her leaving. The chair scraped, harshly this time, as a body was thrust into it with a yelp.

"My husband will hear about this!"

"You're right, he will. And do you know who's going to tell him? Me! I'll get to him before you get a chance to open your lying little mouth." Kurt's tone softened and Nikki could well imagine the deceptive, cold smile turning his lips. "What do you think Ben will say, Abby? Think he'll be happy to find out what his wife's been doing while he was hard at work?"

This was followed by a stifled gasp. "He won't believe you. You can tell him any story you please, but Ben has more faith in me than that."

A tense pause was followed by a growled, "Wanna bet?"

Nikki heard Abigail squirm. This time when the woman talked, her voice was threaded with uncertainty. "This is ridiculous. Your threats mean nothing to me. Absolutely nothing. As I said, tell Ben anything you please. Since you have no proof to back up these ridiculous accusations, however, I don't see the point in involving him."

"The point is this. Six years ago you forged a letter from Nicole that made me leave town when I was needed here most. I want to know your reason, and I'll stop at nothing to get it—that includes bringing you and your husband down. You getting scared yet?" he purred. "Or did you think the Dennisons would keep Ben on knowing what his wife did? Well I've got news for you. They don't like liars and they don't like cheats. They'd let Ben go in a minute"—his fingers snapped—"and then where would you be? How'd you like to spend the rest of your days living in a crummy, bug-infested dugout instead of a cozy cabin?"

Nikki leaned hard against the wall. The breath rushed from her lungs and her head spun, but she kept her ears trained on the room behind her.

"I don't know what you're talking about," Abigail replied weakly. Even Beth would have known the woman was lying. "I didn't write a letter to you from," she tripped over the word, "Nicole or anyone else."

"No? Then what about this? Is this your handwriting?"

Papers rattled. Abigail grew tensely silent.

"Well, yes, but—"

"And this?" More papers rattled. The sound was loud and grating. "What about this? It has your name on it so I don't suggest you deny having written it."

"Mr. Frazier, I hardly see what this has to do with—"

"*This* is the same handwriting that was on the letter I got six years ago, the one that made me leave Snow Creek. You remember, Abby," he sneered, "the one that said 'last night was fun but I deserve better than a dirt-poor cowpoke'. The one that said 'pack your bags and get the hell out, I never want to see your lousy face again'. *The one that destroyed my life!*"

"If anyone destroyed your life, Mr. Frazier, it wasn't me. You seem more than capable of doing that yourself. However, this incident does go to prove that if the high and mighty Miss Nicole Dennison loved you so much, then nothing I could have said or done would have made a bit of diff—*Eeek!* Let go of me!"

"Lady, I have never been so tempted to hit a woman in my life. But so help me, you keep pushing, you keep wagging that acidy little tongue of yours, and I'm going to shove my fist down your throat."

"Put her down."

Nikki took a step, framing herself in the doorway. If she wasn't so angry she would have found the sight of Abigail, scared and being held by her collar, nose to nose with Kurt Frazier, laughable. She wasn't laughing. As a matter of fact, her blood was boiling and she was fighting her own urge to plant a fist down Abigail's throat.

For the first time in her life, Abigail looked delighted to see Nicole Dennison. The feeling was not mutual.

"I said, put her down, Kurt," Nikki repeated as she

stepped into the room. The scent of charred wood from the fire was eaten away by the cloying aroma of Abigail Rollison's perfume. The flowery smell made Nikki's stomach roll.

With a grunt of disgust, Kurt pushed Abigail away. She landed in the chair he had dragged her from with a stifled yelp. He turned away and, plowing tense fingers through his hair, stalked behind the desk and threw himself into the chair. The backrest smashed into the wall in a resounding crash.

There was nothing imposing about Nikki's slight height and stature. There was a hell of a lot imposing about the delicate jaw, hardened in an angry knot, and the deep blue eyes that sparkled with unconcealed fury. Even Abigail had the good sense to look cowered as Nikki slowly, purposefully, approached.

Crossing her arms tightly over her chest, Nikki stifled the urge to reach out and throttle the conniving bitch. She was close enough to feel the heat of Abigail's body, and the feel disgusted her almost as much as the woman who created it.

"Why, Abigail?" she demanded through gritted teeth. Her lips were a tight white line beneath the splash of furious confusion in her cheeks. "What did I ever do to you?"

"Everything," was the instant, feral reply. The woman sneered as her black eyes raked her adversary head to toe. Never before had the raw hatred she felt for Nikki flamed in her gaze the way it did now. "You have everything. The ranch, brothers," her eyes narrowed venomously as she hissed, "a child. I've always hated you, but I hated you more for that. You lord Beth over me at every turn. You lord everything you have over me. When I caught you and"—she jerked her square chin at Kurt"—*him* in the hayloft together—you were acting like the perfect slut, I might add—I knew my chance to change all that had finally come."

"By lying to me? By lying to Kurt?" she spat incredulously. "A lot of good *that* did. What did you hope to get out of it, Abigail? What good did your lies do you?"

"It gave me an incredible amount of satisfaction, and it drove him away. He never belonged here. It was past time he left." Her black gaze flickered to Kurt, who was watching them both with angry precision. "I hurt you and I got rid of him in one fell swoop. What more could I ask for?"

Nikki's hands curled into tight fists. "Why, Abigail?!"

"Because your father was going to make him foreman, that's why," Abigail yelled back. She flung herself from the chair and towered over Nikki, glaring down at her. "Did you think I'd sit still for that after all the work my Ben did on your stupid little ranch? He put his life into this place. Everything he had went into helping the high and mighty Dennisons." Her thick hand slapped her even thicker thigh. "And for what?! He never got anything in return from you people. And he never would. He gave, you took. He gave more, you took more. His best was never enough. He wasn't going to get anything from you Dennisons unless he took it himself."

"Or you took it for him," Nikki murmured, her gaze narrowing on Abigail. The black hair escaping from the severe bun at the woman's nape frizzed around her head, making her look demonic. She looked like exactly what she was: a madwoman hell-bent on revenge. But how crazy was she? How far would she go to right the wrongs she thought had been committed against her?

"Of course!" Abigail shouted. "I love my husband, but he's a fool. He thinks you people are God incarnate." She laughed, a bitter, crazy sound. "He thanks the Lord for every minute he spends groveling in your soil." She thrust her chin high, her gaze daring Nikki, goading her into a response. "I knew he wouldn't take what was his, so I did it myself. *Someone* had to!"

"There are other ways!" Nikki argued. The fury pumping through her blood was a tangible thing. "If Ben thought my father was being unfair he could have come to one of us. *Talked* to us. We would have worked something out."

Abigail opened her mouth to lash out, then snapped it shut. She sprung from the chair and stalked toward the hearth. Her masculine form was an imposing silhouette against the backdrop of dancing flames. The broad shoulders rose and fell in ragged, straining gasps that cut harshly through the air.

A few tensely silent moments passed before she turned back. Her eyes were glassy, devoid of emotion. Her cheeks were a ghostly shade of white, made paler by the darkness of her dress. The black gaze flickered between Nikki and Kurt as though she had never seen them before, then softened with recognition.

"Are we done?" she asked calmly, her dark brows pinched with confusion. "I really must be going. Ben will be home soon, and I want the house nice for him. He does so like his house nice."

Nikki frowned, taken aback by Abigail's abrupt change. "Ben went on the—"

Kurt, who had walked around the desk without Nikki noticing, now placed a warm hand on her arm, stopping her words. It was the first time he had touched her in two weeks, and suddenly Nikki's body was very much aware of that fact.

"Go ahead. We're done." His glaze was harsh as it settled on Abigail. The look in his eyes only added to her confusion.

"Beth," Abigail sighed, a haunting smile spreading over her lips. Nikki's heart tightened with alarm. "Is Beth here? I'd like to say good-bye to her before I leave." Another sigh, this one as light and as carefree as the snowflakes tossing outside the window. "She's such a sweet child. I hope my next child is like her." She blushed—an oddly feminine gesture, so out of place on such a masculine woman—and looked away. "When I have one, of course. It's all I've ever wanted . . . another child."

Nikki looked at Abigail as though she had never seen the woman before. Indeed, she hadn't. This Abigail Rollison wasn't the one she knew as Ben's wife. And she didn't even come close to the lunatic of three minutes ago.

"Beth's taking a nap," Kurt said, his voice still husky with the anger that refused to leave him. "Maybe another day."

Abigail brightened. "Yes, yes, another day." Her gaze fixed on Nikki. No hatred sparkled in her eyes now. Indeed, there wasn't a trace of emotion in the coal-black depths at all. She nodded, then with a swish of her skirts, left.

Nikki whirled on Kurt the second she heard the front door close. She'd forgotten how close he stood, and almost collided with the firm muscles of his chest. She recovered quickly, and took a quick step back. "You don't think that woman had anything to do with—"

"I don't know what to think," he admitted, eyeing her carefully. "I do know that I plan to keep a close eye on her. Check around, see if I can dig anything up. Anything she might be trying to hide," his eyes narrowed, "about herself . . . or anyone else."

"And if she—"

"I'll find out."

Nikki nodded, confident that if there was something damaging to unearth about Abigail, Kurt would find it. "Until you do, I do *not* want that woman anywhere near my daughter."

"*Our* daughter," he corrected darkly. "And don't worry, I don't plan to let her within a three-mile radius of Beth. I don't trust her."

"Gosh, I don't know why." The words dripped with sarcasm.

Kurt's eyes flashed. His hand raised, and for a second she thought he was going to grab her. Nikki steeled herself for the contact, wondering what she would do when he touched her. It had been a long time since he'd really touched her. She missed it.

He didn't. Instead, he rubbed a palm down the whiskers coating his jaw. Whiskers that gave him a rumpled, comfortable appearance. Too comfortable, Nikki thought as she felt her stomach go tight and warm. Her hand burned when she imagined the feel of those sooty whiskers scraping her fingertips.

She took another step back, and almost fell over the chair Abigail had been sitting in. The woolly chaps protected her shin, but nothing cushioned her embarrassment. When she looked up, Kurt was staring at her. His gaze sparkled with steely challenge and a devilish grin tugged at one corner of his mouth. *Oh God, that mouth!* Her skin tingled with peachy memories.

Nikki straightened until her back was incredibly stiff. Brisk steps carried her to the hearth, as far away from Kurt as she could get. She could have groaned aloud when she looked down and saw the faded gold rug beneath her feet.

"What are we going to do about Abigail?" she asked over her shoulder, shattering the silence. "I can't just let this go. I can't let her get away with what she's done."

Kurt shrugged. "What do you want to do?"

"Killing her leaps to mind."

He chuckled at her ready answer, and the sound

helped relieve some of the tension. "Mine, too. But, since neither of us are murderers," he paused while *that* remark sank in, "we'll have to think of something else. Any suggestions?" Nikki shook her head. She'd turned so her back was to the hearth and she was regarding him oddly. "Well, I've got one. I say we boot her off the place and let her fend for herself until Ben gets back. She'll survive. People like her always do." He scowled. "Don't look at me that way. It's what she deserves."

Nikki crossed to the chair and restlessly plopped down on it. "I agree. She deserves worse if she forged that letter."

"*'If'?*" Kurt propped a lean hip against the desk, his expression stormy. His look was long and hard. Nikki looked back, and then some.

The thick arms were crossed with mock casualness atop his chest. The sculpted muscles beneath his thick flannel shirt bunched and strained against the fabric in enticing ripples. When he stretched his legs, his denim encased knee brushed her thigh. Nikki's flesh burned and she pulled away.

"Are you calling me a liar?" he asked darkly.

"No," she sighed, propping an elbow on the chair arm and cushioning her cheek atop the knuckles of her fist, "I'm just confused. For six years I've thought—" Her mouth snapped shut, her eyes widened when she realized what she'd almost said. A quick, shielded glance told her Kurt was not going to let this subject die a natural death. His next words confirmed it.

"What?" he pressed. His expression melted to desperation as, lightning quick, he stood and dragged Nikki from the chair. He pulled her roughly against him. Her giving curves were such a welcome distraction that, for just a second, he forgot what he was going to say. "For six years you've thought what? Nicole, please, don't do this," he groaned before his voice turned hard. "Talk to me, Nicole!"

He gave her a gentle shake, as though trying to rattle the words from her stubborn tongue. He knew what she was going to say, had guessed it a long time ago. Still, he needed to hear the words. Until she could admit her doubt to his face, Kurt didn't stand a prayer of ever changing her mind.

Nikki clamped her teeth shut and fixed her gaze on the horn button, dead center of his sinewy chest. She shook her head, trying to pull away. His fingers bit into her arm, refusing to let her go.

"Kurt, I . . . nothing. I wasn't going to say anything."

"Liar."

Silver lashes flickered up with surprise. Her gaze met eyes that were hard, cold slits that stared into the very core of her soul. His gaze, intent, pulled her in a thousand different directions. Something inside her cracked, peeled away like the crinkling outer skin of an onion; the fragile insides left exposed and frighteningly vulnerable.

Mesmerizied, her gaze lifted. Her gaze caressed the tousled hair framing his face, noticing despite herself how wonderfully the raven curls softened the rugged terrain of his cheeks and jaw. The dent splitting his chin was shadowed but pronounced by the flickering firelight. She searched it out within the concealing, bristly stubble.

God, how he looks like Beth, she thought as she felt the fight drain out of her. She sighed. She was so tired of fighting. So tired of trying to avenge wrongs. How much she wanted to melt against him and let him shelter and protect her. If only she could.

His hands turned from grip to caress. Warm palms stroked her arms, then wrapped around her waist, pulling her close.

Nikki closed her eyes and pillowed her cheek

against his chest. He felt so firm, so strong. His heart drummed in her ear and the sound was sweetly lulling.

"Abigail," she sighed against his shirt.

"Can wait." His cheek rubbed the top of her head. The quicksilver strands felt wonderfully soft against his harder, coarser skin. The contrast was heady. "Tell me what you were going to say, Nicole," he coaxed, stroking her narrow back.

No one called her "Nicole" anymore. That Kurt still did touched her deeply. It tugged at her heart, awakening a part of her she'd thought had been buried with her father.

She shook her head and buried her face deeper. Without her consent, her arms wrapped around his back and she clung to the firm, warm, comforting strength of him. God, he felt good!

"Please," he whispered hoarsely, his breath hot and oh, so sweet against her head. "I need to hear it." The crook of his finger cupped her chin as he dragged her gaze up. His eyes were sharp with uncertainty. "I'll never know unless you tell me."

Nikki opened her mouth to lie, plain and simple. Only nothing was plain and simple when it came to Kurt Frazier. There was only confusion. And passion. A lot of passion. It was rippling through her even now. His body pressed against her, and every solid inch of it seared her flesh.

She sucked in a ragged sigh and drank in the soapy male scent of him. To tell him what he wanted to know would be to admit she was starting to trust him again. That wouldn't be wise. But at the same time, she found she couldn't lie, either. The words wouldn't come.

Her lashes flickered shut—she couldn't look at him—but she didn't pull away. "I . . . thought you hated me because I gave you something I shouldn't have," she said in a rush. "I thought you left that way to get away from me. And I . . . thought you killed my father to hurt me."

"*What?!*" It wasn't what he'd expected to hear. Not at all.

Her eyes snapped open at his angry shout. She tensed in his arms, but Kurt was too busy glaring at her to notice.

"I-it was the only reason I could think of," she stammered. She tried to squirm away, but his grip had turned to iron. It was getting hard to breath. "Why else would you murder him?"

Like storm clouds shadowing the sun, Kurt's expression darkened. "Did it ever occur to you, for one stinking minute, that I *had* no reason to kill your father? Were you so busy trying to pin the blame on someone that you never considered I might be innocent? Sure, why not blame Kurt?!" he ranted. "Lord knows, I wasn't around to defend myself, so what the hell?"

Her anger stormed back full force. "That isn't my fault! *I* didn't ask you to leave. I didn't *want* you to leave!"

"Then why the hell did you send me that Goddamn—?!"

"I didn't send it!" she raged. Then, her voice cracking, added softly, "I didn't send it, Kurt. I would never say those things because I never felt that way. Not about to you."

He looked down at her as though he'd never seen her before. His face was a masterpiece of confusion as his arms dropped to his sides. Twice, his mouth opened. Both times it snapped shut.

"I need some air," he said, his voice ragged as he stepped away and walked to the door. But he didn't leave. Not yet. He turned back toward her, his expression tortured. "I've spent the last few years with some thoughts of my own, Nicole," he sighed huskily, dragging his fingers through his hair. "Not pretty thoughts. Whether you wrote that letter or not, I've spent six very long years thinking you did. And hating you for it."

He paused, his jaw hardening. "Ever since that night in the hayloft, the night I found out you hadn't written the damn thing, I've been fighting these feelings. Fighting the anger, fighting the betrayal, fighting the hatred I've cultivated until it feels like it's a profession with me. I'm trying to forget all that, baby, but it isn't easy. Words like that can eat a man alive. I know. They ate my soul the first time I read them."

"I understand," she whispered softly, her voice barely discernable above the snap of flames. "As much as I've wanted to trust you, I can't." Her gaze fixed on the back of his raven head, which was tilted proudly. "This isn't a storybook, Kurt. We can't patent a happy ending or smooth over misunderstandings just because we want to. And we can't wipe out in a day the anger and pain it took six years to build, even if that anger and pain was founded on a lie."

"I know," he answered, tortured as he pushed away from the door and disappeared into the shadows of the hall.

Nikki watched him go, and felt as though he'd wrenched out her heart and taken it with him. Though his name seared the tip of her tongue, she didn't try to stop him. She couldn't. Words wouldn't fit past the bitter lump of emotion in her throat.

Chapter Twenty-One

A brisk wind howled outside the bedroom window, rattling the panes. Nikki shivered and tossed the heavy black cloak over her shoulders. The hem billowed, then settled in coarse woolen folds around her ankles.

Her gaze shifted to the window. The glass was cloudy. Beyond it, she could barely make out the airy flakes being tossed around on howling gusts of wind. Not only was it snowing again, but it was snowing hard. Another six inches had dropped since dawn, and the sun had risen scarcely four hours ago.

So far, the winter's snowfall had topped all those in previous years. And it was only the middle of December. Worse, the constant storms showed no sign of letting up.

The blizzards were erratic in both severity and occasion. Then, out of the blue, they would stop. Days passed when the warmth of the sun would melt the top layer of snow. But those days, no matter how wonderful they felt to the ranchers, were a danger Snow Creek could not afford.

It was during the warm spells that enough snow melted under the burning sun to form a blanket of ice beneath yet another fluffy coat of snow. The result was layer upon layer of thickly packed snow and ice covering the ranges. It made the ground slippery and treacherous, and not only for the cowpunchers whose job it was to keep watch over the herd. The cattle were suffering. Aside from dragging daily rations of hay to the few steers to be found, nothing could be done to help.

Out of the seven hundred head the drive had left behind, thirty had been lost. Some were cows weakened from labor, a few were helpless calves. Most were from the stock of new Texas imports Pete had shipped in at the beginning of spring—at great expense to the Triple D—to beef up the herd.

The new steers weren't familiar with harsh Dakota winters. They didn't know to dig in the snow to find the sweet, tough grass that grew in thick patches beneath—and that was in short supply thanks to the hot, dry summer. Nor did the Texas cattle seek the protection of the gulches and coulees during a storm. As a result, they either died from starvation, or they died from exposure. Either way, they died; and at an alarming rate.

As Nikki pulled the hood over her head and tucked her hair beneath, her thoughts drifted to Pete, Brian, Mike, and Willy. Lord, how she wished her brothers were here! Between the five of them, these storms and the steady depletion of the herd could be handled. A winter this bad was something Nikki had never faced before, and now she was at a loss as to what to do next.

Who knew when Brian would be back? Nikki had given up hope weeks ago. The other three should have been home by now. That they weren't, and that she'd heard nothing from them, worried her sick. She didn't know where they were. If the drive had reached Bismark before the first snow hit, there was a good chance they'd be home soon. But if they'd encountered problems crossing the ranges—and what trail drive didn't?—if they hadn't reached their destination yet . . .

She shivered and pulled the folds of the cloak around her, snuggling into the warmth, but her thoughts were as cold as the icicles frozen outside her bedroom window. She didn't want to think about what could have happened to her brothers and the rest of the hands had they been caught out in one of these storms.

"Damn, damn, *damn!*" she muttered, the words aimed in the direction of her eldest brother.

It had been Pete's brilliant idea to delay the drive for as long as possible. He'd hoped to fatten the herd the dry summer had left gaunt, thereby pulling in a higher price per head. While the plan had its share of risks, it seemed sound then and the family had agreed. Of course, at this point they'd be lucky to get what herd was left to the station in Bismarck—and fat or lean, they wouldn't get squat for dead cattle! So much for logic and a keen business sense!

Nikki tugged on the gauntlets she usually reserved for riding, then crept to the door. Leaning her ear against the crack, she listened. Silence. Breathing a sigh of relief, she eased the door and slipped into the shadowy hall.

The stairs creaked with her weight. As she neared the front door, she heard Beth's giggles from the kitchen and smelled the tantalizing aroma of freshly baked cookies. Kurt's low, rumbling laughter curled up her spine. Pushing away the pleasant, breathless reaction that raced through her, she slipped out the door.

The snow fell hard, obscuring her vision. The icy wind stung her cheeks and howled in her ears. It tossed the cloak around her legs and found its way through every layer of clothing she'd packed on her body. Two pairs of long johns, flannel pantaloons, a cotton petticoat, and a thick pair of socks she'd found while rumbling through Mike's drawers. She felt as plump as a snowman, and ready to burst at the seams. The layers of clothes made her movements clumsy and awkward.

Still, no matter how many layers she'd packed on her body, it wasn't enough. In two short steps she was chilled to the bone. Her teeth chattered as she crept around the corner of the house and headed toward the married hands' cabins; toward Abigail Rollison, for what she hoped would be the last time. Kurt couldn't have caught a whiff of the flowery cologne she only now remembered smelling the night in the barn when they'd discovered the ladder cut, but Nikki did. And she now knew who it belonged to. Finally, she had some proof!

"Ouch!" Kurt threw the broiling hot baking sheet onto the counter and cursed oven mitts that were too thin. His scorched palm smarted, but he laughed. Never would he have imagined being content to spend a Sunday morning baking cookies with his daughter. Then again, he'd never imagined having a daughter to bake them with.

He pulled the too-thin mitt from his hand and tossed it atop the cluttered counter. His eyes widened with surprise when he realized he rather liked it all. The cookies. Beth. Her mother.

His grin faded. "Kitten, hand me that—" He caught a glimpse of his daughter. "What the heck . . . !"

Beth's face split in a cheerful, open-mouthed smile. Her eyes glistened happily as she slapped at the flour dusting her once-clean body from head to speckled toe. The flour billowed from her calico dress like a cloud of dust kicked up under a pony's hoofs. It powdered to the floor like snowflakes.

"I'm helping you bake cookies, Kurt," she said, quite seriously. But it was difficult to take her seriously when her raven hair was coated with flour—and looked more like the brittle strands of an ancient schoolmarm than the silky black tresses of a precocious five-year-old girl.

"I know that," he replied, wiping a roughened palm down his mouth and trying to swallow back his laughter. He suppressed the urge to reach out and hug her flour-strewn body. "But what..." His mockingly stern gaze raked her. "How did you do that?"

She shrugged and handed him the spatula. "The flour fell," she explained.

"On you?"

"Um-hum. But that's okay. Momma says cookies don't taste good unless you wear them first. Why are you laughing?"

"I'm not," he lied as he turned and began prying the burnt chips of cookie off the baking sheet. They clattered like rocks on top of the waiting plate, the sound only fueling his mirth. Suddenly, he was glad he had no sense of smell. Especially if the fog of smoke curling from the oven and stinging his eyes stank as bad as it looked like it did.

"Can we eat them yet?" Beth asked as she plopped down in one of the kitchen chairs. She eyed the plate. Kurt wasn't the only one who could appreciate a sense-deficient nose!

"That depends. How hard are your teeth?"

"Pretty hard. I've eaten Momma's cookies, and they come out even blacker. Dally's the one who makes good ones. The best! Nice and soft, with golden bottoms."

Kurt set the plate on the table and pulled out the chair next to Beth's. The sound of spindled legs scraping the floor grated on his abruptly sensitive nerves. Plowing all ten fingers through his hair, he looked at his daughter. Sometimes she reminded him so much of Nikki it hurt to look at her.

Beth plucked up a small black cookie and looked at it as if she expected it to walk away. She scrutinized it, turned it this way and that, then tapped it hard against the corner of the table. It didn't crumble. It didn't even dent.

"So when're you going to marry Momma?" she asked sweetly as she nibbled on a charred edge. She grinned at Kurt, unaware of the black crumbs dotting her lips. "I'm glad you're going to be my father, Kurt," she confided. "You're nicer than most of the men Momma knows. Uncle Willy says I could've done a lot worse. I think he meant Mark Winfield."

Kurt's spine stiffened, but he kept his gaze impassive. He plucked a cookie off the plate, but had no intention of eating it; it gave his fingers something to play with. "What about your real father, kitten? Don't you think he'd have something to say about being traded in for me?"

Wiping the crumbs from her chin, she frowned. "No. Since he doesn't know about me, I don't think he'll care. Momma said so, and I know she wouldn't lie. Not to me, anyway."

"She told you that?" he demanded, a knot of fury churning in his gut. He slammed the cookie back on the plate before he broke the hard thing in two. "She told you he doesn't care about you?"

"No, silly, that he doesn't know. She said if he knew about me he'd care, *a lot,* but that he was better off not knowing. She said when I grew up she'd tell me why."

Kurt swallowed hard. This wasn't a safe topic—his mind screamed it, screamed it loudly—but he couldn't stop himself from asking, "What else did she tell you about him, kitten?"

The small lips pursed. Her frown deepened thoughtfully as she ran a fingertip around the jagged edge of the cookie. The narrow shoulders rose and fell, billowing more flour into the air. "Lots of stuff."

"Like what?" Kurt's voice cracked with anticipation. He hated that, but he hated the thought of what Nicole might have told their daughter even more.

"Well," Beth pushed her cookie aside and looked at him squarely, her young mind torn. She liked Kurt; loved him, even. But what Momma had told her was a secret. Still . . . "Momma tells me bedtime stories about him." The dark eyes sparkled under thickly winged brows. "She said he's very handsome. Very brave and strong. She said he once killed a grizzly bear with a knife when it tried to attack her." Her voice hushed respectfully, her eyes rounded. "He tore it to pieces with his bare hands just to protect her! Isn't he great?"

Kurt smiled. The event his daughter referred to rang clear in his mind, although his version was considerably different. There *was* a grizzly bear. A big, black, ferocious monster, who was hell-bent on protecting the small cubs Nicole had accidentally stumbled upon. And there was a knife, but it was sheathed, and the finely honed blade had never seen the light of day.

He hadn't fought the grizzly, though Lord knows he would have if it had come to that. Still, it warmed his heart to think Nicole had embellished the story for Beth's sake.

"And Momma says he's the best broncobuster this Territory's ever seen," she added proudly. "Even better than you"—she smiled apologetically—"no offence."

Ah, now that was no lie, Kurt admitted with his customary lack of modesty. Although he was surprised Nicole had thought this important enough to impart to Beth. What else had she considered important about him? he wondered as his hand snaked out and his fingers wrapped around his daughter's. His skin itched when he thought of the times, back when he'd worked for Hugh, that he'd caught Nicole gazing at him. Even then there had been something between them. Something unspoken but undeniable. Something that sparked every time their eyes met or their hands brushed. Something hot, something sensuous. Something that ran much deeper than lust.

"What else did she say?" he asked, his voice ragged as his fingers tightened around Beth's.

"Oh, lots of stuff." She shrugged, her restless gaze scanning the messy kitchen. "Can we bake more cookies now, Kurt? Before Momma gets back?"

"Back?" His head snapped up and every muscle in his body tensed. "What do you mean 'back'? Momma's resting upstairs with a headache, kitten. Remember?"

"No, she isn't," Beth argued with a maturity that went beyond her years. "She never gets headaches, silly. Beside, she just crept by the window. I saw her."

Kurt craned his neck and looked out the window. All he saw was a murky gray day, with flakes of snow tossing about on a wild, bitter cold wind.

Damn her! Damn Nicole Dennison to hell and back! Kurt swore as his fist pounded the table. The charred cookies rattled on the plate when he thrust himself to a standing position with enough force to make Beth gasp. The chair fell back, crashing to the floor. He couldn't hear the clatter over the furious beating of his heart.

How the hell was he supposed to protect her when she slipped away from him every time he blinked?! And why did the thought of her getting her scrawny neck broken disturb him so much?!

Kurt sucked in an uneven breath. Arching forward, his fingers dug into the table edge in a grip that threatened to crack the sturdy piece of wood in two. His cheeks were flushed, and he felt not unlike someone who'd just been rammed in the gut with the blunt end of a log.

When his eyes flickered closed, he saw Nicole; her

face warm and relaxed in the aftermath of their lovemaking. Beneath his fingers was not solid oak, but satin-soft, quicksilver hair. His body tightened in response, but this time Kurt didn't despise the weakness, he savored it.

No wonder he was so panic-stricken at the thought of someone picking her off. He was still in love with the silver-haired brat. Had never fallen *out* of love with her! The feeling, he was amazed to find, ran deep; it was rooted solidly in his heart, with branches shooting hotly into his blood and loins. The intensity of it all astounded him. Floored him. Panicked him.

She may be spoiled, mule-headed, and thicker than a pregnant cow, but it didn't change the fact that he was in love with her—had been for years. And not just with Nicole, but with "Nikki" as well.

Kurt shook his head in a futile attempt to clear it, but the gut-wrenching feelings were too painfully firm to shake. The same way his mind refused to shake a certain vision bathed in peachy skin, hay, moonlight, and precious little else. A vision whose temptingly round backside he was about to save— again!

After a few hasty instructions to Beth, Kurt thrust himself from the chair. He didn't have to be told where Nikki went. The sudden lurch of his heart told him. How had she pieced everything together so damned fast? And where had she found the proof she'd need to string the killer up? *He* hadn't even found it yet—and he'd been searching for it with a vengeance.

"Abigail, open the door. *Now!*" Nikki raised her fist and pounded for the fourth and last time. Her gauntlets muffled the sound of her knocks. She was chilled to the bone and shivering. Her teeth chattered. The wind howled in her ears, threatening to yank the damp wool hood from her head.

If possible, the snow was coming down harder now. The delicate flakes melted into the cloak as soon as they hit the warmth of her body. So far the cold dampness had only penetrated her hood, chilling her ears until they were throbbing and numb. Soon the moisture would invade the layers of clothes. But Nikki planned to be planted in front of a roaring fire with a cup of something steamy and hot cradled in her hands by the time that happened.

She pressed her ear against the door and heard the muffled creak of floorboards. Her lips compressed as her ragged breath fogged the air in front of her face.

So, Abigail, was inside—she just wasn't answering the door. Well, it was about time the crazy lady found out that a Dennison didn't give up so easily!

Swearing under her breath, Nikki pulled out the dagger she'd concealed in the pocket of her cloak. The hilt felt hard in her cushioned hand, the blade glistened dully in the gray streaks of sun. Her fingers trembled with cold as she shoved the blade in the crack between door and frame. The layered padding of her clothes made her movements awkward and clumsy as she jimmied the lock exactly the way Brian had taught her. The door swung open. Sheathing the blade, she tucked it in her pocket and pushed the door open the rest of the way.

Nikki was hit with a blast of warm air scented with meaty broth. It rushed over her like a lover's caress, and felt almost as good. She didn't allow herself time to enjoy the warmth, but stepped into the house before Abigail could figure out what she'd done and slammed the door shut.

"Well, well, well. If it isn't the high and mighty Nicole Dennison, come to pay call on a lowly hired hand's wife. You'll have to excuse me if I don't welcome you with open arms." The voice lowered to a deadly pitch. "Put your weapons on the table."

Nikki's gaze snapped to the far corner, from where the high-pitched cackling had come. The room was bathed in murky shadows and Abigail, swathed in her customary black, looked to be one of them. What didn't look like a shadow, but was extremely clear, was the rifle the woman leveled at Nikki's chest. Nikki pulled the Colt from her pocket and placed it, as instructed, on the table. Raising her hands, she backed away.

"Don't be a fool!" Abigail shrieked. "I'm not stupid, Nicole. The knife, too, and be quick about it."

Nikki complied, but only for Beth's sake. Abigail collected the weapons and, keeping a careful watch on Nikki, threw them into the pot of boiling stew that hung over the fire. They landed with a plunk, the flames sizzling when liquid sloshed over the sides.

Abigail turned, her grin broad and victorious. "Have a seat, *Miss Dennison.*" She waved the rifle at the benches flanking the table and huffed, "I'll get us a cup of tea. Won't that be something? Me and *the* Nicole Dennison sitting down to tea and cakes?!" The woman frowned, faltering. "Of course, I don't have any cakes, but it would be something just to see us sitting at the same table, wouldn't it?"

Nikki glared at the woman and, planting her fists on padded hips, stood her ground. "I don't want any of your damn—"

"Shut up!" Abigail shrieked. Her boot heels clipped over the creaking floorboards as she approached Nikki, jabbing the barrel sharply into Nikki's stomach. Abigail's eyes darkened with fury when she didn't see so much as a trace of fear sparkling in the large blue eyes. Why wasn't the girl groveling?!

"Shut up and sit down, Miss Fancy Pants,"

Abigail hissed. A warm spray of spit shot from between her clenched teeth, sprinkling Nikki's cheeks. "You're going to have tea with me. A cup of my own is going to touch your dainty Dennison lips if I have to put it there myself."

Nikki wiped a gloved palm down her damp cheeks, a ghost of a smile playing over her lips. One silver brow arched high as the hand ascended, swiping the hood from her head. It sagged limply between her shoulder blades in coarse folds. Tilting her head to the side, she offered up a challenge she knew Abigail wouldn't refuse. "If you think you can, *Mrs. Rollison.*"

"Oh, I can all right." Meaty fingers patted the rifle's carved wood handle with a hollow, tapping sound. "This says I can. It says I can do whatever I want to with you, and that you can't stop me. Not this time. Now sit down!"

"No." Nikki crossed her arms over her chest and turned away from the woman. She walked slowly to the sink, her eyes trained on the window and the snow dancing outside the spotless pane. She was extremely conscious of the fury emanating from the woman behind her. Abigail's outrage flowed over her like tangible fingers wrapping tightly around her rigid spine.

"I didn't come here for tea, Abigail." Clamping her mouth shut, she spun on her heel and leaned against the counter. The cloak's hem whipped around her ankles. The hard edge of wood biting against the small of her back was a welcome distraction. "I came to get rid of you, once and for all." Her eyes narrowed to diamond-hard slits of disgust. "I want you off my land by noon. In case you don't agree, I've sent a man for Sheriff Hardy. He'll make sure you don't linger."

"I'm not going anywhere," Abigail sneered. Her fingers tightened on the rifle until her knuckles were white. A thick index finger twitched over the trigger. "You don't have the power to kick me out. Only your brothers can do that, and they wouldn't dare." The bumpy nose rose high as she looked haughtily down the length of it. "And even if you could throw me out, I wouldn't go. This is my home. Ben and I worked hard for it. I won't give it up."

"Oh, but you're wrong, Abigail. I do have the power, and no compunction about using it. You *will* leave."

The older woman cackled sarcastically, the sound gurgling from somewhere deep in her masculine chest. Hard black eyes raked Nikki head to toe. "Why?" she demanded with a hint of a victorious smile. "Still angry because I had the nerve to come between you and your lover? Is that why you want me gone? Do you think I might do it again?"

"You can try, but I think you'll find it harder the second time around."

"Oh, but it was so much fun!" Abigail taunted with perverse delight. Her lips broadened to a sinister grin, flashing crooked teeth. "You know, I never dreamed Frazier would fall for my letter. He seemed much smarter than that. Of course, I was delighted when he did. It all worked out so perfectly." She sighed. It was a hard, mocking sound. "I don't know. My guess is he was looking for any reason to hightail it out of Snow Creek—as fast and as far away from you and your brazenness as he could get. Wasn't it nice I could provide him with such a perfect excuse?"

Nikki pulled herself up. No part of her body touched the counter as her gaze flickered between the rifle and the woman who taunted her with it. "You are an acid-tongued woman, Abigail!"

Abigail smiled, a cold, heartless gesture that came no where near to touching her glazed eyes. The hammer of the rifle being cocked was loudly ominous against the howling wind. "Perhaps. But you don't have to worry yourself about it. I won't be a problem to you much longer."

Nikki weighed the words. She knew what Abigail meant—and it wasn't that she intended to leave the ranch quietly. Instead of frightening her, the threat brought a wave of disgust. That disgust sparkled in her eyes. "Pull the trigger then, woman, if you think you can. But don't fool yourself into thinking that will end it. My death will be questioned, and this is the first place Kurt will look. He's already suspicious, and itching to kill you. Give him a reason and he won't hesitate." A silver brow arched. "It won't take him long to figure out where I've gone. How quick are you at mopping up blood?"

The woman's gaze glinted evilly. Again her finger twitched on the trigger. "Your blood?" she sneered. "Why would I want to mop it? I'd rather take a bath in it."

"Did you feel that way when you killed my father?" Nikki spat, her voice reflecting every bit of the hatred that filled her rigid body.

It was the last thing Abigail expected to be confronted with and she faltered. The tip of the rifle lowered to a spot near Nikki's knees. Tears, pleas to spare her life—now *that* she'd expected. But not this bitterly calm acceptance of a deed she'd taken great pride in covering. "How do you know about that?" she demanded, jerking the rifle to her shoulder when Nikki moved.

She hadn't know, she'd suspected. Until that very moment, Nikki hadn't been sure. Now the knowledge of who had killed her father burned in her eyes. *My God, Kurt, what have I done to you?* Like a woman punched in the gut, she staggered. The small of her back smashed into the counter, and even through the padding of clothes, she winced at the pain.

"It's true then?" Nikki asked with more calmness

than she felt. Her blood was boiling and it was all she could do not to launch herself at her father's killer. She may not quake with fear the way normal people did, but she wasn't stupid. Her only hope of bringing this killer to justice was to live long enough to do it. Nikki balled her hands into fists that were so tight they hurt, and glared her outrage at the woman—who, she was quickly realizing, was teetering at the brink of madness.

Abigail chuckled, and the sound raced up Nikki's spine. She removed her large hand from the rifle long enough to swipe a few brittle strands of dull black hair from her brow. "Of course it's true, you little chit. The idiot was getting too close. I had to get rid of him before . . ."

"Too close to what?" Nikki demanded.

"To finding out about Ben," she said as though Nikki should already know this. "Hugh couldn't find out. I had to stop him or he would have fired Ben. After all the hard work and sweat Ben put into this place, your father would have fired him without a thought. It would have destroyed Ben." She sneered at Nikki, but Nikki wasn't entirely sure she was the only thing Abigail sneered at. "Your kind doesn't want to hear a man can change the way my Ben did. He's a good man, but that wouldn't have mattered to Hugh once he found out. No, Ben would have been dirt then. A buffalo chip to kick under holy Dennison feet. Or crush."

"Found out about *what?*" Nikki pressed, her temples throbbing with confusion. The woman made no sense. What could Ben have done that would make her father fire him? Hugh Dennison wasn't a man known for letting good employees slip from his grasp without a fight. And Ben, if nothing else, was a good employee. Loyal, devoted, hard working—everything the Dennisons looked for in their help. It wasn't *his* fault he'd married a lunatic!

Abigail blinked twice, her eyes glazed with uncertainty. She shrugged. "Since I plan to kill you, I suppose it won't hurt to tell you the truth." She grinned, but there was a perverse pride in both her expression and her words as she continued, "Ben used to lead the Delhoussey Gang, way back when."

"No," Nikki gasped. Ben? Laid-back old Ben? She thought for a second, and remembered a certain shrewdness in the man's hazel eyes, concealed by his hickish exterior. A slyness she'd always noticed, but overlooked.

"Didn't you wonder why they came here this spring? Weren't you curious about what they wanted with a small, good-for-nothing town like Snow Creek?"

"I wondered, but I didn't lose sleep over it," she murmured. "They've been plaguing the ranges for years. It was only a matter of time before they came here. Are you telling me they came because of Ben?" she asked, still unable to believe it.

"Oh yes. He led them for years—until he married me. *I* made him give all that up." She sighed thoughtfully. "Actually, it was a profitable venture. Rustling marketable cattle is much cheaper than having to feed and nurture an entire herd. When the gang's leader was killed last spring, they decided Ben was the perfect replacement. They were right, of course. My Ben's much smarter than he lets on."

"And he agreed?"

"Oh no, he refused. Ben knows I won't tolerate a husband who disrespects the law."

But you can kill an honorable man in cold blood, ruin another man's life by framing him for the murder, and that's perfectly respectable! Nikki sneered the insanely twisted irony to herself, careful to keep her thoughts from showing.

The heat of the room, coupled with layers of warm clothing, was oppressive. Nikki swayed against the counter, feeling her sweat soak through the cloth packed against her body. The smell of soup still hung heavily in the air. It combined with Abigail's pungently flowery scent to make her stomach churn.

The black eyes sharpened, noting the ruddiness of Nikki's cheeks. She smiled, mistaking the splash of color for fear, and jerked the rifle barrel toward the door. "Come on, then. Out of here. I don't have time to steal Frazier's clothes this time, but there's no one around here to see, anyway."

Nikki's gaze shifted to the door. She raised her arm and mopped the sweat dotting her brow off on her sleeve. She didn't move, nor did she give the woman any indication she was going to. "I'm not going anywhere with you, Abigail."

Abigail's gaze flashed with confusion. She'd expected Nikki to be cowered by now. After all, she had a rifle pointed at the girl's heart, and she knew how to use it. Ben had taught her well. Her tone hardened. "Of course you are. I won't kill you here. Bloodstains on the floor would distress Ben. He does so like his house neat, you know."

"Of course. Heaven forbid we distress Ben," Nikki chided, pushing away from the counter. Maybe she should leave with the woman, Nikki thought. If nothing else, it would buy her some time. Sheriff Hardy would be here soon. Soon, Kurt would find her gone and start a search. That in mind, she headed for the door just as Abigail finished tossing a cloak around her broad shoulders.

Abigail took a quick step back when Nikki's sure strides carried her within arm's reach. It was as though she was afraid Nikki would make a grab for the rifle. She was right. If the opportunity arose, Nikki would jump at it. Unfortunately, the opportunity never arose.

Chapter Twenty-Two

He should have brought a coat, Kurt thought. The bitter wind cut him to the quick. The snow lashed from the sky like the biting end of a whip. It stung his cheeks, melted on the heat of his face and scalp, and dripped coldly into his eyes. Already his clothes were soaked. His feet ached from the cold, his boots crunching over packed snow and ice as he shifted from one leg to the other.

Kurt wiped a palm down his face, knowing he'd weathered worse in the past. If he was lucky, he would again. Right now he was more concerned with Nikki than with freezing to death. He let his concern keep him warm as he hugged his arms around his waist. His gaze was trained on Ben Rollison's cabin.

He'd gotten to the cabin just in time to see Nikki go in. That had been almost fifteen minutes ago. She hadn't come out yet. He was beginning to think the two had slipped out the back door, and was preparing to check out the possibility, when the front door opened. Pressing his back hard against the barn wall, he watched. Like a hawk, he watched.

Nikki stepped outside. Her back was rigid as she gathered the hood over her head. The wind tossed the cloak around her legs. There was nothing in her stance to suggest fear. If anything, she looked like she'd just stepped out to take a casual stroll.

Kurt's eyes hardened to chips of ice when Abigail's hatefully broad frame appeared behind her. Immediately the dark hair was frosted with snow. Brittle strands snapped around her face, clinging to snow-moistened, masculine cheeks. With a cruel jerk of her wrist she jabbed the barrel of her rifle deep into Nikki's ribs. Nikki stumbled down the few steps leading to the deep blanket of snow. They were heading toward the barn.

Kurt felt an angry flame ignite within him—it was all he could do to keep his feet rooted to the hard-packed snow. His hands clenched at his sides uselessly. *But not useless for long*, he promised. Lord, how his fingers itched to wrap around Abigail Rollison's throat! With luck, he'd get his chance soon enough.

Abigail leaned forward and said something that made Nikki glare hotly over her shoulder. It was the only reaction Abigail got, and that seemed to disturb the woman.

Good for you, baby, Kurt encouraged as he slipped around the corner of the barn. The snow crunched beneath his feet. *Get her mad as hell and keep her guessing until I can get to you.*

His heart hammered in his chest as he followed the pair to the barn. Even though a blizzard raged around his head, his palms were sweaty as he eased open the door that led to Stetson's stall from the outside. He didn't know he was praying until he heard himself murmur the words of a psalm his mother had taught him as a child. The words tasted foreign on his tongue, but he muttered them under his breath with a vengeance. At this point, he thought, he'd be a fool to refuse help from any quarter.

* * *

Nikki entered the barn as wordlessly as she'd crossed the yard. She swatted the snow from her shoulders, watching as it rained to the dirt floor, melting on contact. She smiled when a shivering Abigail burst in behind her. The woman's flowery scent was a strong contrast to the smell of hay and horse dung—a pleasant contrast, Nikki thought, since the latter served to drown out the former.

"All right, Abigail," she said, turning. Stetson moved restlessly in his stall at the sound of Nikki's voice. His hoof stomped the hay and hard-packed dirt as an agitated whicker filled the air. Nikki noticed Abigail stiffen. "You're calling the shots, so to speak. What happens next?"

"I kill you," the woman replied gruffly. "And then . . ." Her eyes glazed over as a sinister smile turned her lips. "How's Beth?" Nikki wasn't given time to answer, which was just as well because a sudden lump of fear had clogged in her throat. "The poor child. So sweet. You know, she'll need someone to look after her when you're gone."

Not letting her panic show at that moment was the most difficult thing Nikki ever did. But she did it—for Beth's sake. She met Abigail's gaze and said, "My brothers are more than capable."

"Goodness, no. They're just men, Nicole. They wouldn't know what to do with a child. Beth will need a mother's loving touch. Someone who'll look after her, love her, brush her hair and tie it up in pretty ribbons. I'll enjoy that. I wanted another daughter. After Amy died . . . well, Ben wants a son, but he'll take to a girl just as well."

"And you think you can give Beth all those things?" Nikki asked tightly, ignoring the rest of what Abigail had said. Her muscles went rigid as she measured the distance between herself and the gun. Three steps. Four at the most. But at the end of that short distance was a madwoman practically unleashed.

"Not right away," Abigail replied absently. "Pretty ribbons and material cost money. We don't have much now, but in time we will." The dark eyes sparkled with yet another thought. "I'm sure Pete will be generous when Ben brings in your murderer. If he doesn't get more money in his pay, he'll certainly get a hefty bonus. That should help support the child."

"My murderer?" Nikki asked accusingly. "Why, Abigail, are you planning to turn yourself in?"

A cruel laugh rumbled in the woman's chest. The grating sound made the hairs at Nikki's nape prickle. "I won't have to. My job is to make sure Ben finds enough clues pointing to your lover. Once that's been taken care of . . ." the broad shoulders lifted in a shrug. "I told you, Ben's smart. He'll piece everything together and justice will be served."

"The last time you tried to frame someone, Abigail, it turned out to be poor Ben himself." Nikki knew that Abigail hadn't meant to frame Ben. Leaving the spur had been a careless mistake. Abigail had proved herself to be an inept criminal. Hadn't she tried to kill Nikki, and failed many times?

Abigail's expression clouded. "Framed Ben? Whatever are you talking about? I'd never do such a thing."

Nikki tipped her head. "The spur . . . ?"

"What spur?"

"I thought you'd say that." She inched forward a half-step. Abigail was too busy in her confusion to notice. "Besides, Kurt didn't kill me. *You* did."

"Well, no one has to know that," Abigail spat disgustedly. Her feet shuffled in the dirt. "And no one will."

Nikki started to advance another half-step, but

stopped when the sharp black eyes turned to study her intently. "While you're at it, you'd better provide Kurt with a real good reason to want me dead. Mike and Pete know Kurt and I are getting along now," she lied. "And I'm sure Willy has guessed."

"Willy is a whining little drunkard," Abigail hissed. "He's lucky if he can remember to put his boots on in the morning. I won't have any trouble convincing him."

The truth of her statement stung. Nikki wrapped her arms around her chest defiantly. "Maybe not, but you'll have a bit of trouble convincing Pete and Mike. Look at the proof I had against Kurt, and they still don't believe a lick of it. No, if you don't come up with a damn good reason for him to want me dead, they'll look elsewhere. How long, do you think, before they knock on your door, Abigail?"

The woman's chin tilted up with what Nikki perceived as overconfidence. The handle of the rifle was still buried in her broad shoulder. "They won't," she argued. "Frazier *has* a good reason to want you dead. Especially when it is discovered you'd stumbled on enough evidence to put the noose you keep threatening him with around his neck. Another murder charge would be the least of his worries if it meant saving his hide."

When Abigail glanced down, Nikki took the half-step she'd been waiting to take. Her fingers itched to reach out and grab the rifle, but the opportunity wasn't right. She prayed it would be soon. Just the thought of Abigail Rollison laying claim to Beth made her skin crawl.

"You have this planned out, don't you?" Nikki asked. Her foot rose to take another step, but the other woman's razor-sharp eyes swooped back to her. She balanced her weight on one foot, afraid her rustling skirts would give her intent away.

"Of course I do," Abigail scoffed, then nearly jumped out of her skin when Stetson gave an angry snort. His strong hoof smashed against the stall door, giving Nikki the chance to lower her foot. "What's wrong with that devil?"

"The storm. He doesn't like it. Makes him nervous." Nikki shrugged. Clamping her hands in front of her, she watched a drop of melted snow creep down Abigail's temple. She didn't miss the way the woman's tongue licked at her lips, or the way the black eyes flickered nervously down the center pass. "I don't think he likes you either, Abigail."

Abigail tried to hide her panic-stricken look, but Nikki saw it. "He's just a stupid horse. He doesn't even know I'm here."

"Oh, he knows. He can smell you in the air and, apparently, he doesn't like what he smells." What she said was true. The horse's senses were keen. But she also knew Abigail's nauseating scent wasn't the only thing causing Stetson's agitation. Something other than the storm was bothering the stallion enough to make him want out of his stall. Badly.

Another hoof crashed against the stall door. The sound reverberated around them like a bolt of thunder. Abigail gasped. Nikki cast a quick glance at the woman, and caught a flash of fear in the black eyes.

"No, I don't think he likes you at all," she continued, feeding on Abigail's fear like a spider cocooning its victim in a web of silk. "But don't worry, the stall door's closed. Now, if it were *open* you'd have reason to worry. The last time Stetson took a dislike to someone he tried to trample the poor guy under his hooves. Big, powerful hooves he has, too. Don't you agree?" Nikki gave a delicate shiver, and it was all she could do not to laugh when Abigail's cheeks drained of what little color they had.

"The door *is* closed?" Abigail asked nervously. Her gaze flickered to the center pass between stalls as though expecting the horse to charge down it any second. Her widened gaze shifted to Nikki. "And locked? He can't get out?"

"Of course not," Nikki assured her. Her voice was soft, as deceptively smooth as a glass of aged brandy. It was also edged with the same potent sting. She took another discreet step forward. Abigail's fright had made Nikki's approach much easier.

"He only snuck out of his stall that one time," she continued innocently. Dragging the gauntlets from her hands, she tossed them to the ground. "Brian fixed the door." She leaned forward, and as she unfastened the hook holding her cloak, confided softly, "Actually, he had to make a new one. Stetson knocked the old one down with just his hooves. Imagine that! He must have been awful anxious to get out."

The gun wavered. Nikki swallowed a smile as the clatter continued from the other end of the barn. The noise rivaled the fury of the howling wind. Each crash of hooves against splintering wood made the black eyes widen a little more. The thick fingers trembled.

"Don't you like horses, Abigail?"

"I despise them."

"Pity," she sighed, slipping the cloak from her shoulders. It fluttered to the ground, wrinkling at her feet. She kicked it away. She didn't want anything tripping her when she made her move. "Beth grew up on this ranch. She loves horses. Adores them. If you're going to be her mother, I suggest you learn to like them, too. She won't accept a woman who doesn't."

"I'll see to it she isn't deprived. She can go riding with Ben any time she likes. He can dote on her while

I sit at home waiting for them. I'm sure Beth will understand." The words seemed to shake off some of Abigail's fear. Enough, at least, for her to size up Nikki anew. "What are you doing?"

"Getting ready to die. Isn't that what we came here for?" Her tone suggested she was talking about nothing more dire than the weather. "Have you decided how you're going to kill me yet? Personally, I think you should make it look like an accident. Push me out the hayloft door. Or," the blue eyes sparkled as she tapped an index finger against her chin, "you can get Stetson out here and let him trample me to death. *That* would be good. A bloody mess—Lord knows *I'd* hate to be the one to clean it—but believable." She smiled into Abigail's look of horror as she brushed away the deadly barrel that was close to embedding itself in her shoulder. "Of course, you're free to do as you please. But I wouldn't use the rifle. Too easy to trace."

"Well, it won't be the horse." A shiver overtook the wide shoulders. "They're too wild. You can't trust them, I say." She shook her head and brittle black strands danced around her face. "No, you won't find me anywhere near that beast."

A smile, as cold as it was emotionless, curved Nikki's lips. Her eyes were chips of sparkling blue ice. "But you don't have to. That's the beauty of it. I trained Stetson years ago to come when I whistle. It helps on the trail drives. He's like an obedient dog." She grinned before narrowing her eyes in open challenge. The force of what she was saying was driven home by the stallion's furiously crashing hooves. "Shall I whistle for him now, Abigail? Do you think he'll come?"

For a split second, Abigail hesitated. It was all the time Nikki needed. She brought her arm up in a resounding blow, aimed to knock the rifle from

Abigail's hands. At the same time, she rammed her shoulder into Abigail's stomach. The two fell to the ground with a crash. The wind rushed from Nikki's lungs as she made a grab for the rifle.

Abigail panted in frustration, her thick fingers clinging desperately to the gun, refusing to surrender it from her grasp. She writhed beneath Nikki, who straddled her hips, trying to throw the younger girl off as if she were a bucking bronco. But Nikki had sat atop an unwilling horse too many times to be dislodged now.

They were closely matched. While one was tall, with the leverage of weight and a mind driven by madness, the other was small and nimble, with years of hard work backing each sure move.

Keeping one hand on the rifle, Nikki balled up the other and sank it into Abigail's jaw. The sound of flesh smashing flesh was countered by Stetson's hoof splintering the stall door. Abigail groaned. Blood trickled from the corner of her lips. Its redness made her pale cheeks look ashen in the shadows.

The sound of cracking wood echoed around them. "Do you hear that?" Nikki taunted as she raised her fist to deliver another stinging blow. "Stetson's coming for you."

"No!"

Abigail writhed, her strength fueled by white-hot terror. With a brutal shove of the rifle, she knocked Nikki off.

The ground slammed into Nikki's back, biting at her head and neck. In an instant she was scrambling to her feet, but her movements were hampered by the skirt and the layers of clothes beneath. She wasn't quick enough to stop Abigail from yanking the gun to her shoulder and slamming back the hammer.

* * *

Kurt had been hunkered down in a corner of Stetson's stall waiting for his chance. A chance that wouldn't put Nikki's life at risk. The opportunity never came. Now he would forge his own.

In one throbbing heartbeat he vaulted on top of Stetson's back. It took scarcely half of another to encourage the horse over the battered stall door. Hooves clattered atop the hard-packed earth with muffled thuds. Kurt planted the sharp heels of his boots into the horse's firmly molded flanks and dug his fingers into the silky black mane. Hot breath poured from his nostrils, fogging the bitter air in front of his face. The coldness felt good as it nipped at his lungs with each gasping breath.

He reached the center of the barn in time to see Abigail jerk the rifle to her shoulder. He didn't think, just reacted. The click of the hammer being cocked was loud even against the wind, his ragged breathing, and the muffled clomp of hoofbeats. Before the sound had fallen, Kurt and Stetson were upon her.

He jerked hard on the silky mane. The stallion went up, his deadly hooves flailing near Abigail's head. Her scream cut the bitter air like the honed blade of a knife.

Everything slowed to a crawl. The evil leer that moved across Abigail's face seemed to take hours to form.

Nikki waited for the cold fingers of fear to close around her heart, but all that came to mind was Kurt Frazier's handsomely carved face, and the innocent beauty of Beth's.

She braced herself, waiting to feel the bullet tear through her body, knowing she couldn't prevent it. It didn't come. Instead there was the thunder of hoofbeats. Stetson, snorting, reared up with terrifying majesty from the hard-packed earth. Vapor streamed from his flared black nostrils. In the flickering shadows he looked like a beast spit from the fires of hell. A beast bent on vengeance.

To Abigail, the sight was horrifying. To Nikki, it was exhilarating.

Kurt! Nikki blinked twice before the sight of him sank in. Kurt was there! He clung to the sinewy black back of her horse like the devil himself, his expression darkly vindictive.

To Nikki, things began happening at an alarming rate. Stetson's front hooves smashed to the ground and he cut a quick sidestep. Kurt clung to the horse with his knees, his hands buried in the mane as he fought to keep his seat. The large hooves missed crushing Abigail's toes by mere inches.

Abigail screamed. On instinct, she spun around. The dark folds of her skirt hadn't settled around her legs before she had trained the rifle on Kurt.

Nikki gasped. Fear unlike any she had ever known splashed like ice water in her veins. *"No!"* the single word tore from her soul, echoing off the hay and dirt even as she catapulted herself into motion.

Her head slammed into Abigail's gut. The woman's breath rushed in her ears as the women crashed to the ground. The sound was rivaled by the deafening report of the gun. The bullet lodged in a beam overhead. Shards of wood broke off and sprinkled the dirt below.

Splinters rained over Nikki's head and back, but she didn't feel them. Her gaze was trained on Abigail, her mind's eye imagining Kurt falling from the horse and landing in a pool of his own blood. She pictured him cold and dead, and the image made something inside of her snap.

"I'll kill you, you bitch!" she half growled, half screamed. But it was the voice of a woman as insane as Abigail that rang in her ears, not her own.

When Abigail tried to raise the gun for another shot, Nikki shoved it aside and landed her fist hard on Abigail's jaw. The blow stung Nikki's knuckles, but it was a welcome pain knowing her victim suffered worse.

Abigail cried out, but she was fueled by her own demons.

The gunshot had terrified Stetson, already skittish from the storm. His hooves slapped the dirt as he tried to buck the weight from his back. When his hooves landed next to Abigail's head, close enough for her hair to be pinched beneath the weight, she yelped. It was a momentary weakness. When horse and rider retreated, Abigail channeled her fear into strength. Her struggles increased.

Kurt slipped to the ground just as Nikki knocked the gun from Abigail's hands. But the victory cost her. Abigail seized the chance to shove Nikki off, and Nikki's bottom had no more slammed into the ground before Abigail once again had the rifle.

"Nikki!" Kurt screamed when Abigail slammed the butt to her shoulder and trained the barrel on Nikki. The black eyes were glazed with insanity, past the point of no return.

The hammer clicked into place, but there was another sound to rival it. The sound of the wind whipping the air. The sound of the barn door creaking open.

"I know you told me to stay in my room, Kurt, but I—"

Beth's voice snatched the attention of all three adults. Abigail tensed in surprise, her fingers hesitating over the trigger. It was her last mistake.

Stetson saw the murky light seep in through the door and bolted for freedom. His snorts filled the air a split second before his crashing hoofbeats thundered through the barn.

Beth's eyes widened at the sight of the enraged, charging horse. Her small feet rooted to the spot, refusing to budge as a terrified squeak left her throat.

Nikki didn't see Stetson's intent until it was too late. Kurt saw, but was too far away to reach Beth in time, though he immediately threw himself in that direction. Only Abigail was close enough to attempt to save the child. And she did so without hesitating.

"Oh, sweet Lord. Beth!" Abigail cried, her voice wrenched from her heaving lungs. The rifle was already at her shoulder. She had only to spin and pull the trigger. The bullet shot from the rifle in a nerve-deafening blast.

Stetson snorted in alarm and pain before his black eyes glazed and he crashed to the dirt. The ground shook with the weight of his body slamming into it, and the vibrations trembled up Nikki's watery legs.

Abigail threw down the rifle and rushed to Beth, who stood shivering in the doorway. She reached the child before Kurt, scooping the frightened little body into her arms.

It took Nikki a few seconds to convince her legs to carry her to the trio. She didn't look down at Stetson's dead body as she passed it. She couldn't. The sight, she knew, would be her undoing.

"It's all right," Abigail crooned into the dark hair. "That mean horse won't try to hurt you again. I made sure of it."

"I-I was afraid," Beth sniffled, burying her face in the hard shoulder and clinging to Abigail's neck. Her legs wrapped tightly around the thick waist. "H-he was going t-to—"

"I know. But it's over, honey. I'm here now. I'll protect you." Cold air whipped through the door. Abigail turned so her body shielded the sobbing child from it. The fingers that had moments ago held a rifle on the child's mother with the intent to kill, now stroked the child's soft tresses with maternal tenderness.

Nikki inched to Kurt's side. He'd snatched up the rifle at the first opportunity and emptied it of its shells. He now leaned his weight tiredly against the butt. Nikki placed shaking fingers on his forearm, and drank deeply of the strength that coursed through her fingertips and heated her blood.

The silver lashes flickered up. Her gaze locked with Kurt's and her grip tightened. Though she held his gaze for only a second, six years of understanding passed between them. The contact was broken when Abigail murmured more comfort into Beth's ear.

"I'll take my daughter now, Abigail." Swallowing her emotions, Nikki reached trembling arms out for Beth. Not since the day she was born could Nikki remember needing to hold her daughter quite so desperately.

"Yes," Abigail whispered into Beth's hair, her large arms clinging to the child. She wasn't ready to surrender the child's sweet warmth just yet, though it was slowly beginning to dawn on her that she'd have to soon. "She's *your* daughter, isn't she?"

Nikki opened her mouth to respond, but it was Kurt's voice that filled the air. His tone was gritty, deep, filled with emotion. "*Our* daughter," he said, taking the child from Abigail. He cradled Beth for a minute, then placed her in the welcoming haven of her mother's quivering arms. "Nikki's and mine."

His words curled up Nikki's spine and her arms tightened around Beth. The tears, only a threat before, now streamed down her cheeks, wetting her skin and soaking into the dark head that pillowed her jaw.

"Yes, *our* daughter," she echoed with an acceptance that she had once fought against, but that now hugged her as tightly as the small arms encircling her neck. She nuzzled her cheek against Beth's head as her gaze locked with Kurt's. She couldn't stop looking at him. She didn't want to.

Deep blue meshed with steel gray. Nikki's heart tightened, and the raw emotion in Kurt's eyes stole her breath away. "Our daughter," she repeated softly. "Kurt's and mine."

Chapter Twenty-Three

Nikki couldn't remember a sight quite so pleasing as when she watched Sheriff Hardy arrest Abigail Rollison and cart her off to the jail in Bismarck. She had heard that revenge was not so sweet, that victory was hollow. She didn't believe a word of it. In fact, she came close to weeping tears of joy to know that, at long last, her father's murderer would be punished.

Abigail would stand trial in Bismarck as soon as a circuit judge was available to hear her case. There wasn't a doubt in anyone's mind that she would be convicted.

The only thing that served to mar Nikki's happiness was Kurt. For the two weeks since Abigail's arrest, he'd avoided her. At first Nikki welcomed the distance. His aloofness gave her time to think, time to sort out her feelings, and time to figure out exactly how she could lay the bitterness of the past six years aside and give him the apology she knew he deserved.

He didn't rush her, and after the first week of cool civility between them, Nikki came to the decision that detachment was not what she wanted from Kurt Frazier. No, she wanted something hot, something physical, something that would last a lifetime. But how to get it . . . that was another matter.

Another week passed while Nikki screwed up the courage to tell Kurt she wanted him in her life forever. As always, when it came to herself and Kurt, realization dawned too late. She awoke one morning to find that Kurt was gone. It took Nikki three hours to worm his destination out of Pete. Her decision to follow Kurt to his new ranch in Winston—bought and paid for, Pete told her, with his wages from the Triple D—took days to reach. But once her mind was set, there was no changing it. Pete's offer to accompany her to the Winston town line only strengthened her resolve.

The first of January saw Nikki packing the provisions needed for the journey. That night she went over the ranching duties with Willy. Neither she nor Pete were thrilled to think Willy would be in charge of the ranch while they were gone, but they had no choice. Besides, Willy had changed since the drive. He had returned more self-assured, mature, and he had cut back his drinking considerably. Finding a place as the drive's temporary cook had worked wonders. It had been a small responsibility, but one he had worn with great pride. It was a start.

Pete and Nikki started out at first light.

"Almost there," Pete called from behind.

Nikki grunted a reply.

Three miles back, they'd crossed the Winston town line. Pete, who'd planned to leave Nikki at that point and follow Shelly Winfield's path to Tidewater, had changed his mind. He now rode sullenly beside his sister, his mind on Shelly, and Mike, who'd raced after the coy Miss Winfield the second he'd found out she'd abandoned him, the fickle man.

A quick glance around her told Nikki they were on Kurt's land. She knew it without being told. Her skin burned with his nearness and the tempo of her heart increased with each step that brought her closer to the ranch. And the man who owned it.

The ranch house and outbuildings dotted the horizon, and looked deserted. No hands milled around the houses or split-rail corrals. No horses or cattle stumbled in the ice-encrusted snow. The eight hundred prime head Pete said Kurt had ordered wouldn't be delivered until spring. Except for the lack of livestock, the ranch looked like any other dirt-poor homestead she'd ever seen.

So why does it feel like heaven? Nikki thought.

Curls of smoke wafted from a chimney in the ranch house. The smell of charred wood was strong and Nikki imagined Kurt inside, his sun-kissed cheek warm and golden from the glow of a crackling fire. Her hands tightened on the reins. Her heart gave a disturbing little flutter.

She stiffened, reining Derby in, and was struck again by how much she missed Stetson. Pete edged his brown stallion to the mare's side, but Nikki didn't notice. Suddenly the brisk air fogging her breath no longer existed. Her hands, covered fingertip-to-forearm with heavy gauntlets, tightened around the reins. Breathing was an impossible feat. What little air she could draw wasn't filled with the scent of fresh snow, horses, and a wood fire, but with the memory of Kurt's spicy male sweat.

Nikki groaned. If just conjuring up Kurt's rugged profile did this to her, what would happen when she saw him face-to-face?

It was something that, until now, she'd been too busy to consider. And she wouldn't waste time considering it now. She planted her heel firmly in Derby's flanks before she could change her mind and do as her heart dictated—beat a hasty retreat before she invited Kurt Frazier into her life again. If she didn't feel so strongly that she owed him an apology, she might have done just that.

"Are you sure you want to do this?" Pete called as he spurred his horse to a trot.

"More than anything," she yelled, her voice determinedly battling the wind.

Like the steady pounding of his heart, the ax fell time and again. Its impact vibrated up his arm, throbbed in his shoulders; and did absolutely nothing to relieve his tortured mind.

His breath fogged the air, pouring from his nostrils. In mock contrast to the cold, his body was coated with a sweat that plastered his blue chambray shirt to his arms and chest.

With the blunt end of the ax, Kurt knocked the split log aside and mopped the perspiration from his brow with his sleeve. Leaning against the ax, he glanced at the steadily increasing pile of wood, stacked sloppily beside the stump he used as a chopping block.

His eyes widened. No wonder his arms and back ached. He'd chopped enough wood to keep a fire burning in every room of his newly constructed ranch house for the next year!

He raised the ax and buried it deep into the craggy stump, the muscles in his forearms trembling with exertion. The muffled thump resonated in the air, as did his grunt of disgust.

Drake Frazier had once told his son the legend of King Arthur and the mighty sword, Excalibur. The legend had enchanted Kurt, lodging in his youthful mind much the way the ax now lodged in the stump. Like Excalibur, he doubted the ax would ever come out, he'd buried it that deep. Only a small portion of the blade glistened in the dwindling gray light.

Kurt gave the wooden handle a tug with his work-calloused hands. It didn't budge. He considered kicking it. Then he considered calling upon his own

King Arthur to remove it—in the form of his oldest brother Hank; a taller, brawnier man God had never made!

Both ideas were dismissed at the sound of approaching hoofbeats. Kurt melted into the shadows beside the house, the ax forgotten.

Roughly hewn logs bit at the winter-sensitive flesh beneath his shirt. His gaze picked out the gentle gray and rider. The two visitors were close enough for him to hear the snow crunching under their mounts' hooves. Close enough for him to see the vapor of their breath and the soft silver curls peeking from beneath the smallest rider's hat.

His gut tightened with unbelievable force. He didn't need to see the delicate profile to know who the rider was. The hot rush of blood in his veins told him. That and the exultation quickening his breath until he could hardly breathe for gasping.

A sly grin turned his lips as he clung to the shadows and slipped to the back of the house. He had a surprise in store for Nicole Dennison. A surprise he wouldn't let her refuse. Not this time.

The house smelled of fried venison, coffee, a crackling fire, and sawdust. Letting herself in through the front door, and closing it quietly behind her, Nikki found the scents warm and inviting. Of course, burnt bread, four walls, and any sort of good, solid floor underfoot would have been appreciated. She was half frozen, and tired to the point of dropping. They'd ridden hard to reach Kurt's ranch before nightfall. As it was, they'd barely made it. Already the gray fingers of dusk were stealing in through the windows, casting the room in warm shadows.

Shivering, Nikki's gaze swept the room. It was small but sturdy, with darkly paneled walls and a high, timbered ceiling that attested to its owner's masculine tastes. It was also, except for the unfilled bookcases built into the walls flanking the hearth, completely empty. Empty, if one didn't take into account the man stretched in lazy repose atop the floor in front of the fireplace. The one who appeared to be asleep.

Nikki's heart tightened. It was an instinctive reaction, one that gripped her before she could suppress it. She was glad Kurt was asleep, glad he couldn't see the passion warming her gaze as it roved hungrily over his rugged frame.

He looked wonderful. He looked terrible. Either way, she feasted her eyes on him like a woman starved.

His skin was still bronze, but more from the ravages of wind and snow than from the gentle kiss of the sun. The blue chambray shirt hugged his shoulders. The buttons were free to his waist, exposing a nice wedge of silky black curls and firm flesh. Crystalline drops of moisture glistened on the pelt of chest hairs, as well as the raven strands softening his brow. One arm was thrown casually over his brow, his knuckles kissing the unfinished floor. The muscles of his arms bunched beneath the sleeve and looked larger, more intimidating than she remembered; as though he'd worked hard the past two weeks with little reprieve.

That's where wonderful ended and terrible began.

His eyes, smudged with shadows, spoke of too many sleepless nights. His cheekbones looked higher, the hollows beneath, deeper. The lower half of his face was dark with stubble. The whiskers hardened his already hard jaw, lending it an air of arrogance only hinted at before. The endearing cleft in his chin was hidden beneath. Nikki felt a stab of disappointment. She missed the dent. Somehow, it had always made him look less handsome, but more human; a little rougher, but more endearing.

His steady breaths echoed over the crackling flames, tickling up her spine in slow, rhythmic waves.

Tearing her gaze away, she stepped to the door and threw the bolt. A quick glance said the harsh sound hadn't woken him.

The heels of her boots made hollow clicks atop the bare wood floor as she crossed the room. Her spurs jangled, but she could barely hear the chinking sound over the racket her heart made in her ears. The scent of sawdust grew stronger as she neared the far wall, and the huge stone fireplace.

Towering over Kurt, not close enough for her feet to touch him, she reached out her hands to the fire. She hesitated, letting the delicious heat seep into her fingers and spread up her arms. She then slipped the pistol from her belt and deftly aimed it at a spot dead center between his thick raven eyebrows.

"You deserve this, buster," she growled as, with a smile of pure delight, she prodded Kurt's side. "Now wake up and *strip!*"

Kurt—who hadn't been asleep but was taking great pleasure in studying Nikki beneath a shield of thick lashes—"woke up" with lightning speed. He grunted and rolled to his feet, grabbing soft, shapely thighs as he went. With a struggling Nikki on top, they crashed to the floor.

He twisted when they landed—on purpose, no doubt—so that Nikki came up straddling the firm cushion of his waist. A warm wave of familiar sensation curled through her thighs, pooling in her stomach. Nikki fought those feelings as hard as she fought the man who so easily created them.

"Let me go, you idiot!" she demanded. With one fist she beat on his chest and shoulders. The other gripped the gun.

"Why? So you can shoot me instead of hang me?"

he bellowed, just as hotly. His warm breath blew in her face, giving her pause. "I don't think so, baby."

Kurt lunged for the gun. Nikki, sensing his intent, twisted away. She landed on the floor with a thump, but there was no time to nurse either her wounded pride or her aching backside as she scrambled to her feet.

Kurt threw himself to a stand. One dark brow cocked in challenge as Nikki aimed the barrel at his chest. When he took a warning step toward her, Nikki yanked the hammer back. A loud, echoing, ominous click issued from the gun.

"Don't come any closer, buster, or I'll shoot you where you stand." She raised her chin, her eyes flashing midnight-blue fire. "You know I can do it."

"Haven't we been through this before?" His sharp gaze caressed her face, her hair, her body. The gray eyes burned. "All right, Nicole, I'll play the game. You have a gun, I know you can use it," he conceded, nodding, "but you won't. This time I know it."

"Try me." Her finger quivered on the trigger.

The fire crackled; the sound reverberated through the room like a clap of thunder. Outside, the horses whickered. The wind picked up to a howling pitch. The silence stretched taut. Blue and gray clashed and held. Both gazes shimmered with unrelenting determination. Kurt's hands clenched and unclenched at his sides. Nikki's tightened around the pistol when she realized it was her throat he imagined squeezing tightly in his palms.

"I don't like being held at gunpoint, Nicole," he growled. His thick fingers plowed through his tousled hair. "The first time I understood it—at least I tried to. This time I don't. Make whatever point you came here to make and be quick about it. My patience is wearing thin."

Gaze narrowed, she waved the gun at his chest. "Be glad to—as soon as you do what you're told. Strip, buster. I want to see your long johns in thirty seconds."

A slow look of surprise, mixed heavily with rage, spread over the rugged planes of his face. "You can't be serious."

"I'm dead serious. Now *strip!*"

The muscle in his jaw twitched. "And if I don't?"

"Then I'll shoot the clothes off of you." She smiled coldly. "Twenty seconds to go. Better hurry."

In the end, it took the better part of five minutes for Kurt to peel away his clothes. He did so slowly, exposing each firm inch of flesh with tantalizing precision. He took great pleasure in watching Nikki squirm as each layer was cast aside in a wrinkled heap atop the floor. By the time he'd worked his way down to his thin white underdrawers Nikki's cheeks were flaming, and Kurt was smiling oh, so wickedly!

"Sorry, no long johns." His eyes sparkled a teasing gray as his shirt fluttered from his fingertips to the floor. "What happens now, baby? Or hadn't you thought that far ahead . . . as usual?"

Nikki gritted her teeth until they hurt. Lord, how she wanted to shoot the man! "Now you can kick your clothes over here. Then shush your mouth."

"Then what?"

"You'll find out when you do it!"

Kurt kicked the clothes to Nikki. She stooped, picking up the bundle and tucking them safely under her arm. Kurt watched her closely when she edged over to the window and, after shifting the gun to the hand holding the clothes, eased the pane up.

The room was assaulted with a blast of cold air. Nikki took a deep gulp of it, her gaze shifting between Kurt and the storm kicking up outside. "Pete?" she hissed into the quickly fading light. "Peter Aaron, where are you?"

"Right here. What took you so long? I'm half frozen and tired as hell."

"Quit your whining and take these." She shoved the lumpy bundle into her brother's arms. Hot color splashed her cheeks when Pete's gaze strayed past her shoulder, settling on an almost naked, thoroughly amused Kurt. Had Pete noticed the way Kurt's cotton-thin underdrawers were nearly transparent in the firelight playing behind him?

Pete groaned. "Hell, Nikki, what'd you do to him?"

"Nothing," she barked, shivering with the cold wind that blasted in through the window and whipped at the silver curls clinging to her cheeks and brow. "Yet."

Pete nodded. His grim expression said he didn't want to know what she had planned. "What should I do with these?"

"Take them with you. You said you were going to visit Brian on your way back. Give them to him. Or burn them, for all I care. Just get them out of here."

"All right," he sighed, tucking the clothes under his arm and sending his sister a peculiar look. "I hope you know what you're doing."

"What's she's been doing," a gritty voice rasped close behind, "is playing with fire. What she's about to do"—a strong hand was planted firmly on her shoulder—"is get burned."

Nikki yelped and tried to twist away. Kurt grabbed her other shoulder at the same time she felt the gun being wrenched from her hand. She shot her brother an accusing glare. "What are you doing?" she gasped when Pete pocketed the pistol Kurt had delivered to him. She noticed a trace of Mike's charm in the wry twist of his lips.

"Evening up the odds." He flashed Kurt a smile, the sight of which infuriated Nikki. "Good luck, Frazier. Hope the prize is worth the effort."

"Pete!" Nikki screamed, and planted her heel in Kurt's naked shin. He grunted. "You can't leave me like this! Peter Aaron, you get back here this instant. *And give me my gun!*"

He'd already disappeared into the swirl of snow, but his voice battled the wind. "At the wedding, Sis. If he doesn't kill you before you make it to the altar."

Kurt yanked Nikki inside and slammed the window shut. The pane rattled in its casing from the force as much as from the wind that whipped at it.

"This isn't funny," she panted, suddenly very much aware of the naked chest rumbling with laughter against her back. The heat of the fire was nothing compared with the heat of the man who held her.

"You're right," he grumbled into the silver hair softly caressing his cheek and neck, "it's hilarious."

Supporting their combined weight Kurt dragged her—kicking, clawing, and swearing up a blue streak—to the floor in front of the hearth, where he dropped her unceremoniously on her backside. She landed on the floor with a thud and a yelp.

"So help me God, Nicole," he growled when she started to scramble to her feet, "you move so much as an inch and I swear I'll sit on you. I mean it."

"You've made that threat before," she murmured, but this time his tone said his threat wasn't an idle one. She went dead still at the thought of his brawny weight crushing her fragile ribcage. Her gaze drifted up and her body stiffened at the sight of his lean frame towering over her. The fire cast him in warm orange shadows. The light played over him, caressed him, and made it crystal clear what the scrap of white cloth was concealing. A perfectly base emotion heated her thighs and snatched her breath.

"Wh-what do you want?" she asked breathlessly.

"I could ask you the same thing. After all, you're the one who tornadoed your way into *my* house, thrust a gun in *my* face, and demanded *I* strip." His eyes glinted devilishly, the raven brows slashing a challenge. "If you wanted me naked . . . oh, baby, all you had to do was ask. I've never denied you."

"Louse!" she spat, glad to feel her anger returning. "That's not why I came here."

He chuckled dryly. "No? Then why did you come?"

"To *talk* to you."

"Naked? This may come as a big surprise to you, Nicole, but I'm fully capable of talking with my clothes on."

"You run off when you have your clothes on," she argued. "Three times you've run away from me, and each time you were fully clothed. Keeping you naked is the only way I can be sure you'll stay in the same room with me! Even *you* aren't stupid enough to run outside in the snow without your clothes on!"

"Did you ever think of *asking me?*" he raged. Balled fists rode lean hips. The muscle in his jaw started working. "Did you ever think of saying, 'Hey, Kurt, stick around. I need to talk to you'?"

"No," she answered in a rush of confusion. "I never did."

Kurt sucked in a deep breath and ran a palm down his bristled jaw. He shook his head. "This has to stop, Nikki. We can't go on like this. Me running; you hunting. Yelling and screaming at each other every time we're in the same room together. It's tearing us both to shreds."

Nikki rose up on her elbows, a scowl lacing her brow. "It never bothered you before."

Kurt glared down at her, his hand falling back to his side. "It's always bothered me. I just hide it better than you do."

"If that's true, then why do you keep running away from me?" she demanded, frustrated. "I thought if we sat down and calmly discussed the situation between us—whatever that is—then maybe we could work things out. Maybe, just maybe, we could come to an understanding. But you run off every time I try!"

His gaze grew stormy when she thrust herself to her feet. "I wouldn't exactly call seducing me in your father's barn—how many times now?—a way of coming to terms, Nicole."

"No? Well, what about outside of Coldbrook?" she shot back. "You left me there too."

"You kidnapped me!" he raged. "*After* you'd shot me."

"You deserved it."

"What I deserve is a decoration for patience, and some peace and quiet," he growled tersely. "And that's exactly what I had before you stormed back into my life."

"Well, you can have it again!" Her feet clomped over the floorboards as she stomped to the door. "With my blessings. I hope you rot in it."

"What are you doing?"

"Leaving you to your *peace and quiet*." She wrenched open the door and almost fell back when the wind slammed into her.

"Now who's running away?" he snarled. His hard, challenging words did what they were meant to do—stop her cold. "Take a good look, Nicole, because in the years to come I want you to remember it was *you* who walked out that door. *Not* me."

She slammed the door shut with enough force to rock it on its hinges. "I can't stand this, Kurt," she fumed through gritted teeth. "You're driving me crazy. Either you want me here or you don't. Which is it?"

"Where I want you is in my bed, Nikki," he growled, just as hotly. "God only knows why."

"That won't solve anything," she argued, but weakly. His words ripped up her spine. Just the thought of what he suggested made her legs melt to jam. Sweet, peach jam.

"Maybe not," he sighed, raking his fingers

through his hair. The firelight sparkled over his raven locks. "But at least it's one place where we're guaranteed not to fight."

His bare feet slapped the floor as, in three long strides, he cleared the distance between them. He stopped in front of her; not close enough for their bodies to touch, but close enough. They stood that way for what seemed like hours before the calloused crook of his index finger tilted her chin up.

Reluctantly, Nikki met his gaze. She was close enough to see the turquoise slivers flecking his eyes, close enough to see the spot where each whisker left his silky chin, and close enough to feel his sweet breath kiss her upturned cheeks. The rich male scent of him flooded her nostrils and threatened to drown her.

"How about it?"

"I told you before I didn't come here for that. I came here to talk. I want to . . . dammit! You aren't making this very easy. I—I want to apologize for making your life hell!"

She swallowed hard and tried to tear her gaze away. It wouldn't budge. Her knees turned to liquid, so she reached out and clutched his arms to steady her balance. It was a mistake. She came very close to losing herself to the feel of his tightly bunched muscles beneath her fingertips. *Where the hell is all that good, healthy anger I harbored just a second ago?* she raged weakly. Gone. Gone, as always, to the magic of Kurt Frazier's touch.

"Wrong, baby, you made my life heaven," he groaned finally, huskily. His fingers tunneled into the plush softness of her hair. Her flesh was warm and vibrant beneath his fingertips. The feel of it made his anger smolder to desire. Hunching his shoulders, he pressed his forehead to hers, never once releasing her gaze. "Hotter than hell, but sweeter than heaven."

Her breath caught as he massaged her tingling scalp. She swallowed hard. "Then why did you leave me again, Kurt? Why do you always leave me?!"

"Because you needed time," he answered huskily, "and because staying with you tore me apart. Good God, woman, can't you see what you do to me?! I can't be in the same room with you and not touch you. I can't sleep under the same roof and not make love to you. I wake up in the morning, see an empty pillow beside me, and my first lucid thought is that your head should be on it. Dammit! I asked you to marry me once and you refused. What more do you want from me?!"

Nikki blinked stupidly, trying to push from her tongue the words that clogged in her throat like a dry lump of cotton. Her fingers tightened, burrowing deeply in his flesh. She shook her head, her voice cracking, and whispered, "Lust is nice, Kurt, really it is, but it's not the same as . . . as . . ."

His hands tightened on her face. "As *what?* Say it, Nicole! *Say it!*"

She blinked back the tears stinging her eyes, but her lips refused to form the words Kurt needed so desperately to hear. "Isn't it obvious?"

His eyes devoured her. "Not to a man who wants to be told. Who *needs* to be told. Say it. Please."

"I love you, dammit!" she shouted angrily. And this time she really did cry. Big, beautiful tears. "There, are you happy now that you've seen me humiliated?!" Burying her face in his shoulder, she wrapped her arms around his back. She clung to him tightly, drawing on each ragged breath that tore through the firmly worked chest beneath her ear. His heart was pounding wildly. Almost as wildly as her own.

"Don't think you can use those words against me, buster," she sniffed against his tear-dampened shoulder, "because I won't let you. I won't let you hurt me again, Kurt Frazier. And I'm sick and tired of you leaving me."

Kurt buried his face in her satin-soft hair as the first tidal wave of happiness engulfed him. Happy? Hell, he was ecstatic! His fingers trembled as they caressed her hair, her shoulders, her back. "I'm not going anywhere," he rasped against her temple. "A team of wild horses couldn't drag me away from you this time."

"You've said that before."

"And I meant it each time. Only you listened with your head, never with your heart."

Slowly, Nikki lifted her tear-stained cheek from his shoulder. His eyes were darkly intent as they captured her gaze, and shimmered with white-hot promise.

Kurt grinned down at her and his smile lit up the room. "Give me a lifetime and I'll be more than happy to prove it."

"For Beth?" she asked hesitantly, not wanting to know the answer, but needing to hear it just the same. "You'll stay with me this time for Beth?"

He looked down at her sharply. "Hell, no! I love the kid, sure, but my reasons go way beyond that." He watched as the tip of her tongue moistened her trembling, parched lips. A noise, sounding suspiciously like a groan, rumbled in the back of Kurt's throat. "Open your eyes, dammit! Or are you blind as well as stubborn?"

He grabbed her shoulders, resisting the urge to shake her until her teeth rattled. "Nicole, I've been in love with you since the first time I set eyes on you, but you were too damn young for me to do anything about it. God, I've waited almost my entire life for you to grow up." His gaze lit teasingly on her astonished expression and his grip loosened. "and I may very well die an old man, still waiting."

"You love me? You always have?" she whispered

hoarsely, unbelievably. Her heart felt like it was about to explode, so hard did it pound in her chest. "I mean, after everything that's happened? After everything I've accused you of? After I almost got you hanged? After the letter you thought I wrote but didn't? You still love me, after all of that?"

"Yes, God help me, I do," he sighed, tortured. "I can't say the pain's gone, baby, because we'd both know I was lying."

She glanced at him hesitantly. "Then what are you saying?"

"That our love is stronger than six years of pain and betrayal. That, put in its proper perspective, what happened in the past is just that—in the past. *You're* what's important now. Keeping you in my life is what's important. The past will die, if we let it. Are you willing to try?"

"Oh, God, yes!"

With a groan, Kurt gathered Nikki close. Nikki, not Nicole. The headstrong little spitfire, not the gentle seventeen-year-old. The stubborn wench who'd held a gun on him and demanded he strip, not the delicate creature who'd seduced him six years ago on a bed of moonlit hay.

With a ragged sigh, he pulled back and gazed down at her, his eyes sparkling with all the love in his heart. His voice was thick in his throat as he said, "Nikki, do you remember the first day we met? The day you tumbled from your saddle and landed in the dirt at my feet? Do you remember the way you—?"

"Oh, Kurt, shush up," Nikki sighed and silenced him in the only way she knew how. She kissed him hard, barely noticing when he pressed her onto the floor, but excruciatingly aware of when his body possessively, hungrily, covered hers.

He felt wonderful, and she found herself looking forward to spending the rest of her life in his arms. Of course, there was the small matter of his proposal.

But she simply couldn't bring herself to distract him with words. Not when their bodies spoke to each other with such complete understanding.

With a husky sigh of compliance, she wrapped her arms around his back and pulled him closer. He felt hot, melting into her as though he would gladly die there . . . just as she would gladly die to keep him there. His silky back tickled her palms, his warm breath seared her ear. Nothing in her life had ever felt better than his touch. And nothing ever would.

With a breathless sigh, Nikki decided that the subject of their engagement could wait until later. Much, much later.